In Memory of

Janie (Mary Jane) Maiers

Prairie Song

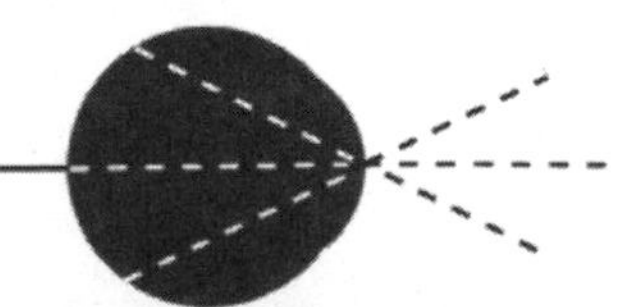

This Large Print Book carries the
Seal of Approval of N.A.V.H.

PRAIRIE SONG

Hearts Seeking Home
Book 1

Mona Hodgson

CENTER POINT LARGE PRINT
THORNDIKE, MAINE

This Center Point Large Print edition is published
in the year 2014 by arrangement with WaterBrook Press,
an imprint of the Crown Publishing Group,
a division of Random House LLC, New York.
Published in association with the literary agency of
Books & Such, 53 Mission Circle, Suite 122, PMB 170,
Santa Rosa, CA 95409-5370.

All Scripture quotations or paraphrases
are taken from the King James Version.

This is a work of fiction. Apart from well-known people,
events, and locales that figure into the narrative, all
names, characters, places, and incidents are the products
of the author's imagination or are used fictitiously.

The text of this Large Print edition is unabridged.
In other aspects, this book may vary
from the original edition.
Printed in the United States of America
on permanent paper.
Set in 16-point Times New Roman type.

ISBN: 978-1-61173-975-6

Library of Congress Cataloging-in-Publication Data

Hodgson, Mona Gansberg, 1954–
Prairie song / Mona Hodgson. — Center Point Large Print edition.
pages ; cm.
ISBN 978-1-61173-975-6 (library binding : alk. paper)
1. Large type books. I. Title.
PS3608.O474P73 2014
813′.6—dc23

2013036166

In loving memory of
William Bert Gansberg, my earthly father.
A man who had an infectious
sense of adventure.
Thanks, Dad!

Have I not commanded thee? Be strong and of a good courage; be not afraid, neither be thou dismayed: for the LORD thy God is with thee whithersoever thou goest.

—JOSHUA 1:9

1

1866, April

Anna Goben's bedchamber spun about her.

Hattie Pemberton, a friend from the Saint Charles quilting circle, stood behind her at the dressing table, weaving Anna's golden-brown hair into a loose chignon. A cord of hair hung on either side of Anna's face while Hattie worked on the back. Anna's stomach felt like it had taken in boarders with fluttering wings, and seeing herself in the mirror above the table wasn't helping matters. Closing her eyes, she gripped the wrought-iron handles on the bench as if she could brace herself against the wave of nausea. Was her sudden decision to marry Boney the reason for the jitters, or did all women feel sick to their stomach and lightheaded directly before they wed?

She'd probably feel less nervous if more of her quilting circle friends had been able to come, especially the married ones. Emilie and Maren had planned to attend the wedding, but then Emilie's father fell ill that morning and Caroline needed Maren's help in the dry goods store.

A twist of hair bounced free, tickling Anna's ear as Hattie's tender hand rested on her shoulder.

Anna opened her eyes and made herself look in the mirror. Concern etched her friend's blue-gray eyes.

Hattie tipped her head, causing the wide brim of her yellow hat to bobble. "You look as if you've seen an apparition. You're nearly as white as the frame on the mirror. Are you feeling well?"

Anna slowly turned her head to the right, then just as deliberately to the left, all the while looking into Hattie's reflection in the mirror. No, she was not all right. Nothing had been right since her brother's death. The void Dedrick's absence left in the family was wrong, and she'd been unable to make anything right since the letter from the Department of War arrived nearly a year and a half ago. She patted the hand on her shoulder. Her friend also knew about the high cost of the war. Hattie's brother had come home last year spared, but her father had died in battle in '63.

"Being ill on your wedding day is a serious problem, don't you think?" Hattie arched her thick eyebrows. "I should let your mother know."

"No need to make a fuss."

"But if you're ill, you should postpone the ceremony."

Anna sighed. Hattie knew a lot about life for her sixteen years, but her mother had little in common with Anna's. Bette Pemberton may be willing to postpone a wedding due to the jitters, but *Mutter* would have no such inclination. Mutter's heart was set on this wedding, her mind made up. Anna regretted the day she'd mentioned Boney's surprising proposal and her refusal.

No, she couldn't postpone the ceremony. The sitting room brimmed with guests. According to Hattie's earlier report, Boney had spiffed up splendidly for the occasion. His boss, Garrett Cowlishaw, captain of the wagon caravan, stood with Boney and the pastor. And three of Boney's fellow trail hands were part of the crowd who had come to see them wed. She couldn't disappoint them. Most of all, she couldn't disappoint Boney.

Drawing in a deep breath, Anna released her grip on the bench and pressed the silk ribbon at her waist. "I'm feeling a bit nervous, is all." She nearly laughed at the absurdity of her understatement. She was far more than a tad or a smidge nervous. She hadn't expected to marry so soon after her eighteenth birthday. Ever, really. Not since Dedrick died, not now that she had to look after Mutter and Großvater.

But marriage to Boney would give her a life apart from them. Somewhat, anyway.

"Anna?" Hattie's voice brought her back to reality. "You're nervous about the ceremony?"

Nervous about all of it. The wedding *and* the marriage. Nervous about the caravan of wagons that would take her and her family away from Saint Charles. She was six when Mutter moved them to the riverside Missouri town to live with

Großvater. For twelve years, she'd called Saint Charles her home. Keeping her reservations to herself, Anna smoothed the lace collar on her dress.

"If you're having—"

"I'll be fine. I'm sure it's customary for a bride-to-be to feel anxious." Was she trying to reassure Hattie or herself? Anna couldn't say with certainty.

"Customary, yes, but to the point of becoming ill?" Hattie lifted the loose curl at Anna's ear and returned to her task. "You and Boney have been good friends for many years."

Anna dipped her chin in a short nod. "Most of my way through school. The year before Boney left for the war, he played Joseph in the Christmas pageant, and I played Mary."

Hattie nodded, her hat brim bouncing again. "Friends, yes. But marriage, well, that's a lifelong commitment." She picked up the strands of hair she'd left hanging and began plaiting them.

Marriage hadn't been a lifelong commitment for Anna's parents. When she was a girl, her father had walked away and never looked back. Anna worried the seam in her muslin dress. Her friendship with Boney was largely based on the past, before the war. He had been the closest friend of her brother, Dedrick.

When Boney returned to Saint Charles a month ago with his condolences for the loss of her brother, she and Boney shared memories and commiserated over the damage the war had done. He witnessed its ill effects on her mother. In their subsequent visits, he said Anna deserved to have a better life, to be cared for instead of having to do all the caring. Then he up and proposed marriage.

"Are you having second thoughts?" Hattie asked.

Second thoughts? Third and fourth thoughts. She felt more like crawling under the bed than standing at Boney's side in front of the pastor. And the cacophony of voices from the other side of the door did nothing to bring her peace. Still, she couldn't change her mind now. Not with plans made and witnesses gathered. Not after the way she'd turned Boney down, then shown up at the men's camp with a change of mind.

Hattie tucked the tails of the loose braids into the chignon, then met Anna's gaze in the mirror. "Boney's return and proposal was a bit of a whirlwind. And this wedding is quite sudden." She lifted an eyebrow. "Are you marrying Boney for love?"

Swallowing the bitter lump in her throat, Anna nodded. Of course she loved Boney. Everyone did. What wasn't to love about him? He was generous and lighthearted. A hard worker. Not only was he a trail hand for the caravan of wagons that would depart Saint Charles next week, but he'd been helping Großvater ready their wagon for the trip. And Boney had loved Dedrick as a brother.

Anna's breath caught. She loved Boney like a brother. Mutter's prompting had influenced her, but it wasn't what had persuaded her to change her mind and marry Boney. *Dedrick.* She'd been desperate to feel close to her brother. When she saw Boney standing in Großvater's kitchen, she felt hope stir inside her. Boney helped her remember her brother.

But was that enough reason for her to marry him?

"Perhaps if you stood and rinsed your face." Hattie glanced at the washstand in the corner.

Anna nodded. Her thoughts had been untangled. It was time she did the same for her insides. It would feel good to stretch a bit. She walked to the wooden stand. While Hattie tipped the pitcher and poured water into the bowl, Anna pulled her washcloth from its peg.

"Thank you."

Hattie returned the pitcher to the shelf. "I only wish there was more I could do to help you."

"You've helped more than you know." More than Anna was ready to say. She still had a question to answer. Was having shared memories of her brother enough of a foundation on which to build a lifelong marriage?

Anna plunged the cloth into the cold water, then wrung out the excess. She'd just pressed the cool refreshment to her face when the door clicked open. She peered over the top of the cloth as Mutter swept into the room, swaying and swerving toward the washstand. Had she been drinking with guests in the house? A wave of heat burned Anna's neck.

Dedrick may have been Anna's motivation to accept Boney's proposal, but Mutter had probably been his reason for asking. Boney thought he could save her from Mutter's unquenchable grief.

Hattie closed the door and joined them at the bowl. "I just finished Anna's hair."

Mutter tugged at the wrinkled sleeves on her shirtwaist. "Anna, you've kept Mr. Hughes waiting long enough." The stench of whiskey hung in the air between them, taunting Anna.

Hattie sighed, her jaw tight. "Ma'am, Anna isn't feeling well."

Again ignoring Hattie, Mutter took the washcloth from Anna and dropped it into the bowl. The splash spotted Anna's pink skirt. "You're excited, is all."

"But this is happening so fast," Anna said. "I don't—"

"Nonsense." Mutter yanked a towel from its peg and studied her. "You still look a little pale, but a brisk walk across the continent will cure that." She pressed the towel into Anna's hand. "Now dry your face and follow me."

It wasn't how she looked that concerned Anna, but how she felt about this marriage. Feelings weren't something Mutter cared to concern herself with.

Anna fell into line behind Mutter, taking slow steps toward the door. The jitters were threatening to topple her when she felt Hattie's hand on her arm.

With one hand on the doorknob, Mutter grabbed Anna's hand, pulling her arm from Hattie's grip. "This isn't the time for lollygagging."

Caleb Reger watched the bride's mother disappear through a side door. He stood beside a bookcase in the corner of the Gobens' sitting room, formulating a list of other things he'd rather be doing. Should be doing. So far, he'd come up with fifteen—inspecting wagons, checking the dry goods store for supplies, studying *Horn's Overland Guide*, washing his socks . . . One week from today, the Boone's Lick Company of wagons would roll out of Saint Charles, headed west. He should've stayed back at camp with Isaac. He didn't need to be here. It wasn't as if the boss were getting hitched. But Garrett Cowlishaw and four of his five hands *were* here. And one of them was about to make a big mistake.

A man didn't take a job on a wagon train then get married right before the long, taxing journey. Boney Hughes had seemed so levelheaded until

Miss Goben showed up at their camp last Friday. The poor fellow hadn't been thinking clearly for days now. And neither was the boss, to be standing up for Boney in the ceremony. Made no sense at all.

The two men stood in front of the hearth, deep in conversation. It wasn't too late for Garrett to talk some sense into Boney. Caleb shook his head. His father would never have agreed to officiate the ceremony. Nor would Reverend Reger have conducted a wedding without a proper courtship and permission from the parents involved. Where he came from, folks didn't marry inside a house. Weddings were sacred rites, deserving nothing less than the sanctity of God's church. Nothing about this felt right.

"You been to a wedding before?" Tiny scrubbed his smooth cheek with a hand the size of a grizzly claw.

"My sister's."

"They take long?"

"They can. Especially if the bride's fussy."

"Your sister, was she fussy?"

Caleb shook his head. "Her ceremony was said and done in less than twenty minutes." Caleb glanced toward the closed door where he presumed the bride was readying herself. Thus far, Miss Goben wasn't quick about it. She had near to twelve folks, mostly men, stuffed into a room with seating for five. Among them were

Otto Goben, the bride's grandfather, Charles Pemberton, who had come with his sister, and Frank Marble, the other trail hand present. Three children crowded around Mrs. Brantenberg and a Mrs. Rafferty, who wasn't going on the caravan.

Another five minutes passed before the bride's mother reopened the side door and stepped into the room.

"Good." Tiny's attempt at a whisper was a wasted effort. "Looks like it'll be over soon."

Caleb nodded, hoping Tiny was right.

Hand in hand with her daughter, the older woman nodded toward Otto. He pulled his mandolin from a side table and started playing an upbeat rhythm. Then she turned expectantly to her daughter.

Without moving into the room, Miss Goben stared at Boney. The color drained from her face. She looked frozen in place as she motioned for Boney to come to her.

Boney left Garrett's side and walked to Miss Goben.

When the music stopped, the bride's mother swept faded brown hair from her face. "Keep playing, Vater."

When Otto resumed the melody, the mother jerked her attention back to the bride and groom. "This isn't—"

Boney raised his hand, one finger lifted. "We need a moment, ma'am."

"But—"

Ignoring the mother, Boney held his arm out to Miss Goben. When she laid her hand on his jacket sleeve, he escorted her out the front door. The bride's mother wasn't the only one left with wide eyes and a slack jaw. Caleb closed his mouth. Miss Hattie Pemberton took quick steps to her brother Charles's side.

Tiny attempted another whisper. "And this? What's this?"

"Unusual."

"Think she went cold on him?"

"May have." Miss Goben was proving to be as fickle as spring weather. She'd told Boney no one minute then shown up at camp with a change of mind, as if playing with a man's heart were an acceptable sport.

Five minutes later, Boney slipped in through the front door, his jacket open and his face long. Tugging his string tie loose, he spoke in whispers to Otto Goben. The bride's mother fought to get a word in edgewise until her father was finally able to silence her. Boney then spoke to Garrett and the pastor before facing the small crowd.

Pressing his felt hat to his chest, Boney cleared his throat. "Thank you all for coming to share in mine and Anna's . . . uh, merriment. While we regret any hardship we have caused you in joining us, Miss Goben and I have decided not to wed."

Murmurs swept across the room until a door creaked at the back of the house and the bride's mother marched out of the room.

Caleb followed Boney and the other hands out the front door.

When they reached the hitching rail, Frank slapped his misshapen felt hat on his thigh and looked at Boney. "When I saw you talkin' to her at that first wagon train meeting, I figured she was trouble. A young woman like that alone at a town meeting? Just ain't right."

Boney shook his head and took off toward camp. Poor fellow expected to be wed and spending the night with his bride. Now, like the rest of them, he was stuck with a bunch of trail hands.

Caleb hadn't remembered seeing Anna Goben at the town meeting. But she was unforgettable now. And Frank was right—she was trouble. Boney was a good man. A better man than deserved having to do Miss Goben's dirty work, having to stand in front of everyone with his heart broken, or at the least his pride wounded. And now the young woman would be traveling west with them.

Unless she planned to back out of the trip too. Wouldn't hurt Caleb's feelings any if she did.

2

Mutter stood in Anna's bedchamber, her fists planted on her hips and her face tight. "Everyone's gone. Including your grandfather."

Anna drew in a fortifying breath. "I didn't intend—"

"I never figured you for bein' so careless, Anna Mae. Men like Boney don't grow on trees like apples, you know."

"I'm only eighteen, Mutter. I hardly think my decision not to marry Boney means I will live my life as a spinster."

"Time moves faster than you think." A shadow crossed Mutter's face. "You just passed up your best chance to escape your life taking care of us."

Anna moistened her lips, giving herself time to think. What was she to say to that? "Boney and I are good friends, nothing more."

"Friendship is a stronger foundation for a marriage than most. If your father and I had been friends . . . well, things might have turned out differently." Shaking her head, Mutter stared at Anna with steely eyes. "You careless fool!" She spun toward the door and slammed it shut behind her.

Defying her weak knees, Anna stepped out of the pink dress and hung it in the wardrobe, her mind hanging on every memory of the past hour. When she'd said she couldn't go through with the ceremony, Boney said he understood her decision. He even looked a bit relieved when she said his proposal meant the world to her but it would be wrong for her to marry him. His gracious acceptance of her last-minute decision had settled her stomach. She'd felt peace about not getting married today.

Until Mutter stormed into the kitchen and followed her to the bedchamber. And when Hattie refused to even attempt to convince Anna to go through with the ceremony, Mutter pitched a fit and sent Hattie home.

Anna pulled her worn calico dress from the wardrobe. A good and honorable man, Boney had seen to the announcement himself. He didn't make her face his buddies or her mother in front of the crowd.

Sighing, she slid the dress over her head. Nothing had changed for her, except that she'd added insult to injury and wasted everyone's time. Her only hope for seeing Mutter or Großvater stand on their own two feet again lay in her family's journey west. The adventure of being active, out in nature, and interacting with other people had to be what would make the difference for Mutter. To make her the strong one again. Anna couldn't bear seeing them withdraw from life—and from her—much longer.

Anna perched on the bench at the dressing table and laced her boots. Mutter was wrong—she hadn't made a stupid mistake calling off the wedding. She and Boney didn't love each other in a romantic way, and Hattie was right to remind her that it mattered. It wasn't fair to Boney that she marry him because of Dedrick, or because she was tired of being the only strong, responsible family member.

Pots and pans clanged on the other side of the wall. The bean kettle. Was that where Mutter had stashed her latest bottle? Her fingers trembling, Anna looped the buttons down the front of her dress. She pulled a shawl from the wardrobe then ventured out into the sitting room. The scent of working men lingered along with the extra chairs they'd gathered for the wedding guests. Mutter had apparently found her consolation and settled into her bed with it.

This was the last place Anna wanted to be. Großvater had the right idea in leaving the house.

Willing herself to step lightly, Anna slipped out thc front door and down the steps. A chilling breeze alerted her to the clouds gathering across the Missouri River. She tugged her shawl tight and took quick steps down the hill toward Heinrich's Dry Goods and Grocery. She preferred to be the one who gave her quilting circle sisters an explanation of her last-minute decision.

When Emilie Heinrich, now Emilie McFarland,

wasn't busy with her courses at Lindenwood Female College, she helped her father in his store. Maren Wainwright had also recently wed and given up her job at the store, but she'd agreed to help out during the rush to provision wagons for the grand departure next week. Anna's widowed friend Caroline was also in Mr. Heinrich's employ. At least until next Tuesday, when she would join the westbound caravan, employed as a nanny for the Kamden family.

At the bottom of the hill, Anna turned right on Main Street and paused for a moment outside the millinery. She'd lost count of the number of hats she'd designed, created, and sold to the proprietor. That and candle sales to Mr. Heinrich had been what had kept her family afloat this past year and a half. She'd make sure to stop at the millinery another day this week to say good-bye. Right now, she was on a mission.

At the next corner, Anna crossed the street and walked the cobblestone sidewalk in front of the Old Capitol Building that housed Johann Heinrich's Dry Goods and Grocery. This time she had no candles to deliver and no shopping list to fulfill, only a desperate need to see the smiles of her friends.

When an ache gripped Garrett Cowlishaw's bad knee, he instinctively bent to rub his leg.

"You okay, Boss?" Caleb, one of his five

trail hands, pushed his derby back on his head.

Garrett straightened. "Yeah. Thanks." The pain easing, he let out a long breath. "Leg just had to remind me it's there."

Caleb pulled a flour sack from the pile. "How many did you say we needed?"

Garrett glanced at the shopping list in his hand. "That and one more should do it. Came for blankets and beads, but, well, Boney still has other things on his mind, and I was coming to the store anyway."

After a quick nod, Caleb added the flour sack to the wheelbarrow they were using to collect supplies. "You suppose he'll be any less distracted, now that the wedding's been called off?"

Garrett shrugged. "I expect so. And he won't have a dithering wife to contend with."

Caleb opened his mouth to speak but looked past Garrett instead, his eyes widening.

"Pardon me?" The familiar voice tensed Garrett's shoulders.

How long had she been there? He hesitated to face her, but turned around anyway. The widow Caroline Milburn pinned him with a fiery gaze, her eyes as green as spring grass. She'd heard him. When he and Caleb had come into the store, Caroline must have been concealed behind the counter in a huddle of customers. Now she stood before him looking like a scorned schoolmarm.

Swallowing the lump in his throat, Garrett

removed his slouch hat. "Mrs. Milburn." He pointed the hat at his trail hand. "You know Caleb Reger?"

"We've met. Yes."

"Mrs. Milburn." Caleb gave her a polite nod, unable to draw her attention.

How was it that the redhead could appear so becoming in a simple work frock and a smudged shopkeeper's apron?

She crossed her arms. Her chin jutted out. "*Dithering wife,* Mr. Cowlishaw?"

He should've known the widow wouldn't let his statement go without a strong rebuke.

"I wouldn't have been surprised to learn you might allow such mockery among your ranks." Her shoulders squared. "But you, Mr. Cowlishaw, purported to be a Southern gentleman—I wouldn't expect such disrespect to fly from your mouth. Whoever the woman, I'm sure she doesn't deserve your harsh judgment."

Garrett let out a huff. "It was a private conversation, ma'am."

"In a very public place."

He couldn't argue with that, but . . . "You were not privy to the whole of the conversation."

Caroline Milburn tipped her face toward the ceiling, her jaw set. "I simply misunderstood your meaning?"

"Probably not. Only the context in which I said it."

She glanced at the clock above the counter. "The wedding?" She uncrossed her arms, her eyes widening. "You were talking about Anna?"

"We were there, ma'am." Caleb raked his hair. "But it didn't happen."

"I don't understand. Anna said—"

"She got cold feet and called it off." Caleb took a step back as he spoke.

She shifted her gaze to Garrett. "Thus earning your reproach."

Unable to resist the opportunity for rebuttal, he offered her a slight smile. "Dithering, as in wavering. Indecisive. That fits Miss Goben where Boney Hughes is concerned, for she's done nothing but change her mind. I simply stated that he is better off not marrying a woman who is not sure of the union, wouldn't you agree?"

Her mouth pursed in a frown, she looked at their wheelbarrow. "Flour. Did you need help finding something else?" she asked, her voice icy.

"Actually, I was wondering about Johann. I heard he'd had another of his spells this morning. How is he?"

Caroline looked at a closed door at the back of the store. "He's resting upstairs. His daughter, Emilie, and the doctor are with him."

"Please tell him we asked after him and offered our best."

She gave him a curt nod. "Now, if you'll excuse me."

"There was something else."

Her chin dipped as she glared up at him. "Well?"

"I ordered blankets."

"Red ones?"

"Yes ma'am." Her narrow-eyed frown told him he was fortunate she didn't have a ruler in her hand, for his knuckles would've surely received a good rapping.

"They're in one of those casks." Caroline pointed toward the crates and barrels along the back wall.

Garrett nodded. "Thank you." He took a step toward her. "Just one more thing."

Her perfectly shaped eyebrows arched.

"We're leaving one week from today—the Boone's Lick Wagon Train Company."

"Yes, I know. Thus the rush on supplies."

He nodded, working the brim of his hat. "It's going to be a difficult journey."

"You made that point in your speeches at the meetings. Hard work. Illness. Hostiles."

"And you'll be traveling with a Scottish family you don't really know, with traditions and foods you're not accustomed to. Carrying tremendous responsibilities."

"You don't think I can eat haggis or handle the Kamden children?"

Garrett kept those doubts to himself. "I wish you'd reconsider and remain in Saint Charles with your own family."

Her shoulders went back again. "You should know by now, Mr. Cowlishaw, that I am not a dithering or wavering woman. Nor am I indecisive."

"You indeed are not."

Sighing, she glanced at the counter where Maren Wainwright held up a cast-iron skillet. "I must help with the other customers."

"Of course." He returned his hat to his head. "Thank you."

She gave them each a sharp nod and walked away.

Garrett grabbed the handles on the barrow a little too forcefully and wheeled it to the back wall.

Caleb lifted a few crate lids and sacks, then turned toward him. "The widow certainly had you doing a dance."

"Never mind that." He let go of the cart and took the crate lid from Caleb. "As Boney found out today, women are complicated."

"Yes." His trail hand sighed. "They are."

"You have a story to tell?"

Caleb shook his head. "We weren't talking about me."

They never were. The young man was as tightlipped as a catfish about himself. In the employment interview, Garrett had asked Caleb about his family and involvement in the war. Caleb was just as mute on those topics as he was about his love life. A hesitancy Garrett shared. He would carry his own secrets on the road west.

"Found the blankets." Caleb lifted a sack from the crate. "We all have bedrolls. Expecting a freeze out on the prairie in July and August, are you?"

Garrett chuckled. "We'll be wishin' for a chill in the air." He shook his head. "They're trading materials for the Indians. They like blankets and beads. A little something I learned on my first run west." While Caleb added the blankets to the cart and closed the barrel, Garrett glanced toward the rack of spice tins where Caroline Milburn now helped a customer, red curls dangling at her neck. So much for trying to get on her good side, or at the very least not aggravate her.

"Boss?"

"Uh-huh."

"Does the widow know you stare at her?"

Jerking his gaze from the counter, Garrett met the younger man's grin. "I wasn't. I don't." He scrubbed his whiskered chin. "I might have been thinking. Have a lot on my mind."

The grin still planted on his face, Caleb held his hands up in mock surrender. "I don't care if you stare at her, Boss."

She would care.

"Just don't get all atwitter and propose marriage to her."

Garrett laughed. "No chance of that. Mrs.

Milburn and I would have to at least like each other before that could happen."

"You're telling me you don't like her?" Caleb's voice dripped with sarcasm.

"She doesn't like me."

"Because you can't help putting your foot in your mouth?"

Garrett sobered in a memory. "First, because of my uniform." To avoid looking at her, he glanced at the shopping list: *coffee, sugar.*

"Same uniform I wore."

"But you didn't step into her path wearing gray trousers and kepi while she waited for word on her missing husband, a Union colonel."

A shadow darkened Caleb's eyes.

"She was with her sister, two nieces, a nephew, and stranded by a broken wagon wheel when I happened upon them." He remembered seeing the accusation and pain in her eyes, and shook his head as if it could set the memory free. "You would've thought I had horns and carried a pitchfork."

"For a lot of folks, we did."

One particular Thursday last fall crowded Garrett's mind. He'd stood before Caroline Milburn, holding a letter from the Department of War concerning Colonel Milburn. He *was* the devil that day. Garrett gripped the cart handles and looked over his shoulder at Caleb. "I might stare at the widow now and again, but that's the extent. Let's leave it at that."

“Whatever you say, Boss.”

Garrett wheeled the cart toward the front of the store. All he did was irritate Caroline Milburn, reminding her of the life she’d never have. He needed to avoid her. A difficult task with her bent on going west with the caravan, thanks to Ian and Rhoda Kamden giving her the means to do so.

He shook his head. He’d best concentrate on his own affairs and the task at hand. “Let’s finish the shopping and get back to camp. You get two sacks of coffee. I’ll find the sugar.”

Caleb nodded and walked toward the mounds of burlap sacks against one wall.

Garrett had just reached for the sack of sugar when he saw Anna Goben outside the front window. Had she looked in through the window, the young woman probably would have turned around. He would have, had it been him. Instead, Miss Goben opened the door and stepped inside. A breeze fluttered the paper sign above the coffee sacks.

Caleb lifted the sack he held to one shoulder. He raised the collar on his coat and looked up. The sack fell to the plank floor, spilling a handful of coffee beans and scenting the chilled air. He glared at Anna. “What are you doing here?”

Miss Goben’s eyes widened like an antelope staring down a gun barrel. “Pardon me?”

That seemed the phrase of the day, at least from any women they encountered. Garrett quickly joined Caleb. “Hello, Miss Goben.” He doffed his slouch hat, and Caleb bent to scoop up the run-away coffee beans.

“Mr. Cowlishaw.” Her jaw tight, she looked around him to the counter where Maren Wainwright took money from a customer. “Have you heard how Mr. Heinrich is faring?”

“I was told he is resting upstairs. His daughter is with him.”

She nodded.

Caleb stood. One hand gripped the sack while the other cupped coffee beans. “The dry goods store doesn’t seem a likely place for you to do your gloating.”

She squared her shoulders, her chin jutting. “You, sir, are a man of ill-formed suppositions.”

Garrett knew he should scold Caleb for his rudeness, but instead he put his effort into hiding the smile that tugged at his lips. He wasn’t one to talk, having had a similar conversation with Caroline Milburn just moments earlier.

“Are you still planning to go west with your mother and grandfather?” Caleb asked her.

“I am. Do you have a problem with that, Mr.—”

“Reger. Caleb Reger.” He arched his eyebrows. “I don’t have a problem with it, but my good friend Boney might.”

“Your *good* friend?” As if surprised she’d said it aloud, Miss Goben looked at Garrett. “Pardon me.”

Garrett nodded and brushed the brim of his hat. He and Caleb both watched Miss Goben walk toward the widow Caroline Milburn, and then he looked at Caleb. "You're not the one staring now, are you?"

"At her? No sir. She's trouble."

Garrett smiled. His exact sentiments concerning Mrs. Milburn.

Hmm. Miss Goben would be a distraction for at least two of his hands. Perhaps it was time he pay her grandfather a visit to question his plans to go west.

3

Sunshine defied the gathering clouds and warmed Anna's face, but still she fought the chill running up her spine.

"The dry goods store doesn't seem a likely place for you to do your gloating."

Caleb Reger may prove to be a good scout for the captain of the wagon train, but he had much to learn about being a civil human being. Did he really believe she'd made her decision not to marry Boney with lightness and merriment?

Anna's footfalls were anything but ladylike as she stomped up Main Street. At least she'd been able to visit with Caroline and Maren for a few minutes. Otherwise, she would've been better off staying home and tangling with her mother. She knew what to expect from Mutter. Mr. Reger's insolence had caught her off guard. Now that she knew he was prone to address issues he knew nothing about, it wouldn't happen again.

"I don't have a problem with it, but my good friend Boney might."

He worried about his *good friend* Boney? Mr. Reger had met Boney mere weeks ago. She'd gone to school with him, played dominoes with him and her brother. She'd known Boney for ten years. Her decision not to marry him may have seemed hasty, but it wasn't in the least thoughtless.

Anna passed Becks' Cobbler Shop. The elder Mr. Beck sat out on the stoop, whittling a pair of wooden shoes. Mr. Beck and his wife, Irene, his son, Arven, and his wife, Lorelei, were among those joining the Boone's Lick Company caravan of wagons. His mallet tapped the chisel lightly, in rhythm with her footfalls. The sound followed her as she drew close to her turn.

If true love was anywhere near as complicated as the lack of it, Anna wanted no part of romance. She was better off going west as planned—a single woman traveling with her family. Somewhere in California, near Hattie and Caroline, she'd set up her millinery. A single businesswoman. That had been her goal before Boney's return to Saint Charles, and it was still an appealing plan.

First, she had to survive traipsing over hill and vale with the sour Mr. Caleb Reger.

"Look out, lady!"

The gruff order stopped Anna in her tracks. A yoke of oxen skidded to a stop not two feet from her. The contents of the wagon they pulled shifted with a crunch. Her heart pounding, Anna couldn't move. The lead oxen offered a wet snort uncomfortably close to her face.

A sharp whistle drew her gaze to the burly man holding the lead rope on the far side. "Good thing I was mindin' what you were doing, ma'am." His thick brows knit together. "Woulda plowed right into ya, if'n I weren't."

"Yes sir. Thank you kindly." Anna dipped her chin in gratitude and took a few steps backward, motioning for him to move forward.

After seeing the tailgate on the farm wagon pass her by, Anna carefully crossed the busy street and started up the hill. Her encounter with Mr. Reger had been a troubling distraction, one that she needed to push from her mind so she could think and pray about what to say when she arrived home.

Life in Saint Charles had been good. Mutter had worked at the millinery and became involved in Mrs. Brantenberg's quilting circle. Großvater had been teaching Dedrick his trade of caning chairs.

They'd been happy here. But the War between the States changed everything. Anna had learned heartbreak could build your faith or tear you down. In the past year and a half since Dedrick's death, she'd watched her grandfather take to his chair and her mother turn to the bottle.

When her breaths became shallow, Anna realized she was stomping up the hill. She slowed her pace, but couldn't hinder her thoughts. If she was old enough to decide to marry a man then choose not to, she was old enough to be heard.

She only prayed Mutter was clearheaded enough to hear her out and later remember what she said.

As Anna approached their light blue house, third from the corner, she saw Großvater sitting on the front porch. Not only was he home, but he sat on a stool with a chair frame balanced on his lap. The once-familiar sight of him working nearly stole her breath.

Now if only he'd quit eating like a sparrow and put some meat back on his bones.

He coughed then rubbed the balding spot amidst his gray hair. "I wondered if you'd be coming back."

"I wondered the same about you."

A slow smile crinkled the corners of his eyes. "A tough day."

Nodding, Anna sank into a finished rocker beside him. "I went to the store to see my friends."

"Did it help?"

She drew in a deep breath. “Some.”

Großvater shook his head. “That was about as convincing as one snowflake in summer.”

“Garrett Cowlishaw and Mr. Reger were in the store.”

He lifted a length of cane from the washbasin and shook off the water. “I don’t suppose that was very comfortable, them working with Boney.”

“I would’ve expected discomfort.”

His hands stilled and his thin eyebrows arched in an unspoken question.

“Mr. Reger felt it necessary to voice his disdain for women who change their minds.”

Großvater threaded the cane through a hole and pinned it with a wedge. “What does he know about it?”

“Precisely.” Anna blew out a long, unladylike breath. Time to change the subject. The insufferable Mr. Reger wasn’t worth another thought. She glanced at the basin then to the chair he was caning. “It does my heart good to see you working.”

He coughed again. She lifted his coffee cup from the table and handed it to him. His hands had gotten so thin and his face was drawn. As much as she wanted to give him a new life—all of them a new life—the trip might be too taxing for Großvater.

“It’s about time I quit skulking and pulled my own weight around here again. You’re young,

Anna. I hoped you would marry Boney just so you could have a life besides caring for me and your mutter. You've done nothing but cook and work and clean since we lost your brother."

Anna looked away from his all-too-familiar grief. Mutter and Großvater had needed her. They still did. How could she have considered marrying, and moving on?

"With my apprentice gone, I didn't care much about caning chairs." He laid another length of cane in the washbasin. "Didn't care about much of anything."

Anna brushed a strand of wayward hair from her face. "I miss Dedrick too. Especially today."

His eyes narrowed. "Was your brother the reason you agreed to marry Boney?"

She nodded. "Being around Boney and talking about Dedrick made me feel less lonely."

Großvater nodded. Grief had robbed him of his appetite and hollowed his cheeks. But here he was, working again.

"Großvater?"

"I can't remember when my name's carried that much weight."

"Mutter thinks I was foolish not to marry him."

"Your mutter, she just wants you to have a good life. Boney is a fine man. Like me, she probably saw marrying him as your chance to escape our grief and find a better way for yourself."

Anna shifted in the chair. "She could've been nicer about it."

Großvater nodded, and dipped more cane in the basin. "I trust your judgment, Anna girl. You've always been real smart."

"I don't feel very smart today."

"Well, then, I say it's a good thing you're trusting more than your feelings." Smiling, he wove the cane across the seat.

The Großvater she knew was climbing out of his grief and coming back to her before they'd even pulled away from Saint Charles.

He stilled his hands again and looked her in the eye. "Boney will be in the caravan. You still want to go west?"

Anna glanced at the closed door beside her. "As far as Boney is concerned, I feel fine." Mutter and Mr. Reger were another matter. And so was Großvater's cough. "What about you? When did you start coughing?"

"Oh, that." He waved his hand. "Just a bother from that can of wildflowers Miss Hattie brought for the wedding. Set a tickle in my throat from the moment she walked in."

She hesitated but decided to accept his explanation. "What about Mutter? Do you think she's strong enough to make the trip?"

"It's given me new hope for the future. I'm praying the trip will do the same for my Wilma."

Anna nodded. That was her hope too, even though doubts daily hounded her heels.

Großvater continued weaving the cane. "Do you think Mr. Cowlishaw knows?"

"I don't know. But Boney does."

He nodded.

"Boney understands and wouldn't speak of our business."

The crease in Großvater's brow told Anna he was concerned. Was there a chance the captain could deny them passage in the caravan because of Mutter?

Anna's spine stiffened. She couldn't let that happen. Somehow, she'd make sure there weren't any bottles in the wagon when they headed out of town next week.

Caroline Milburn scooped a spoonful of boiled potatoes onto four-year-old Mary's plate. Her youngest niece looked up, tears pooling her green eyes. Come Tuesday, leaving Mary in Saint Charles would be nearly impossible. Leaving any of her family would be impossible, excluding Jack. She was all too anxious to rid herself of his company. Her brother-in-law sat in his wicker wheelchair at the head of the table pushing cooked carrots to the lonely side of his plate, his nose rutted in a permanent frown.

"Aunt Caroline, we don't want you to go." Her oldest niece sat across the table, sprigs of auburn hair escaping tired braids. The pleading in seven-year-old Cora's eyes deepened the ache in Caroline's heart. The fact that they'd had this same conversation every day for weeks hadn't lessened the pain it caused.

Caroline didn't dare look at Jewell, for her sister would surely cry again, and she couldn't bear it. Not tonight.

"I need to go," Caroline said.

Mary's little lips pursed in a pout. "Those children don't love you like we do, Auntie Carol-i."

Caroline's breath caught. She couldn't argue with that. She'd only been around the five Kamden children twice and hadn't heard them utter anything but polite greetings to her. How did she expect to live with a new family day and night for four or five months? People she didn't know. Didn't love.

Caroline ran her fingertip along the rim of her plate. "Now that Uncle Phillip is dead . . ." There, she'd said it—Phillip was dead. Not coming back to her. She cleared her throat and finished her statement. "Now that he is dead, I need to make a new life for myself."

"I wish I was goin' with you." The freckles that mapped the bridge of nine-year-old Gilbert's nose belied an innocence his life didn't satisfy. Life with a father who had come home from the war not only missing a leg but his heart as well.

Caroline rested her hand on Gilbert's arm. "I wish you were going too. I'll miss you all." She didn't look at Jack.

Her brother-in-law rolled his chair under the edge of the table. "We're not going, and you are. Now that we have that settled, we can eat in peace and quiet." After giving Caroline a pointed look, his eyes steely, Jack held his plate out to Cora. "Give me more potatoes. At least they're fit to eat."

Caroline bit her bottom lip. It was impossible to do anything in peace with Jack in the house. That was why she needed to leave. She couldn't save her sister from Jack's venom, but she could spare herself. Phillip was gone. He'd want her to move beyond what she'd lost to pursue a fresh beginning without him. And without the ever-present dark cloud that was her brother-in-law.

Working in Heinrich's Dry Goods and Grocery wasn't a bad job, but when her workday was done, she went home to her sister's house. To her sister's family. To her sister's life. Her chance at a family of her own had died in the war, but was it too much to ask for a life of her own?

Caleb hoisted the last sack into the chuck wagon. He added the coffee and sugar to their respective barrels and stashed jerky in the wagon box under the seat. When they pulled out next week, he'd miss Saint Charles. Its brick buildings and clean boardwalks. The redbud and oak trees. The river meandering on the edge of town. He had done a lot of wandering during the war and since, and it felt good to be in one place these past couple of months. But soon he'd be wandering again. This time with a caravan of people he'd met here. Including the vacillating Miss Anna Goben.

In this rare opportunity to be alone, he sank onto the board floor and leaned against a barrel. The moment he and Garrett had left the dry goods store that afternoon, his boss had questioned Caleb's behavior toward the young woman, and he'd thought of little else since. He didn't know Boney Hughes outside of working with him and living in camp these past few weeks. Nor had the jilted groom asked him to fight his battles.

Caleb sighed. Perhaps he had been unfair in his judgment of Miss Goben, certainly in expressing it. Boney's love life was none of his concern, and neither was hers.

When the savory aroma of stewed ham and beans wafted through the front flap of the chuck wagon, Caleb's stomach growled and he stood. It was his night to cook, but Boney had spared them all by volunteering to fix supper.

Caleb slapped his hat on his head, then stepped over the wagon seat and swung down onto the steel tire. Using the spokes of the wheel as a ladder, he jumped off midwheel and landed with both feet on the ground. He fell into line behind Tiny and the others.

Standing at the suspended dutch oven, Boney dished generous portions of beans and biscuits onto tin plates. At the first couple of meals at the camp, the fifth trail hand in their company, Isaac, took the end of the line and sat off on his own. Since then, Garrett made sure the freedman from Savannah was up front and fed. Tonight, Garrett stood directly behind Isaac, followed by Frank and Tiny.

Frank took his plate and looked at Tiny. "There's no way you're feedin' him beans." His Kentucky drawl drew everyone's attention. He glanced at the billowing storm clouds overhead, then at their tent cabin. "Not if there's any chance I'll be cooped up with him."

Caleb laughed along with the others, including Tiny.

Tiny shook his finger at Frank. "I ain't the only one."

Boney pulled two fresh biscuits from the pan and handed Tiny his plate. "Just you remember, 'twas not me tryin' to stand between you and food. I say if we all have beans, it don't make no difference who the culprit is."

Caleb carried his food to a downed log at the campfire and settled beside Isaac.

The sounds from other camps along the creek provided background noise for the clank of forks against tin. Overhead, a cap of clouds had dropped the temperatures near freezing. Caleb raised the collar on his coat then scooped up a big chunk of ham with his beans. He hadn't eaten this good since he'd left home. Now, his boyhood life in Nashville seemed a faded dream.

"Mister Boney." Isaac shook his head. "I's sorry to hear your bride got cold feet." He dragged his biscuit through the dregs of his beans.

Tiny nodded and looked at the rejected groom. "Woulda been a different ending, if the little lady had ever tasted your cookin'." He grinned. "And I was lookin' forward to the shivaree."

Heartache wasn't a light matter. Caleb set his fork on the plate. "If you ask me, that would've for sure been a marriage of inconvenience."

"I didn't ask." Boney's jaw hardened. "And where'd you find so many words for things you know nothing about?"

Caleb swallowed hard. "I didn't mean any harm."

"Well, you can save your pity for someone who needs it. I don't." Boney tapped the spoon on the edge of the pot, knocking off a glob of beans. "Miss Anna Goben is one of the finest women I know." He pointed the spoon at Caleb. "And if I ever hear you vilify her again, I'll tear into you before you've had a chance to swallow your fear. That clear?"

Caleb startled. "Perfectly. I didn't mean to offend you or Miss Goben."

The spoon plopped into the cook pot, and Boney stomped toward the creek.

While the rest of the fellows let out a collective sigh, Caleb hoped Miss Goben wasn't inclined to tell Boney of their encounter in the dry goods store. If anyone had the gift of sticking their foot in their mouth, it was him.

4

Anna dodged mud puddles on her stroll down the hill. The rains had started Tuesday night and hadn't let up until suppertime yesterday. For the past several months, Thursdays had been her favorite day of the week. But today was to be her last in Mrs. Brantenberg's Saint Charles quilting circle. In five days, she would join the wagon train, leaving several of her friends behind.

Watching for the farm wagons and various buggies choking the downtown streets, Anna crossed Main Street and turned toward Heinrich's Dry Goods store. Today, the circle would meet in the apartment over the store rather than out on the farm.

Caroline and her sister, Jewell, waved from the corner, where they waited on Anna. Caroline's niece Mary clung to her aunt's hand. Anna waved and quickened her pace.

"Good morning!" Caroline pulled Anna into a welcoming embrace.

"Good morning."

Mary held up a quilted doll. "I brought a present for my friend. Did you know Gabi is going to . . ." She looked up at Caroline. "Where are you going?"

"California." Caroline's voice cracked, and her green eyes became moist.

"To Cal . . . where Aunt Carol-i is going."

Anna nodded, studying the patchwork doll. "What a nice present."

Mary rocked back and forth, her calico skirt swaying. "Her name is Mary too."

"Such a lovely name. For a dolly, and for a sweet girl." Anna patted the bonnet that contained the child's strawberry curls. She would miss Jewell and her children, but her heart truly ached for the sisters. Come Tuesday, Caroline would leave Jewell and her family behind.

They'd just stepped in front of the display window at Heinrich's Dry Goods and Grocery when the door swung open. Emilie Heinrich McFarland waved them inside. "Come in. Come in. Hattie and Mrs. Brantenberg and all the others are upstairs."

When they'd finished with the first round of hugs, Anna glanced at the potbellied stove in the center of the store where Johann Heinrich sat at the checkerboard with Oliver Rengler. He greeted them with a nod and a wave as they strolled to the open door at the back.

Anna followed Emilie up the stairs. "Your PaPa, how is he?"

Emilie turned and smiled. "More and more ornery every day."

"Then he's doing well?"

"Yes, and he insists that visiting with customers for two hours isn't work, so he'll manage the store while I'm upstairs. With Oliver looking after him." Emilie continued climbing.

Despite the creak of the wooden steps, their friends' voices found their way down the stairwell, and Hattie's cackle was unmistakable. Gabi Wainwright's little face appeared first at the top of the stairwell. "They came!"

Little Mary rushed up the steps, squeezing past Anna and Emilie. "I brought you a present, Gabi!"

Maren's little stepdaughter, Gabi, swung a quilted doll out from behind her back. "I have one for you too." The colors were different and the size slightly smaller, but both were from a pattern Mrs. Brantenberg had shared in the quilting circle.

"They're the same." Mary set her doll to dancing in the air.

Gabi nodded. "Mother Maren helped me make it."

Mother Maren. Anna's heart warmed. Good had come out of the war too. Gabi's father, Rutherford Wainwright, had returned home and found love with Maren Jensen and was building a new family.

In the sitting room at the top of the stairs, Hattie Pemberton, adorned in a straw hat, her mother Bette, a war widow, and both of the Beck women huddled around Mary Alice Brenner and her newborn, Evie. Elsa Brantenberg buzzed about the small kitchen. Plates of sliced almond pound cake, anise cookies, and Berliners lined the countertop.

Maren Wainwright came from the corner where the two little girls played with their dolls. She tucked a strand of blond hair into the braided spiral atop her head then greeted Anna with a hug. "It's not even New Year's Eve and Mother Brantenberg made her filled doughnuts for us."

"Everything looks delicious." Anna sighed. By New Year's they would all have new lives—some of them scattered across the West, others here.

Hattie joined them and pulled Anna into a warm embrace. "Have you seen the quilts yet?" She directed Anna's attention to the back of the sofa where the two friendship album quilts the circle had made lay side by side.

Anna took slow steps to the parting remembrance. One quilt was trimmed in red, the other in a cocoa brown. Each woman had stitched her signature in an album block. Anna ran her hand over the scrap square she'd made for the quilt that would remain in Saint Charles. She'd added her mother's name below hers, even though Wilma Goben, by her own choice, hadn't been part of the group for nearly a year and a half.

With the greetings completed, the women filled their plates at the kitchen counter, then seated themselves at one of two tables extending into the sitting room.

Mrs. Brantenberg sat in a cushioned chair at the head of the table. The blue paisley dress she wore had her looking more chipper than the occasion might call for. When the older widow had blessed the Lord for their time together and thanked Him for the bounty, she cleared her throat and glanced at the quilts draping the sofa. "As you all know, we've made one quilt for those going west and another for those remaining in Saint Charles." She raised an eyebrow, her mouth curving into a grin. "Someone has changed her mind."

Hattie lifted the brim of her hat, peering at their leader. "You changed your mind?"

"Yes." Mrs. Brantenberg's nod was exaggerated and her smile wide. "And I asked Johann Heinrich to marry me."

Anna's mouth dropped open in a gasp that joined several others in the room. She knew the widow and the shopkeeper had been friends for thirty years or more, but marriage?

"He said yes!" Mrs. Brantenberg's blue eyes sparkled.

Emilie stilled her fork midair, a smile tipping her mouth. "They'll marry Sunday after the service, and I couldn't be happier."

"That's wonderful news." The tension on Hattie's face didn't support her statement. "I don't mean to be lemon juice in the sugar bowl, but what about those of us going on the trail? And your family?"

Anna sighed. She would miss having Mrs. Brantenberg on the road with them, and she wasn't even her kin. But little Gabi wouldn't have her grandmother with her, and Mrs. Brantenberg had been like a mother to Maren.

Maren blinked. Anna wasn't sure if her friend was merely focusing her failing vision or fighting tears. "Of course we will miss Mother Brantenberg, but we are happy for her and for Emilie's father. Not everyone gets a second chance at love."

Or a first chance at love. Anna opened her mouth to add her good wishes but fell silent in her thoughts. What if friendship could be enough of a basis for marriage? She was only eighteen, certainly not beyond marrying age, but what if Mutter was right, and she'd turned down her best chance of escaping Mutter's grief? To marry someone who knew and understood her family?

Caleb proceeded up the line of wagons to the next one to be inspected. The sight of six carriage horses in hames harness stopped him cold. Dr. Édouard Le Beau perched on the wagon seat, chin up and shoulders back, the reins slack in his hand. His teenage daughter sat beside him, already taller than her father.

The doctor adjusted the red, cone-shaped hat on his head and spoke in French.

Straightening her back, Mademoiselle Camille looked at Caleb. "Is something amiss, Mr. Reger?"

Caleb removed his derby then wiped his brow with his shirt sleeve. "In the provisions list, Captain Cowlishaw recommended oxen or mules to pull the wagons." He glanced from the doctor to the young woman with hair the color of midnight.

"*Oui.*" That was the only word Caleb recognized before the man's daughter opened her mouth.

"Papa says, 'But I don't have oxen or mules.' "

Dr. Le Beau raised his hands, palms up. More French.

"I have only horses." Mademoiselle Camille raised her eyebrows as her father had.

"It won't be an easy journey." Caleb raked his hair and returned his hat to his head. "Oxen are a much stronger animal, and mules are less skittish."

While speaking, the doctor climbed down from the wagon seat.

The young woman remained seated. "Again, my Papa said, 'I don't have oxen or mules.' "

Caleb drew in a deep breath. "Only horses."

She nodded.

Caleb started his inspection with the lead horses, lifting each hoof to check the farrier's handiwork. As he moved behind each horse, he gave the withers a pat to make sure there was no sign of spooking. He tugged and jangled every part of the harness, hoping to find some reason to reject the whole rig. He finally made his way around the front of the team and back to the wagon. "Tell your father to remember this, if you have trouble with your horses, we can't hold up the whole train."

She translated and her father brushed the base of his hat.

"*Oui.*" Dr. Le Beau spoke another chain of indecipherable words.

"Papa said, 'My horses are six in number, and strong.' " The mademoiselle emphasized the last word.

Caleb nodded. For some folks, hearing the truth wasn't enough. They had to see it to believe it. He was one of those folks, and apparently so was the doctor. No point in wasting his breath. Besides, it'd be good to have a physician along on the trail.

After making his notations on the inspection slip, Caleb signed the paper and handed it to Le Beau. "You're free to go, sir." He regarded the daughter. "Madamoiselle. Tuesday morning at dawn, pull your wagon into line on Boone's Lick Road there." He glanced at the road alongside the Western House Inn, waiting for the young woman to translate.

"*Oui*, Monsieur Reger. *Merci*." The doctor raised his hat then climbed onto the seat beside his daughter and snapped the reins.

Caleb watched as the horses pulled the wagon onto the road. At the sound of his name, he looked over his shoulder.

Garrett leaned on the box at the back of their supply wagon and waved him over. "I've got to go see somebody about the trip. Since that was your last wagon today, you want to come along?"

"Gladly." Caleb had been stuck at The Western House all day inspecting wagons, interpreting the caravan instructions, and answering questions. Getting out and about sounded good. He climbed up onto the seat of the buckboard.

Within minutes, Garrett directed the two horses past the courthouse on Main Street, up the hill toward Lindenwood, and onto a familiar street.

Caleb angled toward his boss. "This *someone* you need to see . . . you failed to mention it was Miss Goben."

"It isn't." Garrett didn't look left or right. "I need to speak to her grandfather."

"But it's where she lives."

The boss turned, looked straight at him. "You have a problem with seeing Miss Goben, do you?"

Caleb folded his arms at his chest. "You think I need to apologize."

"You don't?" Garrett's brow creased. "Was it

my imagination, or did you accuse her of coming to the store to gloat about leaving Boney at the altar?"

Caleb gulped against a dry throat.

"You got yourself spurned by a woman, did you?"

Caleb shifted on the seat. "I planned to marry. Susan told me she wasn't ready to marry yet and asked me to wait until the fighting ended, but I received a message saying she'd married someone else."

Garrett lifted an eyebrow. "Well, Miss Goben isn't that woman back in . . ."

Caleb blew out a breath. His boss was always fishing to learn more about his past. He'd said enough and refused to bite the line. He couldn't. Not if he wanted a fresh start.

"Here's something else to think about." Garrett pulled up on the reins, slowing the horses. "You can bet it'll be a much longer ride west if you set out with enemies. Especially a woman you've alienated."

Caleb gave him a curt nod. "I'll see to it straightaway."

"Good. I knew you had to be smarter than the two of us acted at Heinrich's store on Tuesday." Garrett chuckled.

"How'd you get so sharp about women, Boss?"

"Same way you did . . . stickin' my foot in my mouth, one woman at a time."

Caleb chuckled. Unfortunately, he had but a minute or two to think on what he'd say when he saw Miss Goben.

The wagon rolled to a stop in front of the gingerbread-fronted home where he'd almost attended a wedding. Caleb climbed down from the wagon and tugged his shirt sleeves straight.

Otto Goben sat on the front porch caning a chair, a felt hat shading his face.

Garrett waved on their way up the gravel walkway. "Good day, Otto."

"It is. Come. Sit for a spell, why don't you?"

Caleb followed Garrett to the porch at a slower pace.

Otto nodded toward two freshly caned rockers across from him. Garrett seated himself closest to the front door. Caleb couldn't help but glance at the open door.

"You here on business or pleasure, son?" Otto asked.

Caleb squirmed a little, rested his hands on the arms of the chair and forced himself to lean back. "Business." He looked at Garrett, waiting for him to explain.

"Are the women of the house home?" Garrett asked. "Your granddaughter? Her mother?"

"No, and yes." Otto finished another weave and poked the end through a hole. "Wilma's in the kitchen, but Anna's gone to the quilting circle at Heinrich's store." His blue eyes focused on

Caleb. Had Miss Goben told her grandfather about his rudeness to her at the store? "You need to see her?"

Caleb swallowed the lump forming in his throat. "I do, sir. I mean . . . I have something to tell her."

The elder man grinned, which didn't help Caleb's comfort level any. "Very good then, Mr. Reger. You make yourself comfortable. She should be along sooner than later."

"In the meantime"—Garrett stretched out his bum leg—"I wanted to speak to you about the trip."

"We'll be ready. You been talkin' to old man Gut over at the saddlery?" Otto sat forward, his torso just as lean as his long legs. "I'm workin' day and night to get these chairs done so I can pay off our debts before we go. That what you're worried about?"

Garrett rested against the rocker. "No sir. I have no doubt you're a man who will honor his financial commitments."

"Good." Otto gave Garrett a generous nod. "My wagon's nearly ready. We'll finish packing the bulk of it Saturday."

"About that . . ." Garrett removed his hat. "I have concerns about your family joining the caravan west."

Caleb pulled off his hat and sat up straighter. It'd be better for all concerned, including Boney, if the Gobens didn't make the trip. Garrett obviously had reservations too. He'd assumed his boss was too busy with Boney at the wedding to notice Wilma Goben's unsteadiness.

Otto rolled the caning and set his project on the porch floor, then leaned on the arms of his chair and met Garrett's gaze. "You needn't worry about my age. There's plenty of men exploring, mining, even ranching in their fifties."

Emery Beck was Otto's age, if not older. Did Otto really think that was the concern?

"It's not your age." Garrett glanced first at the open doorway, then at the open window behind them before looking back at the older man. "It's the women." He spoke just above a whisper. "Your daughter doesn't get out much. I don't know her, except for an occasional greeting, but she seems a little—"

"Fragile?"

"Yes sir. It's a very long and arduous journey." Garrett blew out a long breath. "Are you certain your daughter is well enough for the trip?"

"Losin' her son took the starch out of my Wilma." Rubbing his bearded jaw, Otto glanced at the door. "Grief can do that to a person."

Garrett nodded. "It surely can."

Caleb worried the brim on his derby. Was that why Miss Goben had wavered in her decision to marry Boney? Because of her mother's frailties? Because of grief?

"I've given it a lot of thought. And my granddaughter is right." Otto scrubbed his cheek. "We can't just sit here and wallow in Dedrick's death. Languish in our loss. We have to get up and move toward a brighter future."

Caleb gulped. Miss Goben had said that? That was what he was doing, trying to move into a brighter future. Perhaps he had more in common with the young woman than he'd given her credit for.

"If you're worried about my granddaughter being able to make the trip, you can ask her about it yourself." He angled his head toward the road.

Caleb turned. Miss Goben fairly bounced up the street until she glanced at the porch and met his gaze. Her steps slowing, she squared her shoulders.

Following his boss's lead, Caleb rose to his feet. Her steps measured, Miss Goben strolled up the gravel walk toward them.

Caleb nodded. "Miss Goben."

"Mr. Reger." He'd handled ice warmer than her stare. "What is it? You didn't have your full say at the dry goods store?"

Caleb glanced at the hat in his hand. "I owe you an apology."

"You do." A statement, not a question.

Not having a clue what to do with his arms, Caleb let them hang at his side. "I allowed past experience with women to cloud my judgment where your actions were concerned."

"I see." Her lips pursed, she raised an eyebrow. "That is your apology?"

Her grandfather's hand flew to his mouth too late to muffle a snort.

Anna Goben was a tough one. Caleb doubted she'd have any trouble facing down a bear. "Ma'am, I misthought and misspoke, and for that I am sorry. Please accept my humble apology."

"You did. I do." A blush pinked her neck and turned her cheeks red. She moistened her lips. "Apology accepted, Mr. Reger."

"Thank you." Despite the cool breeze causing the curtains in the window to flutter, Caleb fought the impulse to fan himself with his hat. Miss Goben's effects on him were puzzling, to say the least. He wanted to maintain that she was fickle and remain angry with her. But at the same time, he felt her grief over the loss of her brother and the frailty of her mother.

They'd made their peace, but would it make this trip west, in such close proximity, any easier? He still didn't believe the trail was the proper place for this single young woman and her fractured family.

5

A whistled tune floated on the air from Blanchette Creek. Anna looked up from the worktable, her quill poised over the stationery. Her bay pony stood tethered to a nearby tree, ears perked. A crooked row of wagons wearing new white bonnets lined the edge of Boone's Lick Road. Großvater, like many of the other folks in the Company, had sold his house and most of his belongings. Now they were living out of a more portable accommodation, camped between the creek and the road. As of that afternoon, the dressed-up buckboard wagon was to be their home for the next five months. This was their last night in Saint Charles before their Tuesday morning departure.

Großvater busied himself carrying two buckets to the creek while Mutter fussed about in the wagon. It wasn't an easy sell, but Mutter had finally agreed that their westbound journey was her chance at a fresh start. Problem was Mutter had promised she had quit drinking on several other occasions in the past year too. So again, Anna wondered, was Mutter truly preparing her hammock for the night? Or was she using the fleeting privacy to indulge in a hidden bottle?

Try as she might, Anna couldn't make herself

believe getting Mutter to stop drinking would be easy, if even possible. But she couldn't just leave her to herself . . . to her grief.

Unable to swallow her doubts, she had to find a way to be the last one puttering among their belongings. She needed to know just what they were taking with them. She would have the final say about what they left behind.

Still whistling, Großvater strolled up the bank from the creek, his long arms each swinging a bucket of sloshing water. He looked at the stationery laid out on the table and the song stopped. "We haven't left town yet and you're already writing a letter?"

"A note for Emilie. She and her father have been so good to me . . . to us."

Großvater nodded, then emptied the buckets into the water barrel on the side of the wagon. When crates and barrels clunked inside of the canvas cocoon, he stepped to the front wheel. "Wilma, you still in there?"

Mutter poked her head out of the puckered opening. "You're back from the creek already?"

"I am. Can't imagine that you're finding much room for rearranging anything."

Bottles only required careful placement, not a lot of room. Anna swallowed her suspicions. Großvater had enough on his mind.

"Our porch was bigger than this thing." Mutter climbed out over the seat.

"It's only for a short time." Großvater looked toward The Western House Inn, about a quarter mile behind them. A line of other folks from the Boone's Lick Company meandered that direction. "If we don't hurry, all the tables are liable to fill before we can get our supper."

"I'm ready to go." Mutter smoothed her calico skirt and straightened the shawl over her shoulders. "What about you, Anna?"

This might be her chance for time alone in the wagon. "I wondered if you and Großvater would mind going ahead to get our table. My letter won't take but a few more minutes, and I'd really like to finish it before dark."

Großvater nodded. "Very well. But don't be long."

"I won't." At least she hoped so. Anna dipped the quill and lowered her hand to the paper.

When the sound of Mutter's and Großvater's footfalls faded, Anna placed the cork in the ink bottle. She had a job that had nothing to do with the note she was writing to Emilie. And it wouldn't be proper or safe for her to walk to the inn alone after dark. Satisfied they were out of sight, she wiped the quill and returned it and the stationery to her writing box then took quick steps to the wagon. After climbing onto the top of the wheel, she glanced at the various wagons camped along the creek. The Zanzucchi family was scattered from the creek to their campfire while their matriarch prepared supper. Maren and little Gabi Wainwright sat at a table outside their wagon.

Satisfied she hadn't attracted undue attention, Anna scrambled off the wheel, over the seat, and into the wagon through the opening in the canvas. As she did, a bitter bite of regret clogged her throat. She hated sneaking around in order to protect Mutter from herself or the bottle.

Anna widened the puckered gap at the back of the wagon to let in more light, ready to start her search. She'd been listening while Mutter was in the wagon. She'd heard the squeak of hinges and the shuffling of casks and crates. Mutter would be careful to bury a bottle, and what better place than in a crate no one else would have cause to open along the way?

Anna lifted the lid on the biggest crate. Supplies for setting up housekeeping at the other end of the trip. Blankets, artwork, and Sunday dishes lay on the top. After peeling the first layers back, Anna removed two wrapped bundles in the center. The first turned out to be a vase. She unwrapped the second bundle and found an amber bottle. Whiskey, no doubt, Mutter's drink of choice. Anna returned the empty wool blanket to the crate and set the bottle at her feet. Mutter wouldn't have stashed just one bottle. She found another in Mutter's trunk, wrapped in a dressing gown, and a third bottle in a sack of oats.

While disappointed in Mutter, Anna was satisfied with her success. Now to dispose of them. Anna bent to retrieve the bottles.

"Someone in there?"

She'd just grabbed the bottle necks when the gruff, but familiar, voice startled her. The bottles clanged as she released them.

"Who's in there?"

She couldn't let Caleb Reger see inside. Moving quickly, Anna stuck her head out of the opening above the seat. The trail hand stood mere feet away, his boot propped on the tongue.

"It's me. Anna Goben."

His boot slid to the ground and he removed the derby from his head. "I'm sorry to disturb you. But I saw your grandfather and . . . I thought you'd all gone to supper at the Inn."

"I'm joining them shortly."

"When I heard rummaging, I thought there might be an intruder."

"Thank you for your concern." Anna drew in a deep breath. "I was looking for something that had been misplaced." That much was true. Liquor had no place in the new life awaiting Mutter.

"Have you found what you were looking for?"

"I did. Thank you."

"You said you are to join your family." He glanced at the trees, awash in twilight-gray, and returned the derby to his head, causing a tuft of brown hair to stick out over each ear. "It'll soon be dark. Your grandfather wouldn't want you walking alone. Let me escort you."

"Thank you. But I will be ready momentarily, with plenty of light left for the short walk."

Caleb's chest expanded in a deep breath. "Very well." He brushed the brim of his hat. "Good evening, Miss Goben."

"Good evening."

When he turned toward the road, Anna withdrew into the wagon. She detested herself for putting on a false front like some sort of shopkeeper selling cheap baubles. But she hated the alternative even more. Mutter's reputation was at stake. Anna wanted to believe that if the temptation were removed, Mutter could let go of the bottle. Doing so would be that much harder if her secret were out and the Company looked at her as an outsider.

Anna slid the three bottles into an empty flour sack and set them on the grub box, just outside the back of the wagon. She wrapped a dark shawl about her shoulders, then climbed out of the wagon and looked toward the creek below. She wouldn't have to sneak around forever. But for now, it was the only way to give Mutter the chance she needed to start fresh. And if it worked, Anna would also have a new beginning.

6

The next morning, Anna and Hattie stood on the edge of Boone's Lick Road with Emilie. Anna's bay whinnied and tugged against the reins, objecting to the lollygagging. The time had come to leave Saint Charles, but she and Hattie weren't as anxious as her pony was to say good-bye.

Clutching Anna's note, Emilie wiped a tear from her cheek. "Remember to send the circular letters."

Anna nodded. "Every month. We'll mail the first one this side of Independence."

The sound of clomping horse hooves and churning wheels rode the breeze. Distracted, Anna glanced over her shoulder at the line of white-capped wagons inching their way up the hill out of Saint Charles.

She looked at Hattie. "We must go."

After one last hug for Emilie, Jewell, Mr. Heinrich, and Mrs. Brantenberg-Heinrich, Anna and Hattie climbed onto their sidesaddles.

Swallowing the lump of emotion clogging her throat, Anna nodded. She patted Molasses's black mane then sat tall and lifted the reins.

After a final wave, Anna clicked her tongue and Molasses lunged forward behind Hattie's palomino. Although Anna hoped to one day return to this riverside city that had been her childhood home, she knew it wasn't likely. Her back straight, she raised her chin and drew a deep breath, tears blurring her vision.

And under a clear sky as blue as Mutter's eyes had once been, she cantered toward a new life.

Just ahead of the wagons and off to one side, Caleb sat back in the saddle on his Tennessee Pacer. He pushed his derby up on his head and watched the great white snake of wagons wind its way through the spring forest and up Linden Hill.

Garrett and Isaac had left at the first hint of light to ride ahead and make sure the way was free of fallen trees and raiders. Although there hadn't been any raids of late, the soldiers charged with keeping martial law in the area were known to become overwhelmed by the number of bandits that sometimes prowled the route. Boney walked the lead at the chuck wagon, while Tiny herded the livestock at the rear of the train.

So far, so good. They planned to make it as far as Dardenne Prairie by nightfall. By then, they'd have a good idea who the dawdlers and stragglers were.

Despite the sorrowful good-byes back in town, the spirit of adventure flew high. But that spirit alone wouldn't get the overlanders past the Missouri border. He had doubts the Kamdens would make it as far as Independence before pulling their two wagons out of the line, sending Caroline Milburn back to Saint Charles, which was where Garrett said he wanted her. Caleb wasn't so easily convinced.

The four oxen pulling the chuck wagon caught up to Caleb and he waved at Boney, then trotted his chestnut stallion up the line, past the Renglers. Owen, his wife, Sally, and his brother, Oliver. The Brenners and the elder Becks had mules pulling their wagons. The rest were using oxen, all but Dr. Le Beau. But Garrett was right—the risk of delay due to overworked horses was worth it to have a physician traveling with them.

Caroline Milburn walked ahead of the Kamdens' first rig, a simple farm wagon pulled by four oxen. Lyall and Maisie, the two youngest children, walked on either side of her, while Duff and Angus fought over who would hold the lead rope. The older of the two Kamden women sat on the wagon seat with knitting on her lap. At the Conestoga, Blair, the oldest girl, walked beside her mother, Rhoda, holding the lead rope for the team of six oxen that pulled the larger wagon. There was a good chance the Kamden family would be the first to realize they'd packed heavy.

Charles Pemberton and his widowed mother walked beside their oxen. Caleb glanced at the empty wagon seat then at Charles. "Your sister?"

"On horseback. Haven't seen her since we left town."

Caleb brushed the brim of his derby and pulled his horse around. His boss was soft when it came to women. They had far too many young, single ones with minds of their own tagging along on this trip. Straying mules would be easier to keep track of. Nor were mules as stubborn as women. The image of Anna Goben lifting her chin and squaring her shoulders on her front porch filled his mind.

"That is your apology?"

Then there was the memory of last evening when he'd found her rummaging through the wagon. Her refusal of his offer to walk her to the inn hadn't discouraged him from looking out for her. He'd circled around the wagons just in time to see her climb out over the tailgate. She pulled a sack from atop the grub box and took quick steps to the creek, away from the inn. He followed her, far enough away that he wouldn't be detected, but close enough that he could hear the sound of glass clinking in her arms.

On the bank, several feet above the burbling creek, she picked up a rock and dug a hole, then buried the sack of bottles, no doubt. Something he was sure his sister would've done for him, given the opportunity. The Goben family wasn't the only one harboring secrets.

Desperate to forget his secrets, Caleb shook his

head and rode the length of the train, pausing beside the Gobens' rig.

Otto walked with the oxen while his daughter rode on the wagon seat. Miss Goben was suspiciously absent.

The grandfather looked up, adjusting the felt hat on his head. "If you're looking after my granddaughter, she's on horseback."

Caleb chewed his bottom lip. "With Miss Pemberton?"

Wilma Goben, the woman he suspected to be the reason for Anna's evening activities, fidgeted with her shawl. "Last I saw my daughter, she and Hattie were still saying good-bye to Emilie and the others."

"Thank you, ma'am."

Scrubbing his whiskered chin, Otto glanced over his shoulder toward Saint Charles. "Those two are going to be inseparable."

Caleb nodded. And nigh to impossible to keep safe. Moving on, he checked the rest of the line at a trot. No sign of the two young women with the other wagons.

At the end of the caravan, Tiny rode a draft horse, having no trouble standing out among the extra oxen, cows, and horses. "You lookin' for two missin' girls?"

"Miss Goben and Miss Pemberton."

Nodding, the cowboy waved his old felt hat, pointing toward town.

Caleb raised his hand to shield his eyes from the sun. A half mile out, two ponies galloped toward them. Each carried a young woman who was far too independent for her own good.

Tiny snapped a red suspender. "I've been keepin' an eye out for 'em. Figured they'd catch up before too long."

"Thanks. I'll see to them." Caleb lowered his hand to his thigh and pulled his horse toward town. When his Pacer met up with the bay and the palomino, he turned his horse sideways in the road, stopping directly in front of the negligent young women.

"Miss Goben. Miss Pemberton." Remembering the nature of his uncomfortable encounters with Anna Goben in the dry goods store and on her grandfather's porch, he focused his attention on Hattie Pemberton. "I will thank you kindly for minding the rules. The Boone's Lick Company manual clearly states the policy of remaining in reasonable proximity of the group unless permission to do otherwise is granted by a person of authority. That would be Mr. Cowlishaw, myself, or one of the other trail hands."

"We were merely saying a last farewell to our friends." Miss Hattie lifted her chin, allowing him a view of her raised eyebrow under the generous brim of her hat. "Would you count that frivolous and deny us that comfort?"

He made the mistake of looking at Miss Goben.

A grin tugged at her mouth. "I do not count your safety a laughing matter, Miss Goben." Then he noticed the telltale signs of crying—the red that rimmed her blue eyes.

Miss Pemberton straightened on the sidesaddle. "And this, Mr. Reger, doesn't seem the sort of trip you'd want to make without a sense of humor. Or, at the very least, a measure of grace when it comes to saying one's good-byes."

He knew plenty about good-byes. And he'd said enough. Biting his lip, he pulled the reins around, guiding his Pacer back to the wagon train.

It was a good thing he wasn't a gambler. If he were, he might just bet on himself to be the first to turn around as a go-backer. Or at least to head in a different direction. He should, anyway. Miss Anna Goben was trouble.

Anna couldn't help noticing the man riding ahead of her and Hattie. Caleb Reger sat tall in the saddle. An inch or two taller than Hattie's brother, Charles, the trail hand had broader shoulders and a much sharper tongue.

"I will thank you kindly for minding the rules."

"Permission to do otherwise is granted by a person of authority."

Anna remembered his inside-out apology on Großvater's porch. *"I allowed past experience with women to cloud my judgment where your actions were concerned."*

Well, if Mr. Reger cared to know, she could tell him why he'd had sour past experiences with women. For all their chirping, crickets were better listeners. She would do well to keep her distance from him.

Unfortunately, the broad-shouldered Mr. Reger wasn't the only trail hand she wanted to avoid. She and Boney had scarcely greeted each other in passing in the seven days since their almost-wedding. She'd seen him at The Western House last Friday when she and Großvater took the wagon for inspection, but Frank Marble had conducted the inspection. Had she ruined everything and lost Boney's friendship, or had he simply been too busy? She couldn't blame him for washing his hands of her. No man, no matter how gracious, liked to be rejected. Least of all in front of his friends.

Anna shook her head as if doing so could free her of the memory. Dwelling on the past would be of no benefit. Right now, she rode under a clear sky tinted in sapphire hues, through a fresh-leafed forest, toward grassy plains and a new life.

When she and Hattie stopped at their respective wagons, the sour trail hand kept riding toward the front of the caravan.

Mutter waved at Anna from the wagon seat, a smile taking years off her face. She'd obviously not yet discovered her bottles were missing.

"Anna, dear, did you see the hawk back there?" Her mother pointed behind them.

About fifteen feet out, a red-tailed hawk sat atop a dead tree with the confidence of a royal.

"Quite regal, isn't he?"

Anna nodded, unable to remember the last time her mother had referred to her as *dear.* Or had taken note of God's creatures, let alone been outdoors for any length of time. Mutter seemed perfectly fine sitting atop the wagon, even a bit regal herself, her golden-brown hair pinned neatly in place. But Anna knew better. Mutter wasn't fine, and if she wasn't careful, the whole Company would know it.

Anna drew a deep breath and let it out slowly. She'd buried the bottles at the creek, and Mutter would have no opportunity to buy more until they reached Independence. This trip was Mutter's chance to get well, and for that Anna would gladly face Boney Hughes and Caleb Reger every day for five months.

Garrett leaned forward in the saddle, peering through the leafy branches. So far, the road was clear of fallen trees. And he and Isaac Jackson hadn't run into any troublemakers or seen any evidence of raiders in this first stretch.

In the few short weeks Garrett had known Isaac, he'd learned Isaac was a man of few words, and when the freed slave spoke, the words usually rose from careful thought. Resting his hand on his sore knee, Garrett looked over at his trail hand. "I was wondering . . ."

"Yessir?" Isaac's tipped head showed off the scar on the left side of his face.

"We're both from the South and, well, I was wondering about your story."

"My story starts with a woman, Mister Garrett." His voice carried the tension between joy and sorrow.

Garrett draped the reins over his thigh. "I'd like to hear it, if you're of a mind to share."

"Ain't no love as pure as the good Lord's. But my Naomi's love was as close as a man could get. Made of silk and leather, my missus was." Isaac gave a low whistle. "Tender as a new leaf, but Naomi could be tough when she needed to be."

Pulling the reins around, Garrett stopped his stallion and faced Isaac. "She sounds like a very fine woman."

"Yessir, the best one. The only one for me." Isaac dragged his hand across his damp cheek and drew in a deep breath. "No one deserves that kind of treatment, especially not my Naomi."

"No." Garrett's voice quivered. "She died trying to escape?"

His jaw slack, Isaac nodded. “Yessir. And it was my fault she died. I thought we was safe. Till I saw the wall of gray uniforms. I didn’t get to her in time.”

Garrett blinked hard against the tears pooling in his eyes. “I’m terribly sorry for your loss. For all you suffered. That’s how you got the scar on your face?”

Nodding, Isaac brushed his cheek. “Yes. And if it weren’t for the Lord’s surrounding love and goodness . . . well, I’d hate to even have to think about livin’ without that.”

Garrett reined his horse and gave the command to continue up the road. His companion’s faith was a beacon for all who had been lost in a sea of sorrow.

“What about you, Mister Garrett? You can’t be so young that you never had a woman in your life.”

His history with love wasn’t something he cared to discuss. Or even think about.

Isaac wiped his hand on his trousers. “Don’t you worry, if you’d rather not tell.”

Garrett looked at the clearing ahead of them. “I did have a woman in my life.” The good memories were what made him afraid to trust his heart to any woman ever again. They’d set him up for the pain of loss. “I married her.” Garrett blew out a breath. Nobody but family and folks back in Virginia knew this about him.

Silent, Isaac patted the shoulder of the gray he rode. Patience was a real good quality in a trail hand. Especially good for someone facing several months of hard travel with folks with troubles.

"My father owned a tobacco plantation in Richmond." Garrett placed both hands on the saddle and pushed himself upright, trying to ease the ache in his leg. "Unlike most Confederate soldiers, I didn't join the war efforts in a patriot's fervor."

"I know most men didn't have a choice."

"The folks my family considered slaves, I loved more deeply than my own family." He watched as two squirrels skittered up a tree. Anything to avoid looking Isaac in the eye. "I joined thinking I could earn my father's pride and equal standing with my brother. But my heart wasn't in it."

Isaac glanced at Garrett's outstretched leg.

"My regiment was charged with rounding up runaways."

A shadow hid the whites of Isaac's eyes. "That how you hurt your leg?"

"I was standing in front of a boy, barely thirteen, when one of my own men threw a knife."

"Bless my soul." Isaac patted his chest over his heart. "You done stood up for him, didn't you?"

"When I returned to Richmond with my injured leg, the plantation had been burned to ash. Neither my family nor my wife would have anything to do with me."

Isaac's shoulders sagged.

"Now that the telegraph's in most every town, news like what I did travels faster than a lightning bolt."

Except for chirping birds and rustling leaves, they rode the next mile in silence.

Satisfied with the road directly ahead of them, Garrett pulled up on the reins. "This looks like a good place for the Company's noon meal." He turned toward the available grass along the small creek, with room enough for the thirteen wagons and all the livestock. Garrett didn't expect any trouble from outsiders this close to town, but it was best they stay together. He reckoned their caravan had traveled about eight or more miles, and scores of tender feet would need some tending.

Isaac swung down from the saddle. "Truth is, my hindquarters could use a break."

Garrett chuckled. "We're of a like mind, my friend."

A smile fairly lit Isaac's face. Surely God had sent this unassuming man as a liniment for hurting souls.

Caroline turned to face the three youngest Kamden children, now at a standstill behind her.

"My toes hurt." Maisie, the three-year-old, clung to a cloth rabbit.

"Miss Caroline." Nearly five, Lyall always had to be sure he had her full attention before continuing.

"Yes, Lyall."

"My legs hurt." Lyall had a mess of wavy brown hair and a permanent frown on his face.

"Well, I'm hungry." Duff, age six, wore a blue kerchief around his neck.

"I'm sure we'll stop soon for a rest." If not, *she* would take to whining. Caroline looked at each of the drooping children. "When we get to the right place, we'll spread out a quilt and rest our toes and our legs, and fill our empty bellies. I'm sure the captain is just up ahead, waiting for us."

"Pssst. Miss Caroline." The children's grandmother waved her over to the wagon, where she sat perched on the seat like a peacock. Davonna Kamden adjusted her feathered bonnet, a hat better suited to Memphis than the prairie that lay a few weeks ahead of them. "I haven't seen Mr. Cowlishaw all morning. Wherever did our captain gallop off to?"

"Miss Hattie told me Mr. Cowlishaw rode ahead to scout our path."

"Oh no." Mrs. Kamden's gaze darted to the left, then to the right. "Back in Saint Charles, I heard talk of them bushwhackers that raided farms and ranches. Is there going to be trouble?"

Maisie's green eyes widened. "Are those bad men following us?"

Caroline gave the elder woman a look she hoped would encourage keeping such concerns to herself then looked at the little girl. "Maisie, everything is fine. There are no bad men following us." At least not directly.

"Miss Caroline?" Lyall tugged her apron, his face pinched. "How do you know?"

"Mr. Cowlishaw and his brave trail hands are seeing to our safety." She may not approve of Garrett Cowlishaw's Confederate affinities or of his use of the words *dithering wife* in reference to Anna Goben, but she had full confidence in his ability to lead them. "In the meantime, do you think it would be fun to play a game?"

"Aye, let's." Duff pushed his canvas cap back on his head. "I like games."

"Good." Now all she had to do was come up with one. For more than a year, she'd lived with two nieces and a nephew close in age to these three. What would Mary, Cora, and Gilbert enjoy doing to pass the time? "To play the game, we all need to be walking."

"My son gave me a job to do." Mrs. Kamden raised the reins she held in her hand. "I'm not going to play your game."

Whatever the game proved to be, she'd intended it for the children, not for their gran. Something wasn't quite right with Davonna Kamden, and because of it, she was proving to be much more of a challenge than any of the children. And a distraction.

Caroline recalled Garrett Cowlishaw's last attempt to discourage her from making the trip west.

"It's going to be a difficult journey . . . You'll be traveling with a family you don't really know . . . Carrying tremendous responsibilities."

The captain of the caravan didn't think she could meet the responsibilities and complete the journey.

Caroline sighed. Unfortunately, she was no longer sure she could prove the man wrong.

Garrett sat on a tree stump, watching the first wagons pull into the clearing. Following Boney's lead, the others formed a semicircle in front of the stand of oak.

Even in a meadow teeming with wagons, animals, and people, Caroline Milburn managed to capture his attention. The young widow strolled playfully with the three youngest Kamden children in her charge. Caroline spun left and right with Maisie, Lyall, and Duff, her gingham skirts billowing with each spin.

He looked away so as not to be accused of staring.

"Captain!" Three-year-old Maisie darted toward him. "Captain!"

Her brothers joined her. Six-year-old Duff tugged the kerchief knotted at his neck. "What do you see, Captain Cowlishaw?"

Garrett looked at Caroline, who followed the children at a slower pace. "What do I see?"

"Uh, yes. What do you see around you?"

Caroline tipped her head up, raising the brim on her bonnet. Her eyes were as bright green as the new leaves on the trees.

What did he see? A woman who was turning out to be very good with the children, strangers or not. A resourceful woman. A woman who made him wish he hadn't gone to war, or at least hadn't fought on the opposing side. Only their first day on the road and he was already doing a poor job of avoiding her.

"It's a game we're playing. Right now, we are looking for items that start with the letter *c*, *C*aptain *C*owlishaw." A smile edged Caroline's mouth.

"The game is making my toes better." Maisie held up a cloth rabbit. "Her toes too."

Lyall sighed. "Well, my legs still hurt."

"Children." The nanny swatted the air between them. "The captain doesn't have time for our games."

"Aha." Garrett raised a pointed finger, looking straight at Maisie. "I know what I see that starts with a *c*. A cherub." Chuckling, he tapped the little girl on the nose. "I see a cherub."

All three of the children laughed, and so did their nanny. The melody charmed his heart, then caused it to ache. He'd expected to have children with Corliss. No doubt, Caroline had planned on having children of her own before the colonel died.

"Captain?"

Garrett shifted his attention to Lyall, who was bent and rubbing his right leg.

"What about my legs, Captain? They still hurt."

"I'd rub some mint poultice on them to fight the cramping." Garrett patted the boy's shoulder then looked at the woman with a red curl dangling at her neck. "There should be mint sprouting along the creek here. That should fix you right up, Lyall." He brushed the brim of his hat. "Ma'am, you be sure and let me know if you don't find any."

"I will." She moistened her lips. "Thank you."

Now, if only he had a clue about what to use as a salve for his aching heart.

Anna strolled toward the pasture, the lead rope slack in her hand. Four oxen followed at her heels as she mingled with other folks doing the same with their animals. Dr. Le Beau's daughter, Camille, approached with an empty water pail in each hand, her smile warm.

"Good evening."

"*Bonsoir.* Good evening." Long hair the color of coal lay over one shoulder, tied with a forest-green ribbon.

Anna waved as they passed, and Camille's smile

deepened. Camille wasn't more than a year younger than her, and would likely be enjoyable to talk to if they both weren't so busy caring for family and tending to chores.

"Bonsoir," Anna said quietly, trying out the strange word. With her German accent, it didn't sound even close to Camille's version. Camille had already agreed to give Hattie French lessons. If Anna had time, it'd be fun to learn a third language, but she'd be doing well to keep up with the oxen tonight.

Despite the rough start to the morning—having to say good-bye to Emilie and the others in Saint Charles, only to face the fussy Mr. Reger—her first day on the road had been a good one. Mutter had ridden in the wagon seat for most of the fifteen or more miles but seemed resolved to make the most of the journey. If not for her own sake, for Anna's. Perhaps Großvater had convinced her to ease up some. Whatever the motivation, Anna was grateful for the reprieve from Mutter's objections. And if Mutter had looked for the bottles Anna had buried on the banks of Blanchette Creek last night, she kept their absence a secret.

When the lead rope stretched taut, Anna slowed her steps and drew in a deep breath. The fragrance of campfires and cook pots scented the air. With the first day nearly over, Anna turned her thoughts to the previous night. While still camped in Saint

Charles, Mutter had laid claim to the hammock inside the wagon, and Anna had slept curled atop her trunk. Tonight, she'd sleep outside. Großvater had carefully positioned their wagon in the crooked semicircle so she'd have a tree to stretch her hammock to from the wagon.

She watched as Boney stepped out from between two wagons a few yards from her. He smiled but quickly darted away. Anna sighed as she tied the rope around a low branch. She and Boney hadn't spoken more than polite greetings since she'd called off the wedding. She missed visiting with him and hoped they could return to being friends. This would be an even longer journey if she and Boney weren't able to clear the air between them. It would already be plenty long with Mr. Reger questioning her every move.

"More, Mr. Caleb. More."

Anna turned toward the squealing voice. About twenty yards away, near the creek, a passel of children followed Caleb Reger and his chestnut Pacer. Little Gabi Wainwright sat strapped in the saddle, with Mr. Reger's hand cradling her back. Like a shepherd, Blair Kamden herded the younger children, including her siblings, Mary Alice Brenner's twins, and the three Zanzucchi boys.

If Anna didn't have Mutter to look after and supper to fix, she'd be tempted to take Molasses from the pasture and offer rides. That was, if she weren't concerned about doing something wrong within Mr. Reger's line of vision and inviting another of his smoldering speeches.

This evening, he hardly resembled that strict taskmaster. His hat nowhere to be seen and his hair tousled, he sidestepped alongside the horse. His baritone chuckle carried on the air along with the giggles of the children, and the infectious sound caused a surprising burst of laughter from Anna.

Looking up, he smiled at her. One of the oxen jerked the rope, catching her off guard and causing her to lose her footing and her balance. When her attempts to regain stability failed, Anna fell to the ground. Hardly missing a beat, she scrambled to her feet and grabbed the lead rope, embarrassment burning the tips of her ears.

Mean or nice, Caleb Reger was now, officially, an unwelcome distraction.

"Are you all right?" he called.

"Yes." Except that her pride had taken another fall, and any bruise on her backside wouldn't prove nearly as painful.

"Miss Caroline."

Caroline looked up from Maisie's tangled hair. Lyall stood beside the stool.

"When are you going to the creek?" he asked.

She sighed. "Not now, Lyall." Could he not see how busy she was? How busy she'd been all day?

"But my leg hurts worser. And *Mither* said we can't go without the sun."

Caroline glanced up at the purple rays of the sun settling behind clouds near the horizon.

The afternoon walk hadn't been much different from their morning walk, except that she'd run out of games to keep the children occupied. If Angus wasn't helping his father grease wheels and Blair wasn't helping Maren prepare supper, she'd be tempted to have them take the younger children to the creek after the mint for a poultice. Still, it was best she went herself. They didn't need to add poison ivy to their list of complaints.

"Aaaackkk!" Davonna Kamden jumped back and stared at the rope that had suddenly appeared around the butter churn.

Duff gasped as he darted toward her. "Oh no. Gran." Contrition creased his forehead as he quickly retrieved the rope. "I didn't mean to throw it so hard."

His grandmother huffed. "I'll have no cowboys in my kitchen."

"Yes ma'am."

"Miss Caroline?" Lyall asked.

Caroline drew in a deep breath and turned to face Duff's brother. "Lyall."

"The captain said to get polcy at the creek."

"He said I'd find the mint for the poultice at the creek." Caroline's fingers chased a knot to the end of a lock of Maisie's light brown hair.

"My legs hurt too." Maisie squirmed.

"Be still," Caroline said.

"Miss Caroline?"

She didn't bother to look at Lyall. The way this was going, come morning, she'd still be untangling Maisie's hair.

"Lyall." Rhoda stood behind a sizzling cast-iron skillet.

"Yes ma'am."

"Whose idea was it that your sister follow you through the trees?"

He looked at the ground. "Mine."

"It's no small wonder that the limbs went after her braids." Rhoda stirred the potatoes. "Miss Caroline and I are too tired for your nagging. I'll send your father for the mint when he returns from the pasture."

Rhoda wasn't one to have much color in her face, but she seemed even more pallid this evening. And now that Caroline thought about it, the mother of five had gotten a late start on supper because she'd been lying down. Hopefully, she wasn't coming down with something. Caroline sighed, easing the brush through Maisie's hair since Rhoda already had her hands full preparing the meal.

When his mother returned her attention to the skillet, Lyall set the tin plates out on the table. Duff wound his rope and put it in the wagon box while Davonna scooped butter into a small bowl.

Caroline drew in a deep breath. Resting one hand on the top of Maisie's head, she gently pulled the brush through the child's hair with the other.

"Miss Caroline." It was a man's voice, not Lyall's. Caroline turned to face the captain of this traveling circus. Garrett Cowlishaw stood with his weight on his left leg, one hand behind his back and one eyebrow lifted. His smile was too genteel for her vinegary disposition. "About that poultice I mentioned for the children's legs."

"You brought me some?"

He met her teary gaze then showed his hand.

She was surprised to feel herself smiling. "It's a bouquet of mint."

He nodded, bouncing a tuft of light brown hair on his collar.

"I may have to change my mind about you, Captain Cowlishaw."

"Is that good for me, ma'am?"

Her lips pressed together, Caroline nodded.

The captain smiled at the children. "I may just have to bring Miss Caroline a mint bouquet every day. What do you think?"

All three of them nodded.

Was it possible she'd been terribly wrong about Garrett Cowlishaw, after all?

9

Tuesday evening, Caleb dragged the wooden spoon through the dutch oven one more time, then pulled the wrought-iron triangle from the grub box and sounded the dinner bell. He watched Tiny, Boney, Isaac, Garrett, and Frank emerge from various places in the camp. Their two wagons sat in the clearing, facing the road. A comfortable setup, considering they'd been on the road a full day and brought half of the town with them.

Frank set two buckets of water at the back of the chuck wagon, then tugged the misshapen hat from his blond head and slapped it on his thigh, adding more dust to the air. "Been far too long since the noon stop. Good thing you rang that bell when you did."

Using a leather scrap to protect his hand, Caleb gripped the handle of the cast-iron skillet and shoved a flat spatula blade under the biscuits, working them until they loosened. He set the pan on a rock beside the firepit. "Grub's ready."

Whether they were ready for his cooking or not. He'd studied to be a preacher, not a cook.

When Garrett nodded toward the front of the line, Isaac stepped up to the pot.

Caleb scooped a ladle full of soup into a bowl, then pulled a biscuit from the pan. If he'd set the hot morsel on the plate any faster, it would have bounced to the ground.

"Thank you." A smile lit Isaac's eyes. He always took his meals like he'd never been served before.

Caleb repeated the action four times before serving himself. When he joined the others on logs around the campfire, Garrett looked up from his plate.

"I thought we'd have a little meeting over our meal. Catch up on any news from the day." Garrett looked at Caleb. "Any problems while me and Isaac were out scoutin' this morning?"

Caleb set his plate on one knee, wondering if he should tell him about the two young women who hung back in town too long. No sense in stirring that pot. "*Le Doc*'s horses all look good."

The fellows laughed.

"*Le Doc.* I like it." Garrett reached for his coffee mug. "If the horses are gonna give us trouble, it'll be after we hit prairie."

Caleb spooned a bite of potato. The minute it reached his tongue, his nose curled. He shook his head.

"What's wrong?" Tiny snapped a suspender. "You not fond of your cookin' either?"

Caleb shook his head.

Boney's eyes narrowed. "You didn't taste it before you served it?"

"Why would I want to spoil the surprise?" Caleb grinned, half expecting to see a biscuit flying at him.

"I was surprised, all right." Tiny wrinkled his nose, lifting his generous chin. "What is this uh . . . concoction?"

"Bacon and potato soup." Caleb looked at the bread Frank held. "And sourdough biscuits, I think."

Garrett chuckled, sloshing coffee over the sides of his cup. "You'll need a woman to cook for you when you get where you're goin'."

"Humph!" No woman who knew the truth would have anything to do with him.

Frank tapped his biscuit on the front of the log. "What, you're not the marrying kind?"

"I'm not." Caleb lifted his spoon and watched his bland soup plop into the bowl in globs. "But first thing when I get to the other end, I'll hire a cook."

"Uh, Caleb, you didn't tell the boss about those two young women you had to track down."

He followed Tiny's gaze to the corner of the supply wagon, where Anna Goben stood facing him, wrapped in a shawl.

"What's this?" Garrett dropped his biscuit into the soup. "We've already had folks wandering?"

"Not exactly." Caleb blinked. She was still there. "They were delayed saying good-byes."

"You reminded them of the rules?"

"I did." Something about the Company's policy. Authority. Their safety not being a laughing matter. That had to be why Miss Goben was standing there, looking at him. She'd come to him for her apology. Or to chew him out. Either way, he couldn't keep her waiting.

When Caleb started to stand, she shook her head and pointed to the man with his back to her. She'd come to see Boney Hughes.

Anna's heart pounded. She needed to clear the air between her and Boney. That was why she'd come to the captain's camp. But seeing Caleb Reger had only made matters worse. His smile when he'd seen her standing there. The way the corners of his mouth had fallen when she pointed toward Boney.

Boney took quick steps toward her and removed the floppy hat from his head. "Are you all right?"

"Fine. Thank you."

"Otto?" His eyes widened. "Is it your mother?"

"No. She's fine. They're fine. We all are." Anna moistened her lips. "Thank you."

Boney looked down, studying his hat.

Anna drew in a deep breath. "We haven't talked."

"We're talkin' now."

"Not about my canceling the wedding."

"Oh."

"I wouldn't hurt you for the world."

Boney reached for her hand. "I meant what I said that day, Anna. I really do understand."

She appreciated the warmth, given that she'd left her gloves packed away in the wagon. But she didn't feel any tingles or chills like what Emilie described feeling with her husband, Quaid, or Maren with Rutherford.

"You were kind, noble even, making the announcement."

Boney chuckled. "Believe me, I wasn't bein' noble." He met her gaze. "When you said Dedrick was the connection we shared, not a romantical kind of love, I knew you were right. We weren't meant to marry." His sigh spoke peace into the comfortable silence between them.

Anna nodded. "Thank you."

"Happy to oblige, ma'am."

His bow made her smile. Boney would make a fine husband one day.

Straightening, he set his flop hat back on his head. "Your mother did well today?"

"Yes! She spent most of the day riding on the seat, but she seemed to enjoy looking around."

"That's a relief."

"For me too." Anna let out a full breath. "I know we haven't gone far yet, but I really think this trip is the best thing for us."

"You had to do something."

She nodded. "Boney, my brother cared for you deeply. I do too . . . as a dear friend."

His crooked grin showed itself. "The feeling is mutual. You deserve a man who will care for you out of that deeper love you're lookin' for."

A shiver ran up her spine, and she pulled her shawl tighter.

"One more thing, Anna."

"Anything."

"Mind if I eat at your camp on the nights Caleb's cookin' at ours?"

She giggled. "He's really that bad?"

Boney's nod was slow and long.

"Anytime," she said.

"Thank you." Boney squeezed her hands. "You're an angel."

Anna sighed. Why couldn't she be attracted to this man who thought her an angel?

10

Wednesday morning, three—or was it four—sharp blows of a horn startled Caroline out of a sweet dream. For a few fleeting moments, Phillip was alive and picnicking with her on the bank of the Delaware River, at the end of Chestnut Street. There was no place prettier than Philadelphia in the summer.

Davonna Kamden sat straight up atop her horsehair mattress and swung her legs over the side of the flat-top trunks that formed her bed. "What was that?"

Lyall peeked over the edge of his hammock, which hung across the back of the wagon. "It was a horn."

The older woman huffed. "Why, oh why, would anyone be practicing in the middle of the night?"

Lyall spilled out of the hammock and landed on his feet between trunks and barrels. "They're not."

"They most certainly are!" Mrs. Kamden tucked her quilt in at her knees. "Otherwise, the sun would be awake."

Duff laughed from his bed atop a sack of beans. "Gran, Lyall meant the horn player isn't practicing." He grabbed his kerchief off the floor. "Captain Cowlishaw, or one of his men, blows the horn when it's time for everyone to get up."

"Well, they do need practice." She huffed again. "That wasn't enough of a song to make me want to do anything." Mrs. Kamden lay back down on her cozy pallet.

Cozy compared to Caroline's sleeping nook, anyway. At least the top of her metal trunk was flat, but a mattress would have been nice. Every time she tried to sleep on her back, the metal edging jabbed her calves, making her think she would be better off sleeping under a canvas on the ground like Angus and Blair, the two oldest Kamden children.

Duff tied the kerchief at the back of his neck. "Where's my boots?"

"You don't look like a cowboy to me." Lyall laughed, pointing at the wagon box strapped just outside the tailgate. "They're right where you left 'em."

"I'm gonna meet real cowboys when we get to the Wild West." Duff shoved Lyall's shoulder on his way to the box. "I'm gonna be one. Might lass-ooo you while I'm at it."

Shaking her head, Caroline rolled her bedding and stuffed it into her trunk. One thing hadn't changed—she'd woken up surrounded by children. But these weren't her sister's children. They weren't family. How could she ever have left Mary, Cora, and Gilbert? And Jewell?

But if things were better—if Jack would be happier—with her gone, then maybe she'd done the right thing leaving them.

Maisie rolled off the top of her trunk and plopped between some cargo. "Gran's right. God hasn't even waked up the sun yet." Maisie rubbed her eyes.

"After supper last night, your father"—Caroline glanced at Mrs. Kamden—"your son, went over Captain Cowlishaw's morning regimen." She pulled her bonnet on and tied it at her chin. "I suggest we get moving, if we hope to have time for breakfast before Mr. Boney starts this circus parade."

Mrs. Kamden giggled. A reaction Caroline would have expected of the children.

Muted light glowed through the oiled canvas. Could well have been a full moon, but the horn blows meant dawn was breaking.

Maisie jerked away from Lyall. "Did you do that?"

"What?"

"Boy stink!"

"It's that stupid rabbit you carry around."

Maisie clutched her flop-eared cloth treasure. "Is not." Maisie started to cry.

"You did it, Lyall. I heard you." Davonna Kamden pulled her quilt over her head, which was still planted on a feather pillow.

Not knowing what else to do, Caroline slid off the trunk. This would be her first full day with the family, and it was off to a confusing start. Had Ian Kamden brought her along to be the nanny for his children or his mother?

Right now, it seemed both would require her constant attention.

A steaming tin mug of coffee in hand, Garrett stood at the edge of camp, surveying the activity and order of things in first light. Isaac had blown the horn just fifteen minutes ago and in an instant, various families started stirring. Men lit small cookfires and harnessed their teams. Women milked their cows and pulled pots and pans from their wagon boxes. Children hauled buckets of water up from the creek while tending to their younger siblings.

According to his trail hands, everyone did fine yesterday. Most were used to walking, but he'd heard a few children complain about sore feet and legs. Lyall Kamden came to mind, and so did his resourceful nanny. Especially the smile that lit her face when he'd surprised her with the mint for a poultice. She'd called it a bouquet.

He gave his head a shake. He best not be thinking about her or he'd never get anything done.

Garrett looked over at Dr. Le Beau's wagon. Remembering Caleb Reger's nickname for the Frenchman, he chuckled. *Le Doc.* Caleb was a puzzle. His dry sense of humor seemed to battle a serious vein that ran deep. Maybe dangerously deep. Sometimes, Caleb was as intense as a soldier pinned down behind a berm. That had been the case when he'd confronted Miss Goben in Heinrich's Dry Goods store and accused her of gloating.

Apparently, the young man's intensity had flared again yesterday. Tiny had told Garrett about the way Caleb had ridden out to Miss Goben and Miss Pemberton like a sentry at a guard post. Garrett shook his head. He wished he knew what was eating the young man, but he couldn't get much of anything out of him. A good reason to pair him with Isaac.

Le Doc waved, drawing Garrett's attention. "*Bonjour*, *mon capitaine*!"

Garrett doffed his hat in a greeting then

continued his survey. The three Zanzucchi boys crossed the meadow, hauling buckets of water to their oxen. The Rengler brothers pulled down the canvas tent strung from a rope between their wagon and a tree. Mary Alice Brenner, the twins tottering at her side, carried her baby girl to the campfire they shared with Rutherford and Maren Wainwright.

He took a generous gulp of hot coffee. All the wagons and animals had performed well. So far, the only wagons he'd seen lagging belonged to Ian Kamden. He looked at the farm wagon Caroline Milburn managed with the elder Mrs. Kamden. Duff, Lyall, and Maisie spilled out over the seat of the wagon and down the wheel. Caroline followed them out at a slower pace.

As much as he found his youngest trail hand puzzling, he found the young widow to be fascinating. He couldn't think of another woman who would be so determined to go west on her own that she would travel with a passel of strangers to do so.

"Hey, Boss." His youngest trail hand carried a book and was swinging a doused candle lantern. Caleb glanced over his shoulder in the direction Garrett had been staring, his mouth curled in a grin. "If I was prone to gamble, I'd bet you are sweet on the nanny."

Tipping his head, Garrett looked at Caleb. "If we're gonna talk about such matters, we'll need to discuss that doe-eyed face of yours last night when you spotted Miss Goben at our camp."

Caleb gulped, glancing at the Bible he held. "Like I said before, Boss, it don't matter if you stare at the widow. Just so long as you don't get all atwitter and propose marriage to her."

Thankfully, Caroline had been too busy herding children to notice, but Garrett did need to divert his attention from the comely redhead. He glanced at the Gobens' wagon, where Otto's granddaughter was hanging a pail from a hook by the water barrel. "The same goes for you then."

"You needn't worry." The young man sighed like he carried the weight of the world on his broad shoulders. "I won't be marrying anyone."

There was that shadow that followed Caleb around like a storm cloud. Garrett waved his coffee mug toward the Bible. "You read that?"

"I do."

"Good." Garrett looked over at Le Doc's wagon where the Le Beau boys shinnied up a tree, reminding him of the squirrels from yesterday. "You can read a passage before we pull out this morning."

Caleb lifted his chin, his brown eyes wide. "I can't."

"You can't read?" Garrett scrubbed his bearded chin. "You just said—"

"I can read." His voice flat, Caleb tucked the Bible under his arm.

"Every morning just before we pull out, you be ready to read a passage—not a long one, mind you. I'll have someone else do the prayin', if that's what's bothering you."

"Sir." Caleb drew in a deep breath. "I'd rather not."

"I'd rather not tempt calamity, but there's a good chance we'll need to face trials at some point in this journey. Don't you agree that God's truth can prepare our hearts and bolster our spirits?"

Caleb reluctantly nodded then trudged to their camp.

An obvious attraction to Miss Goben. Confident he'd never marry, though still shy of twenty-two. Read the Bible, but turned white as a blizzard when asked to share what he read.

A puzzling young man, for sure.

Wednesday night Anna startled awake. Her hammock swayed, strung between an oak and a hook on the side of the wagon. She'd heard something in the distance but couldn't tell what.

Rubbing her eyes, she looked up into the dark night and squinted to focus her vision. The crescent moon offered enough light to show a clear sky. No hint of lightning or thunder. The company had come through a little berg called Warrenton that afternoon and were camped near a creek. Maybe some hunters or other travelers had set up camp nearby.

Now that she was awake, she heard only sounds she recognized—Großvater's stumbling snore, frogs croaking in the creek, and the incessant chirp of crickets from a few feet away.

Most likely, she'd been dreaming. Whether of walking mile after mile or hearing Caroline's story about the captain bringing her a bouquet of mint for a poultice or falling on her backside in front of Caleb Reger. They had all taken the stage in her sleeping thoughts.

"Bear!"

"A bear!"

Both were women's voices. Not far down the line.

Her heart pounding, Anna rolled from the hammock, tugging her dressing gown free. A rifle blast split the night, and heavy footfalls pounded the ground in the direction of the screams.

"Make noise!" Trail hands' voices, repeating the order, ran by.

The wagon creaked and groaned. Mutter was on the move too.

"There's a bear in camp, Mutter. Stay inside," Anna called.

Mutter hung out the puckered opening in the canvas. "*Vater*! *Mein vater.* Where is he?"

"Right here, Wilma." Großvater scuttled toward them. Huffing and puffing, he scooped a stick off the ground and yanked the bean pot from its hook on the side of the wagon. Whistling louder than she'd ever heard him, he banged on the pot.

Anna joined Mutter on the seat and struck tin plates with spoons, shouting until the other noises began to fade.

"They're quieting down," Großvater said. "Must have chased him out of camp."

Anna dropped the plate and spoon to her lap, sighing in unison with Mutter. "It's over."

"Is it?" Her hands shaking, Mutter tugged a blanket up to her neck. "Someone could be hurt. Or worse."

"You folks all right?" Caleb Reger's voice rose as he stepped into view. "Otto, you here?"

"Yes." Großvater walked into the faint glow of the firepit.

Anna pulled the other corner of Mutter's blanket over her shoulder. The disconcerting trail hand held up a candle lantern. Why did it have to be him? A rifle rested against his left shoulder. "Ladies?"

"We're all fine." Anna clasped her hands to stop the shaking. "Thank you."

"Thank God." Caleb sighed.

"The bear?" Großvater leaned on the wheel. "What happened? Everyone else safe?"

"Our furry guest took a grub box from the Kamdens' table."

Anna and Mutter both gasped. "Caroline? The children?"

"Shaken up but unharmed. The doctor is with

Mr. Kamden's mother, Davonna. She heard the growl and caught the vapors. Seems fine now. We'll need to check on the livestock. May have to round some of them up in the morning before we can head out." Mr. Reger tilted sideways, glancing at the back of the wagon. "If you have any food in that box, we'll need to hang it from a tree. Away from the wagon."

They didn't. But a box of food wasn't all that could make them vulnerable on this trip. Großvater and his weakened constitution. Mutter and her attraction to the bottle. Back in Saint Charles, the captain had warned them of the dangers of the journey, but none of them had seemed real to Anna. Until now.

She wondered suddenly if the hope and new life waiting for them at the end of this journey were worth the risks it would take to get there.

11

Caleb sat in the middle of his bedroll, the graying sky offering a hint of the coming dawn. He draped a wool blanket over his shoulders and rested his forearms on his knees.

The captain expected him to read from Scripture this morning. In front of the entire Company. As if he had authority, or even the right, to do so.

Garrett wanted him to share some sort of word from God for their day, an encouragement for their journey.

Now all he had to do was decide what that would be, and pretend God wasn't being silent. Or at least hope that even if He had nothing to say to Caleb, God would answer the needs of the others. Davonna Kamden came to mind. As did Anna Goben. She slept outside. She could've been killed by the bear last night.

"Mornin', Mister Caleb." Isaac rose from the ground. He was already a big man, but as a silhouette in the early morning hours, he seemed to block out the sky.

"Mornin', Isaac. You get any sleep?"

"Not more than three or four winks." He rolled his blankets. "You, sir?"

"About the same."

"Kept hearin' that bear. Seein' him makin' off with the Kamdens' grub. Not too proud to admit the whole thing had me feeling, well, a lot like that poor woman."

"Faint?"

"Yessir."

A chuckle escaped before Caleb could stop it.

Isaac snapped his suspenders against his barrel chest. "You go on and laugh, sir; it's good for the spirit. But I could make this whole trip without hearin' that word again."

Bear. Caleb resisted the temptation to say it

aloud. Rising to his feet, he looked up at Isaac. He couldn't quite make out the jagged scar on Isaac's face, but he knew it was there. The cheerful fellow had faced much worse than a hungry, cantankerous bear.

"You tellin' me you wasn't scared even a little, knowin' there was a bear trompin' through camp?" Isaac asked.

"I was more mad than anything else."

"Mad? At the bear for disturbin' your beauty sleep?"

Caleb let out a long breath. "Mad at myself. Could have been a lot worse than losin' a box of food."

"Well, you were sure enough quick with that gunshot." Isaac let out a low whistle. "Gave me second thoughts, and the bear too."

"Yes, well, unfortunately, he went the wrong way."

"Only till that hullabaloo started in. More than just Boney that's good with a bean pot." Isaac chuckled.

Caleb pulled his bedding from the ground. He liked spending time with the freedman. No matter the circumstance, he could count on Isaac for a bit of lighthearted fun and encouragement in the midst of it.

Isaac pulled his horn from the bag at his feet. "Done heard the boss asked you to read Scripture before we head out in the mornin's."

Asked wasn't exactly the right word. "I'm going to. Yes. Unless you'd like the honors."

"You know I would, sir. I can't get enough of the Good Book." He sighed, pointing to his head. "But it's all up here, mostly in songs."

"Oh, so that's why you're always whistling or humming."

"Yessir. Never learned to read, but I carry it with me. Sometimes it just wants to come out, all on its own."

Caleb wadded his blankets, wishing he was more grateful for what he had left. And for the abilities he took for granted.

"Seems the boss knew what he was doin', choosin' you. More like a Divine nudge, really. Folks'll be ready for a little steadyin' from the Word."

"I reckon they will."

"A little steadyin'." That's what he needed, and it wasn't a bear causing him grief.

"The Lord works in mysterious ways, don't He?"

Caleb nodded into the early daylight. Was God working in mysterious ways? Or did His silence mean He'd given up?

Anna climbed over the wagon seat and out onto the top of the wheel. The morning had finally come, and its fingers of light seemed to dance across the land as if it knew nothing of the bear's intrusion. Isaac had sounded the horn calling everyone to their morning preparations for the day's journey, so people stirred up and down the line. Anna had spent the remainder of the night curled on top of her trunk. The memory of the camp's guest in the wee hours lingered fresh in her mind. Anna looked on either side of the wagon and toward the trees behind them, where the bear was last seen.

Großvater groaned as he rolled out of the hammock she'd abandoned and attempted to brush down his wiry gray hair.

"It's safe," he said. "The bear is gone." He lifted the loop at the end of the hammock off the hook on the wagon, then untied the rope from the tree. "She's probably snoring in a den somewhere, too full of Mrs. Kamden's *kuchen* and salt pork to move."

"Made for a short night." Anna turned and, using the wheel spokes as a ladder, climbed down from the wagon. "If Mutter and I went back to sleep at all, it was fitful. How about you?"

Yawning, Großvater looked up at the food box he and Caleb had strung in the tree. "I must have slept, because I dreamed about being carried away in the hammock like a fish in a net." He shook his head. "A solemn reminder that we're not at home in the wild."

"The captain certainly warned us of danger, but—"

"We've traveled thirty miles and more without any trouble." Großvater rolled the hammock and heaved it into the back of the wagon. "Having no real trouble can lull you. Maybe it's good we had this incident so early. We will all be more aware."

Anna tied her bonnet at her chin. "You're still glad we're here, I mean, making the move west?"

"I am. I'm feeling better with every day that passes. I think your mutter is too."

"Until last night, anyway."

"Yes, well, we can all do without any more such scares." He chuckled. "When the growling started, I like to have left my skin behind trying to get back here."

Anna nodded. While Großvater lowered the box from the tree, she went to the water barrel lashed to the wagon and scooped out some cold water to splash her face. Just what she needed to be fully awake.

Großvater set the box on the worktable and pulled a match from it. By the time Mutter came out of the wagon, Großvater had the fire popping and the coffeepot boiling, and Anna pulled bread and dry sausage from the box for their breakfast. It'd be a quick one this morning.

Within an hour, they'd eaten and packed up, and Großvater had the oxen yoked to the wagon. Anna gathered with the rest of the Company.

Garrett Cowlishaw stood in front of them, holding a steaming cup of coffee. After delivering a brief summary of the night's adventure, he admonished everyone to take precautions and be vigilant. After a brief pause, the captain motioned for Caleb Reger to step up, which he did, holding a Bible in his hand.

"Yesterday, I asked Caleb here to read a short Scripture passage each morning. As it turns out, this might be the best day to start," the captain said.

"I agree that it is a good idea to get the Lord's blessing." Sally Rengler, Owen's wife, wagged a finger. "But if you had done so on our first two days on the trail, Captain, perhaps that bear would not have attacked our camp."

The captain removed his slouch hat and looked directly at her. "I can't say I agree with your theology, ma'am. I'm not so sure reading Scripture will keep us from having to face trouble as much as it will focus our attention on our Help in those times. The Bible's full of stories about folks with troubles. Good folks. God-fearin' folks."

Expressionless, Mrs. Rengler pulled her shawl tight.

"Caleb, you ready?"

Mr. Reger cleared his throat. With his glum expression, one might think he had been condemned to face a firing squad instead of a gathering of fellow travelers.

"Morning, folks." He didn't look up. "Like the captain said, he wanted me to read to you. Today, it'll be Joshua 1:9: 'Have not I commanded thee? Be strong and of a good courage; be not afraid, neither be thou dismayed: for the LORD thy God is with thee whithersoever thou goest.' "

The last word had barely left Caleb Reger's mouth when he closed the Bible and stepped into the crowd. Anna watched him disappear behind the other trail hands.

Deliverer of chastisements. Entertainer of children. Protector against bears. Helper in the night.

Shy herald of God's holy Word.

Caleb Reger was proving to be a bit of a marvel.

12

The reins slack in his hand, Garrett rode his black stallion up the line from the last wagon. Between the bear's disruption of sleep and the Scripture reading, the Company was slow getting on the road this morning.

Oliver Rengler finished tucking the canvas cover behind the tailgate of their wagon and waved. "We're ready, Captain." His brother and sister-in-law were at the front of the team, pegging the bows to the yoke.

Garrett brushed the brim of his hat in a hello and kept moving.

"I appreciated the Bible reading, Captain." Mary Alice Brenner waved as he rode past. Four-year-olds Thomas and Alice played tug-of-war with a rag doll at Mary Alice's feet while seven-month-old Evie watched from the quilted sling suspended from her mother's shoulder.

"Thank you." He regarded the woman's husband, who looked as if he'd swallowed a lemon whole. "Mornin', Tom."

"Captain." Tom Brenner was always squinting, but this morning his whole face seemed involved in a scowl. "Just slows us down, if you ask me. Folks could be trusted to do their own readin'. If they choose to."

Garrett pulled up on the reins and stopped for a moment. "You're certainly trusted, my friend. It's just that some like to be together with like-minded folks when the Word of God is read. I'm sorry you don't approve of the delay." Garrett waved and continued on his way, the snipping remarks between husband and wife fading into the background none too soon. Seemed judgment was more likely to come from within his own camp than from on high.

The Sunday service would be interesting with such a mix of folks. And most likely conducted without Tom Brenner present. Which was sure to be another source of contention between the couple.

Garrett had just ridden past the Kamdens'

Conestoga, greeting Ian and Rhoda, when he saw Caroline Milburn at the back of the farm wagon.

"Good morning, ma'am."

She looked up, and he doffed his hat.

"Captain." Did the young widow have any idea how distracting the single red curl on her creamy neck was?

Maisie darted toward them with her cloth bunny tucked under one arm. "If we play another game today, you can play too." A wide-eyed smile lit her little round face.

"Thank you, Maisie." He looked at the nanny, wondering how she'd feel about spending more time with him.

Moistening her lips, Caroline loosened the ties on her bonnet. "The captain may have work to do, Maisie."

The green-eyed girl glanced up at his horse. "He can ride his horse while he plays the game."

He chuckled. To a child, it probably seemed that was all he did. "We'll have to see about that, Maisie. But I appreciate the invitation."

Caroline clasped her hands. "Thank you for adding the Scripture reading to our morning routine."

Nodding, he lifted the reins. "I hope it helps. All of us."

"Be strong and of a good courage."

Garrett felt as if Caleb had hand-picked the morning's message just for him. The prowling bear was enough of a challenge for any caravan leader, but he knew from experience there would be more. Much more. He wouldn't think about that right now. Not in the presence of such an intriguing woman.

He straightened in the saddle and brushed the brim of his hat. "Good luck with the game."

Caroline nodded, a smile smoothing her lips and sending tingles up his spine as he urged the horse forward.

"Be strong and of a good courage."

A good message for his heart too. Caroline Milburn wasn't Corliss Huffington Cowlishaw. Corliss would never have ventured west, let alone signed on as a nanny and made up a game to entertain children. She would have called Caroline's *bouquet* of mint a handful of weeds. No, the enchanting widow was not in the least like Corliss.

But neither was he like Phillip Milburn, a Union soldier, a fact that wouldn't serve him as well.

As he rode past the Becks' wagon, Camille Le Beau took long and quick strides toward him, one hand in the air. Her other hand held a lead rope with four horses following her. "Capitaine."

"Good morning, Mademoiselle Le Beau."

"We need to wait for my papa. He is not yet ready to depart."

A sharp huff distracted Garrett, and he shifted in the saddle to look behind him.

Emery Beck had walked up to the back of his stallion and stood with his arms crossed. "His uppity horses got spooked." His beady eyes narrowed. "I knew they'd be trouble."

Garrett straightened, returning his attention to Camille Le Beau. "Is there a problem? Is it the horses?"

"Two of them have run off. Anna's also. Papa and Monsieur Goben are searching."

"I doubt the horses went far." They were lucky only three of them headed for the hills, what with a bear and then all the pot banging and yelling in the night. "I'll get a couple of men to help find them."

"*Merci*, Capitaine. Mama and I will ready the wagon."

When she turned away, he did too. Arguing with Emery Beck would be a waste of time. Hopefully, looking for the horses wouldn't be.

"The LORD thy God is with thee whithersoever thou goest."

And when thou goest. The paraphrase was his.

"Captain, you are wrong to coddle that man and his daughter." Mr. Beck's voice would've carried in a gale. "And their high-strung horses."

Garrett twisted in the saddle to answer over his shoulder. "I'll let you know when we're ready to pull out."

No matter with whom thou goest.

• • •

Caroline added more foodstuffs to the Kamdens' table. During the noon stop, various members of the Company brought victuals of some sort to the wagon she shared with Davonna Kamden and the youngest of her grandchildren. Maren delivered a plate of potato cakes. Mrs. Zanzucchi brought a loaf of Italian bread, and Anna, a plate of smoked ham. Lorelei Beck was the next to approach Rhoda with wild blackberry tarts.

"What a rude awakening." Lorelei shuddered, blond curls bouncing at her ears. "You all must have been terribly frightened."

"Yes. Well." Caroline slanted a gaze toward the farm wagon.

Davonna poked her head out through the puckered canvas. She hadn't stepped a foot off the wagon all morning. She looked at Anna and Lorelei then at Maren. "Did they tell you it was my fault?"

"Your fault a bear came into camp?" Maren squinted. "How is that possible?"

"I forgot to put the box of food away. Left it on the table. I may as well have put a sign on it inviting the bear to supper."

"That's what Faither said." Lyall kicked a rock. "I heard him."

"Never mind that, Mither Kamden." Her lips pressed together, Rhoda let out a sigh that lifted the wisps of hair on her forehead. "Folks have been so kind to bring our dinner. At least come down to eat and visit."

"Mither's right, Gran." Duff pushed the canvas cap back on his head. "You can't stay in the wagon forever. There's no latrine."

Caroline wanted to laugh but didn't dare. Instead, she pressed her lips together and saw that her friends were doing the same thing.

"Son, that is not a proper topic to discuss in front of the ladies, let alone at the dinner table."

Duff looked up at Rhoda and slid the cap off his head. "Yes ma'am."

Sighing as if she carried the weight of the world on her shoulders, Davonna climbed out onto the seat. "My son only talked about the pretty birds and mountains I would see. He said naught about bears."

Duff spread his feet and twirled his right arm. "If I was a real cowboy, I could've lassoed that bear."

"Or at least the grub box." Caroline laughed and so did the others. Except for Davonna.

"Really, Miss Caroline?" Her Scots accent thick, Davonna scowled like a scorned schoolmistress. "You think having a massive animal like that on the other side of the canvas from you—from our children—is a laughing matter? Do you not take anything seriously?"

Rhoda jerked, her eyes wide. "Mither!"

"Miss Caroline was only making a funny, Gran," Duff said.

Davonna pinned her grandson with a somber gaze. "Well, it isn't the least bit funny to think about fighting a bear."

"But I could protect you if I had a horse and a rifle like the captain. Or like Mr. Caleb. Or Tiny. Or—"

"Rhoda, it was a bad idea to make this trip. All these coarse men are putting dangerous ideas into the wee bairns' heads."

"Coarse men?" Garrett Cowlishaw stepped into view, his white slouch hat in his hand like a perfect gentleman. "Ladies."

"Captain." Caroline smiled, though all she wanted to do was laugh. For all the trouble the children and Davonna could be, they were also most entertaining.

Garrett stepped up beside the wagon and held his hand out to Davonna. "Ma'am, it would be my pleasure to assist you. You must be famished by this time."

"Well, I suppose I . . ." She accepted his hand and his assistance to the ground. "Thank you."

"Now, you were saying something about coarse men? Is someone giving you trouble?"

"My grandson."

The captain regarded the boy. "Duff?"

Davonna sighed. "Thanks to you and your trail hands, he is talking about roping a bear like a Wild West cowboy."

"I must say, Duff, I agree with your gran.

For now, you need to leave the bears to us."

Davonna's fleshy cheeks blushed. "I hope I didn't offend you, Captain."

"Not at all, ma'am." He set his hat on his head. "I've been called worse."

Caroline shivered despite the sun's warmth on her arms. She'd been guilty of at least thinking the worst of him.

"I'm glad to hear that." Davonna pulled a tart from the table and took a bite. "Mmm. These are very tasty, Captain, you should try one."

Never mind that Mrs. Kamden wasn't seated with a plate and napkin, and no one else had started eating or even said the blessing.

The captain rubbed his chin in a failed attempt to hide a grin. He met Caroline's gaze, the laugh lines on either side of his hazel eyes deepening. She couldn't help but smile.

It was official: she liked Garrett Cowlishaw.

13

Anna dropped the lead rope, grateful for their noon stop. The oxen team snorted and pawed the ground, ready for their portion of grass. She couldn't say how the oxen's feet were faring but, on this fourth day of walking better than fifteen miles, hers were sore. She needed to take off her shoes and put her feet up, but first she'd make sure her family had something to eat. Since dark clouds loomed on the horizon, the group only planned to stop long enough for quick refreshment for man and animal. The threat of a storm made it all the more critical they gain as much ground as possible before the rains made a muddy mess of the bottomlands.

While Großvater started removing the yokes from the oxen so the animals could eat, Anna set up the small worktable then pulled bread and cheese from the grub box. Mutter unlashed two small cane chairs from the side of the wagon.

"I still don't see how walking miles and miles day after day, sleeping in a suspended rope bed, and cooking over a campfire is supposed to make things better." A scowl creased Mutter's forehead as she ground her favorite chair into the rocky soil on the other side of the table. Mutter hadn't mentioned the missing bottles, but that didn't mean she hadn't searched for them. Their absence could very well be contributing to her bad temper today.

Anna sighed in her exhaustion. They both missed their warm and comfortable beds back home. Why couldn't she believe that was all that was wrong, that Mutter's moodiness had nothing to do with her longing for the drink?

Because she knew better. Mutter had set aside the bottle on several occasions and had never made it through the exasperation and headaches before succumbing to her thirst for deadening relief.

Finished with the yokes, Großvater walked the oxen to the meadow near the pond where the rest of the livestock were feeding. Anna watched as he met up with Charles Pemberton and a few of the others in the field. At least the trip was doing Großvater some good. He'd taken quite keenly to visiting with the Company's men, whether it be standing in a pasture or at a campfire.

Mutter took slow steps to the covered pail that hung from an iron hook at the front of the wagon, then set the pail on the corner of the table.

"Thank you." Anna lifted the lid and peeked inside. "The butter set up nicely."

"Why wouldn't it be churned? It's a very bumpy, winding road."

As Anna spread butter on three chunks of crusty *roggenbrot*, she couldn't help but wonder if her mother was referring to the road or her life. Both were true enough. Mutter hadn't had an easy path. Her husband left her with two little ones. Her son died in the war. For as long as Anna could remember, Mutter's constitution had been as unpredictable as the random twists and turns of the road they traveled today.

When Mutter sank onto the chair, Anna set the bread on the cutting board and met Mutter's gaze. "Are you feeling all right?"

"I'm fine." Mutter sighed, her thin shoulders sagging. "Just tired, very tired."

Anna wished that was all that was troubling her.

"I am wrong to complain, dear." Mutter brushed her graying brown hair off her face and into her faded bonnet, and glanced toward the Wainwrights' wagon. "That poor Danish girl is making this trip with failing eyesight and a child to tend. Doesn't even have Elsa Brantenberg, Mrs. Heinrich now, here to help her with all this work."

"Maren Wainwright." Mutter had already quit going to the quilting circle when Maren joined, but Anna had introduced them at the last caravan meeting in Saint Charles. "Hattie and Bette Pemberton are lending Maren a hand. And Gabi is almost five now and a proud helper." Someone here needed to focus on the positive aspects of the trip. "I sliced a block of cheese for her this morning."

Mutter crossed her arms as if fighting a chill. "I do wish I were more like you, dear. A saint. You always have been."

Like her? A saint? Always have been? Except for the two different days she told Boney she couldn't marry him? If Anna didn't have her hands full of bread and cheese, she'd be tempted to reach up and feel Mutter's forehead for fever. Something wasn't right. Was Mutter trying to get Anna to let down her guard? Let her wander the next berg they passed alone?

Anna removed the wrapping from the chunk of blue cheese, the pungent aroma tickling her nose. "Those of us from the quilting circle, except for Caroline Milburn, are sharing a campfire and the cooking responsibilities at supper tonight. Maren has our album quilt. Remind me to show it to you."

Mutter rested her hand on the edge of the table, causing it to wobble, and quickly let go. Was that why Mutter crossed her arms, so Anna wouldn't notice her trembling?

"I wish I could be of more help to you . . . to everyone. But"—Mutter glanced at the front of the wagon—"I need to rest."

"What about your dinner? You need to eat."

"I can't seem to get warm." Mutter stood and took small steps toward the wagon. "A short nap is all I need. Before my hammock takes to rocking again." She heaved herself up and over the seat, then disappeared through the puckered opening.

Swallowing a bitter bite of concern, Anna slid a chunk of bread and cheese into a red letter sack. She added one of the apples Maren had given her, then took a tin cup to the water barrel on the side of the wagon. The sack and full cup in hand, Anna walked through a bevy of wagons and travelers toward the meadow where she'd seen Großvater head with the four oxen. A few children scampered about with water pails while others managed mules on lead ropes. Before they'd left their noon meal on Tuesday, Anna took count. Sixteen children, including Hattie and Camille Le Beau, not yet eighteen, and Evie, still in her mother's arms. The boys outnumbered the girls.

Großvater waved from the grassy area by the pond. When Anna reached him, he took the sack from her and dangled it as if weighing its contents. "Doesn't feel like enough food for the both of us." He looked at her empty hands. "Where's yours?"

"Back at the wagon. I'm going to sit for a spell and put my feet up."

"Your mutter, how is she?"

Cranky. Shaky. Flattering. "She's resting."

"Good. She seems a bit out of sorts today."

Anna nodded and kissed him on the cheek. "I'll see to her."

"All right. I thought I might visit with Oliver and Owen while I eat."

Anna was on her way back to the wagon when the three Zanzucchi boys breezed past her carrying willow-switch fishing rods against their shoulders.

Back at the wagon, Anna set the two chairs to face each other. Bread and cheese in hand, she sank onto one chair and propped her feet on the other. Sweet relief. She tucked her shawl under her chin and leaned against the welcoming chair.

As she savored the rich rye bread and the pungent blue cheese, Anna surveyed the wagons parked in a line along the edge of the road. She wasn't looking for anyone in particular. That was what she told herself, anyway.

This morning, Caleb Reger had read from Psalm 19 to the travelers from atop a tree stump.

"Let the words of my mouth, and the meditation of my heart, be acceptable in thy sight, O LORD, my strength, and my redeemer."

She probably owed him an apology. He'd only been doing his job Tuesday when he'd come out to meet her and Hattie. She should be thankful for his concern over her whereabouts and safety. Mr. Reger was nothing if not conscientious. And taking one's work seriously was an admirable quality. She'd just prefer that he not stick his nose in their business.

Giggles drew Anna's attention to their wagon. Mutter? Was she dreaming?

Anna sighed, lowering her feet to the ground. She'd told Großvater she'd see to Mutter. Perhaps it was time to wake her and see that she ate something. After setting her napkin and tin cup on the table, she stood.

"*Die gedanken sindfrei . . .*" *Thoughts are free.* The words and tune to the folk song, however muddled, made their way through the canvas.

Mutter was singing in her sleep? Her voice always struggled to find the proper notes, but today even the words were being tortured in her attempts.

Anna took quiet steps to the front of the wagon. She stepped up onto the wagon tongue and gripped the dashboard. This morning, the wagon had smelled of coffee and sweat. Now, it smelled more like peppermint schnapps. Couldn't be. Anna had found three bottles and buried them in Saint Charles.

Pulling back the canvas, Anna peeked inside. "Mutter!"

Her mother startled and sank onto her hammock, then peered over the edge. "Dear, I'm glad you're here." She hummed a little of the tune. "Do you remember the words to my song?"

"No." Anna glanced about her. Satisfied no one stood in earshot, she leaned into the wagon. "You've been drinking."

Mutter pulled herself up, sitting in the suspended cloth. She clasped her hands in her lap like a lady. "I'm feeling better."

She was foolish to have thought four days on the road could cure Mutter. Anna yanked the canvas open, letting in some light and fresh air. She looked around the floor and between the trunks, then up at Mutter's hammock. She didn't see a bottle. But that didn't mean there wasn't one.

"Did you get off your feet, dear?" Mutter lifted her stockinged feet and wiggled them in the air. "It did wonders for me."

Anna opened her mouth to speak, but desperate shouts outside the wagon stopped her.

"Papa! Papa!"

The panic in the eldest Zanzucchi boy's voice sent a shiver up Anna's spine. She turned away from Mutter and watched the lad dart toward his family's farm wagon.

"*Viene*! *Viene*! It's Nicolas! He's hurt!"

Anna's breath caught as she watched Mrs. Zanzucchi run toward her son. She pinched her skirts in her fists, her Italian responses flying like bats at sundown. Alfonzo Jr. pointed toward the creek.

Dr. Le Beau emerged from a stand of trees where his six horses stood tethered. He ran to meet the boy, rattling in French.

Caroline came up from the pond with the youngest Kamden children in tow. "Nicolas fell from a tree. I think his arm is broken."

After a short trip to his wagon, the doctor returned with his black leather bag and followed the boy and his mother toward the pond.

Within moments, Hattie dashed toward the pond with Camille Le Beau at her side, the doctor's daughter and translator.

In the meantime, Mutter continued swinging in the hammock and butchering a good song.

Anna returned to the worktable to slice cheese and bread for Mutter, reminding herself that plenty of folks had far worse affliction than caring for a mother who imbibed and sang indecipherable words off key.

14

Friday evening, Caleb twisted the axle nut with a grunt, then watched Boney Hughes take his weight off the lever pole and lower the wagon to the ground. The other three trail hands were scattered about the camp helping various men grease their wagon wheels. Their boss had a funny way of pairing them. Caleb hadn't figured out if it was conflict or the potential for resolution that Garrett relished most. At least the boss hadn't assigned him the job of digging the latrine.

Caleb glanced at the empty seats around the firepit, then at Boney. "You know, none of the rest of us are as good a cook as you. Ever think about opening a café?"

Boney's hands stilled. "Not for more than a split second, I haven't." A grin lit his narrow face. "Way too much work trying to please everybody's picky palate."

"My sentiments exactly."

"Besides, I'm not all that keen on staying so long in one place. Too much to see." Boney's bushy eyebrows arched. "Kinda funny that you were thinkin' about my future while I was thinkin' about yours."

"Oh?" Caleb set the wrench to the axle nut again.

Boney nodded. "Yeah. The way you read the Bible aloud over us every morning. Like God meant you to be a preacher."

Caleb had been sure of it, that God had made him to preach. That was before he'd gone and done something stupid.

And he couldn't let himself dwell on where that led him.

Boney shook out his hat and returned it to its perch. "Reverend Reger . . . kinda has a r-r-ring to it, don't ya think?"

Caleb swallowed another bitter bite of regret. "Reading isn't the same as preaching."

Bent on changing the topic, he glanced toward Otto Goben's wagon where the elder man sat with his daughter in front of a campfire. "You're at the Gobens' camp a lot now. You and Miss Goben might marry after all?"

Boney chuckled. "You definitely need to work on your sidestep." He lifted the corner of the wagon. "Just an idea, you becomin' a preacher. I'm going west to be a miner. The other fellas plan to be farmers and ranchers. Don't seem like you have much direction yet."

Caleb pulled off the wheel and slathered some grease onto the hub. "Plans change."

Boney nodded. "I know about that, all right. Is that why you asked about me and Miss Anna?"

The wiry fellow looked Caleb in the eye. “Your idea that you’re not the marrying kind . . . did it change too?”

Caleb shook his head. “Just curious, is all, after she came to see you the other night.”

“She came to clear the air between us. I was her brother’s best friend . . . a friend of the family. That’s how we see each other—good friends.” Huffing and puffing, Boney held the lever down while Caleb replaced the wheel. “Me and Anna don’t have a romantical kind of love.”

“People have married for lesser reasons.”

“Not Anna Goben. Nothin’ less than that special kind of love would ever be enough.”

Caleb had thought he and Susan had shared that special kind of love.

But it didn’t matter, because during the war, he’d thrown away any chance of ever being loved again.

Caroline had a few minutes before she had to return to the Kamdens’ camp to help Rhoda prepare supper. Little Nicolas Zanzucchi had broken his arm during the noon stop, extending the Company’s stay. In the extra time, she’d managed to write a short bit for the missive that would go to Jewell and the others of the quilting circle in Saint Charles.

The children were now settled around a central campfire for a reading time with Mary Alice

Brenner. This was as good a time as any to deliver the letter to Lorelei, who was next on the list to add her news, so Caroline double-checked the pocket in her skirt to make sure she had the letter with her. The Becks' two wagons sat at the far end of the line, and she'd seen Lorelei walking that direction from the pasture just minutes ago.

Caroline was about to pass the Zanzucchis' camp when Captain Cowlishaw suddenly stepped out from between the wagons. He skidded to a stop mere inches from her, his eyes widening and his mouth hanging open.

He yanked his slouch hat from his head. "Ma'am?"

Just as surprised to see him, Caroline took a step to the side and pulled her hand from her pocket. The letter managed to follow her hand out, fluttering to the ground before she could catch it.

She bent to retrieve the stationery, but Garrett managed to snatch it from the dirt first. When they had both stood upright again, he held the letter out to her and she reached for it. He extended his arm farther, and she ended up clasping his hand instead of the paper.

His mouth tipped into a grin. Her hand warm and still, she lifted her gaze to his eyes. Even at dusk, they seemed more green than hazel today.

Neither of them looked away as she slid her hand to his fingertips and plucked the letter from them. He swallowed hard, leaving her to wonder if when she'd let go of his hand, he'd also noticed the sudden chill in the air.

Caroline moistened her lips, hoping the gesture would help her push words out of her now dry mouth. "Thank you, Captain."

Was she thanking him for retrieving the letter or for allowing her the warm touch?

"Anytime."

Anytime. Heat rushed to the tips of her ears that surely now matched the color of her red hair. Thankfully, the captain didn't seem to possess the ability to read her mind.

"After all, ma'am, it was my fault you dropped your paper. I didn't mean to startle you."

She cleared her throat as she tried to bring order to her thoughts. "No. There's no need to apologize."

His eyebrows arched. "There isn't?"

"Oh dear." She tapped her chin and fought a smile. "I do see where that might come as a shock to you."

"Yes, well, given our past encounters . . ." Garrett shifted his weight to his left leg. "Let's see . . . My military history. My comment in the dry goods store about a dithering wife. I definitely wasn't off to a good start."

"Perhaps not, but you are forgetting about the mint bouquet."

"That small gesture bought redemption?" He chuckled, the sound surprisingly pleasant.

The letter crinkled in her hands. "I didn't say anything about redemption, but it might have moved you off the starting line."

Another of his crooked grins crinkled the lines framing his eyes. Neither one of them shifted as the silence stretched.

Then he glanced out at the children's reading circle. "Your charges, are they feeling better? With the poultice?"

"Although it seems to be Lyall's nature to complain, the leg cramps have lessened and they're all feeling better."

He nodded. "Nice to know I did something right."

"Yes, well, I wouldn't let it go to your head."

"Not much chance of that." His face sobered, and the laugh lines at his eyes smoothed. "It's been a bit of a rough day, what with the Italian boy coming to harm."

"Children climb trees and fall. Not much you can do about that. Don't be hard on yourself."

His eyebrows lifted again.

"You really are taking good care of us all," she added.

"Thank you for that."

"Anytime." She smiled.

He rewarded her with an even wider smile that brought back the laugh lines.

Anna freed the first chair from its tethering strap on the side of the wagon while Mutter fussed inside. Großvater would need to stretch the canvas to cover the whole wagon before Mutter could retire for the night. A chore that could wait until he returned from the pasture, or from whatever camp he chose to visit once he'd set the oxen and horses out to graze.

This fourth day on the road had been a long one. Mutter had found her drink during the noon stop, and the Zanzucchi boy now wore a sling on his right arm. During their noon break, the doctor tended his first patient on the trail, and the incident had given the captain the opportunity to remind the group that the nature of their journey was such that Nicolas Zanzucchi wouldn't be the last of them to require Dr. Le Beau's services.

"I've seen your großvater do this, but . . ."

Anna looked up. Mutter stood just inside the wagon, leaning on the back of the seat, staring up at the edge of the pulled-back canvas.

"Does he start with the canvas or the hoop, do you remember?"

"That's Großvater's job. We'll let him do it." Anna set the first chair on the ground, out of her way. "I'm sure he'll have it done by the time we return."

Mutter stilled. "Return? From where?"

"You were humming in your hammock when Mary Alice Brenner came by during the noon break."

The corners of Mutter's mouth turned downward. "Oh yes, something about the quilting circle women meeting at her camp for supper tonight."

"Yes." Anna returned to the wagon for the second chair. She'd been looking forward to cooking and visiting with her quilting circle friends. And the sooner the better. "Mary Alice said to bring our own chairs. I'm about ready to head over."

"I'm sorry, dear, but my head hurts."

That was no small wonder. Mutter's drunken humming had given Anna a headache without the numbing benefit of alcohol.

"With all those women there . . ." Mutter sighed. "I just don't feel like going out this evening. You understand."

"I don't feel right leaving you."

Mutter planted a balled fist on her hip. "Meaning you do not trust me."

"You blame me for that?" Anna dropped her hands to her side. "I left you earlier and—"

"I remember."

"Then you can understand why I might find it hard to believe it won't happen again." Anna spoke without looking at her. "This very evening." For all she knew, Mutter hadn't finished off the bottle she'd tipped earlier in the day and wouldn't hesitate to do so this evening.

"So, you're giving up your life to stand guard over me. To be the family *polizist* and make sure I keep your laws?"

Anna's spine stiffened. "That's not what I'm doing, Mutter."

"Then what are you doing?"

"I'm trying to help you. To protect you."

"From a little bottle?"

"From yourself."

"If I can't do as much, what makes you think you can?"

Tears stung Anna's eyes. Indeed, where had she gotten the notion she could make a difference?

"I need to rest, and I don't care to do so out in the open," Mutter said, sounding legitimately tired.

"Rest." Anna lowered her voice to a whisper. "That's the excuse you used earlier to hide. To drink."

"Truth is, dear, you can't protect me any more than I could protect your brother from death in the war."

She blinked back the pooling tears. Mutter had likely never spoken truer words. Anna reached for the strap that held the chair. "Let me get this down for you, and then I'll see what I can do to help with the cover."

Before Anna could set the chair on the ground, she heard a shriek and jerked toward the wagon. Mutter was sprawled across the seat draped with the loose canvas.

Gasping, Anna dropped the chair and rushed up onto the wagon to Mutter. The hoop sagged off to the other side, having sprung out of its sleeve.

Mutter looked up at her, a wince tightening her face.

"Are you all right?" Anna asked. "Did the hoop hit you?"

"No. I just fell. That stupid thing scared me springing out like that, but it didn't touch me."

"Good." Seated now, Anna cupped Mutter's elbow with one hand and reached across to Mutter's shoulder with the other, trying to raise her into a sitting position. Halfway up, Mutter stiffened, another wince darkening her features.

"Am I hurting you? Did you injure your shoulder?"

Looking Anna in the eye, Mutter shook her head. "I might have scraped it. But I'm all right."

When Mutter started moving again, Anna eased her into a sitting position.

Sighing, Mutter brushed wild strands of hair from her face. "Ouch." She twisted her arm, raising her elbow to Anna's face.

"You did scrape your arm."

Mutter lowered her arm and shook her head. "I just don't think I'm cut out for this kind of life, dear. It's too much work."

"I should have helped you. I'm sorry." The words no sooner flowed from her mouth when Anna realized how often she'd spoken words like these. Apologizing when made to feel guilty; apologizing when she hadn't been the one at fault.

She'd told Mutter she would help, if only she'd waited.

Anna pinched her bottom lip between her teeth. Would she ever know another way of life?

"I'm sure your friends are waiting for you. Go on ahead. I can wait for your großvater, or I will go find him when I'm feeling a little better."

The answer to Anna's question was clear: no. She would never know another way of life. "You rest, Mutter. I'll go find Großvater."

"Thank you, dear. I am feeling a mite weak right now."

Anna nodded. Her lips tightened by regret and frustration and sorrow, she set off toward the pasture. She'd glance at the Rengler brothers' camp on the way by, just in case Großvater had stopped there.

"Miss Goben?"

She wasn't of a mind for another lecture, but she turned toward the familiar voice anyway. Caleb Reger walked toward her from the captain's chuck wagon, swinging his derby in one hand.

"Mr. Reger."

"Miss Goben, you were fairly marching. Is something wrong?"

Nothing Großvater couldn't help her with. "I assumed you were poised to finish Tuesday's speech. Am I wrong?"

A red hue touched his tanned face. "Yes, well, about that . . . I wanted to clear the air."

Clear the air. That's the term she'd used the other night when speaking to Boney about calling off the wedding. Anna drew in a deep breath. "Now?" She glanced back toward her wagon. It was probably too much to ask that Mutter be lying down and not tipping the bottle. "It's just that I have a little problem and need to find my grandfather. Have you seen him?"

"He's helping the doctor grease his wagon wheels. This problem you have, is it something I can help you with?"

She might not be able to protect Mutter from herself, but she still had to try to protect her privacy. "No."

His eyes widened as he straightened his back. "You *are* mad at me."

"I didn't mean to sound so sharp."

One eyebrow lifted while his hands worked the brim of his derby.

Anna sighed. "It's the canvas on our wagon. The hoop sprang. My mother needs to rest and—"

"And wants her privacy."

"Yes." She hated to admit unflattering assumptions, but she hadn't figured Caleb Reger to be aware of such concerns. Or to care about them. "I'd rather do it myself, but—"

"Please. Let me help. It's what I'm here for."

She shouldn't. "Thank you. If you're sure you don't mind."

"I'd be happy to help." He set his hat on his

head. “Besides, I’m sure Otto is having a good time visiting.”

Of that, she was certain. She nodded.

When Caleb stretched out his arm, motioning for her to lead the way, Anna did so, hoping for the best. Since she didn’t care to discuss Tuesday’s encounter, she’d best choose the topic. “Do you like being a trail hand?”

He looked her direction, his eyebrows arched. “Yes, to my surprise, I do.”

“You didn’t expect to like the job, but you asked for it?”

Facing forward again, his grip worked its way around the brim of his hat.

“It’s none of my business,” Anna said. “I don’t know why I asked.”

“My guess is that you didn’t want to talk about Tuesday.”

She fought a smile. Caleb was a smart man. And more charming than she’d thought possible.

They closed the remainder of the distance to the wagon in silence. Mutter still sat on the bench, looking forlorn but empty handed.

The moment Mutter looked up and saw the two of them approaching, she straightened and smiled. “Why, Mr. Reger, I wasn’t expecting to see you.”

“Good evening, ma’am.”

She rose to her feet. “Good evening.”

“Mutter, Mr. Reger—”

"Caleb, please."

"Very well." Had his eyes always been a golden brown, or was it just because he was smiling? Anna swallowed and looked away. "Caleb found me before I found Großvater and has offered to help."

Mutter stiffened. "You told him?"

Anna met Mutter's gaze, hoping to ease her concerns about the family secret. "That the hoop has a mind of its own? Yes."

"This sort of thing happens on a regular basis." Caleb's smile deepened, revealing a dimple in his left cheek. "That's good news, actually. With all that experience, I can set the hoop and have your canvas closed right quick."

"I'd like that."

"Just in case I'm fumble-fingered today, ma'am, you might wish to step down from there and stand clear." He lifted his hand to Mutter.

Mutter nodded and accepted his help getting onto the ground. "Thank you."

"You're most welcome, ma'am."

Yes, Caleb was quite charming.

Mutter settled onto one of the chairs Anna had unlashed, as if she were about to watch a show. Turning away from Mutter, Caleb looked directly at Anna. "Are you ready, Miss Goben?"

She gulped. "Ready?"

"The job requires a little height. But I thought if you'd rather do it yourself, I could give you a lift." He circled his arms, clasped his hands, and bent down as if to give her a boost.

Anna dipped her chin, offering the best look of false disdain she could muster with those brown eyes so focused on her. "Thank you." She stepped away from the wagon. "But I'd hate for all the experience you're gaining to go to waste."

Caleb straightened, a grin blooming across his face.

"I can, however, make myself available should you require any assistance," she added.

He fairly hopped onto the wagon and looked down at her. "I will, actually."

Anna's breath caught. Need her help? She'd only offered in jest, certain he would dismiss it. The thought that he might expect her to climb into the wagon with him made her shiver.

"When I get it to this bracket"—Caleb bent over the sideboard and patted the empty steel slot on the side of the wagon—"you push on the hoop and guide it all the way in."

She nodded. She could do that while keeping her feet firmly planted on the ground.

Caleb climbed over the seat with ease and, standing atop the trunk behind the seat, he raised his right hand over his head and lifted the hoop while pulling the loose end in toward the sideboard with his left.

Anna grabbed the end of the wooden hoop and guided it toward the bracket. The force required to bend the wood was more than she expected, and she had to reset her footing with a bounce. Giving a determined grunt, she heaved against the wood, pushing it up into the bracket. She staggered back a few steps and slapped her hands together, trying to downplay the strength she'd spent.

Caleb effortlessly lifted the canvas over the hoop, smoothing out the wrinkles, then stepped back over the seat and pulled the rope that fed through the pucker, centering the opening. In mere moments, he had the wagon covered and ready for the night.

Mutter rose from the chair and admired his handiwork. "That's wonderful. Thank you."

"You're welcome, ma'am." Caleb set his hat on his head and smiled at Anna. "I'd say we make a good team."

Mutter's eyebrows shot upward while Anna's ears warmed.

"Yes, well, you did most of the work." Anna tugged her sleeves straight. "And we are grateful for your help."

"Anytime, miss." Caleb pinched the brim of his derby and nodded at Anna, then at Mutter. "Ma'am."

Anna nodded, and as she watched him stroll toward the Le Beaus' wagon, she found herself hoping she would need his help again soon.

15

Anna breathed in baby Evie's freshness, holding the tightly wrapped bundle against her chest. She'd been around Gabi, Caroline's nieces, and Mary Alice's twins as babies, but none of them were babies anymore.

If she'd married Boney, she could have soon had babies of her own . . .

No! She chided herself for doubting her heart again. She and Boney both agreed marriage wasn't right for them. And she'd vowed to trust God with her heart as well as her mother. If only she were better at it.

Across the campfire, Mary Alice checked the biscuits that were steam baking on top of the kettle. "You've charmed Evie."

"And she's charmed me." Burying her nose in the baby's thin hair, Anna drew in another deep breath. "She smells of soap and talcum powder."

Her hands hidden in quilted gloves, Mary Alice lifted the tin of biscuits from the kettle. "I just fed her, so that sweet smell won't last long." Her laugh made the baby jump.

Anna traced Evie's soft cheek with the back of her fingers. The baby calmed and returned to slumber.

"You look fully at ease in that role, Anna."

Maren sat at a small table cranking the coffee grinder.

She was at ease, which only created a familiar tension. She'd passed up her chance at starting a family of her own. Now, even with Großvater doing so much better, he and Mutter would still need her help to start their new lives.

Mary Alice set the hot bread pan on the table away from Maren's coffee dust. "You know, Anna, Boney Hughes isn't the only single man in camp." Her lips pressed together in a catlike grin.

No one had to tell her that. She'd just watched one charm Mutter and bend a wagon hoop into place as if it were no work at all. And what of the image of him clasping his hands to give her a lift? Charming *and* surprising.

"Mary Alice is right." Maren stilled the grinder. "What about Charles Pemberton? There's nothing wrong with your brother, is there, Hattie?"

"Sounds like a trick question." Hattie tittered. "But I suppose as big brothers go, Charles is all right." She glanced at Anna with a grin that matched Mary Alice's. "Only thing is, you might have trouble finding him if you don't know where to find Camille Le Beau."

A chorus of "Ohs" prompted a round of giggles.

Anna lifted the baby to her chest, letting Evie's head rest on her shoulder.

Hattie pulled the pins from her hat. "That only leaves Captain Cowlishaw, Tiny, Frank, and Oliver Rengler."

Four could play this silly game. Besides, if you can't beat 'em, join 'em, as Dedrick had been fond of saying. "I wouldn't put Garrett Cowlishaw on the list," Anna said. "Not with the way he looks at Caroline."

Mary Alice nodded and gave the stew a brisk stir.

"What about that other trail hand—the ruggedly handsome and mysterious one. Caleb Reger, is it?" Newlywed Maren Wainwright was enjoying this game a little too much.

"Oh! I must have forgotten about him." Mary Alice was the camp master of teasing grins.

Anna let out a long sigh. "He was just at our camp, and you all know it. Hattie waved on her way by."

Hattie's eyes widened in feigned surprise. "Are you saying I'm a gossip?"

Anna and everyone else pinned Hattie with a knowing gaze.

"Very well." Hattie pursed her lips, raising her chin a notch. "I did mention seeing him there. But only because I'm a romantic."

"My grandfather was busy, so Mr. Reger offered to help."

Mary Alice cocked her head, dipping her chin. "Mr. Reger was bending wagon hoops and pulling canvas. You can't tell us you haven't *noticed* him."

Caleb.

"Of course I've noticed him. So has Hattie. He was none too happy with either of us our first day on the road." Though he did want to *clear the air.* No need to mention that part. Or the dimple.

Mary Alice waved her wooden spoon. "You don't have to worry about Hattie where Caleb Reger is concerned. She has her sights set on Boney."

Her face turning the color of ripe tomatoes, Hattie pulled the hat from her head and hid behind it.

Anna leaned toward Hattie. "You do?"

"I don't. At least I have no compelling desire to marry him."

Mary Alice stirred the pot. "You mean, even if you had a clean shot at him?"

"I wouldn't express my feelings in terms of guns and targets, but I do like Boney."

"Then it's a *good* thing I didn't marry him," Anna said, smiling.

"I think so." Hattie grinned, feverishly blinking her blue-gray eyes. "If you think so."

"I do." The moment the words slipped out, heat rushed up Anna's neck, and her friends burst into laughter.

Perhaps she should've let Caleb clear the air between them.

Though as far as she was concerned, he already had.

Caroline dunked the cloth into the dishwater. Mary Alice Brenner's laugh carried to the Kamdens' camp. The threatening storm clouds from earlier had passed without incident, and although the temperature was dropping with the setting sun, the night sky was clear. Dishwater dripping from her hands, Caroline held a clean tin plate out to Rhoda Kamden.

"I'm thankful for your help." Rhoda wiped the plate dry with a thin towel and set it on the corner of the table. "I just don't seem to be able to keep up with it all anymore."

Duff, Lyall, and Maisie busied themselves with Gabi and the other children, playing marbles and chasing a hoop within the camp. After the Zanzucchi boy broke his arm this afternoon, all the parents were on alert. Ian Kamden had gone to see if his services as a wheelwright were needed. His mother was in the wagon fetching her knitting.

Caroline's quilting circle friends had invited her to join them for supper tonight. She should've asked for the evening off. A little laughter would've been good for her. Sitting around a campfire would be sweet relief for her feet too.

She glanced at the circle of three-legged stools Ian Kamden had set out for supper, then handed

Rhoda another clean plate. The sprite of a woman hardly seemed big enough to withstand the birth of one child, let alone five. "I don't know what I'd do without you, Caroline."

"I'm glad to be of help." That much was true. But she couldn't say she was glad she was here, because she'd much rather be at the campfire with her friends.

"I'm sure you'll soon need a break from the children and caring for us." Rhoda carried the plates to the wagon box and glanced toward the Brenners' camp and the sound of Hattie's and Anna's laughter. "For a little time with your friends."

"I'd like that. Thank you." Feeling selfish, Caroline pulled a tin cup from the dishpan. "But I'm fine." Her time with the Kamdens was temporary. Besides, she did have many of her friends on this journey with her. The younger Mrs. Kamden seemed lost and alone even in the midst of her family of eight, with a husband who hardly spoke a word and a mother-in-law who seemed bent on making up for it.

"You get along well with the children." Rhoda took the clean cup from her. "And Mither Kamden is happy for your company."

"Except when that horn blows in the morning and I tell her it's time to rise from her bed."

Rhoda snickered. "I'm glad it's you sleeping in there, and not me."

Caroline raised a teasing eyebrow. The work had given her a purpose, making her feel useful. But she was thankful the job was only for five months.

And she missed her quilting circle friends. She'd take Rhoda up on her offer of time off. Soon.

The senior Mrs. Kamden climbed out of the wagon, clutching a cloth sack. "I can't find it." She walked to the worktable and looked at Rhoda. "I said, I can't find it."

Caroline and Rhoda both glanced at the sack in her mother-in-law's hand. "You have your knitting. There."

"I know that." Davonna Kamden scrunched her face. "I'm not stupid." She laid her hand on her chest. "I'm talking about the locket my husband gave me."

Caroline lifted the biscuit pan from the table. "You went into the wagon to get your knitting."

"I know what I went to do." Davonna huffed. "I decided to look at my locket." She squared her shoulders, broad compared to Rhoda's. "Someone is taking my things."

Caroline stilled. Could someone have really taken the locket from their wagon?

"That seems a drastic conclusion, Mither Kamden. I'm sure you'll find the locket," Rhoda said. "Things like that are easy to misplace."

Another huff from the elder woman.

Cloth in hand, Caroline scrubbed the pan. "I can help you look for it in the morning."

"That would be a waste of precious time." The older woman pressed the knitting sack to her midsection. "If the locket were there, I would have found it."

Ian Kamden strolled into camp, carrying a broken spoke. He looked at least as tired as Caroline's back and legs told her she was.

"Son!" Davonna waved him over. "There's something you should know."

He glanced at his wife then at Caroline, his brow knit together.

"Don't look at them," Davonna said, her voice seeping agitation. "They're hiding the truth. I'm the one who knows what's going on."

Rhoda busied herself drying the clean pan while Caroline retrieved the empty bean pot from a nearby rock.

"Whatever your news, Mither, do I need to hear it this moment?" Mr. Kamden tossed the spoke into the fire then looked at his mother.

"Well, if you ask me,"—Davonna glowered at Rhoda—"this cannot wait."

He sank onto one of the stools and stretched his legs, crossing them at the ankles, then looked at his mother.

Caroline quieted her scrubbing cloth. She shouldn't listen in, but if Davonna Kamden was right about valuables disappearing, and there was a thief in their midst, she wanted to know about it. Mr. Kamden had been milling about with various men. She'd seen him talking to Garrett Cowlishaw before supper. Perhaps he'd heard news of other folks having such problems. She hoped not.

"A thief is an abomination to the Lord." Davonna raised a finger in the air, apparently for added punctuation to her proclamation.

Mr. Kamden frowned. "A thief?"

"Yes." Davonna pressed her hand to her chest. "And we have one among us."

"In the Boone's Lick Company?" Dragging his feet back to the legs of the stool, he looked up at his wife. Rhoda shrugged.

Davonna's nod was slow and deliberate.

Standing, Mr. Kamden glanced out at the encampment of wagons. "I was just with several of the men. No one said a word about a thief."

"They may not know yet, but they surely will."

"Something here has gone missing?"

"It most certainly has." Davonna clutched the collar on her shirtwaist. "The locket your father gave me."

"Anything else? It seems that if someone went to the trouble to go through your belongings, they would have taken other things . . . more valuable things."

Davonna crossed her arms and set her jaw. "It pains me that you think me careless with such a precious gift."

"Mither, I'm only saying that such a small item can easily be misplaced."

"I know who took it."

Caroline lifted the kettle from the dishpan, tipping it toward the light of the fire to see if she'd gotten it clean. If someone had truly stolen the locket, how could Davonna know who'd taken it when she'd only just discovered it missing?

"Who is it, Mother?"

Caroline and Rhoda both stilled.

Davonna leaned toward her son. "I abhor having to say it, but the culprit is our own employee, Mrs. Milburn."

"What?" The kettle slipped out of Caroline's hands and into the dishpan, splashing the front of her dress with dirtied water. "Me? How could you ever think I'd do such a thing?"

"This is preposterous!" Rhoda waved the towel. "Caroline has been nothing but kind and generous with you. How could you ever think she would take the locket?"

Mr. Kamden rested his hand on his mother's arm. "Did you see Mrs. Milburn take it?"

"No. But she was the last one in the wagon before it went missing."

"That doesn't mean she took it. She lives in the wagon."

"You think one of your own bairns is a thief?" Davonna jerked her arm away from him. "Why would they take something that wasn't theirs?"

"Indeed." Rhoda's arm fell, dragging the towel in the dirt. "And why would Caroline take it?"

Davonna tugged her shawl tight. "I've said enough already."

Finally, something they all could agree on.

Mr. Kamden met Caroline's gaze. "The hour is late, and we are all tired."

"So that's it?" Davonna planted her hands on her sides. "You don't care about what I say? About your faither's locket?"

"Not tonight, I don't." He sighed. "I'm sure the captain is ready to bed down as well. If the locket has not turned up by porridge time in the morning, we will go speak to him."

"Very well." Davonna squared her shoulders. "But I do not wish to sleep in the same wagon with her."

The feeling was mutual.

If Caroline weren't dripping wet, she would latch onto a candle lantern and start the long walk back to Jewell and Mary and Cora and Gilbert. Tears stung her eyes. She never should've left her own family.

16

Yawning, Anna pulled the coffee grinder and pot from the box on the back of the wagon. Thanks to her friends' teasing ways during supper last night, she had dreamed of Caleb Reger in her sleep. She and the trail hand had been cheerful, giving the children rides on a cow, until Mutter called out to her from her hammock. A mishmash of her various journey experiences with Caleb.

So far Saturday morning hadn't chased the thoughts of him away as she held the pot under the spigot of the water barrel.

"Anna?" Mutter's voice drew her attention to the table where Mutter pulled a crust of bread from a sack. "Did you hear me?"

Shaking her head, Anna hung the pot from the hook over the fire Großvater had started. "I'm sorry. My mind . . . I was thinking about something else." Someone else.

"I was asking about your großvater."

"He's gone to get the oxen."

"He was awfully slow getting out of bed this morning." Mutter scooped butter from the churn. "I was already up and dressing before he dropped his hammock into the back of the wagon."

Anna nodded. "Yes, and now that you mention

it, he was moving pretty slowly, even at rolling his hammock."

"That's not like him. Since Vater agreed to join the caravan, he's had more energy than I've seen in him since . . . well, you know." Mutter looked away.

Since Dedrick died. Why couldn't Mutter say it?

"Do you think he might be ill?" Mutter asked.

"He didn't say anything about it. Went after the oxen like he does every morning."

"You know your großvater. He wouldn't say if he was feeling *punk.*"

Anna pulled three tin mugs from the wagon box. "I'll keep an eye on him."

Mutter began to slice dry sausage for their breakfast. "And I might talk to the doctor."

"Großvater wouldn't like that."

"Well, I wouldn't like it if he got sick and died on me."

Anna sighed. "Großvater is fine. You'll see." Still she couldn't help but watch for him to return to camp while she freed her hammock from the tree and rolled it.

The coffee seemed eager to boil this morning, sending out a rich aroma. Distracted by Mutter's concerns, Anna realized she may have ground extra into the pot.

Großvater appeared and dropped the lead rope at the tongue of the wagon, leaving the four oxen unattended. “I could smell our coffee two camps down. Works better than a dinner bell.”

Anna poured him a cup and studied his face for any sign of illness.

“*Danke.*” Großvater carried the cup to the table, the steam trailing him. He sank onto a chair and took a long gulp. “Tastes extra good this morning.”

Mutter glanced at the oxen, not yet yoked to the wagon. “Vater?”

After another gulp of coffee, he peered up at her over the cup. “Wilma?”

“How are you feeling?”

“Like everyone else. With my fingers.”

Giggling, Anna handed Mutter a cup of coffee. “Großvater seems fine to me.”

Mutter huffed. “Just as annoying as always, that is for certain.”

“And you’re worrying for naught. You can’t blame me for wanting a little coffee before I go back to work.” He set his cup down and went to the tongue.

“Mornin’, Otto.” Boney strolled up with Caleb Reger at his side. “Anna. Mrs. Goben.” Boney returned his attention to Großvater. “Me and Caleb were just fighting over who was going to get to yoke your oxen for a cup of that coffee and a hunk of Anna’s spice bread.” He looked at Caleb and raised a brow.

“Uh, yes, we were. And I say it should be me.

After all, everyone knows Boney's a better cook than I am. He can make his own bread." He looked at Anna and smiled.

"Well, I am glad to see you," Mutter said, "and will happily give you both a portion and a hot cup if you'll do the rest of Vater's chores for him this morning."

"Sounds like a good deal to me, Otto. We get fed, and you get to watch us work."

"My daughter thinks I'm weak." Großvater shook his head. "When it's just that blamed bear kept me awake the other night, and the memory of its visit hasn't helped me get much sleep since."

"You and me both." Boney gave a low whistle and clapped Großvater on the shoulder. "Show me where to find a coffee mug."

Had Boney seen what Mutter was worried about? Was Großvater not feeling well and trying to hide it? Or was he just grateful for the company? Mutter was no doubt wondering the same things.

When Boney sat down to visit with Großvater, Anna poured a cup for Caleb.

He looked up at her. "So that's my prize?"

"Your prize?"

"The coffee."

Nodding, she smiled and held the cup out to him. "A sip or two might help with the work."

He took the cup, his gaze lingering. "Your smile is worth more than any cup of coffee."

Her cheeks warmed. She tried not to smile, but couldn't help it. "Thanks again for helping us with the hoop yesterday. Seems as long as we're around, you don't have to concern yourself with boredom."

"You are anything but boring, Miss Goben." A smile parted his lips.

She could say the same about him. "I best let you get this job done before the coffee cools."

Caleb returned the cup to her, then bent over the yoke and effortlessly lifted it into position.

Watching him yoke the oxen, Anna couldn't help but wonder if that was what she'd dream about tonight.

At least Davonna Kamden had chosen not to voice her accusation of thievery in front of her grandchildren.

Caroline stirred flour into the dough starter, but her mind and heart weren't in the work. Instead, her thoughts kept returning to the elder Mrs. Kamden's charge. She'd hardly slept a wink last night because of it. When Davonna had gone back into the wagon to gather a few things, Caroline had hoped she would find the missing locket. When that didn't happen, Rhoda had whispered her apologies to Caroline and taken her mother-in-law to the Conestoga for the night.

That had left Caroline to settle the children into their makeshift beds. Of no mind to do anything else, she'd tossed and turned atop her pallet on the lid of her trunk. All she could think about was Davonna Kamden and how much she wanted to get away from her. When she'd first met the elder Mrs. Kamden, the woman had taken an instant liking to her. It was Davonna's idea that her son employ Caroline on the road west to provide her with the means to join the caravan. They'd lived side by side for several days now. Caroline had given no reason to be distrusted. On the contrary, she'd accepted the woman's eccentricities and done all she could to aid her.

Certainly, she wasn't the only one who entertained concerns for the grandmother. Davonna's childish manner had puzzled her more than once. But for her to conclude that the locket had been stolen and Caroline was the culprit . . . Would anyone in their right mind think such a thing?

Nonetheless, the moment the captain of the Boone's Lick Company returned from his early morning scouting trip with Rutherford Wainwright, he was sure to include her in an investigation of thievery.

During this extended midday break, Davonna sat on a quilt under a shade tree up the hill from the wagon. Ian and Rhoda Kamden had gone to the creek with all five of their children.

Caroline covered the bowl of dough starter and returned it to the new grub box Arvin Beck had made for the farm wagon. Rhoda had nearly insisted on staying behind to tend to the dough and peel potatoes, but Caroline needed to be alone. When she wasn't thinking about the events of last evening, her thoughts turned to the quilting circle in Saint Charles and to her sister and nieces and nephew. She missed the weekly drive out to Mrs. Brantenberg's farm with Jewell. She missed cooking meals alongside her sister.

She missed Elsa Brantenberg, Emilie, Johann Heinrich and the dry goods store. She missed sleeping on a soft bed. And, yes, she still missed Phillip. She liked having someone with whom she could share her life. And caring for someone else's gaggle of children and difficult mother-in-law wasn't at all what she had in mind.

"Miss Caroline!"

The voice had become familiar when she worked in Heinrich's Dry Goods and Grocery. Caroline turned toward the gangly young man with the fuzzy beard.

Oliver Rengler glanced at the bucket of potatoes she had yet to peel. "Oooweee. You want some help with those?"

"Yes. Thank you, Oliver." Perhaps having someone to talk to could rein in her thoughts. She pointed to a stool at the back of the wagon. "If you pull that up here, I'll put you to work."

"I'd like that, Miss Caroline." Oliver fairly ran to the stool then back to the table with it. "This is one of those days I seem to be nothin' but in Sally's way."

More often than not, Oliver's sister-in-law seemed put off by him. In Saint Charles, Oliver had spent a lot of time at the dry goods store. The close quarters of a wagon train weren't as accommodating.

"Sometimes, we women have a certain way of doing things—our way." Caroline smiled.

Oliver chuckled. "That's the truth, Miss Caroline."

"I'm happy for your help." As he settled onto the stool at the table, Caroline moved a second pot toward Oliver. "You can put the peeled spuds in this one."

He grabbed a knife and began to peel, taking a little too much potato in the process. "We can have a sport. See who can fill their pot first."

Caroline looked into her tin bowl. "I don't think that would be fair. I have a much smaller bowl."

"Life ain't fair, Miss Caroline. Owen's told me that time and time again."

She drew in a deep breath and let it out on a wistful sigh. "That may be true, Oliver, but I want to be fair."

"I like that about you, Miss Caroline." He started peeling his next potato. "You're nice to people, no matter what."

Caroline nearly choked on his unassuming compliment, which collided with a series of memories. Her judging Garrett Cowlishaw because he'd fought for the South. Her judging Davonna Kamden because the woman talked too much.

"Do you like working for that lady?" Oliver looked over at the dogwood tree and the woman who sat beneath it.

"Actually, I work for Mr. Kamden. I help take care of his children." And his mother.

Oliver dropped the remnant of another potato into his pot and looked up at her, his brown eyes widening. "Remember when I said I could be sweet on you if you wanted me to?"

"I remember."

"We were in the dry goods store."

Caroline carefully slid her knife around the spud, hoping Oliver would notice how little of its flesh she wasted.

"You said you weren't looking for a husband."

She remembered that too.

"You still feel that way?" he asked.

Caroline nodded. As much as she longed for someone special in her life, she feared opening her heart only to risk losing another husband. She couldn't, could she?

"I was just wondering. 'Cause our captain . . . he looks at you a lot."

"He does?"

Oliver's exaggerated nod folded his chin whiskers against his chest. "He looks at you like he really likes you."

If that were true, his interest would change upon today's return from scouting when Davonna Kamden planned to report her accusations. And as captain, he'd be obligated to pursue the charge.

Oliver dropped yet another mutilated potato into his pot. "I seen you look at the captain that way too."

"You have?" She moistened her lips. "You must be mistaken."

Oliver shrugged, a coy grin lifting his thick eyebrows. The youngest Rengler brother was obviously an incurable romantic.

If Garrett Cowlishaw was looking at her, it wasn't in *that* way. Not after the way she'd treated him.

However, their past encounters hadn't seemed the least bit important when she and the captain nearly ran into each other yesterday. When they'd both bent to pick up the fallen letter and their hands touched. He hadn't seemed any more anxious to withdraw his hand than she had been.

Caroline ducked her head to hide a blush. What if Oliver was right?

Garrett pulled up on the reins, slowing his black stallion. While most of the Company enjoyed a much-deserved noon stop, he and Rutherford Wainwright rode on for a look at the road ahead.

He'd known Rutherford for as long as he could remember. They were boys together in Virginia with big ideas and big dreams. Rutherford had gone to Missouri, found a job, then a wife. They'd both suffered heartache in and around the war, but now Rutherford was living a fresh start. He had his little girl at his side, along with his new wife, Maren. And he gave God the credit for helping him find his way through sorrow, for giving him a second chance.

Garrett raised his face to the sky. Could he believe God would do the same for him?

Rutherford slowed his horse, matching Garrett's slower pace, then looked at him. "You plannin' on telling me?"

"What?"

"Your secret."

No point in asking how Rutherford knew he'd been keeping something from him. It was the nature of good friends to know.

Rutherford dipped his chin and stared him in the eye. "Doesn't matter if you're on your feet or on a horse, you always slow down when you're deep in thought."

Garrett nodded and pulled his horse around to face Rutherford. "I'm ready to tell you."

"Good." Rutherford lifted his hat and shoved it back on his head. " 'Cause I wasn't looking forward to wrestling it out of you."

He didn't know why he hadn't told Rutherford. Except that he'd wanted to forget it all, put it behind him.

Garrett lifted himself by the stirrups and sat back on the cantle. “In Virginia, before the war, I was married.” That much was easier than expected, and his buddy didn’t look any more surprised than Isaac had.

After he’d told Rutherford about why he’d joined the war, standing up to his own men to protect escaped slaves, and the consequences, the two of them rode most of the way back to camp in silence, save for the creaks of the saddles and the hoofbeats of the horses.

Garrett looked at the camp below and the surrounding hills. Nothing out of the ordinary.

Rutherford raked his woolly hair with one hand. “You ever think about marrying again?”

Garrett swallowed hard. “Because you did?”

“There are plenty of better reasons.”

Nodding, Garrett urged his stallion toward camp. He didn’t have any trouble coming up with a list of reasons why he wished he were married. The challenge would be finding a woman who would be able to put up with him and his pained leg, let alone care about him in that way. The women back home wanted nothing to do with him.

“What do you make of Caroline Milburn?” Rutherford’s bright-eyed grin told Garrett his buddy knew good and well they were already talking about the young widow.

Garrett drew in a deep breath and opened his mouth. Then abruptly closed it.

Truth was . . . he was tired of his own denials. He could say he admired her, because it was true. He could say she was eye catching. That was true too. But his feelings for Caroline ran deeper than admiration and appreciation, and he didn't have a chance with her.

"Does she know?"

Garrett shook his head. "You think she'd care to know?"

"She doesn't seem to hate you anymore." Rutherford smiled. "I'd say your relations have come a long way."

Garrett laughed until he saw the chuck wagon. Mrs. Davonna Kamden stood beside the front wheel. Wearing a plaid skirt with a polka-dot shirtwaist, she wagged a finger at his best cook.

"Looks like Ian's mother is giving Boney an earful."

The instant Mrs. Kamden saw Garrett riding toward her, the older woman started waving him over.

As they rode up to the chuck wagon, Garrett waved Rutherford on, then swung down from the saddle. "Mrs. Kamden."

Boney took the reins from Garrett. "I'll take him to the pasture, Boss. Give him a chance to graze before we pull out."

Feeling a bit abandoned, Garrett nodded anyway. "Yes. Thank you."

Davonna Kamden smoothed the ties on her

bonnet. "Captain. We'll arrive in Independence in two weeks, is that right?"

"Yes ma'am. That's my plan, anyway."

"Good."

"I don't understand, Mrs. Kamden. Are you in need of supplies? In need of services?"

She blew out an unladylike breath. "It's not me, Captain. You will need to leave someone there."

Garrett frowned. "No one has said anything about an immediate need to leave our Company."

"That's because they're afraid to."

"Afraid to tell me?" He'd all but given up hope of understanding her, and now he was losing patience. And why was her top lip twitching? She didn't seem the least bit distracted by it. "Ma'am, if this person is afraid to tell me they need to stop in Independence, how could you know?"

"That's what I came to tell you, if you would only listen."

Swallowing a mix of irritation and amusement, Garrett met the woman's rigid stare. "Very well. I'm listening."

She glanced around. "In your meetings back in Saint Charles, you said you couldn't abide troublemakers on our journey west."

"That's correct." This was about troublemakers?

Her gaze darted left, then right. "We have a thief in our midst." She fanned herself with her hand.

Garrett jerked to attention. "Thievery is a serious accusation, ma'am."

"Can you tolerate having someone like that in our camp, Captain?"

"No ma'am, I cannot. Who is the accused, ma'am?"

Davonna Kamden looked out over the camp. "You're looking right at the thief." She raised her hand and pointed. "There, at the worktable next to my wagon."

The only people he saw at the end of her pointed finger were Caroline Milburn and Oliver.

"Oliver Rengler. Are you sure this isn't just a misunderstanding?" Garrett shook his head. "Oliver is simple, but he's as honest as the day is long."

Mrs. Kamden tugged the cuffs of her shirt sleeves straight. "Not that poor soul." She huffed. "The young woman is the thief."

Garrett's throat tensed. He coughed hard against the restriction. "Mrs. Milburn? You're accusing Caroline Milburn, your grandchildren's nanny?"

"I'm afraid so. My locket is missing, and she took it."

Of course, he'd have to investigate, no matter how much he doubted the validity of the charge. He was still on shaky ground with Caroline Milburn, and accusing the woman of being a thief would not help his cause in the least.

So much for *his* second chances.

17

Mutter swung a boot over the seat and climbed down from the wagon. "You're still making hats?"

Anna held up her latest handiwork and turned it. "I'm adding the finishing touches to this one, and I'll be done." She hadn't accomplished much else during the noon break, but she had completed two more hats.

"Shouldn't we be on our way by now?"

They both glanced toward the captain's chuck wagon. The elder Mrs. Kamden stood beside it talking to Boney, probably making the same inquiry.

Anna rolled the remaining length of ribbon around her fingers and tucked it into her basket. "This has been our longest noon break."

"Apparently, Rutherford Wainwright has yet to return with our captain."

"I haven't seen them." Anna lifted both hats and stood. "But I've made enough hats for now."

"You are certainly more industrious than I, my dear."

"We're going to need money to start a new life in the West." Anna carried the hats to the back of the wagon and carefully set them inside. "Every little bit will help."

"I could help you make candles to sell. If not

to those in our Company, in the settlements we'll encounter along the way."

"That's a good idea. Perhaps we could get one of these men to rob us a beehive." Anna wasn't looking for another job, but it did her heart good to see Mutter interested in such a task again. Neither of them had spoken further of Mutter's last bout with drunkenness. Nor had there been any more incidents of overindulgence. Or even singing off key. "In the meantime, I thought I'd pay Caroline Milburn a visit. Perhaps she's heard something about our delay." After all, the whole quilting circle knew Caroline kept watch on the captain, whether *she* realized it or not.

"I certainly hope this doesn't delay our arrival in Independence."

Anna didn't need to ask Mutter what her rush was. If she hadn't already emptied the last bottle she'd hidden, she would soon. And then what?

"The city of Independence is our first real milestone of the trip," Mutter continued. "Arriving will make us feel like we're actually getting somewhere."

Anna nodded. "That would feel good." So would selling her hats and buying the supplies to make more.

"Go ahead, dear. You run along to see your friend. I'll put your things in the trunk and pack up the table and chairs."

When Mutter busied herself at the table, Anna

pushed away the notion that she should stay to keep an eye on her and took quick steps toward the Kamdens' wagons.

Feeling a bit warm in the afternoon sun, Anna let her shawl slip to her elbows. Oxen, mules, and horses grazed leisurely in the meadow across the road. A few folks fished along the banks of the creek. The Le Beau boys and several other children, including Gabi, took turns swinging from the board Mary Alice's husband had hung from a sturdy sycamore branch. Anna waved at Maren and Mary Alice as she passed. She looked up the road in time to see Rutherford Wainwright riding toward his camp. He and the captain had returned, so she wouldn't have long to visit with Caroline before the Company pulled out.

Between the Kamdens' farm wagon and their Conestoga, Caroline and Oliver Rengler were seated at a worktable, peeling potatoes.

When Anna arrived, Caroline smiled and stood. "I'm so glad to see you." She pulled Anna into an embrace that seemed a bit intense for a mere afternoon greeting. But then Caroline had seemed sad and withdrawn on the walk that morning. Probably missing Jewell and the children.

Oliver stood. "Hello, Miss Anna."

"Hello, Oliver."

Anna glanced at the two piles of shredded potato skins. "It appears Miss Caroline had a big job to do and found a good helper."

"I surely did."

Oliver shifted his chair to one side for Anna then unlashed another three-legged stool from the side of the wagon. "We're real late leaving."

Anna glanced toward her wagon. "That's what we were talking about. Any idea why? I saw that the captain has returned to camp."

"I think it's Missus Kamden's fault," Oliver said. "She's been over at his chuck wagon workin' her mouth like my brother says I do."

Caroline sighed.

"Caroline, is something wrong?" Anna asked. "Are you having trouble with the children? You seemed to be getting on with them right well."

"I am. If it were only the children."

"Oh." Anna looked toward the chuck wagon then back at Caroline.

Caroline nodded.

Oliver picked up another potato. "You s'pose I should go rescue the captain? Tell him it's time to round us up?"

Before Anna or Caroline could respond, Garrett Cowlishaw took long strides toward them with Mrs. Kamden marching in step, her chin held high.

"Looks like they both been suckin' on lemons," Oliver whispered.

Anna giggled. They could always count on Oliver to come out with the truth, however blunt.

Unlike Anna's mother, the youngest Rengler brother never made you guess what he was thinking.

Caroline stood, holding a half-peeled potato. Anna and Oliver also stood.

The captain removed his slouch hat. "Hello, folks. I'm sorry to interrupt, but I need to have a word with Mrs. Milburn."

Oliver shifted his weight from one foot to the other. "You want me and Miss Anna to leave?"

Caroline slipped her hand into Anna's. Apparently, she wasn't going anywhere.

"Am I in trouble, sir?" Oliver's eyes widened. He looked at Caroline, then back at Garrett. "You don't think we's . . ." A blush rose from beneath his wispy beard. "We just been peelin' these taters. Miss Caroline ain't sweet on me, or nothin'."

Anna couldn't help but smile at Oliver's innocent assumption. Apparently not amused, Caroline gave Anna's hand a squeeze.

The captain cleared his throat. "Mrs. Milburn, your employer—"

"Mr. Kamden?" Caroline looked at the potato in her hand.

"No ma'am. It is Mrs. Davonna Kamden who has expressed concerns."

Caroline dropped the potato into the pan at her feet. "Concerns?"

"Yes." The captain still hadn't looked Caroline in the eye. "She has reported something missing from her belongings and feels you may have some information as to its disappearance."

"A locket, perhaps?"

"Yes. You know of its whereabouts?"

Caroline shook her head. "Only of Mrs. Kamden's accusation."

"Accusation?" Anna tightened her grip on Caroline's hand and squared her shoulders. "What are you talking about?"

"Mrs. Kamden has accused me of stealing her missing locket, and apparently, the captain has concerns about my honesty, as well."

Anna and Oliver both gasped in unison. Oliver started shaking his head.

"I never said . . ." The captain looked at Davonna Kamden then to Caroline. "I am merely doing my job."

Anna drew in a deep breath and looked at Mrs. Kamden. "With all due respect, ma'am, you must have misplaced the locket."

Mrs. Kamden pinched her lips together as Anna had seen little Maisie do when Caroline scolded her.

"Then someone else is to blame," Anna said. "Caroline would never—"

Garrett Cowlishaw cleared his throat. "Mrs. Milburn. Surely you can understand my obligation to consider any and all possibilities."

Caroline arched her eyebrows. "Including the one that suggests I am a thief?"

"Yes ma'am. Facts, not personal opinions, are what I need in order to investigate."

Oliver's chest puffed out. "Investigate? Miss Caroline?"

Anna agreed with Oliver. This woman's accusations were preposterous.

Caroline rested her hand on Oliver's arm. "It's all right. You'll see. Mrs. Kamden is worried sick about her locket, and the captain is only doing his job."

Oliver scrubbed his whiskered cheek. "But—"

"It'll be all right." She met the captain's gaze, now unyielding. "I say we get to the facts."

"Agreed." Mr. Cowlishaw pulled his slouch hat taut. "Mrs. Kamden said she kept the locket in her belongings in the smaller wagon you share."

"That's correct. Along with three of her grandchildren, but all five of them go in and out of the wagon regularly."

Mrs. Kamden stiffened. "You're accusing those innocent children?"

"I'm only stating the facts. That's what the captain said he wanted. And the more facts, the better."

Mr. Cowlishaw drew in another deep breath. "Mrs. Milburn, had you ever seen Mrs. Kamden's locket?"

"I have. She's not worn it on the trip, but I did see the locket once when she took it out of the box to show it to me."

The older woman nodded. “That’s a fact, Captain. So she knew where I kept it.”

“That doesn’t mean I took it. Others—”

“The children, you mean?”

“Yes, and your son and your daughter-in-law. They all knew you kept it in your jewelry case.”

Anna felt like cheering. Not only was Caroline remaining as cool as a crock in a root cellar, she was keeping her wits about her in this ridiculous investigation.

The captain flapped his hat against his thigh. “I see.”

Mrs. Kamden raised her chin. “You see what, Captain Cowlishaw?”

“Mrs. Kamden, I see that this very important matter will require more attention. Further inquiry.” Garrett Cowlishaw returned the hat to his head. “Would you have me do that now, delaying our departure all the more, or might my investigation wait until we arrive at Independence?”

“Very well.” Mrs. Kamden pressed her fingertips to her right temple as if to restrain an oncoming headache. “She is good with the children.”

The captain nodded. “I’ll escort you to your wagon then, and we’ll be on our way.” He cupped the elder woman’s forearm and turned to leave.

Anna added her sigh to Caroline’s. Yes, matters such as this went a long way to help Anna keep her concerns about her own mother in perspective.

At least Mutter kept her insolence to herself. Mrs. Kamden had no such familiarity with discretion.

Poor Caroline.

Now the captain would be required to keep watch on her. And for all the wrong reasons.

Caroline knelt in front of her trunk and set the candle lantern on the floorboard beside her. She pulled the official stationery of the Department of War from an envelope, taking care not to hold the paper too close to the dancing flame. Pressing the folded letter to her chest, she sat back on her heels. The three youngest Kamden children were tucked in and sleep-breathing, Maisie's like the purr of a kitten. Caroline closed her eyes and quieted her spirit.

Thankfully, Rhoda had agreed to move her mother-in-law into the Conestoga until the good captain could reconcile Davonna Kamden's concern that Caroline was a thief.

Caroline blew out an unladylike sigh of relief. This was indeed one day she was glad to see come to a close. The poor woman couldn't actually believe Caroline would take her locket . . . had taken it. Garrett Cowlishaw didn't believe it. She'd seen the vein jumping in his neck and heard the tension in his mandatory questioning.

She'd seen something else in his hazel eyes too. A look she recognized from days gone by. Days with Phillip. Was it possible there was some truth in Oliver's assumptions that the captain fancied her, despite her harsh treatment of him?

Caroline unfolded the sheet of paper Garrett had delivered to her on that cold day last November.

Department of War,
Washington, District of Columbia

Dear Mrs. Milburn,

It is with deepest regret that I write you. Your beloved husband, Colonel Phillip Milburn, served our country well, earning the loyalties of his regiment and indeed the entire army.

Peril beset the good colonel in the Battle of Nashville, 16 December 1864, where the Union had suffered 387 killed, 2,562 wounded, and 112 missing. Colonel Milburn was instrumental in the taking of Shy's Hill, the source of much of the carnage. Though mortally wounded, he led his artillery unit to destroy the entrenchment and the cover it had provided the sharp-shooters of the Confederacy. The Union ultimately prevailed in the battle, with no little thanks to the sacrifice made by your husband.

A brave patriot, your husband. He succumbed to his injuries the following

day, 17 December 1864, and was buried with full military honors near Nashville.
A box of the colonel's personals will be forthcoming. You may expect it to arrive shortly.

With deepest sympathies,
Major Augustus Shnebley,
United States Department of War

Once again, the finality of the letter washed over Caroline. She blinked hard against a ready wall of tears. Determined to cry no more for what was or could have been, she folded the letter and rose to her knees.

"Good-bye, Phillip." If it were safe to do so, she'd burn the letter in the candle flame. Instead, she returned the paper to the envelope and slid her past back into the trunk.

Caroline folded her hands and bowed her head. Following Mrs. Brantenberg's good teaching from the quilting circle, she asked God to take her scraps . . . the mismatched remnants of Phillip's life and death. Saying good-bye to family in Saint Charles. The challenges of caring for the Kamden family. She also gave Him the puzzling piece of new fabric that was her attraction to Garrett Cowlishaw, an unlikely pattern at an unlikely time.

The sound of footfalls quickened Caroline's

heartbeat. Who would be out this late? And so close to her wagon? She blew out her candle in a swift puff. Quiet and still, she watched two silhouettes grow on the oiled canvas.

Caroline felt around for any sort of weapon but only came up with a whittled gun tucked into Duff's boot.

No more steps. Silence.

"Caroline?"

"Rhoda?" She let herself breath again.

Caroline struck a match and relit the candle. The youngest Mrs. Kamden stood at the front of the wagon. When Caroline stuck her head out of the opening, she could see that Rhoda hadn't come alone.

"Mrs. Kamden? It's late." Caroline looked at one woman then the other. "Is something wrong?"

Rhoda faced her mother-in-law, her eyebrows arched. "Mither Kamden needed a word with you."

The elder Mrs. Kamden remained quiet, her hand pressed to her chest.

"Mither?" Rhoda's eyebrows angled upward.

Davonna Kamden moved her hand, revealing a shiny locket dangling from her neck.

"Your locket," Caroline said.

"Yes, dear."

"You found it. Where?"

Davonna shifted her weight. "It's an amusing story, really."

Good. "I could use a little amusement."

"Well, you see, I was knitting in the wagon when my yarn sack fell off my lap. Ian has real good hearing and asked what the jingling sound was. Yarn doesn't usually make much noise."

"It was the locket."

Davonna offered a brief nod, her lips pursed. "Ian found it on the floorboard, chain and all."

Caroline straightened. "I didn't put it in your knitting sack."

"Of course not, dear." Davonna rubbed the locket as if it were a good-luck charm. "I must have put it in there. I'm afraid all this roaming around is making me, well, a little absent-minded."

To say the least.

Rhoda sighed. "I, for one, am happy to have that mystery solved."

Caroline didn't feel as good about the mystery being solved as she would have expected. Now, the good captain would have no reason to make a deeper inquiry into her secret life as a locket thief. Tickled by her sarcastic thoughts, Caroline absently let out a laugh.

"You see, Rhoda," Davonna said, "I told you our Miss Caroline was a jovial sort and would find the whole affair befitting of a hearty laugh."

When Davonna and Rhoda joined in the laughter, Caroline let them assume her giggle concerned the locket. But her amusement quickly gave way to her concern for the elder Mrs. Kamden.

18

Finally alone after five days on the road, Caleb sat at the top of a hillock on Sunday morning. He watched as colors as bright as his mother's spring flower garden streaked the morning sky.

The wagons weren't rolling today. The group had voted that Sundays would be their sacred Sabbath rest, which suited Caleb just fine. Rest sounded real good. He could use the time to do some thinking. His problem was deciding which topic to tackle first. Where he was headed and what he'd do when he got there. Why his boss seemed bent on shepherding him. Or should he concentrate on what he would do about the distraction Miss Anna Goben was proving to be? He'd surprised himself as much as he'd surprised her when he'd told her that her smile was worth more than any cup of coffee. Not the best compliment, now that he thought about it, but she'd seemed pleased anyway.

It had been easier to avoid her before he knew she and Boney only shared the love of two good friends.

The Scripture lay open on Caleb's bent legs, his hand resting on a familiar passage from the book of Psalms. He felt more in common with King

David than any of the other Old Testament men. Not that he was destined to be a king, but his sin, though not the same as David's, had devastated his own people.

Footsteps squeaked in the dewy grass, causing Caleb to jerk. Garrett stood beside him.

"I've only known one other man who was as committed as you are to reading that book. He was a preacher in my regiment." The words came out on a huff as Garrett folded his legs and settled on the ground beside Caleb.

"I read more out of desperation than spiritual fervor."

"All of us carry scars from the war, but not every man turns to God like you have."

Caleb sighed. If only he'd remained consistent in his choice to follow God in the first place.

"That's what I came up here to talk to you about," Garrett continued.

"Desperation?"

Garrett chuckled. "Some might say I'm a little desperate." He plucked a blade of grass and rolled it between his fingers. "It's Sunday. You've done such a good job of reading Scripture every morning. I thought you might like to preach."

The mere thought stung Caleb's heart. "Sorry, but I can't."

"Sure you can." Garrett glanced at the open pages. "It's basically the same as all the other mornings. Only difference is you talk a little about the verse. How about the passage you were just reading?"

Psalm 51. Have mercy upon me, O God. . . . For I acknowledge my transgressions: and my sin is ever before me.

The verse still stung his heart.

"I can't preach." He wasn't clean enough.

"Can't, or won't?"

"Take your pick. I'm not a preacher." Caleb closed the Bible and stood. "It's time I get to my chores."

Caleb took quick steps down the hillock toward camp with Garrett close behind. They'd just reached more even ground, when Garrett broke the silence.

"See you at the breakfast table?"

Caleb nodded and waved his hat, then continued down the narrow path toward the chuck wagon. No need to ask where the captain was headed. To see the Kamden children. Or, rather, their red-headed nanny.

His boss was a good man. Not above jumping in and getting his hands dirty on any jobs needing to be done. The first night the Company set up camp, the captain had been the one to dig the latrine for the women. Garrett also had a touch for teaming up the men who might work best together. Their leader didn't believe in letting bad feelings fester. And no matter how sorely someone tested his patience, he treated everyone with respect. He certainly deserved a second chance at love.

Now, if Garrett would only give up the notion that Caleb would make a good preacher. He cared too much for all of them to pretend he was qualified to be their spiritual leader. He was already crossing the line between truth and lies when standing before the Company reading Scripture like a saint.

He'd already grown fond of many of his fellow travelers, which fed the fear that he'd let them down. He couldn't allow himself to fail the people who depended on him. Not again.

Unfortunately, that anxiety kindled impatience with anyone who didn't follow the rules to the letter. Miss Hattie Pemberton and Miss Anna Goben were among those. Although he'd been right to inquire after them and to remind the young ladies of the Company's policy, he really didn't need to be so abrupt.

He owed them both an apology. He'd intended to deliver one Friday evening when he saw Miss Goben charging toward the pasture, but she had the canvas and hoop on her mind.

Turning toward his camp, Caleb caught sight of a familiar green calico dress. Anna Goben held the lead rope of an ox. It looked like she'd be the first to receive an apology, after all.

Her steps light and the rope slack, she led the steer toward a less populated patch of grass. Were her lips moving? Was she scolding the animal? Comforting it? He chuckled at the thought. But as he drew closer to her, he picked up a melody. She sang in German, but Caleb recognized the tune to the familiar hymn, "Give to Our God Immortal Praise."

Wonders of grace to God belong; repeat His mercies in your song.

She apparently had a better understanding of God's grace than he did.

Just as quickly as his shoulders sagged under the burden of his past, he pushed the memories from his mind. He couldn't change what he'd done on the battlefield. But he could try to right his impolite behavior.

Despite his first impression of Miss Goben, she truly was a marvel. She cooked, helped her grandfather with the livestock, fetched water, looked after her mother, created hats, yoked oxen, and slept in a hammock suspended between a wagon and a tree. Those weren't all standard activities for a female who was also an eye-catching young woman.

Caleb slowed his steps.

Fact was, he'd found Anna Goben intriguing from the moment she'd summoned Boney Hughes away from the altar. And then approaching him on her grandfather's porch, her shoulders squared. Then, again, the evening he'd followed her to the creek bank and watched her bury what he was sure were bottles of liquor. Friday evening, he'd caught her watching him intently while she pretended to busy herself at the grub box on the back of the wagon. From what he'd seen of her, it didn't seem there was anything she couldn't or wouldn't do to provide for and protect her family.

And she sang about God's grace and mercy. To an ox.

He chewed his bottom lip. If he was thinking so highly of her, it might be best he maintain some antagonism between them. Fondness and affections weren't something his heart could afford.

Caleb was in the process of turning around, about thirty feet from Miss Goben, when she looked up.

With no choice now but to follow through on his original plan, Caleb joined her beside a young willow. "Good day, Miss Goben."

Her face pinked. "And to you, Caleb." She glanced around them. "I didn't see you there. Anna. Call me Anna."

"Anna." He pulled the derby from his head.

Her gaze rose to the top of his head, and a bashful grin brightened her blue eyes.

"My hair?" He looked that direction as if he could actually see his hair and then, smiling, raised his right arm.

"On the top. Your left."

He switched hands and brushed his hair. "Better?"

She nodded.

"I heard you singing."

The pink in her cheeks deepened.

"You have a lovely voice."

"Thank you." She glanced at the rope in her hand. "I was just moving one of our oxen."

"Mind if I walk with you?"

"I don't mind, but I'm not going very far." She looked at the steer. "It seems he's feeling a bit cantankerous this morning."

Caleb grinned. "I know the feeling. That happened to me last Tuesday morning."

A smile tugged at the corners of her mouth.

"When I saw you out here, I thought this might be a better time to clear the air."

"I would've said you did as much the other evening when you helped with the wagon."

Caleb matched her easy pace, swinging his hat at his side. "Yes, well, thank you. But there was nothing official about it."

"All right, then. Let's clear the air."

"Good. It's just that I have a job to do, and I wish to be cordial with everyone in the Company. I don't want any ill will between us."

She stopped and looked him in the eye. He saw no sign of ill will, and what he thought he saw made him weak in the knees. Curiosity? Interest? Attraction?

Caleb cleared his throat, hoping his imagination would take the hint. "I became concerned when I learned that you and Miss Pemberton weren't with the wagons." He sighed. "I overreacted."

"Yes, well, at least now I am quite familiar with Company policy."

"Please forgive my curtness."

"You were only doing your job, keeping track of wayward women."

He chuckled. "Perhaps, but I really don't aim to make your trip miserable."

"That's good news. I agree that our travels will be more pleasant if we're cordial, free of any ill will." She moistened her lips.

Did she have any idea how distracting she was?

"You were new to Saint Charles when you took the job as a trail hand. My guess is you're from Tennessee or Georgia, maybe Kentucky."

"Good guess. I'm from Tennessee." But it hadn't been home since the war. "You went to school with Boney. Does that mean you've lived in Saint Charles all your life?"

"Since I was six." She stopped and let the lead rope drop to the ground. "My father left me, my mother, and Dedrick in New York. That very week, we climbed into a stagecoach and came to Missouri to live with my grandfather."

"I'm sure it was hard to leave your friends behind there, but it can't have been any easier to leave the place where you last saw your brother alive."

She shook her head, holding his gaze. "No, but

I felt we had to make this trip if there was any hope of crawling out of our grief. It's been really hard on my mother. And on my grandfather."

And on her. Trying to be strong for them. He could see the strain of it in her eyes.

Sighing, Anna tucked a curl of golden-brown hair behind her ear. "What about you? And your family?"

"I have one sister. And my parents."

She raised an eyebrow, as if waiting for more. "They're all still in Tennessee?"

"As far as I know, they are. I haven't seen them since the war." For all he knew, they counted him among the dead. Something else he didn't care to think about, let alone say.

"I'm sorry, Caleb."

"For what?"

"For whatever it is you can't say."

"Thank you."

The air between them was certainly free of ill will, but it was nowhere close to being free of secrets.

Caroline greeted the two Beck couples on her way by their campfire. Rhoda had given Caroline time to herself this morning before the Sunday worship service. Davonna had found her missing locket, but the fact that she had jumped to disturbing conclusions remained. And so did Caroline's concern regarding the older woman's well-being.

She shook her head. Time to put the whole Kamden family out of her mind, for now, and think about someone else. Maren Wainwright. Whenever Caroline was tempted to feel sorry for herself, she thought about Maren. Here she was on this long journey to the unknown—a newlywed, stepmother to a four-year-old, and losing her eyesight because of some mysterious condition. And all without Mrs. Brantenberg, the woman who had become like a mother to her in America.

When Caroline arrived at the Wainwrights' wagon, Maren sat at the worktable cutting up potatoes and Gabi was still inside dressing. Rutherford came up from the stream, a bucket of water in each hand. After they greeted each other, he poured the water into the barrel lashed to the side of the wagon.

Rutherford captured his bride's hand. "I'll leave you two to visit. But I'll be back in time for breakfast." He pulled Maren toward him and kissed her on the forehead.

Caroline looked away while a niggling question taunted her. Would she ever love and be loved again?

Rutherford waved good-bye and strolled toward Garrett's chuck wagon.

A sweet, happy song floated from Maren's wagon, and Caroline looked that direction. "It sounds like Gabi is enjoying a little time to herself. As am I."

"You'll have breakfast with us?"

"Yes, if you're sure."

"I'm sure, and Gabi will love the company too." Maren pointed toward the three-footed skillet on the cookfire. "The spider pan, as Mother Brantenberg liked to call it, should be hot enough by now. Mind if I cook while we visit?"

"Not at all. I like to watch other people work."

Smiling, Maren rose from the stool. Before she could straighten, she began to teeter.

Caroline lunged forward, holding her arm out to catch her, but Maren quickly regained her balance.

"Are you all right?" Caroline asked.

"Yes. Thank you. I must have stood with too much haste." Maren took slow steps to the campfire, tugging her apron straight.

Caroline looked at the spread of fixings on the table. "What can I do to help you?"

"You want to slice onion for the potatoes or cook the bacon?"

"I'll take the onion." Caroline reached into the tow sack and pulled out an onion. She found a knife and while she sliced, Maren started the bacon to sizzling.

A few moments later, Maren turned to her, blinking, something she did a lot of to help refocus her vision. But this time she didn't look well. The color drained from her face.

"You're not well. Are you?" Caroline asked.

Shaking her head, Maren twisted away from

the fire. She jerked her apron skirt to her mouth and began to retch.

When her friend's wave of sickness passed, Caroline carefully removed the soiled apron from Maren, set it on the ground under the wagon, and took over tending the bubbling skillet.

"How long have you not been feeling right?"

"Two or three days."

"Mostly in the mornings?"

Maren nodded.

Caroline looked her in the eye. "You could be expecting."

"Now?" Tears glistened in Maren's eyes.

"Does Rutherford know you haven't been feeling well?" Caroline could scarcely hear herself for all the popping and sizzling in the skillet.

"No. He's busy every morning tending to the animals." Maren pressed her hand to the waist of her calico dress, a tear sliding down her cheek. "I'll talk to Dr. Le Beau tomorrow. I don't want to disturb him on a Sunday." Her bottom lip quivered. "Gabi is old enough to do a lot for herself, but a baby—"

Suddenly, Gabi stood beside them, holding up her cloth dolly. "Here's my baby."

Neither of them had seen or heard the child climb out of the wagon.

Maren looked away, brushing tears from her face.

Caroline scrambled to fill the silence. "After

breakfast, maybe you'd like to go with me to help Miss Mary Alice with baby Evie."

Gabi's woolly brown curls bounced. "Yes."

So much had changed for all of them in the past few months, and Caroline couldn't help but wonder if Rutherford would choose to turn back when he found out Maren was carrying his child . . . on what his friend Garrett Cowlishaw called a treacherous journey.

Today, Caroline couldn't say she wouldn't return to Saint Charles with them.

19

Caleb squirmed on his sparse allotment of log, bumping Tiny's arm on one side and Frank's shoulder on the other. All three of them shifted. The last Sunday service Caleb had attended wasn't all that different from the one being held at the center of the circled wagons. The sky served as the ceiling. The grassy ground, the church flooring. A mishmash of logs and stools took the place of pews in the same way they had just over a year ago at Centralia. But Caleb couldn't remember there even being a sermon, let alone who had delivered it. That Sunday morning, he'd somehow roused himself enough to attend.

No. Someone had dragged him out of the tent.

Billy.

A familiar pang seared Caleb's gut and shot into his chest, and he crossed his arms against the onslaught.

Garrett had insisted all of the wagon train's leadership attend the service. Probably saw it as part of his role as the group's shepherd. Most members of the caravan were present, including the immigrants who didn't speak English. Even Wilma Goben, whom he'd rarely seen outside of her camp. Anna's mother seemed to appreciate isolation as much as he did.

Raised in the church, attending Sunday services had once been second nature to Caleb. He had looked forward to the gatherings. But that was before . . .

His gaze darted to Mama Zanzucchi and the cross dangling from her neck, then to little Gabi Wainwright who sat in front of the group between Maren and Rutherford, her fingers tracing the holes on the flute she held. He shouldn't be here. Didn't deserve to be here. He was a hypocrite, a sinner who didn't belong in the midst of these good people.

When Garrett cleared his throat and seated himself on a tree stump, Rutherford stood with a zither at his side and set his Bible on the stool.

"Welcome to the Boone's Lick Company's first worship service."

The oldest Zanzucchi boy translated for his

family while Le Doc's daughter translated for hers.

"Our esteemed captain asked me and my family to provide some music before I share my story with you."

Mrs. Rengler stood, wearing a hat too small for her head. "Excuse me, Mr. Wainwright, but I have something to say."

Owen tugged her calico sleeve. "Sit down, Sally."

"I will not." She turned her back on her husband and faced the boss.

Garrett stood. "Mrs. Rengler?"

"Captain." Her back stiff, she lifted her generous nose in the air. "I'm not sure he should be in our church service." Without turning her body, she jerked her head to where Isaac sat on a stool at the back of the ragtag congregation. Following Mrs. Rengler's gesture, the whole group turned in their seats. Husbands and wives gasped and murmured. If the count of hats bobbing were to be compared to those swaying back and forth, the group was about evenly split.

Emery Beck rose to his feet. "I agree with Mrs. Rengler. Fighting for the abolishment of slavery is one thing, but inviting the coloreds into our worship services is another entirely."

Caleb's shoulders tensed. Tiny and Frank both leaned forward. They all knew this test of Garrett's leadership had been coming. They also knew he'd rather eat broken glass than let an innocent be abused or allow anyone to question the worth of any man.

"I see no one in this congregation who is above or below anyone else. It is not our place, especially in the eyes of our Maker, to judge any of His created beings as less valuable than ourselves." Garrett scanned the group, not focusing on either of those standing.

"You didn't even fight on their side," Emery spat.

"Now you have me confused, Emery." Garrett's gentle tone belied the sharp set of his jaw. "Are we in church? Or are we not?"

Isaac stood. "I can go, Boss. I don't want to be any trouble."

"You're not." His voice steady, Garrett looked from one dissenter to the other. "If Mrs. Rengler and Mr. Beck are uncomfortable with our way of doing things, they are welcome to dismiss themselves from this service and conduct one of their own, if they so choose. They are not, however, permitted to cause such a disruption here."

Mrs. Rengler sank to her chair. Emery, on the other hand, slapped his hat against his leg and stormed off.

Garrett looked at Rutherford. "What was that you were saying?"

"Welcome." Rutherford set his fingers to the zither, and his wife and little Gabi lifted their flutes and began playing "A Mighty Fortress Is

Our God." Most everyone joined in, singing in English, French, German, or Italian.

Miss Hattie Pemberton stood, turned toward the group, and began moving her arms as if she were a musical director. Unfortunately, the movements bore little connection to the melody. She had just ushered in the second stanza when Mrs. Wainwright's flute dropped to her lap then tumbled to the ground. Rutherford swiftly set his zither on the stool and cupped his arms just in time to catch his wilting wife.

"Mother Maren!" Gabi's cry tore Caleb's heart. The group had already suffered a child breaking an arm. Now this, and they were only six days into the demanding journey.

If disease were to strike them and spread . . . Caleb didn't want to think about what could happen.

Dr. Le Beau darted toward Rutherford, shouting orders over his shoulder. The oldest of his sons ran to their wagon while Caroline Milburn suddenly appeared with a cup of water. When Maren Wainwright stirred, whispers ensued in the inner circle and murmurs rippled through the gathering again.

Within moments, Rutherford carried his wife to the bench where the widow Milburn cradled Gabi in her arms. His hand on his wife's shoulder, he looked out at the concerned crowd. "It is with joy that I make this announcement."

More murmurs.

"It appears my dear wife is going to give me a son or a daughter."

Sighs of relief replaced the murmurs as Gabi shouted, "A baby!"

Knowing Rutherford had lost his first wife in childbirth, Caleb begged God's protection on them all.

Folks swarmed the family, offering well-wishes and advice. What began as a simple church service had quickly given way to a public announcement. Now, everyone knew the Wainwrights' business. This traveling town didn't allow for privacy.

Caleb went to stand behind the crude seats. How did he expect to keep his failings in the past where they belonged?

He fought the nagging fear and drew a deep breath. His secret was safe. No one knew.

Except for him, and the pit of his stomach.

Anna couldn't remember the last time she'd felt this good. Not only was Mutter out of the wagon, but she was seated beside Anna in a worship service. The last time Mutter had attended a service was branded upon Anna's memory. The following Tuesday, Mutter received the telegram from the Department of War saying her beloved son had fallen in a barrage of enemy gunfire. Mutter hadn't gone to church since. Anna felt her throat tighten at the remembrance. She refused to let the past tarnish this moment. Her new beginning. Mutter and Großvater's fresh starts.

"Before she was my wife . . . before I ever believed I could love again, Miss Maren Jensen" —Rutherford smiled at Maren, now settled comfortably between Caroline and Gabi— "showed me what it meant to allow oneself to be guided by the lamp of God's Word. To trust the path He has for you, even when you can't see the way. Especially when you can't discern the direction, trusting His ability to navigate rough waters." Rutherford Wainwright stood before them in the midst of his own second chance. Reuniting with his daughter after a four-year absence, finding a new wife, and having a baby on its way.

Lord, please strengthen Maren with Thy divine grace.

Anna reached for her mother's hand, praying the same for her. For all of them, including Caleb.

Following the service and a noon meal, Hattie and Mary Alice brought their busy work to Anna's camp for a visit. Mutter had gone into the wagon to rest, causing Anna to wonder about any more hidden bottles.

Now, Anna sat at the worktable, feathers, ribbons, and hat blanks spread in front of her. Word was they'd roll into Independence in less than two weeks. The city had long been the jumping-off point for most westbound overlanders. Independence was certain to have at least one millinery and dress shop, and Anna was determined to have five hats ready to sell to the proprietor.

Hattie Pemberton was the only person Anna knew who would continue to wear a Sunday bonnet while doing her mending. Her friend pulled a needle through a wool sock and glanced toward the wagon. “It did my heart good to see your mother at the service this morning.”

Anna nodded. “Mine too.”

Bending to the quilt where Evie slept, Mary Alice pulled the corner taut. “I surely wish my Tom would join us for church.” She sighed then lifted the knitting from her lap and resumed her work. “Says he can’t believe in a God who would allow people to kill one another.” The words had no sooner left Mary Alice’s mouth when she gasped. “Oh dear. You both buried . . . Forgive me. My husband would say I live with my foot in my mouth.”

“No need to apologize.” Anna wove a peacock feather through the band on the straw hat she was designing.

“Anna’s right.” Hattie smoothed the toe of the sock. “Neither one of us are porcelain dolls that break at the mention of our losses.”

Anna looked up to respond. Instead, she watched Boney and Caleb walk toward them. Hattie and

Mary Alice had apparently noticed too, for they both quieted. Still dressed in clean Sunday shirts, the two men were engaged in deep conversation as if they'd lost track of where they were headed.

Hattie pinched the brim of her hat, her pinkie finger extended. "You two gents look mighty serious. Solving all of the world's problems, are you?"

Boney lifted the floppy hat from his head. "Just discussing how lovely you look on this fine Sunday."

"You are quite the flatterer, Mr. Boney."

Anna nodded in agreement, though it wasn't Boney who held her attention, but the man with the disarming brown eyes. The one who couldn't tell her the secrets behind them.

"It's good to see you again, Anna."

"And you, Caleb."

Boney cleared his throat. "Anna. Caleb. Since when did you two become so friendly?"

"Since he helped us with the wagon."

"And I heard her singing to an ox." Caleb grinned, revealing the dimple in his left cheek.

Anna pressed her hand to her lips. She was able to stifle the giggle, but not the memory of standing in the pasture with him and not wanting to be anywhere else.

Boney chuckled and slapped Caleb on the shoulder. "S'pose we better move along and let these ladies get back to their work."

Both men brushed the brims of their hats and walked away, but not before Caleb caught her eye again and dipped his chin.

She needed to guard her heart against the distraction that was Caleb Reger. She needed to concentrate on her work and on seeing to Großvater and Mutter's well-being.

Didn't she?

Garrett took quick steps past the supply wagon. Away from the swagger and bluster of his trail hands, he tugged his sleeves straight and smoothed his collar.

The good Lord willing, the caravan would arrive on the outskirts of Independence on Saturday afternoon, but that had little to do with the grasshoppers sprinting in his belly today. He waved at the Becks on his way by their breakfast fire, then cut across toward the farm wagon that housed the three youngest Kamden children and a certain redhead.

He had to find out how permanently he'd alienated Caroline Milburn in his attempts to appease Davonna Kamden.

The Kamden camp was quiet. He didn't find the family at their wagon. The young widow turned nanny wasn't there either. The Kamdens had likely gone to the creek, and it wasn't hard to guess that Caroline would take the opportunity for a break. He looked up at the grasses and trees behind the wagons and saw her seated on a quilt under a cottonwood tree.

While he didn't wish to disturb her, he did prefer to speak to her without interruption. He repositioned his slouch hat and tugged his coat straight before taking long strides toward the tree. He'd only stay long enough to plead his case for having no choice but to follow up on Mrs. Kamden's claim that Caroline had taken the locket.

When she saw him approaching, she stood and adjusted her straw hat. To block the sun or her view of him? He couldn't say until she looked up, straight into his eyes.

His mouth went dry. All he could hear was her speech in the dry goods store about him purporting to be a Southern gentleman yet referring to Anna Goben as a dithering wife. Yesterday, he'd questioned Caroline about being a thief. Coming to see her so soon was a bad idea.

"To what do I owe the honor of *this* visit, Captain Cowlishaw?"

He shoved his hands into his trouser pockets. "I count it a pleasure you're still speaking to me, ma'am."

"And well you should." She tugged her apron straight and met his gaze. Her lips were pursed, but a teasing sparkle lit her green eyes. Emeralds: the only thing that would come close.

Now the dryness affected his throat. No woman,

including the one who had left him and moved on, had ever affected him as Caroline Milburn did.

She moistened her lips. "I suppose you've heard the wonderful news by now? Mrs. Kamden found her locket."

"Yes." He pulled his hands from his pockets and then quickly returned them. "It was wonderful news, but no surprise. You are many things." *Passionate. Resourceful. Patient. Determined. Lovely.* A flush warmed his ears. "But a thief? No." Unless he considered the fact that she may have stolen his heart while he was looking. *Staring,* according to Caleb.

"You believed in me."

"I can't help myself."

Her warm smile sent a chill up his spine. "Thank you, Captain."

"Garrett, please."

"You were only doing your job, Garrett. And you're actually good at leading our sundry bunch of sojourners." She hadn't looked away from him. He knew, because he'd been *staring*.

She glanced down at her black boots then drew in a deep breath and moistened her lips. "Was there something else?"

Yes. A kiss would be real nice. And premature.

He blinked. "Only to say that I'm glad the matter of the locket is settled."

"Not as much as I am."

"And to say that I'm disappointed."

"Disappointed?" Her lips pushed into a pout. "You relished the idea of seeing me on trial, did you?"

"Actually." He swallowed hard. "I was looking forward to having the excuse to see you more."

One of her eyebrows shot upward.

He'd said too much. Why couldn't he have settled for her speaking to him at all? He blew out a long breath. "I'm sorry if that bothers you."

She tucked an errant red curl into the loose knot of hair at the back of her neck, then met his gaze. "Surprisingly, it doesn't."

"It doesn't?" Those were all the words he could push past the knot in his throat.

"I would, however, prefer more pleasant circumstances than an investigation into my secret life as a locket thief." Her lips curved into a coy smile, begging to be kissed.

"So, you wouldn't mind if I came around more often. Maybe to whisk you away for a walk?"

A slow grin lifted her mouth. "A two-thousand-mile walk isn't enough for you?"

He chuckled, giving himself time to think. Was she actually open to another idea, or was that just wishful thinking on his part? "Perhaps Anna Goben would let you borrow her pony for a Sunday afternoon ride sometime."

"I'll ask her."

While the grasshoppers in his belly jumped for joy, he gave her a quick nod, lest she change her mind. “I best leave you to your solace, then.” He brushed the brim of his hat and turned back toward camp.

Either he had missed any indications of Caroline Milburn’s growing attraction toward him, or the young woman was simply desperate to escape the Kamdens.

Either way, he would enjoy her company.

20

Hattie spread several of her hats from one end of the Pembertons’ camp table to the other. Anna studied them with a designer’s eye for style and grace. Any hats she made wouldn’t be as flamboyant, of course, but she did like the placement of feathers on the yellow hat and the ribbon banding another.

“Anna?”

She looked at Hattie, who sat beside her at the table. Had she ever seen her friend in public without a hat on her head?

“I think Boney likes me.”

Anna lifted a red straw hat and tipped it, looking at the angle of the brim. “Everyone likes you. Why wouldn’t he?”

Hattie sighed. “You know what I mean. Likes me in a way that could lead to *amour.*”

Hattie being the romantic that she was, of course *love* would be one of the first words she'd want to learn. In any language.

"You know Boney better than anyone here. What do you think?" Hattie asked.

"I think he's a fine man, who just two weeks ago was ready to marry me for reasons other than *amour.* I think you should give him a little time." To say the least.

"I can do that. Why, we've got at least another four or five months together on the road."

Anna nodded, at a loss for how to answer such a self-assured declaration. If only she possessed even a thin slice of Hattie's confidence. About wearing sometimes preposterous hats. About learning another language. About men. It didn't seem there was anything her friend wasn't willing to attempt.

She, on the other hand, found herself tongue-tied whenever Caleb Reger showed up. Never worse than when he appeared in the pasture Sunday morning and told her she had a lovely voice. Why couldn't she be as comfortable as Hattie was with men? She hadn't had much experience around them. Boney moved to Saint Louis, the war broke out, and Dedrick died, all at about the time she was reaching courting age. All those who were left in town were women, children, and old men.

"Hmm." Hattie nudged Anna's shoulder toward

the center of camp. "Speaking of fine men, I'd say Mr. Reger seems most eager to see you."

He was practically marching, his arms swinging at his sides. "Too eager. Something is wrong." Anna set the hat on the table and stood. "Caleb? What's wrong?"

"It's your grandfather. He's hot with fever." Caleb held his hand out to her, obviously intending to take her to Großvater.

"Let me know, Anna," Hattie said.

Anna nodded but didn't look at Hattie. She snatched Caleb's warm hand.

He led her onto the open road. "Me and Boney took him to your wagon."

At the far end of the line. "Boney's there?"

"Yes. When I left, a couple of the guys were going to move Otto's hammock in closer to your camp."

"Thank you." Short of breath, Anna pressed her free hand to her throat.

Caleb slowed. "I'm sorry. I didn't mean to drag you."

"I just have shorter legs." Slowing, she drew in a deep breath. "My mother? Is she all right?" Except for probably wishing she had a bottle.

"She was doing some cooking and got frightened when she saw him. But Boney gave her a job to do and that seemed to calm her."

Boney had a way with Mutter, and Caleb had a way with Anna. A way of always being there when her family needed him. Anna glanced at their joined hands.

"What happened?" She meant the question to concern Großvater, but she could just as well have been talking about her and Caleb.

"He was playing dominoes with Boney. Didn't quite seem himself but said he was fine."

"He said he'd been working too hard and not getting enough sleep?"

Caleb nodded. "Yes. Same as Saturday morning when Boney and I noticed he was moving pretty slow."

"The doctor?"

"I stopped there first. He and his daughter headed down there straightaway."

Tears welled in her eyes, and she blinked hard against them. She needed to be strong. For Mutter.

Caleb squeezed Anna's hand, sending another wave of warmth through her and making it even harder to quench the tears. "Your grandfather will be all right. They both will."

She nodded, hoping he was right. But she knew too much. She knew how fragile Großvater and Mutter were before they ever left Saint Charles. If something happened to Großvater . . .

The closer they came to her camp, the faster Anna's heart pounded.

After another squeeze of her hand, Caleb let go. A chill shimmied up her spine as she stepped over the tongue on their wagon.

Großvater lay in his hammock, now tethered to the same tree as hers at one end and the front wagon wheel on the other. Boney's arm held Mutter off to one side while Dr. Le Beau examined Großvater. Camille stood opposite her father, holding her papa's medical bag.

When Mutter saw Anna, she broke free from Boney and darted toward her. "Your grandfather is very ill." Her tears flowing, Mutter stepped into Anna's embrace.

"The doctor will help him. He'll be all right." Anna prayed she wasn't lying and looked at Boney, who stood beside the firepit. "Do we know anything?"

Boney shook his head. "No word yet."

Dr. Le Beau left Großvater's side and approached them, Camille at his side. "He has a high fever," his daughter translated.

"Why? What is wrong with him?" Mutter's volume escalated with each word.

Anna laid an arm across Mutter's back. Caleb and Boney stepped up beside them like book-ends. She didn't understand it, but just having Caleb at her side seemed to give Anna strength.

"Papa says he does not yet know the cause, but that we must break the fever. It is the reason Monsieur Goben trembles." Camille tucked threads of black hair behind her ear while communicating with her papa. "He asks of any other symptoms you might remember."

“Coughing,” Mutter spit out. “Vater was coughing. He said it was the wedding flowers.”

“That was two weeks ago, and he only coughed for two or three days.” Anna shuddered. She’d heard stories of sickness on the trail west that devastated caravans. That was fifteen and twenty years ago, but if this was cholera or yellow fever . . .

“Vater has seemed out of wind and tired since . . .” Mutter raised her hands and let them drop. “I don’t know.”

“Saturday is when we first saw him return with the oxen and rest before yoking them.” Anna struggled to fight the fear welling inside her. “He insisted nothing was wrong. Nothing serious. Mutter was worried and wanted to talk to the doctor then. I should have—”

Caleb seized her hand, drawing her attention to his brown eyes. “This isn’t your fault, Anna. You could not have known.”

“Monsieur Reger, he is right.” Camille pulled a small cloth sack from the black leather bag. “Willow-bark tea is known for bringing fever down. We’ll give him that first.”

“Boney had me boil water. I’ll use it to brew the tea.” Mutter took the dried bark.

When Mutter went to the kettle hanging from a hook above the firepit, Anna decided to ask the question tearing at her heart. “Camille.” Anna looked directly into the seventeen-year-old's face. "Could this be something contagious?"

Camille sighed. "Papa does not believe it to be so. Your grandfather is the only one reported sick, and fever is all he is suffering. But we will be keeping an eye on others in the Company."

"Thank you for all you're doing." She hated feeling helpless. "When you talked about the tea, you said *first.* What else can we do?"

"We need to cool your grandfather with a wet bed sheet."

"I know about that from the war." Caleb pulled a pail from a hook on the wagon. "I'll take a bucket to the creek."

"I'll get the bed sheet." Anna took quick steps to the wagon and scrambled onto the spokes and over the seat. In mere moments, she found a sheet in her trunk and carried it outside.

"Your grandfather is asking for you." Camille glanced toward the hammock, then took the sheet from Anna and stepped out of her way.

Her heart quickening, Anna approached Großvater.

"Anna." His weak voice tore at her insides. His eyelids fluttered open, and she looked into his unfocused eyes.

"I'm here." Drawing in a fortifying breath, she captured his hand. Its warmth seared her skin and tightened her throat. She couldn't lose him. Mutter couldn't bear it.

“I’m so sorry, Großvater, I should’ve known you were sick. I should have—”

“Take care.” His chest heaving, he struggled for breath. “Of your mutter.”

“Everything will be all right. Don’t waste your breath trying to speak right now.”

“Take care of her.”

Tears stung her eyes again. “Only until you get better.”

“Otto, we have something for you to drink.” Boney stepped up with Mutter. Mutter held a tin cup, the steam mingling with the tears staining her face. Boney helped Großvater sit up enough to take a drink. “Now, I know you prefer your strong coffee, but when men get sick, the womenfolk like to make us pay for it by stickin’ tea in our faces.” Boney braced Großvater with one arm and used his other hand to support the cup. “Tonight, it’s your turn.”

While Boney and Mutter got the tea in him, Anna took the sheets from Camille and met Caleb at the bucket several yards away.

“How is he?”

Tears pooled her eyes. “He’s so hot. And weak. He could barely speak.”

Caleb rested his hand on her forearm. “I’m praying with you, Anna.”

She nodded. “I’m so glad you’re here.”

He took the sheet from her and dunked it into the water pail. When it was soaked through, he pulled it out. "You take two corners, and I'll take the others."

Following Caleb's lead, Anna pulled the sheet taut, and they waved it up and down until it billowed in the air. Then they took quick steps to the hammock. Mutter stepped away with the cup, and Caleb laid the cold sheet over Großvater. His trembling intensified, and Anna's insides shivered in sympathy.

"I'm sorry, Großvater."

Camille stepped up beside her. "You did the right thing. You will see."

"I hope you're right. I hope I do see him better."

"The sheet warms quickly, so you'll need to repeat this several times."

Three hours later, Anna lay in her hammock, listening to Großvater's sleep breathing and thanking God. The shivering had finally stopped, and the fever had broken as the moon arced overhead. When Dr. Le Beau and Camille left, Mutter had gone in to her bed. Boney and Caleb lingered for a few minutes while Anna got more tea into Großvater.

The doctor couldn't say for sure what had caused the fever, but since it had broken, he believed Großvater would be well again. His peaceful sleep told Anna it was true, but sleep still evaded her.

Now, all she could think about was Caleb. The way he'd found her. Held her hand. Stood beside her. Helped her with the sheet. Said he was praying with her. In just one week, her estimation of him had drastically changed.

And for the better. By leaps and bounds.

21

Caleb dropped the last hoof after cleaning and checking them all for cracks. He had already saddled his Pacer and tied up his bedroll. The doctor said Otto would need to take it easy for a few days to regain his strength, so Anna would be needing help with their work.

Isaac gave a low whistle. "You sure are whippin' through them chores this mornin'."

"Like you had a fire under you." Tiny twisted his head as if to see a fire at Caleb's feet.

Frank chuckled as he backed the oxen into position in front of the chuck wagon. "He's in such a hurry I'm surprised he didn't offer to pay us to do his work."

"Go." Boney stood and pushed his flop hat back on his head.

Caleb met his gaze. "You mean it?"

"Yeah." Boney nodded. "I'll finish up for you."

"You're not coming?"

"Naw, you go on ahead." Boney waved toward the Goben camp. "She'll be glad to see you."

Too anxious to see Anna—all of the Gobens—Caleb didn't take the time to question Boney further. Instead, he went to the washbasin and scrubbed his hands clean.

"Just one thing, Caleb," Boney said.

Caleb tucked his shirt into his trousers. "Yes, I'll tell them you sent greetings, and I'll let you know how Otto's doing."

"Okay, that and one more thing."

Caleb nodded, finger-combing his hair.

"Anna never once looked at me the way she looks at you."

So, it wasn't his imagination. Even before the crisis last night, he was sure he'd noticed something different in her eyes. And definitely Sunday when he'd found her in the pasture.

"Anna is strong, but it don't mean she can't be hurt." Boney's eyes narrowed. "Don't you be the one to do it."

"I won't." Caleb no sooner made the promise when the few sips of coffee he'd swallowed soured in his stomach. He'd been so determined not to care about a woman or to invite a woman's affections. Until Anna. Now what was he to do?

Boney should be the one going to check on Otto, Anna, and Wilma. Despite that fact, Caleb's feet carried him down the line, past the Becks, to the Gobens' camp. Could've knocked him to the ground with a feather when he saw Otto sitting in a cane chair with his feet on one of the rocks circling the fire.

Caleb opened his mouth to speak, but when Otto tilted his head toward the hammock on the far side, he forced his mouth closed. Anna wasn't up yet. How had she slept through Isaac's horn blasts? Through the chaos up and down the line? It wasn't like her.

He seated himself on a chair beside Otto and whispered, "Is Anna all right? She's not sick, is she?"

Otto shook his head. "I don't think she gave in to sleep before the sun started peeking over them trees."

"She was very worried. We all were." Caleb studied the man's face for any signs of illness. His eyes were focused this morning. "You sure you should be up so soon?"

"Might feel as weak as a fresh kitten, but no fever."

"That's good news. But you don't think hitting the road today would be too much?"

"I may have to kick my daughter off the seat, but I'll be ready to go."

Relief washed over Caleb. He knew Otto well enough to know he wouldn't want to delay the train, and Caleb didn't want to leave the Gobens behind. Thankfully, Otto knew he wasn't well and was willing to ride.

"Just so you know," Otto drew in a deep breath,

"I wasn't so sick that I don't remember those freezing sheets you plopped on me."

"That wasn't my idea."

Otto arched his eyebrows. "You think that matters?"

Caleb chuckled, keeping the sound beneath his breath.

"You're a good man, Caleb. I knew it that day on my porch back in Saint Charles."

"Thank you, sir." He was trying to be a good man, if that meant anything.

"But I see trouble in your eyes." Otto's face sobered, the lines at his mouth now smooth. "My guess is that trouble latched onto you in the war."

"Yes sir. It did."

"That's your business." Otto's eyes narrowed. "My granddaughter is mine."

"I want to protect Anna too."

"You've grown fond of her."

He swallowed. "I have, sir."

"How fond?"

"Probably too fond."

Anna had all but stopped breathing, trying not to move. Given what she'd just heard, it wasn't an easy task.

Caleb was fond of her.

She shouldn't have been surprised to learn that. Not after last night, when he'd sat with her at

Großvater's bedside. The way he'd held her hand, squeezed it. Gone to the creek for a bucket of water and helped her put the chilled sheet on Großvater. The way he'd remained at her side until Großvater's fever broke and he'd come through the worst of it.

He couldn't know she was awake, that she'd heard him. Not now, anyway.

But what was she to do? It didn't seem he intended to go anywhere soon. And while that fact brought her comfort, she desperately needed to make a trip to the latrine. In addition, the sounds stirring in the camps around them told her she was likely the last one out of bed. How long had Caleb been here?

"You're still asleep, Anna Mae?" Mutter's voice.

Anna popped her eyes open. "Mutter? You're up?" Mutter was standing at the wagon, filling the coffeepot from the water barrel.

"Yes, I'm up."

Lifting herself into a sitting position, Anna looked at the other hammock. "Großvater?"

"He's up too. Over in his chair, visiting with a guest."

"A guest?" The acting might not earn her a place on a stage in San Francisco, but hopefully it was enough to convince Großvater and Caleb that she hadn't overheard their conversation.

"Good morning, Großvater. You are well?"

"For a man who had to drink bitter tea and have

a cold sheet draped over him as if he were half-dead, I can't complain about how I'm feeling this morning."

He was on the mend if he could pretend he wasn't complaining when he was.

Anna glanced at Caleb, who had changed his shirt and combed his hair. "Good morning."

He stood. "Good morning, Anna. I, uh, came to help."

"Good. Otherwise, he might be tempted to do too much." She gave Großvater a warning glance.

"I'll go fetch the oxen and get them yoked." Caleb took his hat from his knee and set it on his head. "I would invite you to go with me, except, well, you're still in bed."

"Oh dear." Anna jumped up and tugged her sleeves straight. She'd been too tired to change into her dressing gown, so she still wore yesterday's rumpled clothes.

Caleb, Mutter, and Großvater all chuckled.

"I'll see you when I get back," Caleb said.

Anna nodded and smiled at the man who was fond of her.

"Probably too fond."

What did that mean? He was fond of her and wished he wasn't? He was fond of her, despite his attempts to guard his heart? Something they'd have in common, if that were the case. Or he was so fond of her that it was too late to turn his heart around, even if he wanted to?

Anna sighed as she stepped onto the wheel and up into the wagon. To save time in her morning ablutions, she'd use the chamber pot instead of making the trek to the latrine.

She, too, had seen the trouble in Caleb's eyes. What man didn't come home from the war without bringing at least a measure of trouble with him? Who could witness such horrors—brother killing brother—without it taking a piece of his own heart? His trouble could be overcome.

At least he had returned from the war. At least he had a chance at life. And perhaps she would have a chance too.

22

Anna was up early Saturday morning, brushing her hair and anticipating Caleb's early visit. He'd come to their camp the past three mornings since Großvater had taken ill and helped fetch water, yoke the oxen, and pack up camp, and then ate breakfast across the table from her. She glanced at the hand he'd held, remembering the tenderness in his eyes when he told her of Großvater's illness and the warm surety of his touch when he guided her to Großvater's sickbed.

If a man's true character was revealed in his benevolent response to someone else's pain and need, then Caleb Reger had proven himself a compassionate and admirable man. Anna gave her hair a twist and pinned it on her head. Despite her assertion that she should avoid emotional attachments to tend to the needs of her family, the brown-eyed trail hand from Tennessee was capturing her heart.

"Morning, Otto. Ma'am." Caleb's visits could be timed with the first rays of sunrise illuminating the wagon canvas. She liked that about him too.

Anna stepped out over the seat. Four oxen stood at the tongue. Caleb leaned against the wheel, his back to her, but he quickly straightened and turned her direction.

"Good morning, Anna." He offered his hand.

"Good morning." Anna set her hand in his, watching as his fingers curled over the top of hers, sending a shiver up her arm and into her heart.

Mutter looked up from the potatoes she was slicing. "Thank you for bringing the oxen again this morning."

"Yes." Großvater warmed his hands at the fire ring. "I don't like needing help, but I appreciate the help nonetheless."

"It's my pleasure." Caleb may have been speaking to Großvater, but it was Anna he looked at as she stepped down from the wagon.

The brown-eyed trail hand *had* captured her heart. As surely as if he'd lassoed it with Duff Kamden's cowboy rope.

Mutter stared at their still-joined hands.

Caleb let go. Too soon.

"If you and Anna would like to fetch some water, we could have a full barrel when we roll out," Mutter said.

"Yes ma'am." Caleb lifted the pails off the hooks on the side of the wagon and handed one of them to Anna, a smile widening his mouth.

Davonna Kamden waved from the road, apparently on her way to the latrine. The older woman made frequent trips that direction. Anna returned her wave then followed Caleb past the back of the wagon and down to the creek in relative silence. The handle on her bucket squeaked in time with the questions swirling her thoughts.

What was happening between her and Caleb? It seemed God had used Großvater's illness to bring them together. But she didn't know that much about him, and there was that matter of the trouble she and Großvater had seen in Caleb's eyes.

When they arrived on the creek bank, Anna cleared her throat and looked at him. "Sunday, when you came out to the pasture to clear the air?"

"I remember it well." He bent at the creek and looked over his shoulder at her. "You were singing to the ox. A most inspiring song. 'Give to Our God Immortal Praise,' I believe it was."

"Yes." Anna stepped closer to him. "One of my

favorites, but it really wasn't for the animal's benefit."

"Whatever you say." That wide grin lit his brown eyes. In the morning sun, they looked the color of her polished walnut jewelry case, where she kept her finest possessions.

Anna moistened her lips, trying to remember where she was going with her initial question about last Sunday. They both knelt at the water's edge. "That day, I learned you came from Tennessee."

Caleb looked out at the rocky creek, silent. If he was truly fond of her, she needed to know what troubled him. She knew some about loss and sorrow, and maybe she could help ease his pain.

Anna drew in a deep breath. "When I asked if your parents and your sister were still in Tennessee, you said you didn't know for sure; that you hadn't seen them since before the war."

His face sobered. "I haven't."

"If Dedrick had done that . . ."

His jaw tense, he dunked his bucket into the water, getting the sleeves of his shirt wet. "I'm not Dedrick."

Tears pricked her eyes. "I know that."

Caleb set the full bucket on the bank. "Why do you care so much about my family? About my past?"

"Because I'm fond of you too."

He jerked to face her, his eyes wide. "*Fond* of

me? You were awake. You heard what I said to your grandfather." It was a statement, not a question.

"I didn't mean to overhear you. But, yes, I did."

"Then you also heard Otto say he saw trouble in my eyes." Caleb took her empty bucket. "Anna, I'm trouble. I didn't want to care for you, but I do. And now—"

"Now you can help me understand. You've been separated from your family since the war, for years. Why wouldn't you want to see them as soon as possible?"

"It's thorny, Anna." He scooped up more water, splashing it over the sides of the pail. "I made mistakes. I did things I'm not proud of."

She stared at the buckets filled with cool, clear water, all the while sorting through muddied thoughts. What could be so terrible that he'd feel set apart from hundreds of thousands of other soldiers who returned home with regrets?

"I love my family too much to go home," he said.

She didn't have to understand to know that fact hurt him deeply. "I'm sorry."

"I am too." He stood and cupped her elbow, helping her up.

"Caleb."

He looked her in the eye.

"I'm glad you care about me."

He rewarded her with a knee-weakening smile.

"We'd better go back. Garrett will be ready for me to read soon, and he'll wonder where I am."

Anna smiled. It was unlikely anyone in the camp wondered where Caleb was or where he'd been the past several days. Everyone already knew.

She wasn't about to complain. They both had past experiences too personal and painful to discuss. Just one more thing she had in common with Caleb Reger.

Garrett couldn't help but notice the spring in Caleb's step as he left the Gobens' camp and headed to the chuck wagon. For a young man who started this journey so sure he was beyond marriage, he seemed to be falling hard for Anna Goben.

Garrett felt a smile tugging at one side of his mouth. Caleb wasn't so different from him.

"Garrett?"

He jerked his attention back to Caroline's creamy face and that red curl gracing her long neck. The Kamdens were gathered around the firepit, while he and Caroline stood on the road's edge.

Caroline sighed, her lips pursed in a contrived reproach. "I was saying that Caleb has been a big help to Anna and her family these past few days."

"Above and beyond duty, really."

She raised a thin eyebrow. "Much like you

coming around here more often than necessary, perhaps?"

"Who says it isn't necessary?"

"Not I." Her demure smile could melt a glacier. "It does my heart good to see Anna and Caleb getting along so well."

Garrett nodded. "Yes. I suppose we weren't the only ones who started off on the wrong foot and got over it."

Caroline laughed. "I'm not saying Anna had as big a challenge as I did."

He opened his mouth and dropped his chin, feigning surprise and indignation. All to hear her melodious laugh again.

"Capitano! *Mi scusi*, Capitano." Mrs. Zanzucchi shuffled toward him with Alfonzo Jr. at her side.

Garrett removed his hat. "Mrs. Zanzucchi. Alfonzo." He looked from one to the other.

"Good morning, Captain," the boy said. "Mama needs to speak with you."

As soon as Garrett nodded, Mrs. Zanzucchi started rattling in Italian. Her hand motions didn't help him understand any better.

"Mama is very upset," Alfonzo Jr. translated. "She keeps her silver teapot in a box in our wagon, but last night she took it out to polish it. She set it on the table and went to fetch my brothers."

More Italian.

"Mama says we have a thief in the camp."

"I knew it!"

They all turned toward the voice. Davonna Kamden stood at the front corner of the farm wagon.

"I tried to tell you myself, Captain," she said. "And now it turns out I wasn't the only one missing things."

"Ma'am, if I remember correctly, your locket was found. Are you saying you're missing other things?"

"I'll have to see about that." She looked at Mrs. Zanzucchi and shook her head. "In the meantime, what do you intend to do to find this poor woman's possession?"

"I will conduct an investigation." He looked at the boy. "I'll talk to the members of the Company."

Davonna huffed and wagged her finger at him. "And you should have that Southern man read the Ten Commandments this morning. He needs to read about the sinfulness of stealing."

Garrett pressed his fingers to his temple, hoping to ward off the headache forming there. "Ma'am, we'll put that off for another time. I'd prefer to conduct my investigation quietly."

"Good idea. That way you can surprise the thief . . . sneak up on her." Davonna gave Caroline a sideways glance, her eyebrows lifted. "Or him, if it turns out that way."

Caroline's crooked smile told him she, too, had doubts about it being a quiet inquiry.

• • •

Caleb carried his supper plate to the far side of the campfire and sat on the empty stool between Isaac and Frank.

"I saw you all making the rounds today. Thanks." Garrett stretched his legs out in front of him, holding his plate at his chest. "Let's hear what you found out, if anything."

That morning, he'd told them about Mrs. Zanzucchi's visit and her missing teapot. He'd given them each a couple of families to talk to, and asked Caleb to make inquiries with the Brenners and the Renglers about missing anything or noticing anyone near the Zanzucchis' camp Friday evening.

"I'll start." Tiny stabbed a bite of ham with his fork. "I talked to both of the Beck couples. None of them reported anything missing. Didn't notice anything out of the ordinary at the Zanzucchis' camp last night." He shook his head. "That doesn't mean Emery didn't have plenty to say about everything else."

Garrett nodded. "Anything I should know about?"

"He doesn't approve of the way Mama Zanzucchi lets her boys *run wild.*" A slow smile bunched Tiny's full cheeks. "Oh, and one of Le Doc's horses has a case of the scours and left a surprise on the road in front of his camp."

"Ha!" Boney slapped his pant leg, sending dust

up to mingle with the smoke. "What goes around comes around."

Caleb nodded, hoping that wasn't entirely true. Unless it pertained to only his most recent actions. Anna Goben had a way of bringing out the best in him.

"Nothing about anything missing or having seen anything," Boney said. "I did get an earful from Tom Brenner about his disdain for being forced to listen to the Bible every morning."

Garrett nodded. "Yeah, he hit me up with that same complaint."

Caleb took a biscuit from his plate. "Sally Rengler suggested I search her brother-in-law's things."

"Oliver? She thinks he may have taken Mrs. Zanzucchi's teapot?" Garrett sighed. "What did you tell her?"

"I asked what made her think of Oliver, and she didn't have any credible reason. Only that he was slow minded and bound to do something like that." Caleb bristled, remembering the way her nose went into the air every time she spoke Oliver's name. "I said I'd talk to him, which I did. He didn't know anything about it either, and said he felt real bad for Mama Zanzucchi and that she was a really nice lady and made the best noodles."

"Hey, Boss." Frank Marble raked his dusty blond hair. "You asked me to talk to the Gobens about things gettin' pilfered, and I found out somethin' really interesting."

"Oh? Let's hear it."

"It seems someone might have stolen Miss Anna Goben's . . ."

Caleb's shoulders tensed.

"Heart." Frank cackled and pinned Caleb with wide eyes, and his mouth puckered for a fanciful kiss. "You know anything about that, Ca-leb? When I asked ol' Otto if there was anything I could do to help out, his granddaughter was all too anxious to pipe up and sing your praises."

"Now, you've gone and given me indigestion." Boney reared back and belched. "Not sure it's good to talk about such things over food."

Garrett cleared this throat. "Doesn't sound like any of you heard any reports of anything else missing."

Isaac shook his head. "The Le Beaus and the Pembertons were all fine. No complaints."

"Good. I hate this sort of stuff. Becomes easy to get sidetracked and distracted from what's most important."

Isaac added a log to the firepit. "Seein' to the safety and well-bein' of all these folks has got to be rough."

"Exactly right, Isaac." Garrett drained his coffee cup. "I'll go talk to the Zanzucchi family after supper. I'll tell them we'll keep our ears and eyes open, but that for now we've not received any other reports, nor found the pot in question." Garrett rubbed the back of his neck. "You all let me know if you hear anything new."

Caleb nodded, his thoughts centered on how to get back at Frank for his ruthless teasing. Maybe a surprise in his cornbread ingredients the next time it was his turn to cook.

23

Caleb perched on a log, watching the sun sink through the last of the Missouri trees. Warming his hands on the tin cup, he gulped fresh coffee. He and Isaac had left the Company after breakfast. While it was true the number of westbound overlanders had dwindled considerably in the past ten years, Independence was still the main jumping-off point. The end of April through the beginning of May was the prime time of year for starting west, and enough camp space and grazing would be hard to come by. Garrett had sent him and Isaac ahead of the wagons to scout for their arrival tomorrow.

One of the farmers he and Isaac talked to near Lake City had sent them this direction—a nice wide spot along the Little Blue River. A company smaller than the Boone's Lick group camped up the road, but the river was close and the grasses plentiful enough for a two-night encampment.

When the last ribbons of color faded, Caleb returned his attention to the campfire, where Isaac roasted the rabbit he'd snared. His trail mate sang while he cooked. Sang or hummed or whistled while he did most anything. Despite the scars down the left side of his face and neck and despite the savage way in which his wife was taken from him, Isaac was a cheerful soul who said he found his peace and rest in the goodness of the Lord.

Caleb sighed. Isaac should be the one reading the Scriptures every morning. He didn't just talk about peace; he *knew* peace.

His boss, and shepherd of the roving flock, probably figured Caleb could learn something from Isaac. But their situations were different. Isaac hadn't been the one who kept making the mistakes and doing wrong. He had only to forgive others.

"Mister Caleb?"

"Yes?"

"That night in Saint Charles when you told Frank you wasn't the marrying kind."

Caleb drew in a deep breath. He should have known the subject would come up again.

"Did you mean it?"

After a few seconds of listening to the kettle of beans bubbling over hot coals, Caleb looked up at Isaac. "I did. I loved someone once. Thought I did, anyway. A wisp of a girl named Susan, almost pixie-like with the smallest freckled nose."

Isaac gave the rabbit a turn on the spit and stirred the beans.

"I thought she loved me. She said she did." Caleb picked bark off the log and threw it onto the embers. "We planned to be married in time. She was sixteen, and I was seventeen." The flames sparked and popped. "The war broke out and I went to fight. Later received word that Susan had found someone else."

Isaac topped up Caleb's coffee cup then refilled his own. "You're plenty young. You want to find someone else to marry one day, don't ya?"

"I do." Caleb pressed his hands against the cup's warmth. "But I won't." His first answer was the accurate one. He might have one day married Anna, if things were different for him. If he hadn't been responsible for so many deaths. If he knew she wouldn't turn her back on him if she knew the truth. If only.

"Hmm." Isaac pulled the roasting stick from above the fire and studied the browned rabbit. "He's done. And the beans are hot. No reason we can't eat while we talk."

"About something else." Caleb set his cup on a rock, stood, and held out his plate for his portion. "It's best I don't think about all that. Some men make mistakes."

"Like both of them two on the crosses, either side of our Lord Jesus?"

It wasn't that simple.

"Both guilty. The man who believed, Jesus told him He'd see him that day in paradise." Isaac separated the rabbit and put the meaty back half, a ladle of beans, and a biscuit on Caleb's plate. "Don't think God woulda sent His Son to die to give us grace we didn't sorely need."

Isaac was the one who would make a good preacher. Garrett should ask him instead.

Caleb took his supper to the log and sat down. When Isaac brought his plate over, they both bowed their heads, silent.

The horses nickered. The sound of a snapping twig popped Caleb's eyes open. They weren't alone. Jumping up from the fallen tree, he nearly toppled his plate. A hairy man draped in buffalo skins walked out of the darkness and into the light of the fire.

Caleb's heart pounded. He'd done it again. He'd let someone sneak up on them. He started for his bedroll where he'd left his rifle.

Isaac motioned for Caleb to stop. "Evenin', Mister."

The intruder walked straight to the fire and warmed his hands.

Isaac hadn't moved from his tree stump. "You hungry? We got some grub, if'n you are."

Caleb swallowed hard at the memories of intruders.

"We got coffee too."

The hairy man shook his head then studied the kettle of beans.

Isaac stood and held his full plate out to the man. "I'm Isaac, and this here's Mister Caleb."

In one swift move, the trapper took the plate then squatted close to the fire. When *Skins* started eating, Isaac motioned for Caleb to do the same. He did, never looking away from the strange man.

How could Isaac be so trusting? so calm? fearless?

When the trapper had dragged his last bite of biscuit across the plate, he studied Isaac. "You two ain't from around here." The words came out in a mumble. His mouth hadn't even moved.

"No sir." Isaac took the empty plate from him. "Scouting for a caravan of wagons."

"That rise over there."

Caleb followed the man's gaze upstream, to where they'd seen a low hilly area before dark.

"Black bear and her cubs live up there. Hunt down here."

"Good to know," Isaac said. "Much obliged."

Skins raised his hand, then turned and disappeared into the trees.

Caleb dropped his plate and cup in the wash bucket. "I should've been paying attention." He started pacing. "Shouldn't have let him sneak up on us like that. Should've seen him coming."

"Mister Caleb, I don't know what happened or

what that mistake was you talked about, and I don't need to know." Isaac laid his hand on Caleb's arm. "But for someone who reads the Scripture as much as you do, you don't seem none too familiar with God's grace."

Caleb nodded then walked away from the firelight.

While Isaac got his supper, Caleb ducked under the makeshift tent he'd tied to a branch and rolled out his bed, but he didn't expect to get much sleep. He planned to be on guard for vagrants and beggars. And bears. He couldn't make that mistake again.

Anna moved the small worktable as close to the campfire as she dared then sat down with her parchment and quill. Crickets chirped and tree leaves rustled in the breeze. Smoke from various fires floated on the cool night air, glowing in the light of the almost-full moon.

The Company's children had quieted, tucked in for the night. Anxious for morning, Mutter had gone to bed. Großvater had turned in early too. Most of the camp had settled in, except for the handful of men still wandering about.

Anna had adorned all the hats she'd brought with her. Now seemed the perfect opportunity to pen a letter to Emilie. The city of Independence would have a post office, and if she made haste, she'd have the letter ready to mail when they arrived tomorrow. Leaning over the table, she dipped the quill into the ink and set it to paper.

Dearest Emilie,

She wrote in German, the language she shared with Emilie and Mrs. Brantenberg. Mrs. Heinrich, now, she reminded herself. So much had happened in the two and a half weeks since they'd left Saint Charles that Anna scarcely knew where to begin.

We are well. I pray the same for all of you. We are all anxious to hear news from you and the others.

Your father? How is he faring? And Mrs. Heinrich? Much happened so quickly in that last week before our departure that I still have to remind myself that Mrs. Brantenberg is your father's wife.

Caroline sorely misses her sister and the children. Although seeing the beauty of lush meadows, streams, and uncountable animals has been a feast for my eyes, I miss delivering candles to the Dry Goods and Grocery. I miss seeing you.

Anna leaned against the chair while a memory carried her back to the day of her canceled wedding. Caleb Reger in the store, spilling coffee beans on the floor. Much had changed between them since then. Since the first day on the road when he'd scolded her and Hattie for lingering in town. The way he'd jumped in to help her and Mutter with the wagon canvas. The way in which he'd looked at her since that day in the field with the ox hadn't escaped her notice either. The way he'd held her hand and comforted her. She couldn't say for sure what it was that blazed in his brown eyes, but it was no longer condemnation.

Yes, he was a much more complicated man than she first thought.

Adding her sigh to the hoot of the owl off in the distance, Anna returned the quill to the page.

Do you remember a Caleb Reger? One of Garrett Cowlishaw's trail hands.

The one who, along with Mr. Isaac, had left camp on his Tennessee Pacer directly after breakfast that morning. Truth was Anna had noticed far more about Caleb than she cared to admit, even to herself.

Mr. Reger is not entirely rude and distant, as I first thought.

Rather charming, in fact. She left that out of the letter too.

Oh dear, she hadn't realized how much Caleb Reger occupied her letter. Her thoughts.

She would miss seeing him early tomorrow morning and hearing his deep voice recite Scripture. He read with authority, and yet she heard a longing there too. No doubt, his troubling war experiences. Much of her fellow travelers seemed weighted by such memories.

Perhaps God had brought her—all of them—on this road for something more than just a long walk to a new home. She prayed it was so.

An owl hooted from a distant tree, probably protesting Isaac's snores. Caleb was used to them. He rolled over and stared at the glowing canvas, lit by embers in the firepit. How was he to sleep with thoughts of roaming trappers, hungry bears, and the thief on the cross?

"You told Frank you wasn't the marrying kind. Did you mean it?"

And impossible thoughts concerning Anna Goben.

He'd thought he loved Susan. Her pixie-like looks and freckled nose was all he'd told Isaac about. All he really remembered was her looks. That didn't sound like love to him now. And it didn't sound at all like the way he saw Anna Goben.

A strong young woman who valued her family enough at least to try to do what was right by them. She'd lost her brother and left the only home she'd really known to provide a fresh start for her grandfather and a mother whose unpredictable moods looked all too familiar.

Wilma Goben had no husband, and she'd lost her son. She had every right to be bitter and moody.

What had been his excuse?

His father was honorable, a godly man who had only wanted what was best for his son. His mother had been proud of his every achievement, and his sister adored him. He had a bright and purposeful future as a preacher. But then that future had gone up in gunfire and smoke.

And it wasn't Susan's fault. She'd probably done him a favor. He wouldn't have wanted to marry a woman who didn't truly love him. He had no one to blame but himself. It was his choice to follow the bottle, to ruin the life he no longer deserved.

God, why did it have to be this way?

His family didn't know if he were dead or alive. They probably still blamed Union soldiers for his death or capture.

Neelie had probably made him an uncle by now. A boy? A girl? Perhaps several. It had been at least five years since the wedding. He wanted to know her children. To see if Neelie's daughter pouted like she used to, to hear his father preach again and to see his mother smile.

His gut clenching, he rolled over again. He

couldn't face any of them. Not if he wanted to keep his secret. Not if he wanted to protect them from the truth. He had no choice but to make a family of people who didn't know his past and couldn't be hurt by it.

So why couldn't he have just done his job as a trail hand—scouting, guarding, helping—and kept his distance? He was supposed to have protected himself from the possibility of any attachments. Kept his emotions from becoming so tangled.

He had managed it up until the point when he no longer found Anna Goben annoying. Until she stopped squaring her shoulders and jutting out her chin, angry with him. Until that day she accepted his help with the wagon canvas. And out in the pasture with the ox, when she said she was sorry for whatever it was he couldn't say.

Caleb scrubbed his whiskered face. He'd begun to care for Anna, and she could be hurt by the truth. He was horrified to think she cared about someone so despicable.

He tossed from side to side for several minutes.

God, why?

"Some men make mistakes." His own words taunted him.

Why did they have to die? Why would You make so many families grieve the loss of their sons because of me and my horrible mistake? If You're so loving and ever present, why didn't You stop me?

"Like both of them two on the crosses, either side of our Lord Jesus?"

The memory burned. What was he missing? What was he supposed to do about those two sinners?

"Don't think God woulda sent His Son to die to give us grace we didn't sorely need."

What was it that Isaac understood about it all?

Why can't I forget?

What can I do?

Why don't I feel forgiven?

Silence.

Caleb caught the bottom of the tangled wool blanket with his stockinged feet and pulled it straight. When his foot slipped from the blanket, he bumped the tent pole and knocked the canvas loose. The tent toppled on him and he fought against it, flailing his arms and legs.

"Mister Caleb?"

He stilled, letting the heavy canvas settle over him.

"You all right, Mister Caleb?" Isaac asked.

"Yes." Another lie.

"With all that thrashing, I didn't know if you were sick or maybe sufferin' a nightmare."

"Sorry I disturbed you. Go back to sleep."

"All right, then. You too."

Anna Goben had pushed her own grief aside to see to the needs of her family and friends.

That was what he had to do.

Caleb shoved the canvas off his body and straightened the blanket to cover himself.

Garrett and a whole Company of people needed him to set his own concerns and desires aside to see them safely to their destination. And that was what he intended to do, with or without God's help.

Despite his own pain. His past failings. He would just have to pile them all on his back and carry them. A reminder of what he could've been. Maybe he would eventually learn to live with them, but his back wouldn't support much more.

Making him all the more determined to never fail again.

24

The next morning, a scraping sound woke Anna and she opened one eye. Darkness greeted her. She lifted her head. The noise hadn't come from Großvater's hammock, farther out between two trees.

Whatever the noise, it didn't matter. The horn hadn't sounded yet. Settling her head back onto the pillow, she listened, waiting for the hammock to quit swinging. The noises had come from inside the wagon. Mutter was up. Why so early?

Mutter stuck her head out the back flap.

"It's Saturday, dear. You know what that means."

It meant she wouldn't get any more rest. "Some of us are still trying to sleep."

"We're going to the city today."

Großvater walked up, rubbing his eyes, his hammock rolled under one arm. "Wilma, we've gone by many towns—Warrenton, Columbia, Boonville—since we've left home. What's so special about Independence?"

"Don't be silly, Vater. Independence is bigger. Besides, we'll be there for a couple of days. The rest will do us all good."

Anna buried her head on the pillow. "Speaking of rest, I wish to return to sleep."

She'd just closed her eyes when the horn blasts started.

Maybe she'd get some rest in Independence. She rolled out of her swinging bed and untied the ropes at the wagon and at a young buttonwood tree. Großvater started the cookfire. Remembering the letter she'd written to Emilie, Anna took quick steps to the table where she'd left the paper folded under the inkwell the night before.

Now that she thought about it, she was anxious for their arrival in Independence too. Or at least, their arrival to the campsite where Caleb Reger awaited them.

Caroline walked the road with the youngest of the Kamden children. Most everyone's feet had developed calluses that protected them against blisters. In the meantime, the mint Garrett gave her for a poultice helped calm the children's leg cramps and her nerves.

Angus, the eldest of the five Kamden children, held the lead rope for the canvassed farm wagon while his grandmother rode in the seat, munching a hard, dry biscuit. After another battle to get his mother going after the horn blew, Ian Kamden told Davonna she could ride until they came to any uphill stretches. The elder Mrs. Kamden seemed strong of body but hadn't adjusted to the constant change the journey forced upon them. Caroline didn't understand why she preferred the torturous bumps and rattles of the wagon to standing on her own two feet.

"Miss Caroline."

"Yes, Lyall?"

"What will you do in the city?"

"She'll prob'ly buy a dress or sumpin'." Duff whacked a bush with the stick he'd been carrying. "That's what ladies do in the city."

Caroline smiled. As much as this family exasperated her at times, she was thankful for the children. She still missed her sister and being called Auntie, but these little ones had eased the pain of separation some. "Actually, I expect our camp will be a few miles out of town, and I'm not planning to make a special trip into Independence."

No, she had other plans.

"We get candy." Maisie licked her lips. "Faither said so."

"If there's a confectionary," Duff said.

Lyall kicked a rock. "Or if the general store has candy."

"Me and Floppy"—Maisie raised her cloth bunny into the air—"are getting a pink rock candy."

Their expected arrival in the city of Independence later that day didn't hold much shine for Caroline, but the promise of tomorrow—Sunday—dangled before her like a bauble for a princess. If six months ago, even two months ago, anyone would have told her she'd look forward to spending time with a man like Garrett Cowlishaw, she would have pronounced them daft. But things were ever changing. All around her, as well as in her heart.

Maisie tugged on Caroline's skirt. "Can I walk with Gabi? Or the twins?"

"If she gets to do that, I want to walk with Jules and Henri." Lyall kicked another rock. "Their Mama lets them catch frogs."

"Then she cooks 'em." Duff licked his lips.

"Just their legs!" Maisie shook her head in disgust.

"You ever eat a frog, Miss Caroline?"

"No." She scrunched her face, just to hear the children giggle. Lyall's laugh sounded like an out-of-practice foghorn. "I can't say I could ever consider frog legs a treat." She looked at Maisie. "But if you want to bring me back a rock candy, that I *would* enjoy." Caroline tapped her chin. "What do you say we have a visiting walk?"

"Is that another game?" Duff twirled his stick.

"Not exactly. While we walk, we'll visit with different families. That way you'll each see your friends." Caroline looked ahead to the Gobens' wagon. They'd start with her friend.

"We like that game." Maisie gave Floppy a twirl, dropping her in the dirt. Maybe Floppy would get a scrubbing too.

"First, we'll walk fast to catch up with Miss Anna's wagon so I can speak to her, then we'll wait for the others to catch up to us."

After Caroline explained their plan to Angus and his grandmother, she took Maisie's hand. Duff and Lyall joined them with quick steps up the line of wagons.

Anna walked on one side of the team while her mother held the lead on the other. No doubt hearing the children's chatter, Anna turned and smiled. "We love company." She gave Caroline a quick hug then looked at the children. "How is everyone today?"

"I'm getting candy tomorrow." Maisie waved her cloth bunny. "Floppy is too."

"Miss Anna, Miss Caroline's never eaten frog legs," Lyall said. "Have you?"

Anna tugged the brim of Lyall's floppy hat.

"No. I've never eaten frog legs, and I don't care to."

Lyall chuckled. "That's what Miss Caroline said."

While the boys walked ahead of them, Caroline moved closer to Anna. "We're on a visiting walk to see our friends."

"That sounds like fun."

"Not 'til I see Gabi." Maisie wiggled her bunny as if it were doing the talking.

Caroline drew in a deep breath. "Since we're all a little impatient today, I best get right to the point of my visit. Your horse."

"You need Molasses? Not this afternoon, I hope. If we arrive at camp early enough, Mutter and I will ride into Independence."

"Tomorrow. For a ride."

Anna lifted the brim on her bonnet and leaned toward Caroline. "A Sunday ride?"

"Yes."

Her eyebrows lifted higher. "With thecaptain?"

Caroline glanced at the little girl at her side and nodded.

Anna nodded, her grin brightening her blue eyes. "It's about time you two noticed each other's finer qualities."

"I agree."

Anna's grin deepened. "Molasses will be yours tomorrow. Have you ridden?"

"Thank you. Yes." Hopefully, in the lapse of time since her last ride, she hadn't forgotten what she'd learned. "And Anna, Garrett and I aren't the only ones who should . . . uh, note each other's finer qualities."

Anna blushed with pleasure but then glanced at her mother. "I don't know."

Caroline knew what her friend wasn't saying. "I'm sure your family wants you to find love."

A shadow darkened Anna's blue eyes. "I'll think about it."

Caroline waved good-bye to Anna, slowing her pace to wait for the Wainwrights to catch up for Maisie's visit with Gabi.

Anna had let her family's needs consume her, but Caroline knew she wasn't so different. She'd let her ties to Phillip bind her heart. Anna may not be ready to accept a man's attentions, but Caroline was finally beginning to feel like she could. Again.

Anna shifted the lead rope to her other hand. She was tired of looking at the back of the Le Beaus' wagon. Tired of walking the road.

But mostly, she missed Caleb. A most surprising and foreign feeling. All she'd thought about since Dedrick died was how to help Mutter and Großvater feel better. How to make enough money to support them. What to cook that might make them want to eat again. How to protect Mutter from herself and the rumors swirling about her in Saint Charles.

Until encountering Caleb Reger at Heinrich's Dry Goods store. Until he looked up and saw her, and spilled coffee beans on the floor.

Boney had done the Bible reading these past two mornings, but it wasn't the same. She missed seeing Caleb at their camp for early morning trips to the creek with her to fill their water buckets. She missed hearing his laugh. Seeing his smile and that lock of hair that stood at attention when he removed his hat.

A huffy sigh drew Anna's gaze to her chestnut horse and Mutter sitting on the sidesaddle. She'd been riding since their noon stop. "I'm beginning to wonder if we'll ever arrive at Independence."

Anna nodded. "I'm fighting that notion too, but the camp shouldn't be too much farther."

"I hope not. Or there won't be time to go into town before supper."

"And the millinery won't be open on Sunday."

"That's right. You've worked so hard making those hats." Mutter pulled Molasses to a stop and climbed down.

"I suppose we'll have to leave setting up the camp to Großvater. Do you think he's up to it?"

Mutter nodded. "It's been a week and a half since his fever, and he says he already feels better than he has since we left Saint Charles."

Which meant Großvater had mostly likely accepted Caleb's recent help only to appease Mutter's concerns for her vater's well-being. Or for Anna's sake. Either way, Caleb's assistance had afforded her more time with the intriguing trail hand.

"Besides, the way Caleb hangs around our camp lately, he would no doubt be happy to help Vater."

"If he isn't going into town."

"My guess is that if you are, he will." A smirk brightened Mutter's blue eyes.

"Afternoon, Miss Anna. Missus Goben." Isaac Jackson sat large on the back of his gray, his flop hat in hand. Anna straightened. He had gone on the scouting trip with Caleb.

"Good afternoon, Isaac. You had a good scouting trip, did you?" Anna asked.

"Yes ma'am. Had me a good time visitin' with Mister Caleb."

"He's a pleasant man." Anna glanced behind Isaac, looking for a Tennessee Pacer that wasn't there.

A grin widened Isaac's face. "He stayed behind at the camp we found."

"Oh."

"Just a mile on up the road, is all. At Little Blue River, this side of Independence."

"That's good news," Mutter said. "Thank you. My daughter and I plan to ride into town this afternoon."

"That shouldn't be a problem, Missus Goben." Isaac glanced up at the sun. "Got us a few hours of light left." After setting his hat on his head, he raised his reins. "Best let the boss know about it all."

When Isaac rode on up the line, Anna exchanged lead ropes with Mutter and climbed onto Molasses. Riding her horse the last mile might pass the time more quickly than staring at the wagon in front of them. She wouldn't have much time with Caleb at camp, but she hoped to at least see him before she and Mutter rode into Independence. Maybe Mutter was right, and he'd go into town with them.

Less than half an hour later, Anna rode Molasses into the camp at Little Blue River. Großvater was helping Mutter, guiding their wagon into place. Boney stood beside the chuck wagon at the front of the line, and the last of the wagons soon rolled in, completing the semicircle. But she didn't see Caleb on either end.

Anna looked at Mutter. "I'll be right back, and then we can go on into town."

Mutter nodded. "Don't be too long."

Anna clicked her tongue for Molasses to move forward. Caleb could have been behind the line, guiding the first wagons into place.

"Anna."

Her shoulders relaxed as she twisted toward the familiar voice. Caleb appeared from behind the chuck wagon and strolled toward her.

"There you are," she said, unable to control the size of her smile.

"You were looking for me?" A grin showed off the dimple in his cheek. "You missed me?"

"I did."

"I'm glad to see you too." He rolled his derby in his hand. "Anna, I had a lot of time to think out here last night." Drawing in a deep breath, he held it for a few seconds then blew it out through his teeth. "I have something I need to tell you. When you've set up camp, do you think we could go sit by the river?"

Anna's breath caught. "I'd really like to, but I need to ride into town with my mother. Those hats I've made since we left Saint Charles?"

He nodded.

"I'm hoping to sell them to the millinery in Independence, and the shop will be closed tomorrow."

"Of course."

"I'm sorry. It's not that I don't want to sit with you . . . to hear what you have to say."

"I understand."

"Are you going into town this afternoon?"

"I rode in this morning with a list of supplies. Told the captain I'd stay here this afternoon to help folks grease up their wagon wheels and such." Caleb shook his head. "Now I wish I hadn't agreed to that. I'd rather go back into town since that's where you'll be."

Anna smiled, despite the fact that she felt torn. She'd rather stay here since that was where he'd be.

"We'll camp here until Monday. Perhaps we could have some time alone tomorrow?"

"I'd like that. Yes."

Mutter rode up on Großvater's sorrel with Boney on his mule at her side. "Caleb, are you coming with us?"

"No ma'am. Thank you. Seems I have work to do around here." He set his hat on his head and looked at Anna. "Have a nice time."

"Thank you. And I'll see you when we get back?"

"I hope so."

When Caleb strolled toward the Zanzucchis' wagon, Anna looked at Boney. Her friend wore a grin as wide as the river. "We'll need to stop by the wagon to pick up the hats," she said.

Now, thanks to Caleb, all Anna could think about was getting to town and back as quickly as possible. Her curiosity mounted as she wondered what it was Caleb needed to tell her. More about the depth of his feelings for her? Perhaps his intentions? Or was it the secret that sometimes clouded his eyes and weighed on his shoulders?

She glanced at Mutter, who rode beside her. If he did share his past mistake and regret, should Anna confide her secret?

25

Saturday afternoon, Anna glanced out at the bench in front of the millinery, where Mutter awaited her. She slipped the dollar notes into her pocket and fairly floated out the door. The kindly proprietor had purchased all five hats from her. Before Anna left the store, she'd helped pin the puffed hat onto the silver head of a customer.

Mutter was right to joyously anticipate this day and their arrival in the fair city. Independence, Missouri, was grand in its appearance, especially the view of Courthouse Square, the site where she was to meet the others who had ridden into town. The stately brick building with a chimney on each of four corners was trimmed in white marble, as was its magnificent spire. A wood-rail fence ringed the manicured lawns. Horse-drawn carriages, families on foot, and road-ready wagons with clean white cloth dotted the surrounding streets.

Mutter waved, her smile a warming sight.

As Anna approached the bench, she fanned her fingers and wiggled them.

Mutter's eyes widened. "You have no hats!"

"She bought them all." Anna sat on the bench.

"That's wonderful, dear." Mutter patted Anna's

knee as she had when Anna was a young girl.

Anna wanted to feel like that little girl again—innocent and trusting—but she'd seen the sack on the other side of Mutter. It wasn't big enough to hold a bottle, but that didn't mean Mutter hadn't purchased one. But when? Every time she'd looked, Mutter had been seated on the bench.

Sighing, Anna rested against the back of the bench. What kind of daughter would distrust her mother, not believe someone she loved could get better? Be better?

One who had heard too many promises that hadn't been kept.

Mutter smoothed her shawl over her calico sleeves and looked out at the square. "This city is quite charming, don't you think?"

Anna breathed in the sweet scent of bread baking in the shop up the street. "Like an oasis. You were right, Mutter; it is nice to be in the city at least for a day or two."

Mutter shifted on the bench to face her. "Dear, I don't think a day or two here is enough." She clasped her hands on her lap. "I think we should stay."

"In Independence? For how long?"

"To live."

"But we haven't even left Missouri."

Mutter stared at the Square and heaved a deep sigh. "It wasn't my idea to leave."

Anna shivered, pulling her shawl higher on her

neck. What about her friends? Caleb Reger? She was just beginning to appreciate his *finer qualities*. Could she watch them all leave her behind? She hadn't come this far to stop now, had she? Surely Mutter didn't mean to give up now. Anna hoped a new place and a fresh start would do Großvater and Mutter good. Do them all good. That was, after all, why she'd suggested they move west.

She twisted on the bench to face Mutter. "What about Großvater? He's enjoying the journey."

"The trip made him very ill. We could have lost him." Mutter pressed her lips together.

"But we didn't, and he's quite well again. And I've not seen Großvater so happy in a long time."

Mutter drew in a deep breath, straightening against the back of the bench. "We'll ask him what he thinks we should do."

If Mutter insisted on staying, Großvater would give in to her. He, too, was eager to please his little girl. He'd do anything if he thought it would keep her clearheaded.

"All right, Mutter." Anna saw no benefit in aggravating her mother right now and spoiling their time in the city together.

"Oh." Mutter pulled the sack from the bench and held it up. "I nearly forgot why I walked down to the general store." She glanced at the sign board swinging in the breeze a couple of shops down.

"You went into the general store?"

"Why, yes, dear. Where else was I to find this?" Mutter slid a block of beeswax from the sack. "We talked about the two of us making candles, remember?"

Anna nodded. She remembered Mutter's suggestion, but hadn't expected her to follow through. Again, she felt guilty for distrusting Mutter. Maybe the change she'd been praying for long and hard was finally beginning.

Anna followed Mutter into camp at a slower pace. They'd remove the saddles from the horses at the wagon before walking the sorrel and the chestnut to the pasture. As they rode in, she'd kept an eye out for Caleb but hadn't seen him. It was just as well they not talk just yet, since he had decided to tell her more.

If there was any chance Mutter could talk Großvater into remaining in Independence, Anna wasn't ready to hear what Caleb had to say to her, let alone face him knowing she may not be continuing on with the caravan. Mutter knew how fond she and Caleb had become of each other. How could Mutter ask her to even think about watching him ride away?

Once the horses were settled, she'd take a bucket to the river for washing water. It might also be a good time to look for feathers or weaving grass to make more hats for the next town.

By the time Anna arrived in camp, well behind

Mutter, Großvater's horse nickered at the back of the wagon where it stood tethered to a wheel. Mutter was poking around in the wagon box while Großvater bent over the ground near the work-table, kicking through the grass and leaves.

Anna climbed down from Molasses and tethered her horse to a low branch. "Großvater, did you drop something?"

Standing, he let out a rush of air, his cheeks puffing. "I don't think I did, but I have to be sure."

"It's not in here." Mutter closed the lid on the box and looked at Anna. "Your großvater is missing the timepiece Dedrick gave him."

Anna looked at the contents of Großvater's valise littering the table. His felt hat sat on the corner. The pocket watch had to be there, somewhere.

Großvater's shoulders sagged. "The Christmas before he left."

"Could it have fallen out of your pocket?"

"Wasn't in my pocket. Had it right there"—he jabbed his finger at the table—"next to my jerky. I had just wound it." He resumed his methodical search through the grass.

Anna heaved her saddle onto the wagon's wheel to let it dry out some. "I'll take the horses to the pasture, then I planned to go to the river for water."

Großvater peered up at her. "I already filled the barrel."

"I want to get more to have extra to wash up before the meeting tonight."

Mutter sighed. "Meeting? I had forgotten about that." She looked at Anna, her shoulders squared. "We were going to talk to your großvater, remember?"

"Not now, Wilma." Großvater yanked his hat off the table. "We'll take care of the horses, Anna. You go on ahead to the river." He pressed his hat onto the gray hair that circled his bald spot. "Mrs. Zanzucchi is missing her silver teapot. You know what the captain said. If I can't find my pocket watch, I need to tell Boney or one of the trail hands about it going missing."

"You think someone took it?" Anna pulled a red letter sack from the wagon box and stuffed it into her skirt pocket. Next, she lifted a bucket off its hook on the side of the wagon. She would be surprised if there actually was a thief. A grumbler or two, yes, but no thief. "Why would they want your watch, and how would they know to even look for it?"

"Stranger things have happened, I suppose."

Anna groaned. "Yes. Things like Davonna Kamden accusing Caroline of taking her locket, then finding out it had been in her knitting sack all along."

"That woman is forgetful."

"And you're not?" Mutter's lips curled into a grin.

"Only when you've told me things I didn't care to hear. Or plan to remember." He set his fists on his hips and frowned down at the table. "I set my timepiece on the table with my valise. Went down to talk to Ian Kamden about a spare wheel. Left for no more than ten minutes, but when I came back, it was gone."

Anna ruffled the grass at her feet. "I don't have to go. I can stay and help you look."

"No." Großvater shook his head. "It's not here. I have searched the table, the valise, and the ground." He tugged open the mouth of his trouser pockets. "I emptied all my pockets."

"I'll be back in a few minutes, then." Relief washed over Anna as she strolled through the trees on a footpath that would eventually take her to the river. She was sorry Großvater's timepiece was missing but not sorry for the delay in discussing Mutter's request that they remain in Independence.

Mutter wouldn't be put off for very long. She'd have her say. In the meantime, Anna intended to enjoy a little peace and quiet. She allowed herself to wander down the path, looking under bushes and in low branches for feathers and anything else she could collect in her sack and use to make an interesting arrangement on a hat. She stopped and peeked into a hole in a blackberry vine that hid an empty bird's nest.

She'd just bent to pick it up when she heard

twigs snapping behind her. Only a few yards away, by her judgment.

A bear. They were still in the woods of Missouri, where they'd had a black bear raid their camp. How could she have been so careless? She didn't have any pots and pans. Only a pail, a cloth sack, and a few feathers.

The uneven footfalls came closer. Maybe if she stayed low and still, it wouldn't find her. A reasonable plan, except for the pounding of her heart.

Caleb stood in the river, his boots off and his pant legs rolled to his knees. He took the block of lye soap to the muddy trousers he had splayed across a rock and began scrubbing. Finished with his current camp duties and unable to escape his thoughts, he'd decided to take care of one of his personal chores.

He shook the trousers in the running water and watched the brown suds flow downstream. If only redemption were as easy as dunking and scrubbing. What he wouldn't give to watch his past wash away like unwanted mud. He swallowed another chaw of regret. What was done was done. And even if he could undo the last eleven days since Otto's illness to protect Anna's heart, he wasn't sure he would. But neither could he go on living a lie and still look into Anna's pure blue eyes.

Caleb slapped the trousers against the rock and scrubbed some more. Finally satisfied he'd done all the scrubbing needed, he dunked the pants in the river for a rinse, then wrung them out. Back at the shore where he'd left his socks and boots, he laid the wet trousers over a bush and pulled his boots on. He was about to unroll his pant legs when a piercing scream tore through the air.

A woman was in trouble. And she was close. The scream had come from behind him, upstream and in the thick woods. Leaving the soap and the clean trousers behind, Caleb bolted up the bank and into the trees.

Where was she?

"Stay away!" He knew that voice.

A loud grunt followed the yell, and Caleb's legs couldn't carry him fast enough.

"Anna?"

"Caleb!"

He turned toward the voice and fairly leapt the last few yards to the edge of a small clearing. Anna stood at the far side. Because of the shadows in the trees on the other side of her, he couldn't make out who or what had frightened her.

Caleb pulled his knife from its sheath at his waist. He could see that Anna wasn't moving, and neither was her apparent attacker. Calling up on his wartime training, he made his way around the clearing, staying just inside the trees. As he drew closer, even in the waning light, he could make out the trapper he'd encountered the night before. Anna held an empty pail between her and the trapper as if it were a medieval shield, while the mountain man stood in front of her, his arms raised in surrender.

Caleb stepped into the clearing. "Skins?"

Anna glanced at Caleb, still wielding the bucket. "You know this man?"

"He came to camp last night. Had supper with me and Isaac." Caleb glanced around them. "I thought you went to town. What are you doing out here?"

"We returned." Her lips were trembling. "I was collecting feathers to make more hats."

Caleb studied Skins. "What happened?"

The trapper shrugged.

"I bent down to pick up an abandoned bird's nest and heard something coming. I stayed down, hoping whoever or whatever it was wouldn't see me. When I did finally look up, he was towering over me."

Skins grunted and shrugged. "Quiet like a mouse, this girl." He looked at the blackberry bush at Anna's feet. "Had no idea she was down there."

Caleb nodded. "Anna, I'm sure Skins didn't mean any harm."

"I didn't know that." She drew in a shuddering breath and set the pail down.

Skins tugged his buckskin jacket straight. "I'll be by your camp for a plate."

"We'll have one for you." Caleb and Anna both watched as the trapper ambled back into the forest.

"When I first heard his footfalls, I thought it might be a bear."

"He does look a bit like one."

"Back in Saint Charles, I was used to seeing river rats, as Großvater liked to call them. But not mountain men." Anna shook her head. "What was all that?"

"The reason I called him Skins. A raccoon-pelt hat. A bear-hide coat. And I'm guessing there's some skunk in there somewhere."

She smiled, thinning her lips. "I'm sorry I screamed and scared you."

"I'm just thankful you're all right." He took a step toward her. "Anna?"

She nodded.

He placed his fingertip under her chin and lifted it.

The bucket hit the ground.

He leaned in closer, his lips touching hers.

Anna had just sunk her fingers into the hair at his neck, when the sound of someone or something fast approaching jerked them both to attention.

Boney stumbled to a stop in front of them, huffing and puffing, and staring at Caleb then at Anna. "I thought I heard you scream."

Caleb backed away from Anna. "She did. You did."

"Yes." Anna moistened her lips and glanced at Caleb. "A mountain man surprised me."

"I take it she ain't talkin' about you?"

Caleb shook his head, thinking about how cold and dry his lips felt right now. "Skins. The fellow from last night. I told the boss about him."

Boney glanced back at the trees and then out into the clearing.

"He's gone now."

"Yes." Anna moistened her lips again and smiled. "And everything is fine."

"Is it, now?" Boney looked them both up and down. "You sure?"

"I'm sure." Anna didn't take her gaze from Caleb.

Caleb smiled. "Well, then, we'd better get back."

"Good idea." Boney glanced up at the sky. "It'll be dark soon."

Anna cleared her throat in a most unladylike manner. "I need to get supper before the meeting."

When Boney showed no signs of leaving without them, Anna smiled and took the first step back toward camp.

Caleb motioned for Boney to follow her, then fell in line behind them and brushed his lips with the back of his hand. He'd wanted to tell Anna the truth about himself today, but their kiss was almost enough to give him hope that his past mistakes couldn't change the way Anna felt about him.

26

Garrett stood beside his campfire and looked out over the Boone's Lick Company gathered before him, most seated on stools or chairs. A few folks had ridden into town before supper, but as far as he could tell, everyone else was accounted for. Anna Goben was easy to find with Caleb wedged between her and Otto. She and her mother had obviously returned from town. And so had the Rengler brothers and Arven and Lorelei, the younger Mr. and Mrs. Beck. And there was Dr. Le Beau, scarcely visible standing behind his wife. The children played off to the side with a wooden hoop and a leather ball except for young Alfonzo Zanzucchi, who had remained with his parents to translate.

Garrett looked up at the graying sky and cleared his throat. "We'd best get started. Many of you have children to settle into bed."

Mrs. Kamden waved her arm.

"A question, Mrs. Kamden?"

"Tomorrow is Sunday, Captain. You do intend to observe the Sabbath, do you not?"

"Yes ma'am." Garrett was careful not to look directly at the woman standing beside her, for Caroline Milburn was a different kind of distraction altogether. “We’ll hold our camp until Monday morning. From here we’ll head to the river and stay there overnight.”

“Captain, Papa wants to know, are we making good time?” At seventeen, Camille Le Beau had the poise and maturity of a much older lady. “We are to pick up more medical supplies at Fort Kearney. We will arrive there the beginning of June?”

Not with all these interruptions, they wouldn’t. Garrett forced a smile. “We are making good time, but we have only just begun.” He waited for her to translate into French, and the Zanzucchi boy into Italian. “We could encounter difficulties that slow us down. But hopefully we will not.”

Emery Beck stood, holding his whittling knife in one hand and a half-carved wooden shoe in the other. He looked directly at the doctor. “Difficulties with animals that aren’t fit to haul a loaded wagon over a frontier trail, for instance?”

Garrett gave the ruddy-faced Mr. Beck a sharp look and drew in a deep breath. “So far, all the animals are faring well, including the doctor’s horses. And your concerns about them are old news.”

Dr. Le Beau jumped to his feet, shaking a fist. Apparently, his daughter had translated the cobbler’s comment. The doctor rattled off several chains of words in French.

Garrett didn’t know French, but he knew enough

about body language to know the doctor wasn't merely reciting the finer qualities of his six quarter horses.

Apparently, Emery Beck knew it too. His eyes steely, he shook the wooden shoe at Le Beau. "Being a doctor doesn't give him the right to spread his shoulders and go against policy."

"Captain." Camille Le Beau's sharp voice silenced the crowd. The young woman stood beside her father, already two inches taller than him. "Papa said Mr. Beck should take more care with the knife he's wielding and the wood he's butchering, and leave the horses to us."

"Butchering?" Emery huffed. A muscle twitched in his jaw. "Well, the doctor can ride his uppity horses to the nearest port." He dropped his knife and marched toward Le Beau. "Go home."

Tiny stepped in front of the cobbler, elbows out. The cobbler halted midstep. The other trail hands fanned out. Caleb and Frank with the Le Beaus. Boney and Isaac stood on either side of the fray.

Hattie's brother, Charles, appeared beside Camille, towering over everyone around him. His shoulders squared, he faced Emery Beck. "All this bluster . . . coming from a German immigrant."

Hattie's gasp was one among a chorus.

Emery Beck looked around Tiny. "You say that as if I'm Irish." He jerked his gaze to where the Zanzucchis stood. "Or Italian, for that matter."

The boy didn't translate, but still Mrs. Zanzucchi offered a rebuttal in Italian. Her husband tugged at her coat sleeve, a wasted gesture.

Emery's chest puffed out. "Charles, you didn't seem to mind when Germans stocked dry goods for your trip"—he looked at Otto Goben—"or caned chairs for you."

Charles shook his head. "I only meant that neither you nor any of us have the right to point a finger at someone else and declare them unworthy of equal rights."

"Well said, Charles. Thank you." Garrett waved his slouch hat. "Gentlemen, we'll have no more outbursts. Understood?"

The doctor and Emery Beck gave him a tight nod and returned to their stools. Le Doc had no sooner settled than Caroline Milburn stepped up beside Camille Le Beau and spoke in whispers. Garrett followed their gaze to Ian Kamden who walked away from the crowd, his arm bracing his wife. Le Beau took quick steps to his wagon while Caroline accompanied his daughter to the Kamdens' Conestoga.

If the younger Mrs. Kamden had fallen ill, he needed to know about it. All the more reason to get on with this meeting.

"Folks, my concerns lie with the threat of illness and accidents, raging rivers, and howling winds that can splinter even the sturdiest of wagons." Garrett returned the hat to his head. "My intention is to keep you all informed of our progress, and any new developments. That is the reason for our gathering this evening. These next several weeks, the settlements and stage stops will peter out. Water is in short supply on the prairie, so make sure your water barrels are in good shape and topped up before we roll Monday morning."

The majority of the Company nodded, and family members whispered to one another, no doubt assigning additional duties. Good. He needed them to take the real issues seriously.

Anna carried her chair back to the wagon. Unlike the others in the camp, she wasn't talking about the argument between Mr. Beck and Dr. Le Beau, Rhoda Kamden's need for the doctor, or even the lack of civilization looming before them.

No, the conversation in town with her mother held Anna's attention and begged the question: If Mutter was serious about staying in Independence and mentioned it to Großvater, what would he say?

And if Großvater sided with Mutter as Anna feared he would, what would she do?

The memory of Caleb's kiss wouldn't let her give up and say good-bye to him so easily.

But she knew from Caroline's experience with the captain that he wouldn't allow a single woman to make the trip without a man in her party. For her, that was Großvater, but she couldn't ask him to leave Mutter alone in Independence.

Anna needed to keep going. Needed to get past Dedrick's death and Mutter's desperation. She had to believe she could, that God had a purpose and a plan in all of this.

Mary Alice was right—Boney wasn't the only man in the camp. And she had definitely noticed Caleb.

No. Anna shook her head. Marriage wasn't the answer. It couldn't be. If she couldn't marry Boney despite their long friendship, she'd never be able to marry someone simply to continue with the wagon train. Doing chores together, taking walks to the creek, and sharing a brief, interrupted kiss didn't mean Caleb intended to marry her. She didn't know what it meant, but she was desperate to stay and find out.

Back at the wagon with Mutter and Großvater, Anna set her chair at the cookfire but she had no intention of sitting down. Instead, she pulled her hammock from the wagon and slid the loop at one end over a hook on the wagon and played out the rope to tie it around a tree. Perhaps if Mutter saw her preparing her bed, she would do the same and forget the ridiculous notion to give up so soon into the journey.

"Vater." Mutter carried her chair to the fire. "There is something we need to talk to you about."

Anna sighed, her lips pressed together. Mutter hadn't forgotten. Nor had she lost her determination.

Großvater pulled up the third chair and added a dried branch to the fire before sitting down. "Have the two women in my life been plotting against me?"

Anna shook her head. More like Mutter was plotting against her.

"Nothing like that, Vater." Mutter lighted on her chair beside Großvater and waved Anna over. "Come sit with us, dear."

Anna let go of the end of her bed, watching the ropes drop to the ground. Hopefully, her dream of a fresh start out west wouldn't do the same. Should she let go of it and let it fall, or hang on? She'd never done well standing up to Mutter. Neither had Großvater. But maybe it was time one of them did.

Anna wrapped the ends of her shawl over her arms and seated herself.

Flickering light from the fire showed the deep lines framing Großvater's mouth. "This seems serious."

It was, especially if he voted for setting up housekeeping in Independence. Anna opened her mouth to speak but wasn't fast enough.

"Anna and I had a lovely time in Independence this afternoon, and we came up with an idea. A wonderful idea."

We? Anna rubbed her arms, battling a chill inside and out. If Mutter wasn't going to clarify her involvement, Anna would. "It is Mutter's idea."

"And you don't like it?" he asked.

Anna shook her head. "Mutter wants to stay in Independence."

"To live?" Großvater stood, looking at Mutter. "You've come so far. We all have. Why would you want to quit now?"

"Anna makes it sound bad. Like I'm giving up. That's not what I'm doing, Vater. My daughter was wise to lead us out of Saint Charles, to drag me out of the pit I was in. I did need a change. But I'm better now. And you were terribly sick just eleven days ago. Now it seems the poor mother of all those children is ill. Not to mention the thief in our Company." Mutter straightened in her chair, stacking her hands on her lap. "Must we deplete ourselves and our resources completely, chasing an unknown future in the Wild West, when Independence is a fine city?"

Großvater paced between the fire and the back of the wagon.

Anna watched him, trying to discern what he was thinking and prepare for what he'd say.

Mutter stood, looking small and frail. She reached for the knot at her neck and untied her bonnet strings. "Making our home in Independence would give us the new beginning and still let us remain in our beloved Missouri."

God, help me. Am I being selfish? Should we stay? If that's what's best for Mutter, please change my heart. Give me peace.

Großvater warmed his hands above the flames then returned to his cane chair. "You are right, my dear *tochter.*"

Anna's heart sank.

Mutter smiled and sat down, perched on the edge of her chair like a bird expecting a worm to come to her.

"Your Anna is wise. We were smart to let her lead us out of our Egypt." Großvater lifted his arms, swiveling side to side. "Out here, on the road, I feel freer than I have in years."

"But, Vater, what about that frightening fever?"

"And all the help we received?" Großvater met Anna's gaze, his look tender, then turned back to Mutter. "Wilma, it has taken great courage to come this far. Courage I feared our losses had taken from us." The fire crackled, drawing his attention. "Will we doubt God now when He has brought us this far?"

Mutter rose from her chair and crossed her arms. "And what if the West isn't our promised land?"

Großvater held his hands up to the fire. "What if Moses had given in?"

When the crowd had dispersed, Garrett looked at his men. "That was some meeting."

Isaac gave a low whistle. "Yessir. I'm afraid those two men left on their own; someone could get hurt."

"We'll just have to see that it doesn't happen."

Garrett glanced toward the Kamdens' Conestoga.

"No one likes to lead or trail Emery Beck's wagon." Boney shook his head. "That man is pure sour, and nobody wants it rubbin' off on them."

They all chuckled. Leave it to Boney to make sure they had a laugh before the day was through.

"I think I'll leave you fellows to think on that while I go check on Rhoda Kamden," Garrett said.

"She's got five children. She's probably just . . . uh, fruitful." Frank shoved his hands into his pockets.

"Be that as it may, Caroline seemed quite concerned about her."

"And you're quite, uh, concerned with Mrs. Milburn." Tiny pressed fingertips to his round cheeks and lolled his head.

"Love is in the air, all right." Boney locked gazes with Caleb. "But it seems to be avoidin' most of us."

Garrett sighed. He had a feeling something was afoot he should know about, but he didn't have the patience for it now. "I'll leave you all to sort that out for Boney." He waved and walked up the line, looking straight ahead until he reached the Conestoga.

Ian and his mother, Davonna, stood outside talking with Dr. Le Beau and Camille. "Captain." The father of five sighed. "We didn't want to disrupt the meeting."

"Don't worry about that. You certainly weren't the first ones." Garrett smiled.

Ian nodded. "I figure Mr. Beck and the doctor's hurly-burly was enough to make any of us sick." His voice flattened on the last word.

"Any news?" Garrett asked, looking from Ian to Dr. Le Beau.

"I thought perhaps she carried another child, but the doctor doesn't seem to think that's the cause of her pain."

"Does she have a fever like Otto Goben had last week?"

"No." Ian shook his head. "Only sharp pain that started in the mid o' her belly. Mostly lower, on the right side now. She was ne'er sick with any of our bairns."

Garrett was sure the Scotsman hadn't spoken so many words to him the whole time they'd been on the road. He glanced from the doctor to the daughter. "What do you think is wrong?"

Camille translated. "Papa says no, it is not like Monsieur Goben's ailment. He is not sure of the cause. But no one else has made complaints of any such sign. We will keep watch for any others who take ill."

"Good. Thank you." Garrett looked up just as Caroline peeked through the opening in the front of the wagon.

"I thought I heard your voice." Caroline looked

through the darkness, toward the clearing. "The meeting is over, then?"

"Thankfully, yes."

She turned her attention to Ian. "Rhoda is asking for you." That said, she stepped over the seat and down the wheel spokes.

Ian nodded, then looked at Davonna. "Mither, could you go see about the children?"

Davonna huffed.

"I'll let you know if anything changes, Mither."

Caroline glanced at the grandmother. "I'll be along in just a few minutes, Davonna."

When the older woman skulked toward the farm wagon, Dr. Le Beau and Camille followed Ian up and into the wagon.

Garrett looked Caroline in the eyes, a mesmerizing green even in the faint light the campfire offered. He swallowed and glanced toward the Conestoga with a nod. "How is she?"

"The pain is easing. Hopefully, it was just a fluke. The children . . ." Caroline lowered her voice. "And her mother-in-law can be a handful, at times."

"Yes. I do know a little something about folks bein' a handful." He shook his head. "Under the tree last Sunday, you praised my leadership."

"I remember that."

"Well, I'm certain tonight you were having second thoughts."

"Not at all." She pressed her hand to the lace

collar, drawing his attention to the red curl dangling at her neck. "I think it takes strong leadership skills to refrain from knocking heads together when grown men forget how to behave."

"I like the way you think." Garrett rubbed his bearded chin, holding her gaze. "You may think me uncaring for asking, under Mrs. Kamden's circumstances, but—"

She lifted an eyebrow, her mouth tipped in a crooked smile.

"Will you need to help out tomorrow, or can we still plan on taking our horseback ride?"

"I'm still counting on it." Caroline clasped her hands below her waist. "If need be, Lorelei Beck or Hattie can sit with Rhoda or help Davonna with the children."

"That is good news, ma'am. Real good news."

She tilted her head. "I think so too, Captain."

Suddenly, he was all the more anxious to welcome tomorrow.

27

Anna had mixed feelings about Rutherford Wainwright's prayer of benediction. She wasn't ready to leave the service yet. Not if it meant parting company with Caleb. He stood on one side of her, Großvater on the other. Mutter hadn't joined them.

She and Caleb hadn't had a chance to speak privately since their kiss and Boney's interruption yesterday. She hoped they would have an opportunity this afternoon, but Großvater would expect his supper soon.

Großvater set his hat on his head, her signal that it was time to go back to camp.

Caleb brushed her hand, sending a shiver up her spine, and she met his brown-eyed gaze. "Anna, will I see you later?"

Nodding, she moistened her lips. "You could join us for supper if you'd like."

Boney sauntered up. "You comin' to Sunday supper too?" he asked Caleb.

Anna's mouth dropped open. "You're coming?"

Boney grinned. "Do you have to sound so disappointed?"

"I'm not. Just surprised, is all." Anna looked at Großvater.

Großvater nodded, and she was pretty sure she saw a twinkle in his eyes.

"The more the merrier is how I think." Boney clapped Caleb on the shoulder. "We accept."

Caleb nodded, a grin deepening the dimple in his cheek.

The more the merrier, unless you're interrupting a kiss. Or you were once the intended of the woman who invited another man to supper. Anna sighed, and took the lead to their camp while the men talked about greasing wagon wheels, fording rivers, and trappers named Skins.

She served the food, and soon everyone was happily filling their stomachs.

Caleb took a second bread roll from the basket. "You made these?" he asked Anna.

"I did. And the veal *potthast.*"

"Best I've ever tasted."

Anna moistened her lips. "You like German foods?"

"I do now."

Anna's cheeks warmed.

Boney cleared his throat. "I wouldn't be too flattered, Anna. Caleb's told me he likes my cookin' too."

Anna smiled.

"Him, on the other hand." Boney looked at Caleb, his mouth turned up in a grin. "Well, Caleb's cookin' can leave a wild animal feeling hungry."

Caleb peered at Boney over his forkful of potato.

Boney shrugged. "Just sayin, you're gonna need a woman who can cook."

Grinning, Caleb looked directly into her eyes. Good thing she was seated. "It's the truth."

Großvater lifted his coffee cup. "Which part is the truth?"

"Otto's got a point there, Tennessee," Boney

said. “You agreein’ your cookin’ is too bad for even a wild animal, or you lookin’ for a woman who can cook?”

Caleb scooped a generous bite of veal onto his fork. “Yes.”

Anna pressed her bottom lip between her teeth but was still having trouble containing a giggle. This was more fun than she would’ve guessed possible.

“Well, I can see we’re gettin’ nowhere with Caleb. Not while there’s still food here.” Boney glanced at the wagon. “Where’s your mother? Is she ill?”

Anna drew in a deep breath. “She wasn’t feeling her best today and decided to rest before our departure in the morning.”

“My daughter is pouting.”

“Großvater!” Anna squared her shoulders.

He shrugged. “These young men need to know right here and now that you women pout.”

Anna drew in a slow, deep breath, refusing to offer any hint of a pout. Boney’s and Caleb’s mouths tipped into not-so-subtle grins.

Großvater focused on the young men. “When females don’t get their way, that’s what they do. At any age. Every age.”

Caleb glanced at Anna, mischief brightening his face. “That’s good to know, sir.”

“My daughter, she wants to stay in Independence.”

Boney set his half-eaten bread on his plate, no doubt surprised and concerned. But it was Caleb's reaction, not Boney's, Anna cared most about. She met his pensive gaze.

A frown creased Caleb's sun-kissed brow. "You're not leaving the Company, are you?"

"No," Großvater said. "I told her no."

The smile on Caleb's face added to Anna's joy. In their first meetings, she wouldn't have guessed the two of them could be friends, but now . . .

Boney blew out a long breath. "Safe to say we're both thankful you're staying with us."

Caleb looked straight at Anna. "Yes, very grateful."

Anna nodded, her list of reasons not to leave Caleb Reger growing fast. His willingness to lend a helping hand to anyone who needed it. The tenor of his voice when he read Scripture. His good humor in Boney's relentless teasing. The way he smiled after every bite of her cooking . . .

Caroline stood beside Anna's horse, Molasses. Had horses grown taller, or was she shrinking? When Garrett Cowlishaw suggested a Sunday ride, she'd ignored the fact that it had been nearly six years since she'd ridden a horse.

Yet, here she was in a skirt, with a man who rode a horse every day.

It seemed she had only three choices. One,

attempt to climb up by herself, risk falling to the ground, or worse, dangling with her foot caught in the stirrup. Two, tell Garrett the truth, that she felt insecure about her riding skills. Or three, she could suddenly feel ill and cancel the ride.

Talking herself into spending time with any man other than Phillip, much less this particular one, had been no easy task. Steeling herself, Caroline turned to face her companion. Garrett stood beside his black stallion looking every bit a seasoned horseman.

"Mr. Cowlishaw."

"Garrett."

"Garrett." She dropped her hands to her sides. "I'm not a horsewoman."

"You've never ridden?"

"Twice. But it's been a long while."

He smiled. "I didn't consider that being from the city, you may—"

Caroline raised her gloved hand to stop him. "I'm not opposed to riding. I'm just not sure where to begin so as to land on the saddle"—she looked at their feet—"and not on the ground."

His chuckle tender, Garrett stepped toward her. "Not that I'm an expert in the art of landing in a sidesaddle, mind you, but I'm happy to help."

She pressed her lips together, holding back a giggle. "Please."

Garrett held the stirrup for her. When he pointed to her left foot, she took the prompt and raised her leg. Once she had her foot in the stirrup, Garrett moved to her side and placed his hands around her waist. Her breaths quickened. Until now, no one but Phillip had ever touched her in such an intimate way. The blend of amusement and aware-ness she detected in Garrett's eyes did nothing to calm the flutters in her stomach.

"Are you all right?" he asked.

She was better now than she'd been in a long time.

When she nodded, Garrett lifted her into position, helping her right leg over the pommel.

Caroline settled into the saddle then took the reins from him. "I am quite certain that went much more smoothly with your help than it would've without it. Thank you."

Garrett swung into the saddle on his stallion and leaned toward her. "You're most welcome, ma'am." He brushed the brim of his white hat.

"Caroline. Please call me Caroline. You did, after all, keep me from taking a tumble." She smiled.

"I'm happy to oblige." He lifted the reins. "Are you ready, Caroline?"

Yes. No. Nodding, she raised her eyebrows. "I think so." *Please let me be ready, Lord.*

Garrett clicked a command to the horses, and they sauntered across the lush meadow toward a stand of trees. Molasses's first steps made Caroline feel like cream sloshing in a bucket. She gripped the front edge of the saddle with her right hand to steady herself. Soon, her body began to sway with the bay's steady rhythm.

Following Garrett, she couldn't help but note that he'd given her space to reacquaint herself with the feel of a horse in movement without the embarrassment of a watchful eye. A helpful teacher, and a thoughtful one too.

She managed to ride up beside the stallion and guide Molasses to match the pace of the taller black horse. Garrett glanced at her but remained silent, looking peaceful and at home on horseback. Or with her?

Enjoying the solace, Caroline looked up at the flawless blue sky, watching a yellow bird flit from a primrose bush to a box elder. She couldn't have asked for a more perfect day.

They'd ridden in silence for a few minutes when she sensed Garrett's attention. She met his warm gaze and smiled. How long had he been watching her?

"You're feeling all right?" he asked. "Comfortable?"

"I am." On the horse, and with him.

Garrett glanced at the grassy ground, then back up at her. "The last time you rode a horse, it was with your husband?"

"Phillip's uncle had a ranch outside of Philadelphia, and we rode there a time or two."

"Has it gotten any easier?"

The sincerity in his eyes told her he wasn't talking about riding a horse.

"Easier than it was when you first handed me the letter from the Department of War? Yes."

"I'm glad." Garrett shifted on his saddle. "I know it's been difficult."

"It has, but—"

"You're here."

She nodded. "Yes." With him. And enjoying his company. A vast improvement from her feelings mere weeks ago.

They'd ridden a ways farther from camp when Garrett stood in the stirrups and stretched his right leg.

"Does the leg pain you much?" she asked.

His brow creased. "Only when I ride."

Caroline's breath caught and she pulled back on the reins, halting her horse. "But you ride every day. We're riding—"

His boyish grin stopped her midsentence. "I'm tugging your leg now." He chuckled, his face turning red. "I know it was mean, but I couldn't help myself."

Good; he also had a sense of humor. He definitely possessed many intriguing layers. For show, she slapped the air between them and he ducked. Yes, she was already enjoying getting to know the man leading the caravan.

She pulled the reins around and signaled for her horse to resume his slow gait. "If you don't mind my asking, how did you injure your leg? When we first met, my nephew Gilbert asked if you'd been shot, and you told him you hadn't."

"Yes. I remember." He sat back down. "He's a bright boy. You must miss Gilbert—all of them—Mary, Cora, and your sister."

He obviously remembered Jack too, since he'd failed to mention her brother-in-law in the list of those she was likely to miss.

"The injury was a knife wound." He flexed his leg before settling his boot into the stirrup. If Phillip were able to tell her what happened in battle, would he? She guessed not.

Concerned with her sensibilities, her late husband would've kept the experiences to himself. She was wrong to ask Garrett to talk about the war. He probably thought her unladylike to inquire. Even forward. Brash.

Gripping the front of the saddle, she straightened. "I'm sorry. I shouldn't have asked."

"Don't ever think that. I want us to know each other."

Her skin suddenly warmed, and she pressed her hand to her collar. "I want that too." No, Garrett Cowlishaw was not Phillip Milburn. And as much as she'd loved Phillip, her curiosities concerning the man beside her mounted.

"It happened in a battle, but not in the kind of battle you might expect."

"I don't understand. It was an accident involving a fellow soldier?"

"Phillip no doubt joined the Union army as a patriot, convinced he was fighting for a noble cause."

"He did." His callous repetition of the stark difference between him and her late husband awakened her indignation, but she pushed it down. They needed to at least hear each other out. "Phillip believed in the *United States.* He fought and died for the freedom of all men."

Garrett nodded.

He had nothing more to say about it? Perhaps she and the captain getting to know each other wasn't such a splendid idea after all.

"As you know, I was a Confederate soldier."

"Our first point of contention."

"Yes." His horse stopped in front of the stand of dogwood trees. "There's a log over there. Mind if we sit for a spell?"

"Probably a good idea." If he got her mad enough, she was liable to twitch her ankle at the horse's side, giving Molasses the wrong idea.

He dismounted, then helped her down, and they walked the few feet to the log and seated themselves.

Garrett removed his hat and straddled the fallen tree, facing her. "Caroline, I didn't fight with my squad. Don't get me wrong. When I needed to, I fought to protect my fellow soldiers. But I didn't join the army because I agreed with their cause. It's a poor excuse and makes me sound weak, but I joined because I was afraid of my father most of my childhood. And desperate to please him."

"Your father made you go to war?"

"As far as he and my brother were concerned, I had no choice but to go in gray."

Caroline worried the seam on her calico skirt.

"A time came when I'd had enough." He slapped his hat against his leg. "My squad came upon a family of runaways."

"You were stabbed trying to capture runaway slaves?"

Garrett looked away.

Her stomach knotted. This was a mistake. She didn't want to know.

"Trying to protect them," he said.

Her breath caught. "Trying?"

Tears brimmed in his eyes. "He was a boy. Thirteen."

She pressed her hand to his tensed arm. "He didn't make it?"

His shoulders sagged. His head turned side to side like a slow pendulum.

Tears stung her eyes and burned her cheeks. "But you were willing to give your life to save him." Her heart breaking, her voice cracked. "You tried to save him."

Every horrible thing she'd said to Garrett when they first met assaulted her like fiery arrows.

She'd treated him like a criminal. Like an enemy. Why, she'd all but accused him of personally killing her husband.

She slid her fingers down his arm and gripped his hand. "I was awful to you. Can you ever forgive me?"

Giving her hand a gentle squeeze, Garrett looked her in the eye. "I already have." He let go. "Caroline, there's something more you should know about me if we are to spend more time together." He glanced at the horses. "Together like this, I mean."

Drawing in a deep breath, she nodded.

"I was married. Corliss and I were married only months before I went to war."

Was married. Were married. "Your wife died? All the time I was grieving the loss of Phillip, you knew what it was like . . . how I felt?"

"My grief wasn't the same. My wife didn't die; she left me."

She followed his gaze to the closest tree, where two squirrels scampered up the trunk and out onto a limb.

"Corliss said she wanted nothing to do with a traitor."

"I'm so sorry." Her head was beginning to understand what her heart had apparently already known—Garrett was indeed a man she admired. A man she could love.

28

Tuesday morning, Garrett looked out over the Kansas River, just west of Independence. After driving through the jumping-off city yesterday, the Company had camped on the riverbank. Today, a small paddle wheeler would carry the wagons across the river two at a time.

The Becks were to be first. Caleb guided Emery, Irene, and their animals onto the flat deck of the ferry, while Frank directed Arven and Lorelei with their wagon.

In order to place a couple of his men on the other bank early, Garrett waved Boney and Isaac into line with the chuck wagon behind Tom and Mary Alice Brenner's mishmash conveyance. The rest of the Company would have more time on the bank while waiting for the little boat to cross and return. But still it was important they all line up and ready their wagons for the river.

Feeling a bit like Noah with his ark, Garrett lined up the remaining wagons two by two. He motioned for Caroline and Rhoda Kamden to pull the farm wagon up behind the Renglers' tidy wagon. He had decided to separate the Kamden wagons. One, because of the added weight of the Conestoga and the large family. Two, because something wasn't quite right with Davonna, and Ian would have his hands full caring for his mother. Oliver Rengler would help Mrs. Kamden and Caroline keep track of the children. Ian Kamden and his mother would ride over in the Conestoga with Rutherford, his family, and their smaller wagon.

The Gobens would ferry over with the Le Beaus. The Pembertons with the Zanzucchis. Once everyone had been safely transported, he and Tiny would ferry over with the supply wagon.

The paddle wheeler worked against the flow, crossing the river at an angle. Its little steam engine grunted and puffed great clouds of smoke and mist. When the Becks started across, Garrett walked the muddy ruts toward the river until he came to the chuck wagon.

Holding a strip of jerky in one hand, Boney pushed his flop hat back on his head. "The line's lookin' good, Boss."

Garrett gave him a quick nod. "So far. Just wishin' this was the last load over and not the first."

"Me too." Boney bit off the end of the jerky stick. "There's no doubt that river crossings have come a long way since your first two trains."

"They have. Ready-made ferries save time and keep folks and their animals dry."

Nodding, Boney looked up the line. "You done all you could to prepare the folks, and they look plenty ready to me."

It seemed so. He hoped so. Garrett glanced at the grub box. "You have any idea what would help sweeten the wait for me?"

A grin widened Boney's blue eyes. "Doughnuts. That's why you came to see me?"

"That, and your cheery self."

"Just happened to save one for you, Boss." Boney unlatched the box and pulled a sugar-coated doughnut from a sack.

Garrett took a big bite, the sweetness of sugar teasing his tongue. "You're a good man, Boney."

"Thanks. But if I didn't have my cookin' to make me so well-liked . . ."

Garrett laughed. "Those skills don't hurt you none."

"Speaking of skills . . ." Boney pushed his flop hat back on his head. "Couldn't help but see how good you were at teachin' the widow how to climb onto Anna's horse Sunday."

He'd known the teasing would come. "You didn't have enough work to keep you busy?"

Boney swallowed, his Adam's apple bobbing. "Plenty o' work. Just lookin' out for ya." He glanced up the line at the Kamdens' wagons. "For you. And for the ladies."

"Speaking of the ladies, maybe I should shift the order of things . . . put you on the ferry with the Pembertons."

"Is Miss Hattie bribin' you again for my attentions?"

Garrett laughed, earning a grunt from the lead oxen. "You know you like it."

"I do, actually. Miss Hattie is full of vim and vigor." He put the last of the jerky in his mouth. "Wouldn't mind, though, if she didn't wear such big hats."

Garrett couldn't have asked for a better mix of trail hands. Each one brought something different to the Company. He didn't know Frank very well yet, but he could always count on Boney for good food and a hearty laugh.

"Captain!" Mrs. Davonna Kamden waved both arms.

Garrett popped the last bite of sweetness into his mouth. Licking the sugar from his fingers, he took long strides toward the Conestoga. Ian had a three-legged stool in each hand and was stuffing them through the canvas opening.

"Is there a problem, ma'am?" Garrett asked Mrs. Kamden.

Ian startled, catching a chair leg on the canvas. "Captain?"

"Your mother waved me over."

Ian shrugged, then freed the chair and continued with his task.

Davonna lifted her chin. "That's what I want to know, Captain. Is there a problem?"

"Ma'am?"

"Rhoda and Miss Caroline aren't crossing the river with us."

"No ma'am." He bit his bottom lip, asking God for the right words for his explanation. Before meeting Davonna Kamden and Caroline Milburn, he'd never prayed so much. Not since the war, anyway.

"My son said you were sure to have a good reason for separating me from my grandchildren." She knotted her hands at her thick waist. "I'd like to hear it."

"Yes ma'am, I do."

Empty handed, Ian sank onto the wagon seat, giving Garrett his full attention.

Garrett glanced at the Wainwrights' wagon where Rutherford unlashed a chair from a sideboard. "The Conestoga weighs a lot. And you have a very large family."

Davonna quirked an eyebrow.

He smiled when a more palatable explanation came to mind. "Ma'am, I thought with Mrs. Wainwright having a child to care for and being *with child,* and her own dear mother being all the way in Denmark . . . Well, I thought it would be good for her to have a woman accompany her, and you seemed the perfect choice."

"Oh."

"But if you would rather—"

"No. No." She shook her hands, as if to dismiss her concerns. "I could see where I would be a help to them."

"Very well." He may have to apologize to

Rutherford and Maren later as the older woman could be a bit fussy, but hopefully she wouldn't be too smothering.

Mrs. Kamden patted his cheek. "You are a smart man, Captain."

Ian nodded, grinning, an uncharacteristic feature for his face.

Garrett brushed the brim of his hat then walked toward Caleb and Frank, who stood at the river's edge in front of the Kamdens' farm wagon. Rhoda Kamden stood off to one side visiting with Owen's wife, Sally Rengler. Oliver Rengler had little Maisie Kamden up on his shoulders. Her sweet giggles mingled with Caroline's soft laugh.

He was smart placing Oliver and Caroline on the ferry together. Oliver would look after her and the children, which was good. So why the pesky niggle in his gut?

Well, it wasn't jealousy. He wasn't that childish. Besides, Oliver was more like a kid brother to Caroline than anything else. His discomfort likely had more to do with the fact that he didn't want to leave Caroline's side. Sunday she'd rested her hand on his arm and shed tears for him. He wanted to be the one leading the wagon with her. Riding the ferry with her. Waking up next to her. The thought sent heat rushing up his neck.

Thankfully, her attention was drawn to the river. When the paddle wheeler made it to the far shore, the pilot waved the white flag and started chugging back toward them. “It looks as if it’ll be our turn before too long.” Caroline turned to him, stretching a red curl at her neck.

“Uh, yes.” *Our turn.* Garrett glanced at the gaggle of children at her side then looked into the green eyes that could easily hold him spellbound. “Be safe.”

“I intend to. The children and I are going to look for fish.” She was still fiddling with that curl.

He looked at Duff and his ever-ready rope. “No trying to lasso the fish, buddy.”

“No sir. Mither told me I have to throw my rope into the wagon before we get on.”

“Smart woman. I’ll see you all on the other side, then.” Garrett doffed his hat. “Caroline.”

Absorbing her warm smile, he walked back up the line of wagons. Time to check in with Rutherford and Maren Wainwright, and little Gabi.

Within a couple of hours, several pairs of wagons had safely made it across the river, including the two belonging to the Kamdens. A row of camps had sprouted up on the opposite bank. Boney was right—river crossings weren’t nearly as intimidating as they had been even six years ago.

The Gobens and the Le Beaus were on the ferry now, and the Pembertons and Zanzucchis were up next. All three Zanzucchi boys chased one another with sticks, the youngest wearing a splint on his right arm. Garrett shook his head, his teacher's voice ringing in his ears. *"Boys will be boys, but not in my school they won't."* At least on the road, the boys had more room to be boys.

And a doctor along to treat broken arms.

Alfonzo Jr., the eldest, dashed toward him. "We will go soon, Captain, no?"

"Lord willing. Yes. Yours is the next wagon on the ferry." Garrett glanced up the line at their wagon and watched as a chair landed at Ermalinda Zanzucchi's feet in her attempt to lash it to the wagon. Minutes ago, he'd seen the senior Alfonzo headed for the bushes.

He could send the boys to help their mother, but allowing them to expend some of their boundless energy before confining them to the boat seemed the wiser thought. With a few quick strides, Garrett approached Mrs. Zanzucchi. The petite woman spoke to the chair as if it understood Italian, her hands active in the conversation.

"Ma'am?"

He had yet to see her without a soiled apron. "Ah, Capitano." She looked at the chairs, rose onto her tiptoes, and glanced at her worn shoes. "I too wee." She spread her fingers and lowered her hand in increments.

"Too short. Yes." She smelled of tomato and oregano. "Please. Let me help." He rescued the chair from the ground and from the scolding. When he'd finished lashing the last chair onto the side of the Zanzucchis' wagon, Garrett turned back toward the river.

"Anna!"

Distant screams and whinnies followed Caleb's piercing cry.

"Captain!" Frank ran to the water's edge.

Garrett followed close behind, nearly tripping over Caleb's saddle, left on the shore. "What in the blazes is happening?"

"Don't know, Boss," Frank said.

The Pemberton and Zanzucchi families flanked them at the river's edge.

Caleb's Tennessee Pacer kicked through the river toward the ferry with him on its back, already twenty yards out from shore.

"I heard a commotion on the ferry." Charles Pemberton's hand rested on his sister's shoulder. "Then the screams started."

"Me and Caleb heard it too." Frank raised his arms. "He yanked the saddle off his horse and took off before I knew what he was doing. Rode the shore, then went in downstream from the ferry."

Garrett shielded his eyes from the sun, straining for a better look. One of the wagons hung off the edge of the flat deck. Garrett looked at Frank. "Eight and the pilot on board."

"And several horses and oxen."

"Can you see? Are they all accounted for?"

"I can't tell from here."

His heart pounding, Garrett ran into the river up to his knees with Frank close behind him.

"I don't see Miss Anna." Frank's voice faded. "Or her mother."

Garrett didn't see them either. "Lord, have mercy!"

Please, God, no.

Caleb spit and sputtered, fighting to lean forward. His Pacer's legs churned the chilled water below them. The spray gurgled up and over Caleb's shoulders, threatening to steal his breath. Stinging his eyes. He never should've read Garrett's Oregon Road guidebooks. The drowning statistics taunting him, he tightened his grip on the horse's neck.

The ride would get him to the women faster than he could swim. For as long as possible, he'd force his cramping arms and shoulders to hold on for dear life. For Anna's and her mother's lives. He'd been watching the paddle wheeler when Le Beau's quarter horses reared. The wagon shifted and Wilma Goben tumbled from the ferry's edge. He was already pulling the saddle off his horse when Anna dove into the river. He'd ridden along the shore and gone in downriver, hoping to intercept the women. They probably wouldn't be able to swim against the river's flow.

Pressing his thighs to the withers, Caleb jerked his head up, trying to catch a dry breath, desperate to get a look at the water ahead of him. He could at least see the ferry. Hopefully, the pilot would signal, direct him to Anna and her mother. First, he had to get close enough. Right now, he couldn't be but a third of the way.

The Pacer huffed and snorted, slanted against the current battling his legs. Not sure which hurt worse, his throbbing head or his aching limbs, Caleb rounded his shoulders again for a better grip on the horse's slick neck.

A swell of water caught his legs, lifting him from the horse's back and twisting him. The horse went under. So did he. They'd hit the channel, and he didn't want to bet the Pacer could manage it. Time to let the horse return to the shore.

Caleb let go and rolled free. Gasping and coughing, he rose to the surface, not far from the wide-eyed horse, which was already turning toward the shore. Caleb captured a deep breath then dug his arms into the water and swam.

Lord, help me. Help us all.

His shoulders aching, Caleb paddled furiously and kicked his legs. Pausing, he surfaced to catch his breath and check directions, blinking to clear his eyes. The ferry came into view, turned to the current, holding its position. Now to find Anna and her mother. A red bandana tied to a stick caught his eye. The pilot stood at the bow. "Over there!" He pointed the stick to Caleb's left.

Caleb tread water, looked around, and willed his

aching lungs to draw a deep breath. Suddenly, he spotted movement about ten yards upriver of him.

Anna? Or her mother? She disappeared. If he didn't hurry, she'd pass him headed downstream.

His chest felt like it could burst, but he plowed through the water, anyway. They had to be all right.

Please, Lord, spare them.

"Here!" The voice sounded a world away, but it was Anna's.

Thank God!

Her head barely above the surface, Anna bobbed in the current, one arm wrapped around her flailing mother's chest.

"She can't swim!"

"I'll take her." Before she could pull her daughter down for good, Caleb wrapped his arm around the older woman, pinning her swinging arm. But she kept wiggling and kicking, fighting his grip. "Wilma!" he shouted through the water bubbling in his face. "It's Caleb. Be still."

She still fought.

"We'll all die if you don't let me save you! Save Anna!"

The woman relaxed, her legs dangling. Paddling with his one free arm and kicking both legs, Caleb was barely able to keep their heads above water.

He had to save Anna too. But how?

Shivering and coughing, Anna looked so helpless. "Can you swim?" he shouted to her.

She nodded and slipped under the surface for one terrifying second. "Yes, but not much longer. Go. Take Mutter."

Not with Anna too tired to swim. "I can't leave you."

"Caleb!" Otto's voice.

Caleb jerked toward the ferry that had been piloted closer. Dr. Le Beau and Otto stood at the rail, holding a pole out to him. Now, all he had to do was get Wilma to the pole and talk her into grabbing it instead of his neck.

He kicked harder against the depths and lifted her up enough to keep her face out of the water. The boat and rescue pole may have been close, but they felt miles away in this test of his endurance. But Anna still needed him.

"Mrs. Goben, there's a pole. I need you to grab onto the pole."

She went limp in his arms. "I can't." The alcohol on her breath was unmistakable.

"You have to." Caleb started peeling her arms from his neck. "Anna is still in the water."

"Caleb!" Anna cried. The current was carrying her away.

"Anna!"

Otto shouted something in German. The only word Caleb understood was Wilma. But she let go of him and latched onto the pole.

As soon as the doctor and Otto had a hold of Wilma, Caleb kicked off toward Anna.

The current had carried her several more yards downstream. He forced as much out of his arms and legs as he could, yet it didn't seem enough. He still had a few yards to go when he saw Boney reach Anna from the other side.

Thank God. Caleb relaxed and waved. He'd never been so happy to see his wiry friend. He even looked forward to his teasing when this was all said and done. When Anna and her mother were both safe.

Caleb held out his hand as Boney and Anna approached and helped carry her to the boat.

29

"You are well?" Großvater glanced at Mutter then returned his attention to Anna. "Both of you?"

"Yes." They had survived. But she was a long way from feeling *well.*

"You can take care of her?" he asked.

Anna gave a curt nod, taking the lead rope from him.

"I'll help the Le Beaus then." Großvater wasted no time trotting off to the hobbled wagon.

Anna gave the rope a tug. The wagon groaned as its wheels slogged through the mud, voicing her sentiments. The blanket Mrs. Le Beau had wrapped her in was now soaked through. She was wet, cold, tired, and angry. And all the hugs and celebration hadn't helped any.

Out of the mud and now on dry soil, Anna trudged toward the camp.

Yes, she would take care of Mutter. It was what she did. That, and pretend her caring was enough. Pretend Mutter's condition was temporary, that everything would be all right.

But everything wasn't all right. Mutter wasn't all right, and neither was she.

Anna knew the truth. Worst of all, she could no longer ignore it. She could no longer pretend she could live with the lies. She wasn't strong enough to bear Mutter's grief. Not with the weight Mutter had given it.

The day she'd called off the wedding, Mutter had called her careless and she was right. Anna had been a fool to think she could change her mother. Only God could do that. Mrs. Brantenberg had told the quilting circle He was the only One who always saw and always heard; that He could heal a broken heart. So why wasn't He helping Mutter?

When the wagon shuddered and creaked and the oxen groaned, she slowed her steps.

Mutter caught up to Anna, matching her pace. "We have much to be thankful for, dear."

Anna couldn't look at her. "Thankful it wasn't our wagon that slammed onto the rail and broke a wheel?"

"Yes. That, and we saw the good Lord has indeed blessed us with dear friends."

"Strong, wet friends." Anna spoke over her shoulder. "Friends who risked their lives for us."

Mutter's feet sloshed in oversized boots. She'd lost her shoes to the river, and Maren had brought a pair of Rutherford's to the shore for her. "I was frightfully scared."

"So was I, Mutter." Yes, petrified to face the truth.

"Dear, you were brave to jump in after me."

"On the other side of the river . . ." Anna was talking more to herself than to Mutter, her voice low. "While Großvater and I were visiting with the others, waiting for our turn to cross, you went into the wagon." She stopped and faced Mutter.

"I'm sorry I scared the horses and scared you." Mutter looked back toward the river. "I didn't mean to."

She never meant to.

Anna drew in a fortifying breath. "I didn't see any bottles in Independence, but you bought drink in the city. When you bought the beeswax. I thought I smelled whiskey on your breath when we were boarding the ferry, but I refused to think you'd do such a thing."

Mutter shook her head, water spraying from her stringy, wet hair. "Anyone can trip. Remember that time we were at the parade and you stumbled over a curb?"

Anna was done giving her the benefit of the doubt. "You didn't just lose your balance, Mutter. You staggered into those horses and spooked them." Anna shivered. "I hate to think what could've happened. I could've lost you."

"But you didn't. We're fine."

Anna swallowed hard past the lump in her throat. Caleb and Boney had risked their lives to save her and Mutter. What would she say to them? To the Le Beaus? And the captain? Did they know Mutter had been drinking?

Anna led the four oxen to the line of wagons that had formed. When their wagon was in position, she climbed up to the seat and set the brake. "Mutter, you can go in and change your clothes."

Mutter looked Anna over from her soggy bonnet to her soaked boots. "What about you, dear?"

"I'm fine." Another lie. Had they ever told each other the truth? "First, I need to see to the yokes and take the animals to the corral." She climbed back to the ground and slid in behind the oxen.

Mutter nodded, then climbed up onto the seat. "I'm sorry."

Anna shrugged the blanket off onto the wagon's wheel and bent to unhook the chains.

When the four animals were free of the tongue, she pulled the yoke pins and guided the heavy beam to the ground. Then she led the oxen to the open grass and hobbled the bull. Now it was her turn to peel off her wet clothes and warm herself before the sun completely disappeared.

A small fire burned a few feet from the wagon. Mutter wasn't outside. She wouldn't have lit a fire. That was always Großvater's job or Anna's. Anna glanced up the line to where Oliver stood, a wide grin on his face. He had built the fire for her. She waved her thanks and stepped up the spokes onto the top of the front wheel.

Climbing onto the seat, Anna peered into the wagon. A candle lantern glowed atop the salt barrel. Mutter sat on her trunk, dressed in a dry skirt and shirtwaist, her hair up in a twist.

When she let out a belch, Anna saw that Mutter held the neck of a flat-sided bottle—a whiskey bottle.

Anna scrambled over the seat and into the wagon. "You're drinking? You could have drowned! I could have drowned trying to save you, and you're drinking?"

"I was cold. Just needed a couple swallows to warm me."

"You think it can make you forget what happened? What you did?" Anna wrenched the bottle from Mutter's grip and stomped to the front of the wagon. Leaning over the seatback, she reached through the flap and tossed the bottle at the fire. The bottle hit the rocks and shattered, causing a fireball to rise, filled with smoke and steam. She turned back to face Mutter.

Mutter stood, clinging to the ribs of the wagon, her face twisted and her eyes bulged. "What did you do?"

"What I should've done a year ago." Anna jerked the lid open on her mother's trunk and dug until she found another bottle. After stomping to the wagon seat, she repeated her actions. While the glass crashed and the foul liquor went up in flames, the heat from the explosion warmed her face and fueled her determination to find all of it this time.

Her heart pounding, Anna climbed back through the puckered opening and searched another of the crates she'd seen Mutter hover around. When Anna found another bottle, she sent it to the same fate as the others. Her face still hot from the flames, she returned to Mutter. All she could do was stare, her whole body quivering.

"That's the last one," Mutter cried. "You don't know what it's like."

"What? Losing someone you love? When you lost your son, I lost my mother. I'm still alive, Mutter. What about me?"

Her lips pressed together, Mutter charged past Anna and out over the seat. She should stop her from going out on her own. Protect her. Care for her. But she wasn't strong enough.

Instead, Anna sank to the floorboard, letting her tears fall.

• • •

Caleb followed Wilma Goben, keeping distance between them. Wearing a dark skirt and shirt-waist, her hair pinned up in a loose twist, she ducked behind the back row of wagons toward a tree-lined draw.

While waiting for his dry clothes to cross the river in the supply wagon, he'd decided to go to Otto's wagon and check on Anna and her mother. He'd just escaped the mob at the paddle wheeler when he heard breaking glass and a loud *whoosh.* At the Gobens' camp, a ball of flames shot into the air. Plumes of smoke followed. After the second plume, he was close enough to their camp to see Anna climb out onto the seat and toss something into the fire.

No one had to tell him what had happened. Instead of burying her mother's bottles this time, she'd sent them to the fire. In the river, he'd smelled the liquor on Wilma Goben's breath. He'd seen Anna storm away from the shore. She'd held the lead rope taut, pulling the oxen as if they were her burden to bear.

She knew her mother had been drinking and caused the trouble out on the river.

Now, Caleb followed Wilma Goben into the draw, fighting his trembling insides. Where was she going?

Away. He knew from experience all she wanted was to get away from herself. From those she'd hurt. From anyone who knew her.

And this was his fault. He'd had his suspicions before they'd ever left Saint Charles. He should've told Anna he'd seen her carry a sack toward Blanchette Creek and bury what he guessed were whiskey bottles. Instead, he'd let Anna and her mother hold on to secrets that could've claimed their lives. Only God knew what would happen to Wilma Goben now if he didn't stop her.

Mud from the river bottom weighted his wet boots just as surely as the Saint Charles memory tugged his heart. Wilma kept moving, her pace as unsteady as her gait. The setting sun would soon give way to twilight.

Following directly behind her, he took longer strides. "Ma'am. It's Caleb."

She jerked, losing her balance. Mrs. Goben fell, landing in a heap on the sandy bottom of the wash.

"You've had a busy day, ma'am." When she made no effort to stand, Caleb sank his knees into the sand beside her. "Your hair is still wet, and the sun is sinking fast. Why are you out here?"

"You're out here. I might ask you the same question. Why?"

"I followed you."

She huffed, then pushed a thicket of graying brown hair behind her ear and looked at him. "It wasn't enough that you saved me from the deep?"

"I don't know. Was it?"

She looked everywhere but at him. “What do you know about it?”

“It?”

“Drinking. That’s why you’re here.”

“I know some about it, ma’am. Too much.” Caleb drew in a deep breath and let it out. “I had a problem with the drink myself.”

“That’s what you think I have?”

“You don’t?”

“That’s what Anna told you, that I have a drinking problem?”

“I didn’t talk to your daughter.”

She repositioned her skirt to cover her bare feet.

“I saw the flames in your firepit. Then I saw you running away from the wagon, and I wanted to be certain you were all right.”

Wilma Goben crossed her arms, staring at the sand and sagebrush surrounding them. “Why should I tell a stranger anything?”

“Because he pulled you out of the river?”

“But you weren’t on that ferry. You don’t know anything about what happened.”

He sighed. Nothing about this day had been easy. “That’s right, ma’am. I wasn’t on the ferry. Not when I saw you go overboard.”

“I was feeling a little dizzy with the boat moving on the water and all. I lost my balance and fell into that doctor’s flighty horses.” Wilma sighed. “I feel bad about his wagon.”

He'd heard from Le Doc that she was unsteady and had gotten too close to the horses.

"You were so kind to come in after us," she said, continuing. "You and Boney. Angels, both of you."

"I can't speak for Boney, ma'am, but I'm no angel." She was looking at him, but she still wouldn't look him in the eye. "We care about you and your daughter."

She pinched her bottom lip between her teeth. "The doctor's wagon, is it all right?"

"A wheel broke up and was lost in the river. All that's left is the hub and a couple of spokes."

Her lips pressed together, she shook her head.

"You could've drowned." His voice cracked. "Your daughter could've drowned trying to save you." He'd deal with those emotions later. Right now, he didn't want to let Wilma Goben off the hook. He was desperate for her to see the damage her drinking could do. Before it was too late.

Before she allowed liquor to stand between her and her duty.

Before she let down everyone who trusted her . . . everyone she cared about.

"My vater is helping the doctor with his wagon?" she asked.

"Yes." Caleb swallowed the memory of coming out of his stupor and finding Billy and the others in his squad dead. He had to do what he could for Anna's mother. "My guess is you started drinking after your son died."

She looked up, her chin quivering. “You know about Dedrick?”

“Boney told me they were good friends, that Dedrick died in the war.”

She pressed her hand to her cheek as a mother would to her child’s face. “Dedrick was a good boy. When he died, I felt so empty. It’s a cold life without my son. The drink, it warms and soothes the ache inside.”

He nodded. “I know how that feels. To lose someone you love, and all you want to do is forget.” A shiver raced up his spine. “To feel better. Warm again.”

Tears streamed down her face.

Caleb blinked hard against his own tears. “Before the war, I had big plans. I was going to be a preacher. Then something happened that hurt me deeply, and I soon started drinking with friends.”

“It wasn’t like that for me. I did it on my own.”

“Ma’am.”

She finally looked him in the eye, her face drawn and gaze teary.

“For some of us, it takes catastrophe and heartbreak before we can see what the love of liquor is doing to us. And to the people we say we love.”

Wilma mumbled something under her breath and wiped her eyes.

“Please, Mrs. Goben, don’t let that happen to

you." Caleb pressed his hand to her forearm. "Stop imbibing before there's any more heart-break."

"Turns out you're not a stranger, after all."

"No ma'am."

Not a stranger to any of it, which concerned him. His father had said the same words to him on the back pew of his church, and he hadn't heeded the warning.

30

Her tears spent, Anna put on dry clothes and grabbed Mutter's shawl. Mutter had left the wagon without it. Without supper. In her stockinged feet. She pulled Mutter's only other pair of shoes from her trunk. Großvater hadn't come to the wagon yet. He was probably still busy trying to make things right for the Le Beaus. If she didn't see to Mutter, who would?

Anna pulled the candle lantern from the top of the salt barrel. Her hands full, she set the supplies on the end of the seat then climbed out. She'd hoped Mutter would have returned by now, but she hadn't, and it would soon be nightfall. The footfalls she'd heard when Mutter ran away had come from behind the wagons, so that was where she would start.

The Boone's Lick Company's policy probably indicated that she should contact the captain in such situations, but she wasn't in the mood for a fuss. Or for offering any explanations as to why Mutter had gone off with wet hair and no shoes at dusk. Besides, there was a strong chance Mutter hadn't made it as far as the riverbank before propping herself against a rock to practice her speech.

She'd taken her last drink. She'd never tip a bottle again. And that was a promise. She'd never meant to hurt her baby girl. It pained her to know that I'd lost my mother to grief . . . to the bottle. How awful. Knowing that would make all the difference. She would choose her daughter over the bottle. Without hesitation.

Tears brimmed Anna's eyes. The first part of the speech she'd heard before. The second part was just as much a lie. It was all just empty words. In the meantime, Mutter could be asleep under a tree somewhere without so much as a shawl to wrap around her. Or she could be lost.

Either way, it was Anna's job to take care of Mutter. Raising the candle, she trudged toward the trees. But she hadn't walked more than ten steps before the mental image of a bear walking away with the Kamdens' grub box stopped her. They were still in Missouri, or at least close to its edge. What if there was a bear out here?

No need to think the worst. That had nearly

happened on the river. She could've lost Mutter altogether.

The brisk night air chilled her neck, making her grateful her hair had dried quickly. Or maybe it was remembering the bear's roar that gave her gooseflesh. She tried to tug her shawl tight with her hands full and dropped the boots. Anna had bent to pick them up when she heard Mutter's voice. And Caleb's too?

Straightening, she looked up, toward a sandy draw. Mutter walked her direction, resting her arm on Caleb's.

Relief swept over Anna. She sighed. She'd never misjudged anyone as she had Caleb. He'd been her rescuer—not once today, but twice. This time, how had he known they needed rescuing?

Mutter waved with her free hand.

"Where did you go?" Anna asked.

Mutter let go of Caleb's arm. "For a walk."

Anna looked at Caleb, his shirt still wet and clinging to his chest. "Where did you find her?"

"She was in the draw."

"How did you know?"

"I was coming to the wagon to check on the two of you when I saw your mother heading that way." Caleb brushed wet hair back from his face. "I followed her to make sure she was all right."

"Thank you." Did he think Mutter was all right? Had he any idea of her bad habit? Keeping her questions to herself, Anna turned her attention to

Mutter. "We'd best get these boots on you. Then we'll go have some supper before we rest."

"Yes. This has been a long day."

Second longest. She had been sure the day she learned her brother had died would never, ever end.

When Mutter had laced her boots, she looked up at Caleb. "Thank you for everything, Mr. Reger."

"Yes ma'am." He looked at Anna and opened his mouth as if to say something but didn't.

"I'll see her to the wagon. It's not that far. Thank you. Again." Anna dipped her chin then cupped Mutter's elbow. After watching Caleb turn toward the river, she started walking to the wagon.

"He's a nice young man, Anna." Mutter lifted her shoulders in a deep breath. "Very helpful too."

"Oh?"

"Yes. He sat with me for a while, you know."

"Did you talk?"

"Of course we did. I *can* be sociable, now and again." Mutter snickered. "Especially with someone like him."

"Someone like him?" Compassionate and protective. A lifesaver.

"He knows life can be cold, dear, and that drink can warm and soothe the ache inside."

Anna faltered and nearly dropped the candle lantern. "Caleb? He said that?" They couldn't be talking about the same man. Caleb didn't drink. He couldn't.

"Yes dear. He said he, too, drinks for the same reasons."

Mutter wouldn't make up that kind of story. She'd been encouraging Anna to consider Caleb. And he'd already begun to draw her affections.

"Don't look so distressed. He knows drinking is a habit that can cause heartache, and we're going to help each other do better."

Anna's throat burned. Mutter was family. She had to listen to Mutter's speeches, but Caleb could keep his to himself.

By the time the paddle wheeler inched toward the west bank of the river, Garrett was fit to be tied. Not only had two of the paying travelers gone into the water, so had two of his trail hands. How was he to keep everyone safe in that kind of chaos?

The Le Beaus' hobbled wagon sat on the shore with several men huddled around it. But a disabled wagon was the least of his worries. He could have lost them all.

When the wet Pacer at his side whinnied, Garrett looked past the crowd to where Caleb stood up on the bank. He'd start with the young man who took off into the water on his horse and contend with Boney later.

As soon as the ferry grounded and the plank swung down, Garrett barreled off the boat, holding the lead rope for Caleb's Pacer.

"Boss." Caleb took the rope from him and

hugged the horse's neck. "Thanks for bringing him over. My saddle?"

Garrett looked at the wagon trailing him. "Tiny's got it on the supply wagon."

Caleb pulled his wet shirt out from his chest. "My dry clothes too."

Garrett nodded. "The Gobens? How are they faring?"

"The women are fine, Boss. Safe at their wagon."

"And Boney?"

"Ornery as ever. Already cooking."

Garrett glanced at the Le Beaus' wagon.

"They're fine too. Le Doc's wife, daughter, and the children are with thc Pembertons for supper." Caleb pointed to the Pemberton camp. "Otto Goben helped Arven Beck pull what was left of the hub off the wagon. The rest of the men are retying his load while they wait for Tom Brenner to bring a new wheel. He should be able to get one at a small settlement up the road."

"They'll have it ready to roll by morning?"

"That's what they said."

Garrett watched his stallion pass, tethered to the back of the supply wagon. "There's more I need to know."

Caleb's brow creased. "Boss?" He had yet to look Garrett in the eye.

"Looked to me like somebody was throwin' kerosene on their fire. What do you know about that?"

The trail hand looked away.

Garrett gripped Caleb's elbow. "I have my suspicions, but you need to tell me what you know." He let go. "For all our sakes, including Anna's."

"It was liquor. Anna found some bottles in her mother's things and tossed them into the fire."

"Wilma Goben had been drinking before she boarded the paddle wheeler, hadn't she?"

Caleb nodded. "After Anna tossed the bottles, her mother ran away. I followed her into the draw. We had a good conversation."

"You told her you know about her drinking?"

"I did. Yes. And I think, at least, I hope the frightening events of the day were enough to scare her into temperance."

"I'm afraid you may be a little naive when it comes to drunks."

A shadow darkened Caleb's eyes. "I know more than I should, sir."

Garrett was more curious than ever about his trail hand's family history, but he couldn't get into it right now. Too much to tend to before twilight left them with only moonlight and candles to work with.

"So much as a hint of her hittin' the bottle again, and the Gobens are headed back to Missouri with the first go-backers we see."

Caleb set his jaw. Ready to admit it or not, everyone knew he was sweet on Anna Goben.

It made no difference to Garrett how Caleb felt about Anna. It couldn't matter. Not to a leader who had close to four dozen folks to look out for. "You know what her mother did. She put everyone and everything on that ferry in harm's way. And you know as well as I do that because of her drinking, her daughter, you, and Boney could have lost your lives."

Caleb rolled the lead rope around his hand. "But we didn't."

"This time."

"They'll be all right, Boss. Anna saw to it her mother doesn't have any liquor left in the wagon."

"Until she talks someone else out of theirs or we reach an outpost."

"We need to keep a closer watch on her, is all."

"Well, it won't be you or Boney doin' it. You two are heading out to do some scouting. Thursday or Friday. I'll let you know when I decide which it is."

His jaw tight, Caleb nodded and then walked his horse toward the pasture where the others grazed their animals.

Caleb and Boney both had too much emotion invested in the Goben family to be objective. Garrett needed to be the one to keep watch after the Gobens, starting first thing in the morning. In the meantime, he'd check the progress on the wheel.

• • •

Tuesday evening, Caroline sat on the floorboard, wedged between her trunk and a barrel. The friendship album quilt from the Saint Charles quilting circle warmed her legs. Her bent knees held the journal that supported a sheet of stationery.

Davonna Kamden, having grown tired of her knitting, lay on her horsehair mattress repeating the Twenty-third Psalm.

"The LORD is my shepherd; I shall not want."

Maisie's peaceful face glowed in the lamplight. Lyall and Duff had finally drifted off to sleep too.

"He leadeth me beside the still waters . . ."

The verse brought to mind the day's events. The water was anything but still when Anna and her mother disappeared into its depths.

Oliver had been helping her and Rhoda set the wagon when shouts from the bank summoned those who had already crossed back to the river's edge. Caroline had watched in breathless dread as they'd lost sight of Wilma Goben. Then Anna. And watched in relief as Caleb and Boney reached Anna and her mother and brought them to safety. She'd celebrated with the others as all four boarded the ferry, dripping wet and chilled but alive. Safe.

"Yea, though I walk through the valley of the shadow of death . . ."

Caroline had heard the talk on the riverbank. It was no surprise to hear the proclamations that Wilma Goben liked her drink. Caroline had lived in her brother-in-law's house for too long not to recognize the signs. She'd piggy-backed on her sister's sorrow, trying to protect the family secret. Time after time, she'd heard Jewell make excuses for Jack. Before long, she'd started doing the same thing. To protect the family. But from what? Secrecy didn't change the truth, and shrouding it in darkness only added loneliness and fear to the hiding.

Poor Anna.

"Thy rod and thy staff they comfort me . . ."

Caroline smoothed the stationery and dipped the quill.

My Dear Sister, Jewell,

Hattie started writing the quilting circular yesterday. We will all add to it. But I wanted to pen a more personal letter for you alone.

I hope you and the children are well. Jack, too. In fact, I pray he is better.

Was it too much to hope he was less crabby, kinder now that she was gone?

I am well. Except for missing my family, I am feeling better than I have felt since Phillip left for the war. Most days, we travel fifteen to twenty miles. The walking is doing me good. Seeing the beauty of God's vast creation warms my heart as the sun warms my skin. Having the three youngest Kamden children and their grandmother to care for is at times a great challenge, but the work gives me purpose. And—

Mrs. Kamden paused before continuing her recitation.

"Thou anointest my head with oil; my cup runneth over . . ."

Jewell, this past Sunday, I went for a horseback ride. With Garrett Cowlishaw. Yes, the very same man I rebuked when, a stranger, he stopped to help us with the broken wagon wheel. Garrett and I will ride again this Sunday, weather permitting.

Caroline stilled her hand and moistened her lips. Oh, how she wished her sister were here for a chat over tea. She had so much to share with her. Trying to sort her thoughts, she dipped the quill again.

I feel a change, Sister. I loved Phillip and gave him my heart. Some might say that because Phillip died, my heart is mine to give again. But thinking about another man with affection feels foreign. And wonderful.

Do you think it wrong for me to want to love and be loved again?

31

The memory of Anna's face the night before, wrought with fear and pain and then relief drove Caleb up the line of wagons toward the Goben camp.

The past several days had passed in a swirl of early morning chats with Anna, reports of thefts, Sunday supper with Anna, countless interruptions, river rescues, and pep talks. All since he'd made the decision to tell Anna the truth and all since he and Anna kissed on Saturday. Truth was, he was long overdue for another kiss.

He cared deeply for Anna despite his resolve not to. He might even have loved her. The problem was Anna's family depended on her for their well-being and there might not be a permanent place for him in her life. He admired her commitment to her mother and her grandfather, but it was wrong for them to expect so much of her.

Anna deserved a life of her own, of her choosing, regardless of what her mother decided to do with hers. Wilma Goben would either let yesterday's frightening river incident and his frank talk with her in the draw help her change her course, or she wouldn't.

Either way, he couldn't stand by and let Anna end up like Billy and the others in his squad—victims of his disastrous choices. Anna needed to know the truth about him, so she could see what her mother's bad habit could . . . would do to her.

The campfire at the Gobens' wagon was abandoned. The yoke was empty. Anna's hammock was down, and breakfast things were set out on the table, so the women had to be close by. Caleb stood still, listening. He didn't hear any voices on the other side of the canvas, so perhaps Anna had stepped away for a moment.

A sudden groan drew him closer to the wagon.

"Anna?" Wilma's weak voice sounded a mile away. "Is that you, Anna?"

"No ma'am. It's Caleb Reger."

"Oh. I'm afraid I'm under the weather today." Another groan. "Do you see Anna?"

"No ma'am. I thought maybe she was in with you."

"I haven't seen her yet this morning. I can't blame her. I caused a lot of trouble yesterday."

"I heard you groaning. Are you in pain?"

"My head is pounding something fierce."

Caleb nodded as if she could see him through the canvas.

"What are you doing here?" Anna's voice behind him sounded as if she'd run into Skins, not a man she'd kissed just days ago. "My mother is still in bed."

Caleb turned. "Yes. I mean I knew she was still in the wagon." He swallowed. "I came to check on her. To see you."

Anna set a full bucket on the ground beneath the water barrel. "Now is not a good time." She wasn't looking at him.

"What's wrong? What happened?"

Her shoulders squared; her lips pressed together.

"Anna, I understand you being upset."

"You do?"

"Yes, of course I do." He took a step toward her. "You had a very trying day. And night."

"And now I have work to do." She backed away, still avoiding his gaze.

"I can help. Let me help."

"Not this time." Anna wiped her hands on her apron. "Please go."

"But—"

"Please."

"Very well. If that's what you truly want."

"It is."

His throat tightening, Caleb brushed the brim of his hat. "I'd ask the good doctor if he has any catnip herbs in his apothecary. Catnip tea might help your mother with her sick headache."

Her jaw set, Anna spun and walked to the box at the back of the wagon.

That was his answer. There was little chance he'd have a permanent place in Anna's life. She'd chosen to take the weight of her mother's bad habit on her shoulders. He couldn't compete with Anna's dogged determination to do what she deemed right by her family. He couldn't argue with Anna's need to fix her mother, to try to protect her. He'd watched his sister try to do the same for him.

But it wasn't *his* past that had come between him and Anna, it was her present.

"Anna," Mutter called.

Anna sighed. She wasn't in the mood for conversation. Not with Caleb Reger. Not with Mutter.

"Anna. Come here, please."

Against her will, if she had any, Anna climbed up the spokes of the wheel and knelt on the wagon seat. "What is it, Mutter?" She didn't bother to whisper. "Großvater will be back soon with the oxen, and I need to get his breakfast."

She looked through the puckered opening in the canvas. Mutter lay on her side in the hammock, holding her head. "Why were you so rude to Caleb? And after all the nice things he's done for us."

Tears stung Anna's eyes. She couldn't tell

Mutter the truth—that she now wanted nothing to do with him because of his drinking. Why she still cared about Mutter's feelings after all the pain she'd caused, Anna couldn't say, but she did. Blinking back the tears, Anna stood. "I'm taking care of you and Großvater. Isn't that enough?"

Mutter groaned. "Don't you want more?"

She did. "Not with Caleb, I don't." Not anymore. "Now, while you rest, I'm going to see the doctor."

"Good morning, Anna." Captain Cowlishaw's voice came from behind her.

She wondered how long it would be before he showed up to revisit yesterday's happenings. She turned and climbed off the wagon.

"Good morning, Captain."

"You said you were going to see the doctor?"

"Yes. For some catnip for tea."

"You have a headache?"

"It's Mutter. After all the excitement yesterday—"

"Yes, I'll need to speak to her about that."

"I'm afraid she's not feeling well this morning."

He stepped up to the wheel and spoke into the canvas. "Ma'am, I need to have a word with you."

Anna raised her chin a notch. "My mother is still in her bed."

"It is official business, Anna. I must speak to her."

Her shoulders sagging, Anna nodded. Perhaps

it was best they were turned around and sent packing. Not seeing Caleb every day wouldn't lessen the pain she felt, but it would make letting go of him easier.

"Mutter, you need to come out," Anna called.

Mutter groaned. "Give me a moment, Captain."

"Yes ma'am." He turned toward Anna. "If you'd like to go find the doctor, I can see to your mother."

"Yes. I will do that and return shortly." She'd done all she could for Mutter, and now it was time Mutter faced the consequences for her actions. If nothing else made a difference, perhaps confrontation by authority and the public humiliation that went along with it would.

When Anna returned to the wagon a few minutes later, Mutter sat on the seat alone, her head in her hands. Anna pulled a tin cup from the wagon box and filled it with steaming hot water from the kettle that hung over the campfire. While it steeped, she carried the cup to the wagon.

Mutter looked up, her eyes red and her cheeks wet with tears. "This is so hard."

Anna's breath caught. Was Mutter going to tell her they couldn't go on with the caravan; that she'd lost Anna's chance to go west with her friends? To start a new life there?

She set the cup on the seat and climbed up.

Mutter looked at her. "Did you see the doctor? Did he give you what Caleb said?"

“Yes.” Anna picked up the cup and sat beside Mutter. “What did the Captain say?”

Mutter took the cup from her. “He wanted to know what happened to me yesterday. On the ferry.”

“What did you tell him?”

Mutter took a sip from the cup and wrinkled her nose as she swallowed. “I told him I lost my balance.”

Anna sighed.

“Then I told him I was frightened to cross the river and that I took a little whiskey to settle my nerves.”

“You did?”

“Yes.” Mutter drank more of the headache remedy. “But he already knew I’d been drinking.”

“What else did he say?”

“That he couldn’t allow me to put the whole company at risk because of my reckless behavior.”

Anna’s chest tightened. “We have to turn around, go back to Saint Charles, don’t we?”

Mutter huffed. “No, dear. All the captain said was that if I take another drink of alcohol, we will have to leave the caravan.” She drained the cup and looked at her. “Is that what you want? Do you want to turn around?”

“No.” Anna shrugged. “I don’t know what I want.”

“That was apparent when you chased that nice young man off with your foul mood.”

"Never mind that." Anna drew in a deep breath. "Did you tell the captain about Caleb?"

"No, dear. That's not my place."

"But you told me."

"I only told you because you are my daughter, and you have feelings for him."

Feelings she now had to deny. For her own sake.

32

Friday morning, under the coral ribbons of dawn, Anna rolled her hammock and tucked it into the wagon. Mutter sat on a trunk wearing a fresh dress. Looking uncharacteristically peaceful, she pulled a brush through her hair.

"Mutter?"

She turned toward the opening and smiled at Anna. "Good morning, dear."

"You're out of bed?"

"The horn sounded, and there's breakfast to fix and things to do."

"Yes." The same thing had been true the last two mornings, but Mutter had spent them both in bed. In fact, she'd been sequestered in the wagon since the incident at the Kansas River. Anna climbed into the wagon. "Your headache?"

"Is all better." Mutter sounded bright and

clear. "I feel good today. Except that I am so hungry. I think we should have potatoes with our sausage." She raised her hairbrush. "I'll make popovers too. You said you brought Emilie's receipt with you?"

"Yes, but—"

Mutter raised her hand. "Really, dear, I'm fine now."

Neither of them had spoken a word about the bottles Anna had thrown into the fire. She wanted to believe that was behind them now. And not another breath had been spent discussing Caleb Reger either. But it didn't mean she hadn't thought about him.

Mutter pinned up her hair and tied a yellow calico bonnet at her neck. "You've been working so hard. You need to let me help."

Anna nodded, starting to believe for the first time in a long while that Mutter *could* help.

"You take your time, dear." Mutter climbed out over the seat, then looked back in at Anna. "You and Vater have been doing all the work the past few days. I intend to pull my weight."

Anna knelt at the washbowl atop the salt barrel and splashed water on her face. Refreshed, she toweled her face dry. Next, she pulled a cotton skirt and shirtwaist from her trunk.

Pots and pans jangled just outside in the wagon box. It felt good to have a break, to not be the one doing the work and making the noise. She wanted to feel as confident as Mutter did that Mutter was ready to face the day's tasks. Anna knew she had no choice but to let Mutter try.

In the meantime, she would spend her extra minutes readying herself this morning. She may even take the time to plait her hair.

While Anna dressed and tidied the wagon, sausage sizzled over a cookfire and the aroma of potatoes and onions wafted in through the canvas and set her stomach to growling. She couldn't recall the last time Mutter had cooked a full meal. Long before they'd left Saint Charles.

Anna pulled her bonnet from the hook on one of the bows framing the wagon and set it on her head. As she tied the ribbons, she heard the plodding footsteps of the ox team approaching.

"Tochter." Großvater had returned from the pasture.

"*Guten morgen*, *Vater*!"

"*Guten morgen*!" Großvater's voice echoed the surprise in Anna's heart. "Is our Anna sick?"

"Anna is well, only slower than I am this morning."

Straightening her bonnet, Anna poked her head out through the opening.

Großvater stood at the tongue, setting the yoke on the first two oxen. He looked up at her.

"Mutter is right," Anna said. "I can't keep up with her this morning."

His eyebrows arched.

Anna climbed over the seat and down from the wagon. "Mutter is feeling better."

Großvater glanced at the steaming skillet on the cookfire then at the worktable, where Mutter rolled out dough. "My tochter is cooking?"

A smile edged Mutter's lips. "Vater, I was cooking long before I ever birthed Anna." She shook her head.

Großvater chuckled as he backed the two lead oxen into place. "I'm glad to see you remembered where you had hidden your spunk."

Mutter held up a wooden spoon and twirled it between her fingers.

Anna giggled. Instantly, Mutter and Großvater had taken her back in time to one of their prewar sparring matches.

"Good morning, folks."

Anna looked up to see Garrett Cowlishaw walking up the line toward them.

"Good morning, Captain." Mutter wiped her hands on her apron. "You're just in time for break-fast."

He sniffed the air. "Makes we wish I hadn't already eaten, ma'am. Smells real good."

"Perhaps the next time you come to check on me."

Garrett removed his slouch hat. "Yes ma'am. I'd like that."

Anna met the captain's gaze. "She is feeling better than she has in a long while."

Großvater stepped away from the yoked oxen. "My tochter is cooking. That should tell you life is good."

Garrett rolled his hat in his hands. "It does all our hearts good to see you up and about, ma'am."

"Mine too, Captain. That was one nasty ailment." Mutter removed the pan of popovers from atop the dutch oven. "But as you can see, I am alive and well."

"Yes. And I'd best let you get your breakfast. I'll see you out for the Scripture reading, then."

"We'll be there." Mutter spoke before Anna could come up with an acceptable excuse not to join the gathering.

Twenty minutes later, they'd finished eating and the three of them had worked together in the cleanup. The wagon was packed and ready to go. Anna stood with Mutter and Großvater between the Kamdens and the Zanzucchis. Caleb stood beside Garrett in front of the Company, his Bible open and his hat tucked under one arm. His hair, the color of ground coffee, dusted the collar on his denim shirt.

When he looked directly at her, she looked away. On this third day since Mutter's revelation, she didn't find it any easier to ignore him.

Caleb cleared his throat and pressed a finger to the open pages. "This morning, I will read from the Apostle Paul's letter to Ephesus in Ephesians, chapter 2, verses 8 and 9.

"For by grace are ye saved through faith; and that not of yourselves: it is the gift of God: not of works, lest any man should boast."

Caleb closed his Bible. "According to my friend Isaac Jackson"—he glanced at the freed slave standing on the sidelines—"God wouldn't have sent His Son to die to give us grace we didn't sorely need."

Anna shuddered. Was he referring to Mutter or to himself? He had to know Mutter would tell her of his problem. And now he was trying to say she needed to have more grace?

Settling back against the cantle of his saddle, Caleb studied his scouting companion and the old flop hat that shaded Boney Hughes's narrow face. Boney insisted on riding a mule, said they fit him better. As usual, Boney was chewing on some-thing. Probably jerky, since he never had to spit. How was it possible he could always be eating and not add an ounce to his girth?

Boney swung his gaze toward Caleb. "You want to talk about Anna. Go ahead."

"Tuesday night, after the boss crossed the river, he gave me a talking to. Questioned our judgment, yours and mine."

"Yeah, he chewed on me the next mornin'. Was none too happy about us takin' to the river after Anna and her mother."

"You think we had a choice?"

"Not a lick of a chance we coulda done anything else." Boney scrubbed his whiskered chin. "When I seen you take off on your horse, I knew something was wrong. Had to help."

Caleb couldn't speak for Boney, but he knew he was having trouble thinking of much else besides Anna. She was a distraction, a delight, and a frustration—all at once.

"The boss all but said me and you don't think straight when it comes to the Gobens."

Caleb nodded. Couldn't deny it was true. For him, at least. "He told me if Wilma gets to drinking again, he'd have to turn all three of them back. Can't take the chance of her causing any-body any more grief."

"I believe he'd do it." Boney's brow furrowed. "Sure don't wanna see that happen. Anna really has her heart set on a fresh start out west. And then there's you and your feelings for her."

Caleb's tension was causing a cramp in his neck, and he reached up to rub it. "There's nothing there."

"I helped with your chores all those mornings so you could be with Anna." A crooked grin lit Boney's blue eyes. "And the kiss I saw?"

"I remember." And now he wished he could forget the kiss altogether. He blew out a long breath. "For all the good my feelings are doing either of us."

"I knew somethin' must have happened. I've been seein' way too much of you."

"Has Anna said anything to you since our, uh, swim Tuesday?"

"You mean, about her mother's drinkin' and all?"

"About me."

"Anna hasn't been out and about much, and the boss is keepin' me too busy for idle chattin'." Boney shook his head. "No. What are you expectin' her to say about you?"

"I don't know. She turned me away Wednesday morning. I've been busy too, but when I have seen Anna, she's been quick to look away and busy herself. I thought we were, uh, starting to enjoy each other's company."

"This started when you discovered her mother's problem with drinkin', right?"

Caleb nodded. "Yeah. After my suspicions were confirmed, anyway."

"She's probably red-faced about the family secret bein' out."

"Anna doesn't need to feel embarrassed. Not around me."

"You tell her that?"

"I will." Caleb leaned forward as his horse climbed an incline. "First chance she gives me."

Over the rise lay a lush green valley. An ideal place for their camp tomorrow night, except for the village of tipis clustered along the creek.

Caleb pulled back on the reins, slowing his Pacer.

"Looks like we'll be sharing the valley with the mission Indians the boss told us about." Boney stopped his mule, stood in his stirrups, and looked to the horizon.

Caleb didn't see any Indian scouts, but it didn't mean they weren't there. "We've got us some pretty skittish folks. You think they'll be all right having Indians for neighbors?"

"I sure hope so, 'cause that's where we'll need to camp." Boney looked out over the valley. "I say we pay 'em a friendly visit." He pulled a slab of jerky from his pack and clicked his tongue at his mule.

Caleb took jerky from his pack too, then pulled his horse around to follow Boney's mule down a muddy path toward a stand of about twenty tipis. Women dressed in deerskins busied themselves around firepits while men dressed in elk hide stood and watched them wander in. Children wearing loincloths chased one another with sticks in some kind of a game. The scent of smoke permeated the village. Buffalo skins hung on frames, drying in direct sunlight.

Boney glanced at Caleb. "Hunters and gatherers. Nomads like us."

Caleb kept his head facing straight ahead, but his eyes were busy surveying his surroundings.

As they approached the center of the village, Boney held up the gift of jerky. "Afternoon, folks."

A trim young man wearing a felt hat stepped forward from one of the frames. When he offered a short sentence in a language Caleb didn't understand, the children ran toward Boney's mule chattering and laughing. An older man joined the young one. They each reached for one of the offered gifts.

When the younger man took the jerky from him, Caleb removed his hat and pointed at the creek. "Hope you don't mind, but we'd like to camp our wagons up the creek tonight."

The man standing beside Caleb's horse spoke undecipherable words to the man standing with the children, then smiled up at Caleb. "You make coffee then?"

Caleb nodded, chuckling inside. "Yes. You come see us. We'll have coffee at the campfire."

The older man held up his bundle of jerky and gave Boney a sort of salute before walking away, with the others falling into step. The greeting was brief, but Caleb took it as a good sign. They weren't seen as any kind of threat. And this band obviously wasn't Lakota, the tribe farther north, infamous for causing problems.

The wagon train could camp close by for the night. There didn't seem to be any hostility or fear among the villagers. If only that were true for the band of travelers known as the Boone's Lick Company.

33

Anna guided Molasses toward a hillock up the road from camp. The Indians with which the Company shared the pretty valley weren't anything like those talked about in the dime novels. The children had played with the Company's children, and several of the Indian men sat around campfires, drinking coffee and swapping stories. So far, it seemed to be Großvater's second favorite moment on the trip. The first was the previous morning, when he'd returned to camp to find Mutter cooking and sassing him.

The Company had made good time this morning, walking through a rolling countryside that held no rivers to ford and no surprises but for a large herd of antelope. Tonight, the camp would feast on roasted meat. For now, Anna saw their break for the noon meal as an opportunity for a little time to herself. She reined Molasses to a stop under a shady oak, swung to the ground, and pulled her sack from the pommel.

Looking out over the land, she could see for miles and miles and almost felt like one of the captain's scouts. This must be how Caleb felt, riding ahead and seeing the lay of the land before the others. No sign of outposts, rivers, or Indian villages today. Just a hill here, and a draw there. Off in the distance, she spotted a row of what looked like three ants wearing soiled white hats. Probably wagons belonging to go-backers. The sight reminded her of the captain's ultimatum to Mutter. If she took to the drink again, Anna's family could be counted among those returning to Saint Charles.

Anna untied a small quilt from behind the saddle and laid it out on the grassy ground. Settled on the quilt, she reached into the sack for the napkin that held her sandwich. She asked the Lord's blessing on her noon meal then unfolded the cloth. Savoring the tangy taste of Mutter's fresh sourdough bread, Anna let her mind roam the memories of the past five days. Mutter had gone from a stumbling drunken sot to someone bedridden and in need of care for two days, to a clear-headed, hard-working companion. At the same time, Caleb had fallen from lifesaver to someone who saw nothing wrong with Mutter's life. Her past life. At least, Anna hoped the drunkenness was in their past. With Mutter feeling so well lately, it was easy to believe her need for alcohol was behind her. Easy to believe that breaking those bottles set Mutter on the path to sobriety.

But then, she'd gotten rid of Mutter's bottles before. And what of Caleb's family? Was that why he hadn't returned home after the war? Because his parents and sister had emptied liquor bottles to no avail?

Anna shook her head. She needed to think about something else. Someone else. The quilting circle. That was what she needed, more time with the other women. It would be good for Mutter too. Back in Saint Charles, Thursday was the circle day. But Thursdays, like most other days, were spent walking. Sunday afternoons, however, seemed the perfect time for quilting together.

When Anna had finished her sandwich, she returned the napkin to the sack and pulled out her Bible. Since Caleb was reading God's Word each morning for the Company, her personal reading had become sporadic, lost in the rush of preparation for retiring for the day or starting a new one. Drawing in a cleansing breath, she opened to Proverbs, chapter three.

"Trust in the LORD with all thine heart; and lean not unto thine own understanding. In all thy ways acknowledge him, and he shall direct thy paths."

She leaned against the tree and closed her eyes, letting the memories of the past several weeks wash over her. Mutter had accused her of trying to be the family law, trying to protect her from herself.

"If I can't do as much, what makes you think you can?"

Indeed. Anna loosened the ties on her bonnet and let her arms drop at her sides. What made her think she could change Mutter if Großvater couldn't and God chose not to?

That was the hardest question of all. Why wasn't God changing Mutter? Or at least changing Anna's own heart so Mutter's choices wouldn't hurt so much.

Her own understanding and her path were her biggest problems. She'd make plans based upon her understanding, and then plans would change. And that would make her angry. Then she'd try harder.

She wanted to trust the Lord with her heart. With her plans. Always. That was her intention. Why was it so hard for her?

Twigs snapped behind Anna. Her eyes popped open. She slapped her Bible shut and set it on the quilt.

"Anna?"

She scrambled to her feet and faced a chestnut Tennessee Pacer. Caleb Reger sat in the saddle, looking every bit the Southern gentleman, his back perfectly straight and the reins suspended in his right hand.

"I didn't purpose to startle you, I—"

"You didn't." Anna bent to pick up her Bible and the sack, then looked up at him.

His slanted grin gave a full showing of teeth. As he pulled off his hat, a wave of hair settled on his ear.

Anna slid her Bible into the sack. “Perhaps you did startle me some. But it’s all right. I took my meal up here. Then I was reading. I’d closed my eyes to think. I was thinking.” She was talking too much.

Caleb’s grin hadn’t gone anywhere. He leaned over his saddle horn, bringing his face closer to hers.

She needed to return to camp. Now. She needed to get away from Caleb before she lost her resolve to avoid him. She didn’t like him. She couldn’t like him. Not if she wished to protect her heart. She scooped the quilt off the ground and folded it. “You shouldn’t have followed me.”

“I saw you ride ahead of the Company by yourself. When Garrett was ready to move the wagons and you hadn’t returned, I decided to come find you.” Caleb straightened and scanned the horizon. “I’m glad I did. I’ve wanted to talk to you.”

Anna swallowed the lump in her throat. After making her care about him, he’d finally decided to be honest with her, to tell her the truth about himself? Now that they’d been on the road together for nearly a month. Too late. She knew all she needed to know. Ignoring him, Anna stuffed the quilt into the sack.

He swung down from the saddle and stood directly in front of her.

She pulled Molasses’s reins from the branch.

"I was getting ready to rejoin the Company."

His jaw tightened. "You were leaning against a tree with your eyes closed, relaxed. Until you saw me. You've been avoiding me since the night I brought your mother back from the draw. Why? If you're embarrassed—"

"Embarrassed?"

"Because I know about your mother's drinking."

He really thought mere embarrassment would be enough to keep her away from the man she cared about?

"Anna, if you're feeling ill at ease because I know you broke the bottles in the fire, you needn't."

She slid the strings of the sack over the pommel, noting that the Boone's Lick Company was on the move. "I'm not embarrassed."

He blew out a deep breath. "We kissed. That meant something to me. And now, you've been avoiding me. I'm desperate to know why."

She set her foot in the stirrup and lifted herself into the saddle.

"Anna." He stepped forward, capturing the reins at Molasses's withers. "If it's not embarrassment, then what is wrong? What have I done to make you angry?"

"I had to choose." Anna glanced at the last of the wagons passing on the road below them. "We're late. With the captain's talk of buffalo stampedes, prowling cougars, and sneaky Indians, my mother will be worried about me. I need to catch up."

"We were friends." He put his hand on her forearm. "And I thought we were becoming more than friends."

She did too. But that was before she learned he and Mutter shared the same secret. She stared at his hand.

He abruptly let go of her arm, went to his horse and swung up into the saddle. "You mean you chose your mother over me? You don't have to. Why are you so angry with me?"

She pulled her horse toward the road, and looked over her shoulder at Caleb. "I didn't say I was angry with you, you did." She gave Molasses a nudge, and settled into a gallop toward the wagons, refusing to look back.

About five miles down the road, Anna spotted the telltale drippings of a honeycomb in the branch of a dead tree and urged Molasses off the road.

She wasn't at the tree two minutes, hardly enough time to come up with a plan, when a mule sauntered in her direction. Its slender rider brushed the brim of his floppy hat and smiled.

"You figurin' on knockin' that thing down for the wax?"

"And the honey."

"This I gotta see."

"I think it's been abandoned." She studied the

hive for another moment, then looked Boney in the eye. “So you and Caleb are taking turns keeping watch on me?”

Boney nodded. “And on your mother.”

“The captain visits our camp every morning.” Anna sighed. “That isn’t enough?”

“I thought you might appreciate a little help with the hive, but if you’re viewin’ my visit as an intrusion, I’ll kindly take my leave.” Boney pretended to nudge his mule.

“Don’t leave.” She drew in a deep breath. “I’m actually glad to see you.”

“Good.” Boney slid off his mule and pushed his hat back on his head. “I was startin’ to think you were disappointed it was me, and not Caleb, who showed up.”

He jerked his head in the direction they’d come from. “I saw you two jawin’ up on that knoll.”

“If you’re keeping such good watch on me, you know I went to that tree by myself. To be alone.”

“Woo-weee! None too happy he joined you, huh?”

Ignoring the conflict raging inside her, Anna shook her head. More like she’d been glad to see Caleb, but upset with herself because of it.

When Boney pulled his rifle from its buckskin scabbard, she backed her horse farther away from the tree. Just in case the hive hadn’t been as abandoned as she suspected.

He jabbed the branch with his rifle barrel,

knocking it and the hive to the ground. "So, you're fumin' at him, not embarrassed?"

"You're the one who told Caleb I was embarrassed?"

Boney's eyes widened. "Just a theory, since you've been avoiding him."

"You two spend a lot of time talking about me, do you?"

"Not a lot. A time or two, is all." After waiting to see if angry bees appeared outside the hive, Boney swung the branch over the back of his mule and tied it behind the saddle. "You're telling me you don't have *feelings* for him?"

"I *can't* have feelings for him." Anna met Boney's blue-eyed gaze. "Let's leave it at that."

34

Sunday, after a quick midday bite to eat with his men, Garrett saddled his stallion and rode down the line. If ever a company of wagons had crammed all they could into a week, this was the one. Reports and investigations of thefts, the ferry crossing disaster, and Dr. Le Beau's resultant wagon wheel troubles. Two of his men trying to cover up Wilma Goben's problem with the bottle, and his uncomfortable encounter with Anna and Wilma Goben the next morning. Not to mention the daily sniveling about the dust and the weather, as if that were within his control. All of that since his pleasurable horseback ride with Caroline last Sunday. To say he was anxious for this second ride would be a colossal understatement.

When he arrived at the Goben camp, Anna had her chestnut pony saddled for Caroline, and the redhead sat in the saddle looking every bit a seasoned rider. Wilma Goben sat at the table sorting a stack of fabric, while Anna stood beside the horse, talking to Caroline.

Garrett doffed his hat. "Ladies."

"Captain." Wilma smiled, looking well and sober. So far, so good. Anna gave him a tight nod.

Garrett studied Caroline from her wide-brimmed hat, to her relaxed hold on the reins, to her boot in the stirrup. "You certainly look ready for a ride."

"I am." Caroline lifted the reins. "I'll see you after a while, Anna."

Anna waved. "Enjoy yourselves." Her voice was tinged with a sullen wistfulness, hounding his curiosity about what had transpired between the young woman and Caleb.

Caroline pulled the reins around, directing her horse beside his, and gave him a wide-eyed nod.

Smiling, he clicked his tongue, directing his mount onto the road. The pony stayed in step beside him with no apparent prodding from Caroline. "One might think you'd been practicing your horsemanship all week."

"Hardly." A playful smirk added light to her emerald-green eyes. "But I'd say after the topsy-turvy week you've had, you've earned an afternoon that didn't involve worrying whether I could stay in a saddle, wouldn't you?"

"I agree wholeheartedly." He looked directly into her eyes, feeling as if he could get lost in them. Or found. "And, Caroline . . ."

She nodded, her gaze fixed on his face.

"I can't think of anyone else I'd rather spend my afternoon with, worry or not."

"Thank you."

He'd hoped for more. Perhaps an admission that she felt the same way about spending time with him. Instead, they rode in silence up a side trail toward a grassy hillock.

He looked over at Caroline. "Have you talked to Anna? Her grandfather seems to be doing well."

"Yes. Anna said he is stronger every day." A shadow crossed Caroline's face, tightening her features. "But she doesn't seem as well off."

"Something seems to have flipped for Caleb and Anna since her mother fell into the river. For days, Caleb was dashing off to their camp early every morning and going for walks to the creek with Anna."

Caroline nodded. "And the next thing you know, she's avoiding him. Ever since that day at the river, Anna has been keeping to herself."

Garrett nodded. “I was hoping you might know what happened.”

“I wish I did. I noticed also and asked Anna about him, but she’s being tight-lipped.” A sigh lifted an errant strand of hair on her forehead. “I thought maybe Caleb had said something to you.”

“Only that Otto was strong again, and the Gobens no longer needed his help.”

“My guess is it had something to do with her mother, but it’s just a guess.”

A good guess. At the top of the rise, he gave the horses a low “Whoa,” which brought them both to a stop. While he was sure Caroline knew about Wilma Goben’s struggles with alcohol, he didn’t wish to bring it up. The memory of meeting her sodden brother-in-law back in Saint Charles was still fresh in his mind. And although he knew she was all too happy to be out from under the man’s roof, her sister was still there.

Caroline looked out at the meager forest. “It’s much more open here than I was used to back along the Missouri River.”

“Yes. One of the big draws west—wide, open spaces.”

“I can’t wait to see the mountains and the desert. All of it.”

And he couldn’t wait to show it to her.

Caroline loosened the bonnet ties at her neck. Had she read his thoughts?

She moistened her lips. “Rhoda says the pain

left her about a week ago and hasn't returned, but she still seems a mite puny to me."

"When I asked Ian about her yesterday, he said she was fine, but sometimes we men can be a bit, well—"

"Oblivious?" An eyebrow lifted and her mouth tipped in a grin.

He chuckled. "I was going to say unmindful. But, yes, oblivious may be more accurate. To his credit, Ian does have good reason to be preoccupied. Seems his mother is constantly pecking at him about one thing or another."

Caroline nodded. "That she is, which reminds me. What has come of your investigations? Have you received any more reports of things missing?"

Garrett shook his head. "Thankfully, no. The two I have are plenty puzzling. Who in the caravan would want a teapot and a pocket watch badly enough to steal them?"

Caroline shrugged. "Both silver. And they were taken from two separate camps. Keepsakes with sentimental value." She tapped her chin as if trying to think like a sheriff in a Beadle's Dime Novel. "You said Mrs. Zanzucchi and Otto Goben had left the missing items on their tables?"

"That's what they both said."

She tucked an errant strand of hair beneath her bonnet. "So whoever it is isn't going into a wagon looking for things to steal."

He nodded in quick agreement. "They may have

simply walked by, saw the items sitting out in the open, and decided to take advantage of the opportunity."

"You've had no luck finding out if anyone was seen near those camps at those times?"

"No. Children and people of all ages are coming and going all the time in just about every direction. The pasture. The latrine. The creeks. Hunting firewood and kindling. Working. Playing."

"I suppose it could be a child." She stretched the curl on her neck. "I have learned from recent experience that it's difficult to keep an eye on children at all times."

"Sally Rengler thinks it could be Oliver."

"That woman needs to have a second thought, then."

He chuckled.

"What, pray tell, is so funny?"

He straightened and took on the air of an expert. "Well, ma'am, if you must know . . . it's you."

Her eyebrows shot skyward. "Me?"

"Yes." He gestured with his hand, like a barrister in court. "Your passion. For answers. For the downtrodden. For justice. I love that about you."

"You do?"

"I do." His neck warmed.

Her face pinked. "I feel the same about you."

"Oh?" He pulled his horse around to face her.

"Yes. I can't think of anyone I'd rather spend an

afternoon with." Her hat tipped up, revealing a purposeful expression on her face. "And, in case you're wondering, I'm not just saying that because a horseback ride with you means a break from my responsibilities with the Kamdens." She moistened her distracting lips. "I really am enjoying our time together."

Clearly, there weren't going to be enough hours in this afternoon.

A lifetime of hours with the fervent and alluring Caroline Milburn wouldn't be enough.

35

Anna added two more river rocks to the canvas sack she carried, then walked back toward the wagon. Großvater knelt at the new fire ring, forming the first layer of rock.

"Do you think we'll need another load?"

Großvater looked up at the burden she carried. "If we do, I'll go get it." He watched as she bent and let the rocks tumble from the canvas. "Anna."

She knelt at the small circle of rocks across from him and looked up.

Großvater held a rock midair as if he were weighing it. A frown dulled his eyes. "I wish I could bear it all for you."

Anna didn't know for certain what Großvater

meant, but she nodded anyway. She guessed that he was referring to Mutter. That he'd make life better for both of them, if it were in his power to do so.

"But you and I both know I can't carry your burdens." He added the rock to the ring and peered up at her. "Any more than you can bear your mutter's sorrow."

Anna sat back on her heels. "I know I can't take care of her, not the way I wish I could. But she is doing better."

"And if it doesn't last? Then what will you do?"

Tears stung her eyes. "How can you give up on your own daughter?"

Großvater's sigh tore at her heart. "I won't ever give up on my Wilma, but I have no say if she's given up on herself."

The tears rolled down her chin.

"Anna, don't throw away your life."

"That's not what I'm doing."

"Isn't it?" He stared at her, *into* her, his face solemn. "What about Caleb? He's the first man I've seen you take a fancy to, and you've turned him away."

"You don't know all there is to know about him."

"I don't think you do either."

"I know enough."

"You know enough to make a judgment, but not enough to hear him out?" He twisted a rock into the circle, making it fit.

"He's been talking to you?"

"He tried, desperate to know what he did or said that hurt you." Großvater pushed himself up from the ground, taking the sack with him. "You're not going to tell me what he did to end up on your bad side?"

"It's just better this way. He has a job to do. We don't need his help any longer. And I don't need the distraction."

She took over for Großvater and began to stack rocks more forcefully than she needed to, trying to convince herself she didn't need Caleb, didn't want him in her life. It was best for her to concentrate on Mutter's well-being; success in that area was all she truly needed.

Garrett pounded a tent stake into the root-bound soil. As of today, the Boone's Lick Company had been on the road one month. Slowed down by the fording of several streams this afternoon, the wagons hadn't covered as much ground today, but they were still making good time. He moved to the far side of the tent and set another stake. If they kept this pace, they'd arrive at Fort Kearney in less than three weeks.

The last two Sundays had been his favorite days on the road thus far. The day after tomorrow would be his third Sunday horseback ride with Caroline Milburn, and he couldn't wait. She had a way about her that had him caught—hook, line, and sinker. A perplexing blend of compassion and spiritedness, independence and appreciation for society. Her porcelain-doll looks pitted against an iron will. Crossing to the third stake, Garrett realized that if he didn't pull himself out of his daydreams, he was sure to pound a thumb.

"Boss!"

He followed Frank's nod. The redhead of his dreams marched toward him, her skirts pinched and raised to the tops of her boots.

"It's Davonna."

"Again?" Garrett blew out a breath. "What is she upset about now?"

"She's missing!"

His mouth went dry.

"She left camp to fetch a bucket of water from the stream. I thought it would be okay. It isn't that far."

"When did she go?"

"Just over an hour ago."

"I'm sure she's fine. Probably just decided to sit and enjoy some peace and quiet." At least he hoped so.

"About thirty minutes ago, Ian went to the stream and walked it a ways but didn't find her. We're all worried."

"Understandably." He shared their concerns that something wasn't right with Davonna. "Where is Ian now?"

"He went back out with a candle lantern."

"Tiny and Isaac are out scouting," Garrett said, his mind searching for a solution.

"The sun is nearly down. We have to find her before something terrible happens."

"I agree. I'll get a search party together."

"I'm going to look for her too."

The intensity in Caroline's green eyes told him any objection would only delay her involvement.

"All right, but you'll stay with me." He faced Frank. "Send Caleb out. Then you and Boney round up several teams of two and three. Make sure each team has a rifle with them."

"Will do, Boss."

While Frank took quick steps to the chuck wagon, Garrett went to the sycamore where he'd tethered his stallion and met Caroline's gaze. "We'll walk, but I want to have a horse with us in case Davonna is injured or ill."

Caroline squeezed his hand, and they set off into the twilight together.

36

Caleb tromped upstream through waist-high prairie grass. He carried a medical kit over his shoulder and gripped a candle lantern and his rifle. Staying on the bank just above the stream for a better view of the surrounding area, he searched the grass for any sign of disturbance. Anna's mother had been easier to track in the draw. He'd seen her leave the camp.

Wilma Goben and now Davonna Kamden. Garrett was right. Women weren't designed for the trail. That was all there was to it. The day-in-and-day-out demands were too rigorous and emotionally taxing for the female constitution.

An image suddenly confronted him—Anna sitting peacefully on the quilt under the tree, her Bible laying open on her lap. He'd have to count Anna as an exception to the rule. He'd hate to consider this trip without having her along, even if she was angry with him and wouldn't say why.

When Caleb reached a stand of trees, he stilled his steps, listening. "Mrs. Kamden?"

"Caleb?"

It wasn't a woman's voice, but it did have a Scottish ring to it. "Ian?"

The broad-shouldered man stepped out from between some trees. "I can't find her either." He pressed his hand to his forehead. "Mither's not right. My wife tried to tell me. Miss Caroline too. But—"

"There's a search party out looking." Caleb hadn't heard much come from Ian's mouth before now, let alone detected any emotion. It made him miss his own mother all the more. He clapped Ian on the shoulder. "We'll find her, Ian. Much of the party is covering both sides of the creek.

Why don't you loop back around toward camp?"

"In case she comes back on her own. Good idea."

Caleb hooked his thumb on the rifle at his shoulder. "We'll fire one shot to say we found her. Another to say she's unharmed."

Ian nodded before walking away.

Caleb started farther up the hill, praying someone found Davonna soon. First, the Zanzucchi boy's broken arm, then Otto's fever, Rhoda Kamden's recurring pain, and Wilma's near-drowning. The Company was already on edge.

An owl hooted from a far-off perch, a family of prairie dogs whistled nearby, and coyotes yipped and howled in the distance—all a part of a prairie song. But no hint of Davonna Kamden.

He'd only walked another thirty yards or so when he heard another song familiar in the prairie—a woman's cry.

At least it sounded like a woman. Or was it only wishful thinking?

Caleb held the lantern up behind him for light to scan the area. "Mrs. Kamden? Davonna?"

Silence. If she wasn't here, where was she?

Then the cry turned to wailing. It had to be her. Caleb made his way toward a bluff at a crook in the stream. At its base stood a clump of dogwood trees. A silhouette lay in a heap beneath them, her body trembling with her sobs. A shawl covered her head.

"Ma'am?" He didn't see any threat to her, but still she cried and trembled. He took careful steps toward the trees. "Mrs. Kamden, it's Caleb Reger."

Finally, she lifted her head. Tears streamed down her blotchy face, and her eyes were swollen.

He swung the pack to the ground and knelt beside her. "Are you hurt? Did you fall?"

She shook her head, her wails rising. "Look!" She ran her hand over the dirt in front of her.

Caleb noticed the rock beyond her knee and the freshly plucked bundle of sunflowers beside it. A piece of paper stuck out from under a jagged edge. She had stumbled upon a grave.

"Mrs. Kamden, I need to fire my rifle to let Ian know I've found you." He pulled the rifle from the scabbard and fired a shot. The second shot was to let Garrett know she was unharmed and he could return her to camp on his own.

She reared up on her knees. "Shush." Pressing a finger to her lips, the disheveled woman shook her head. "Quiet!" She spoke in a whisper. "A bairn . . . only a wee bairn. And now he's a boy asleep in God's arms."

Caleb nodded, fighting the emotion clogging his throat. He knelt beside her and pulled the water-stained slip of paper from under the rock. Sitting on his legs, Caleb unfolded the crinkled note and read in silence.

Here lies my precious son Michael Eugene Stetson. Gone far too soon at six days, but now cradled in God's loving arms. I am made to travel on without him. Please leave flowers of beauty as you pass.

From a bereaved mother, thankful for the time she had with her boy, but ever hungry for more. Pauline Stetson

Davonna Kamden patted the heads of the wildflowers as one would stroke a newborn's soft curls. "I picked these for Michael. Every one of them."

Caleb nodded then refolded the note and tucked it back under the rock. They should get back to camp. But with his heart equally heavy, he couldn't budge.

"Mr. Caleb?" Her lips quivered.

"Yes ma'am."

"Why do babies have to die?"

His whole body trembling, Caleb looked away from her pleading eyes. Cupping his face in his hands, he finally allowed himself to shed tears for Billy and the other eight men in his squad.

Anna trudged through tall grasses along the stream a few feet behind Hattie and her brother. A candle lantern hung at her side, but she hadn't lit it yet. Hopefully someone in the search party would find Davonna Kamden soon so they could all return to camp before dark.

A glance at the sinking sun told her that wasn't likely.

"Something isn't right with that woman." Charles spoke over his shoulder. "Seems a bit daft to me. Probably wandered off and can't find her way back."

"That is why we have to find her." Hattie marched ahead of her brother. "Imagine what could befall her if we don't."

Three of them bunched together looking for her wouldn't do much good, but Anna couldn't sit back at camp and do nothing. Not when that poor woman was out here somewhere. Alone. She could have fallen and hurt herself.

Sadly, Anna found herself in agreement with Charles's theory, if not his exact description. At first, she thought the elder Mrs. Kamden just a little peculiar. Back in Saint Charles, she'd known a few folks considered *different* from other folks. The trapper back at Little Blue River would definitely qualify as such. Indeed, his differences were obvious and had frightened her.

That day, Caleb had kissed her. Stepping around a rock, Anna pressed her fingers to her lips. That day, she'd kissed him. That day she'd been so sure she'd found a man she could love.

Anna shook her head. She'd been wrong.

And this evening wasn't about Caleb Reger. It

was about Davonna Kamden. That was who she needed to think about. That was why she was out here, to help find Mrs. Kamden.

Hattie stopped and raised her hand, signaling for Charles and Anna to stop and be quiet. They did, and after a few seconds she shook her head. "I thought I heard something."

"Probably someone else in the search party." Charles shifted his rifle to his other shoulder. "Awhile back, I thought I heard Caleb calling her name."

Anna resumed her steps. She could do without hearing Caleb's name again this evening. Picking up her pace, she caught up to Charles. "Davonna buried her husband in Memphis, then boarded a paddle wheeler bound for Missouri. Grief could be causing her odd behavior."

Hattie glanced back at them. "Anna's right. Drastic change can affect a person. The poor woman hadn't been in Saint Charles but a few months before her son carried her off for parts unknown."

Anna sighed. Like she'd done to her own mother.

A rifle blast stopped them all midstep. They remained frozen in place until a second shot.

Charles shifted the hat on his head. "That was the signal to say someone found Ian's mother and that she isn't harmed."

"Thank You, God."

Anna's heart echoed Hattie's short prayer.

Charles pointed to the right, up from the stream. "They're not far away either." He turned toward the shots.

"Since she's all right, we can go back," Hattie said.

"Best to see for ourselves, sis. *Not harmed* doesn't mean they couldn't use help."

Hattie nodded and looked back at Anna.

Anna was ready to get back to camp before full darkness claimed the day, but she didn't dare try to do it alone, lest she end up needing the search party herself. She pulled a match from her apron pocket and lit the candle lantern, then fell into step with the brother and sister. Within a few minutes, they'd reached a bluff at a crook in the stream and a cluster of dogwood trees. Charles stopped suddenly, quietly, and raised his hand. Hattie stopped, and Anna stepped up beside them.

She saw the silhouettes of two people sitting on the ground beneath one of the trees.

Anna took slow steps past the others. Stopping a few feet out, she lifted the candle toward Mrs. Kamden. "Are you all right, ma'am?"

"How can I be?" Mrs. Kamden shook her head. "A baby has died."

"A baby?" They only had one baby in their midst. Evie Brenner. It couldn't be her.

"Mrs. Kamden found a grave." The man stood and helped Davonna to her feet, then, after dragging one forearm across his face, he pointed to the ground with the other.

"Caleb?" In the faint light from the candle, she could see that redness ringed his eyes.

Garrett and Caroline rushed toward them from the left, Ian Kamden from the right. "Mither! I was so worried."

Davonna patted her son's cheek. "I am well. Mr. Caleb is a very nice man, you know. The baby made him sad too."

Ian shook Caleb's hand. "Thank you for finding her. For taking care of her."

Caleb nodded, looking straight at Anna but not saying a word.

He had told her the day he kissed her that he had something to tell her, something she needed to know. What if she was wrong not to hear him out?

She squared her shoulders. No.

No matter how desperate she was to believe Mutter could change—that her near-drowning would reform her—there was better chance that Mutter's struggle would continue. No. She wasn't judging Caleb. Not really. She just knew that hearing him out wouldn't make a difference. She couldn't give her heart to a man she knew would break it time and time again, as Mutter had. He'd make promises he couldn't keep, regardless of his desire to do so. Because of alcohol.

"Anna?" Hattie laid her hand on Anna's arm. "I asked if you wanted to walk back to camp with Caleb."

"I don't."

She couldn't.

37

Saturday morning, Anna walked the road with Maren Wainwright, whose plaited blond hair circled her head. The Danish immigrant suffered from what a doctor in Saint Charles referred to as Night Blindness, with no known cure. And yet Maren possessed a quiet strength and grace Anna desired for herself.

Little Gabi Wainwright and little Maisie Kamden skipped ahead of them, singing to their cloth doll and rabbit. The girls' songs about the birds and rocks tickled Anna, but also pricked her heart. Would she forever be responsible for Mutter and Großvater, or would she one day marry and have a family of her own? She'd started to believe she might . . .

She shook her head. Never mind what she thought. Or felt.

It didn't matter.

But still, last night's image of Caleb on the ground with Davonna Kamden, mourning the loss of a baby he didn't know, disturbed her. He hadn't behaved like he'd been drinking. Instead, he'd seemed wrought with grief.

Anna brushed a blade of grass from her apron. Whatever happened to her resolve to lean on God's understanding and to trust Him to direct her paths? She should be thankful God had allowed her to discover the truth about Caleb before she'd let her heart follow him. They'd already kissed. A mistake.

"Your mother? Is she well?" Maren tucked a windblown curl behind her ear and blinked feverishly.

Anna looked at her friend. "Yes. Thank you. She seems to be feeling better than she has in a long while." Anna tugged the brim of her bonnet to better shade her eyes from the sun. "In fact, she's been doing most of the cooking lately."

"Yes." Maren nodded. "She brought us some of her *kartoffelpuffer* this morning. Even better than Mother Brantenberg's potato pancakes." She pressed her finger to her mouth. "You know you can't tell Elsa I said that."

"Don't worry, she won't hear it from me." Anna smiled. "But I know the secret ingredient."

"Do tell."

"She adds garlic to the hot oil. Says that's what adds flavor. And wards off rheumatism."

"Rutherford asked her for the receipt. Perhaps she can teach Gabi how to make them."

"I'm sure she'd be happy to."

And what a great idea to get Mutter involved with the others. Being around children was good for one's spirit. One of the great blessings of being on the trail with all these families.

"Anna." Maren looked at her, blinking. "You are a good daughter."

Anna looked away, fighting the legions of doubts that plagued her.

"Even before we left Saint Charles, we all saw you." Maren laid her tender hand on Anna's sleeve. "Despite your own grief, you worked to provide for your family. And here on the road, you've done everything you can to care for your mother."

"Thank you." Anna patted Maren's hand. "You are a good friend."

"I know it can't be easy."

Anna shook her head. "No, but we all do what the Lord gives us to do. You are a good example of that, from the very day you boarded the boat in Copenhagen. Now, you're on a wagon caravan crossing this wide desert, all the while anticipating a child." She glanced at the girls scampering ahead of them, then returned her focus to her friend. "You're feeling better these days?"

Maren nodded, bouncing her braided crown. "No more fainting. I count that good."

"Yes, well, you did gain everyone's attention for Rutherford's sermon that Sunday."

Maren giggled, her face turning pink.

"What was it Caleb read this morning? I can't remember."

"From Romans, the fifth chapter?" Maren looked ahead at the two girls. "That's far enough ahead, Gabi girl." She turned back toward Anna. "Something about glorying in tribulations."

"Yes." Anna sighed. "Knowing that tribulation works patience. Patience, experience; and experience, hope."

"I suppose that means we'll both have an abundance of patience by the end of this trip?" Maren smiled.

"Good." Anna swatted a fly away from her face. "I could use a greater measure of patience."

"Me too." Maren pointed at the two little girls twirling just ahead of them then faced Anna. "He's a bit of a surprise, that man."

"Rutherford?"

"Him, too. But I was thinking about Caleb. A man who reveres God's Word. And always helping folks, like your grandfather and Mrs. Kamden."

"Yes." Anna couldn't argue with any of that. Caleb was like no man she'd ever met. Quiet. Smoldering. Emotion in check, but just barely. Sensitive. Compassionate. But if what Mutter said was true, he had a secret Anna couldn't abide.

"Rutherford and I—Gabi too—are excited about the music celebration tonight. You're planning to come, aren't you?"

Anna gulped. Großvater had mentioned the plan over breakfast. She hadn't yet come up with a good enough excuse not to participate. But she couldn't go.

"Your grandfather is playing the mandolin. Rutherford will play his zither." Maren arched her eyebrows. "With all the troubles your family has had lately, a little fun would do you well."

That much was true, if not for the fact that she was trying to avoid Caleb, and it would be even more difficult to do at a Company dance. Especially since he was convinced she was angry with him and he was bent on learning why.

Caroline pulled the hand mirror from her trunk and studied her reflection. Except for the fact that she'd been traveling across the country on foot for a month, out in the elements, she didn't look too terrible. After supper, she'd managed to wash her face and brush out her hair, which now was swept into a chignon. If only her feelings could be so easily contained.

With the attention Garrett Cowlishaw had been paying her the past few weeks, her mind had started thinking about the possibility that she could marry again. The realization that she cared for Garrett tangled her feelings all the more. This wasn't his first wagon caravan. He heard the call to adventure and answered it. He'd traveled this way twice before. In their time together on

Sunday afternoons, he'd said nothing about wanting to settle down. He'd been married once already. At one time, he may have planned to have a family, but he could have decided not to marry again. Did he even mean to remain in California once he'd seen the wagons safely there?

"How-de-do, Miss Caroline!" Davonna Kamden's face appeared through the puckered opening in the canvas. "Dear, the family went ahead. I said I'd wait for you, but I can't—"

Caroline held up her index finger. "I'm nearly ready." She tucked the mirror into her trunk then pinned a small hat on her head. She handed her candle lantern to Davonna and carefully climbed over the wagon seat. Her feet on the ground, Caroline smoothed her blue dress and repositioned her lace shawl.

"You look lovely, dear."

"Thank you. You do, as well." Davonna wore a starched green, puff-sleeve dress, and a warm smile that crinkled the soft creases at her eyes. Caroline raised her arm and bent it as a proper escort would.

Her smile deepening, Davonna rested her gloved hand on Caroline's arm. "I already have dance partners."

Plural? "The music hasn't even begun, and you've received multiple requests?"

She held up her other hand. "Three dance partners, in fact. Mr. Tiny. Mr. Lyall Kamden." A finger wiggled with the mention of each name. "And *your* Captain Garrett."

"He isn't my Captain Garrett." The statement left her feeling a bit cold.

"Well, dear, I don't believe he has a clue about that." Davonna tittered.

Their Sunday horseback rides had everyone making assumptions about the two of them. But she couldn't afford to presume Garrett Cowlishaw's attention meant anything more than companionship to him.

"Oh my stars. I was wrong. Four menfolk reserved a dance with me." Davonna shook her head. "How could I forget about Oliver?"

Caroline swallowed her amusement. "You do have a full dance card."

Davonna nodded then looked out at the camp. "It's so lovely."

They'd circled the wagons for tonight's gathering. Garrett and the other men built a firepit in the center of camp. Red and orange flames pirouetted in a light breeze. The children played off to one side and a small band assembled itself on the other. A table held various refreshments—pies and other desserts. Lorelei Beck had made macaroons. Everyone looked as if they'd been polished—clean and fresh.

Caroline looked up. Out here on the open prairie, even above a fireglow, the sky sparkled with myriad stars. An especially lovely night.

"Ladies." Garrett walked toward them, his beard neatly trimmed and his hair combed into place, all except for that one wave that liked to frame his temple.

A handsome night. Or at least *her* captain was handsome tonight.

Davonna removed her hand from Caroline's arm and laid it on Garrett's. His grin undermined Caroline's footing. Thankfully, he held his other arm out to her. The warmth of his skin through his chambray sleeve did little to steady her as he led them toward a circle of chairs, stools, and benches.

"Captain, seeing as how you were so prompt, I'm awarding you my first dance."

"I am most honored, ma'am." He looked at Caroline, his eyebrows arched in a question. "The second dance on your card?"

"It's yours."

And maybe, if she was bold enough, she'd take the opportunity to ask if this was his last caravan west.

Anna seated herself at the worktable across from Mutter. She couldn't remember the last time she'd seen her writing a letter.

Anna pulled a sheet of paper from the desk kit and flipped it over to the blank side. This was as good a time as any to add to the quilting circular. Lorelei had handed her the letter during the noon break. She could tell Emilie and the others in Saint Charles about how well Mutter was doing and that the adventure seemed to have added several years to Großvater's life.

Mutter stilled the quill in her hand and looked up. "What do you think you're doing?"

Anna dipped her chin in surprise. "Writing a letter seemed a good idea."

"It isn't. Not for you."

"Why not?"

The screech and squawk of instruments being tuned momentarily drew their attention to the center of the circle of wagons. "You're not going to be young and attractive forever. You need to find a husband. Now."

"I'm only eighteen." Besides, what did writing letters have to do with aging? And what did going to a campfire gathering have to do with finding a husband? Even as she thought it, Anna knew the answer and the name that would soon be on Mutter's lips.

Mutter drew in a deep breath. "The West is not the friendliest of places for single women." Her eyes were clear and focused. "You'd do well to marry."

"And what if I value my unencumbered young womanhood?"

Unencumbered? That was laughable too.

"Dear, your life is anything but unencumbered." Mutter shook her head. "You know it as well as I do. I never meant to stand in the way of your happiness."

Anna pulled a second quill from the leather pouch. Was that what Mutter was doing? Standing in the way of her happiness?

No. It wasn't Mutter's bad habit, but Caleb's that had discouraged her to follow any notion of romance with him.

The sprightly twang of Großvater's mandolin suddenly courted Anna to dance. Next came the lilt of Boney's harmonica. Her girlfriends would be there. All good reasons to go.

"I'm the reason you didn't marry Boney. I'm the reason you're avoiding Caleb. And I'm the reason you don't want to go to the gathering tonight, aren't I?"

Anna shook her head. "No, you are not the reason for any of those decisions I made." She glanced at the stack of stationery at Mutter's hand. "Are you writing to someone in Saint Charles?"

"The letter is to my sister." Mutter pointed the quill at her. "And don't you think I don't know you purposely changed the course of our conversation."

Anna shrugged and offered a weak smile.

"Little Elva. I'll always think of my baby sister that way. Anyway, your aunt planned to leave Germany, to join us in America. It's been eighteen years." Mutter hung her head. "That's what happens when you sit around writing letters. Nothing!" She sighed. "Time passes."

Anna slid her piece of stationery back into the

writing kit. Mutter needed a lively distraction even more than she did. "I'll go to the campfire gathering, and I may even dance a step or two." With Gabi or Maisie or Duff Kamden. Any of the children. "I'll go if you'll come with me."

Mutter sighed, dropping her chin.

Anna stood and held out her hand.

Mutter didn't budge. "I'm not going to drink while you're gone, if that's what concerns you. Even if I wanted to, you made sure all the bottles were destroyed."

Anna knew full well that many of the wagons about them carried liquor. Dr. Le Beau considered himself a connoisseur of fine wines, and the whole Company had gathered in the center of camp. Mutter could easily . . .

Anna pressed her hand to her bosom. What a dreadful thought to have of your own mother.

"I don't wish to *police* you, Mutter." Surprisingly, she actually meant it. Anna glanced toward the music. "You said it yourself, time passes. And I think it may be time we both had a little fun."

Mutter made a noise between a gasp and a grunt. But she gathered the paper and inkwell, then marched to the back of the wagon and set them inside. "Very well. If the only way I can get you to enjoy society with young men is to join you, then let's be on our way."

Enjoy society with young men?

There was only one young man who held her interest.

Feeling more like she was headed to a funeral than a celebration, Anna plodded toward the music and the dancing. Neither one of them looked any better than they had while walking the road just over an hour ago, but Anna found it hard to care.

She and Mutter had no sooner found empty seats when Caleb approached them. He didn't look like he'd been riding the road all day. Not in the least. Freshly combed hair dusted the collar on his blue twill shirt.

"Good evening, ma'am."

Mutter smiled. "And to you."

"How are you doing?" Caleb looked into Mutter's eyes. "Well, I hope."

"Thanks to you. And to Anna, yes." She leaned toward him as if to share a secret. "You are too?"

Caleb gave Mutter a nod.

Anna swallowed hard. Mutter had said she needn't worry about it, that they were going to help each other. And now the two of them were openly talking about their drinking, and how they were doing with the avoidance of it. Anna felt her hands curl into fists and forced them to relax.

"Good evening, Anna." Caleb's gaze was far too attentive. "I'm glad you came."

"Thank you." She could be polite. No sense in causing a scene and ruining the party.

“Katie’s Beau!” Frank called, signaling the first dance—a Virginia reel.

Caleb held his hand out to Anna. “May I have your first dance?”

She’d set that snare herself. Actually, Mutter had. But she may as well get the dance with him over with. Then she’d busy herself dancing with Mutter and the children.

Anna placed her hand in his, trying to ignore the calm she felt in his touch. Caleb held her hand high as they waited for the opening notes.

“Thank you for dancing with me, but I’m still waiting for an explanation.”

She pressed her lips together. This wasn’t the place to share her answer.

“On the knoll, I asked you why you were angry with me.”

“I remember.”

“You told me you hadn’t said you were. But you are angry. My sister used to act the same way when she was mad.” A frown line formed above his nose.

“Do you mean to say she pouted?” He could be so charming. How cruel that she’d become so fond of him, only to find out he wasn’t the man she thought him to be.

His cocoa-brown eyes narrowed. “Are you pouting, Anna? Ever since the night I found your mother in the draw, you’ve acted as though it pains you to look at me. Why is that?”

It did pain her to look at him. To think about him. But she couldn't tell him that. When she started to pull away, Caleb tightened his grip.

"Anna, did I do something?"

While everyone around them danced, they stood still.

"It's not you I'm angry with." How could she be? No one was perfect. She couldn't judge him. But neither could she offer him her heart.

"Who, then? Tell me. Maybe I can help."

Tears stung her eyes. "Myself."

He let her go, dropping his hands to his sides. "You're angry with yourself? I don't understand."

"I can't care for you, Caleb." Anna spun toward her wagon.

"Can't? Or won't?"

She didn't look back.

38

"God!" Caleb knelt on the far side of the creek and cried out. His Bible lay shut beside a candle lantern on a nearby rock. He'd not slept all night. The minute he started to drift off, painful memories assaulted him in a barrage of distorted images and sounds. Hearing his mother's cries. Seeing the disappointment and heartache written in the lines on his father's face. A debilitating headache. Waking up to find his fellow soldiers dead. He was sick of the secrets.

"I can't care for you, Caleb." Anna's declaration mocked him. She couldn't care for him, and she didn't even know the truth.

Caleb thrashed the prairie grasses that fashioned his irregular altar. "God! What am I to do?"

He wanted to know peace the way Isaac did. Despite the scars on his face, the emptiness of his arms, and the wounds in his heart, the former slave enjoyed freedom from his past.

How, Lord? How?

"If we confess our sins, he is faithful and just to forgive us our sins, and to cleanse us from all unrighteousness."

"I *have* confessed!" Time and time again, he'd pled for forgiveness.

He knew the promises in First John. He'd recited them many times. He'd prayed them.

But he didn't *feel* forgiven. Cleansed. He didn't *feel* righteous. He jammed his balled fists into his thighs. "What would You have me do? I don't know."

"But if we walk in the light, as he is in the light . . ."

Swallowing hard against the acid burning his throat, Caleb raised his face to the darkness. The Scriptures he'd read and intended to preach now felt like swords piercing him to the core.

Walk in the light.

What did that mean? How was he to walk in the light when he carried such darkness?

I am faithful.

The voice wasn't audible, but clear, speaking directly into his spirit. Trembling, Caleb fell on his face.

I am just to forgive your sins. I AM.

My blood cleanses you from all sin. I have made you clean.

Walk in My Light.

When he raised his head, morning light cast stripes on the trees along the creek. He crawled to the rock and opened his Bible to a verse from the book of Hebrews.

"For the word of God is quick, and powerful, and sharper than any two-edged sword, piercing even to the dividing asunder of soul and spirit, and of the joints and marrow, and is a discerner of the thoughts and intents of the heart."

"You know my heart, Lord. Take it. Heal it."

His spirit calmed. His breaths deepened.

Caleb snuffed the candle. It wasn't what he knew in his head or what he felt in his emotions, but what he believed, that brought peace. He couldn't understand how he could be forgiven. He hadn't felt forgiven, so he didn't believe God would forgive him. Had forgiven him. He'd been clinging to the faint light of his understanding while missing the bright and shining Light of the world.

Resting against the rock, Caleb fanned the pages to the book of John. At the eighth chapter, his finger touched the truth in verse twelve.

"Then spake Jesus again unto them, saying, 'I am the light of the world: he that followeth me shall not walk in darkness, but shall have the light of life.' "

He had committed the Scriptures to memory but not allowed them to change his heart.

Caroline spread her patchwork quilt on the ground beneath a crab-apple tree.

After last night's musical festivities in celebration of being several weeks closer to California, she knew the answers to her most personal questions. Yes, she could finally let go of her dreams of having a life with Phillip. She could allow herself to find love again. And this afternoon, watching Garrett Cowlishaw stroll toward her carrying a picnic sack, she was certain she had found love again. Despite his limp, which she knew was painful at times, he wore a smile that was surely tailor-made for her.

But it seemed Garrett still had questions he needed to answer. Could he trust again? Love again? Was he ready to make a home, to start a family?

"I thought this day would never come." Garrett held the picnic sack out to her.

When she reached for their food, he held tight

to the sack. Her stomach fluttered as she looked at the pleasing lines of his face.

"I'm glad you came, Caroline."

"On the ride?" She gave their tethered horses a quick glance. "The picnic?"

"On the walk west." He let go of the sack, and not certain her legs could hold her up any longer, she sat down with it.

Garrett lowered himself to the quilt, knelt, and faced her. "I'm glad you ignored my counsel to remain in Saint Charles."

"So, you're glad I'm stubborn?"

"I wouldn't go that far." His better-than-gold grin tipped his mouth. "But your persistence did come in handy."

"That's an acceptable answer." Caroline moistened her dry lips. "I'm glad I came too. On the road. And riding. Now. With you."

The glimmer in his hazel eyes told her he might kiss her. Instead, he reached for the sack and handed her a soda biscuit. Silently, they each raised their biscuits to their mouths and took a bite, neither of them looking away. The salty, flaky biscuit was every bit the best she'd ever tasted.

Garrett lowered his crumbly morsel. "Would you like to marry again?"

Thankfully, she'd already swallowed her bite, because right now just catching a breath seemed challenge enough. "I didn't think so," she said.

"And now?"

"I may. If the right man came along." She gave him a shy smile.

His eyes widened. "I hope it's okay that I'm praying I can be that man."

She nodded. "Is that a proposal, Captain Cowlishaw?"

"As a matter of fact, it is. But not a very proper one, I'm afraid." He rose onto his left knee and reached for her hand. "I didn't think I would marry again either. But that was before I loved you."

Tears of joy welled her eyes. "That, sir, is a proper enough proposal for me." She clasped Garrett's other hand then leaned forward, her lips finding his in a kiss that had been well worth the wait.

When Garrett finally pulled back, he cupped her cheek. "If that's a yes, I must say, I do favor them."

"Yes! Let's marry. I may have loved you from the day you joined our trail game and said *c* is for 'cherub.' "

Riding back to camp, Garrett didn't think he needed the horse beneath him. He felt like he could float all the way to the Rockies. God had given him a second chance at love, and Caroline had said yes. He'd seen Caroline back to the Kamdens' camp and returned to his own.

Caleb sat at the worktable between the

Company's two wagons, engaged in a game of dominoes. Otto Goben sat across from him, tapping his bearded chin. Caleb nodded Garrett's direction then played his last wooden tile.

Otto blew out a long breath and looked up at Garrett. "This young man is good!"

"Thank you, sir." Caleb shook the man's hand. "You put up a fine fight."

Otto stood and faced Garrett. "I'm the last of eight fellows—all lost to him. Best go check on my animals before supper. Although, supper might be late with all that gasping and tittering going on over at my wagon. A gaggle of women there."

"Ah yes, the Sunday quilting circle, or such." No doubt where Caroline would be going with their news.

When Caleb started stacking the dominoes, Garrett raised his hand to stop him. "Not so fast. I haven't had a shot at you yet."

"You think you're good enough?" Caleb said with a grin.

Otto gave a low whistle. "Boy, oh boy, sorry to miss this battle, but I've got to get moving." He stretched out his back then waved and headed across the pasture.

Caleb started flipping the dominoes over. Garrett seated himself and joined in.

"I was a little surprised to see Otto here. You invite him over for a talk, did you?"

Caleb peered at him. "To talk about you and Caroline Milburn?"

Garrett chuckled. "That dry humor of yours is the best."

"I'm glad you think so."

The serious tone in Caleb's voice no doubt meant he hadn't talked to Anna today, but Garrett would ask anyway. "I take it you haven't talked to Anna about last night?"

"No." Caleb shook his head and flipped over the last domino. "Only God knows how it will all work out." He shuffled the tiles in a figure-eight motion. "Feel like I need to give her more time."

"Otto tell you that?"

A grin brightened Caleb's eyes. "He did."

Garrett nodded, giving the dominoes a swirl. "Sounds like good counsel, and from a man who would know." Each of them pulled their starting pieces and stood them on edge.

"You and the woman you're sweet on rode back into town wearing wide smiles."

Garrett straightened and sighed. He may as well have a little fun. He wasn't above distracting Caleb from the game to win. "I think I may have proposed."

"You think?" Caleb jerked upright, bumping the table and knocking over most of the tiles. "You may have asked a woman to marry you, and you don't know for sure?" He scrambled to right his tiles. "How is that possible?"

Garrett chuckled. "Did I say I *think* I may have proposed? No, I'm pretty sure I proposed." He gave Caleb an exaggerated nod. "And she said yes!"

"It's about time you smartened up."

"What? You're the one who told me not to get all atwitter over her."

"Since when did you start listening to me?" Smiling, Caleb slapped his double six on the table. "You thought you could distract me, with all that woman and marriage talk, didn't you?"

"Can't blame a man for tryin'. Knew that was my only chance." Garrett smiled then looked Caleb in the eye. "I have a feeling things are going to work out for you and Anna too. Just can't say how. Or how soon."

39

Wednesday, Anna had taken turns with Großvater. For the past couple of hours, he'd walked holding the lead rope while Anna quietly put one foot in front of the other. Now it was her turn to lead. Mutter had spent most of the day riding on the wagon seat.

When the wind caught the brim on Großvater's hat, he pulled it off and shoved it into his back pocket. He looked over his shoulder at Mutter. "Your headache any better, tochter?"

"Yes. Some. *Danke.*" Mutter signaled for Anna to slow the oxen. "If you want to ride your horse for a while with the other men, I can walk with Anna."

"I thought I might." Großvater stepped around to the tongue of the wagon and helped Mutter down from the seat. "You didn't eat much at the stop."

"Don't worry, Vater. I'm only tired."

Großvater narrowed his eyes.

"I'm feeling fine. Did me good to be out of the wind for a spell."

He scrubbed his weathered cheek. "With Rhoda Kamden feeling punk again, I—"

"I'll eat some bread." Mutter tied the straps on her bonnet. "Anna will see to it."

Anna nodded, remembering the day she'd become her mother's keeper. Even before Dedrick died. She wasn't much older than Gabi on the day she'd watched her father walk out and found her mother on the floor, sobbing. That night, her mother had dropped her married name, and they became Gobens.

"We can't gossip about you if you're stuck to us like prairie dust." Mutter flapped her hand at Großvater. "Now, shoo."

Shaking his head, Großvater turned toward the livestock at the back of the train.

Anna opened her mouth to remind Mutter to eat something but just as quickly rememb her resolve to trust Mutter to take care of herself.

"Speaking of Rhoda and her ill health, what is she to do with her mother-in-law and all those children when your friend Caroline marries the captain?" Mutter shook her head. "Didn't you say they were talking about being wed while we're in Fort Kearney?"

"That's what Caroline said."

"Well, according to the captain's announcement, we'll be at the fort in a couple of weeks. Does she not plan to live with her husband? And, if so, where?" Mutter looked over the land, her brow furrowing. "In the grass?"

"All good questions, Mutter. I hadn't thought about it, but with Rhoda and Davonna—"

"And what of all those men? Is she to live amongst them, and cook for them?"

Anna smiled. "You know Boney better than that. He's not going to let her take over his chuck wagon."

Mutter snickered. "All this talk of cooking is making me hungry." She glanced back at the grub box lashed to the far side of the wagon. "If you'll slow the animals, I'll get me some bread."

Anna obliged her, pulling back on the lead rope and congratulating herself for not nagging Mutter about eating.

Mutter was at the grub box, when a buckboard rolled up from behind. The dapper gentleman at the reins doffed his top hat as he passed on

Anna's side, his cargo clinking and clattering. Probably headed for the next stage stop or outpost to sell his wares.

When Anna heard the grub box close, she picked up her pace to match the wagon in front of them.

Mutter walked up beside her, slipping a crusty bite of bread into her mouth. "I haven't seen your großvater this satisfied in years."

Anna nodded.

"Even though he lost to Caleb, he said he had a good time playing dominoes on Sunday. It could become a tradition, you know?" Mutter's eyebrow lifted.

Anna dipped her chin then glanced at the bread in Mutter's hand. Mutter may need encouragement to eat today, but Anna didn't need to be goaded or spurred toward Caleb.

"And you, Anna, are you glad to be making this trip?"

Her hesitation surprised her. The trip was her idea. Upon her insistence. Of course she was glad, wasn't she? "Yes. I still believe the change is good, that a little adventure is good for the spirit." So what if things hadn't gone as she'd expected. She'd learned that expectations and assumptions weren't the best measuring sticks.

"You still feel that way when you look around?" One hand perched at her waist, Mutter pointed to the rolling countryside and knee-high grasses surrounding them.

"Not exactly adventurous."

Mutter shook her head. "Windy, and the same. Like we're walking past the same weed, crossing the same draw, and seeing the same hill in the distance. Over and over, the same."

Anna couldn't argue. The monotony of the past couple of weeks had niggled at her, too.

"I miss seeing trees." Mutter sighed. "And not just crabapples or redbuds."

"We'll see plenty of trees when we get to the Rockies and the Sierras."

"Let us hope I can wait that long, dear."

Anna was pondering the meaning of Mutter's statement when the oxen stopped suddenly, pushing against the horse tethered to the wagon in front of them. The train had come to a halt.

Mutter tensed. "Why did we stop?"

"Someone probably has a tired animal or a broken spoke."

"Then why hasn't Caleb or one of the other hands ridden by to tell us so?"

Anna shrugged and stepped out of the line to look ahead. "I can't see anything from here."

"Indians!" Davonna Kamden's fearful cry caused a wave of rumbling up and down the line.

Mutter left Anna's side and scrambled up onto the spokes of the wagon and over the seat.

"We don't really know that there are Indians," Anna said. "Mrs. Kamden, uh, gets excited over nothing sometimes."

“Come in here with me, anyway.”

Anna shook her head. “I need to see to the animals if we’re going to be stopped for a while.”

The oxen reared against the yoke, trying to give themselves some space.

Mutter poked her face through the pucker in the canvas. “What was that?”

“Just the cows letting the horse know they don’t like the situation.”

“Well, they’re not alone.”

Anna sighed. She was weary of all this too but wasn’t about to admit to it. Not when it had been her idea.

“It’s Indians!” A man’s voice. Oliver Rengler’s?

“That wasn’t Davonna.” Mutter didn’t come to the opening in the canvas this time.

“No. But even if it is Indians, I’m sure there’s nothing to be afraid of. We’ve seen the villages and camped near them. The captain is probably only exchanging niceties.”

“I hardly think that’s a good idea.”

Shouts began riding the wind. “They’re blocking the road!”

Anna’s heart raced.

“There’s twenty of ’em.”

The oxen snorted and stamped the ground. Anna’s sweaty palms were barely able to grasp the lead rope.

The shouts continued. “They’re dressed for war!”

"Your großvater is out there!" Mutter cried.

Anna stepped out around the Becks' wagon as far as the rope would allow. "I still don't see any Indians, Mutter." Or Großvater. Or Caleb or Boney. As a precaution, she moved back behind the Becks' wagon.

"I have to lie down," Mutter said.

Anna listened as Mutter climbed onto a crate, then a barrel, and into her squeaking hammock.

Within a few minutes, Großvater rode up, his face free of tension. "Had us a little excitement."

"Was it Indians?" Anna asked.

"It was. About ten of them."

How was it that Mutter had come from this man? One would've thought he'd just participated in a sport, not faced a potential enemy.

"Friendly Indians who wanted a toll."

"A toll?"

Großvater nodded. "That's what the captain called it. A trade, of sorts. He gave them some blankets, and they were happy."

"If it was a trade, what did they give us?"

"Directions, bead necklaces, and an open road." He glanced around, then up at the empty seat. "Your mutter get scared?"

Anna nodded and pointed to the wagon.

He swung down from the saddle. "Did she eat?"

"A morsel."

A shadow deepened the wrinkles framing his blue eyes. "I wish all this wasn't so hard on her."

A wish Anna shared. But in her heart, she knew the trip wasn't really any harder for Mutter than daily life in Saint Charles had been.

40

Sometime before the horn blew Thursday morning, a light rain started and added a steady rhythm to Anna's steps on the road west. Rutherford Wainwright had read from the Scripture that morning since Caleb had left early to scout with Frank. That suited Anna just fine. Of course, she was happy for Caroline and couldn't begrudge the talk of her plans to wed Garrett, but it seemed all Anna could think about was her disappointment in Caleb and how foolish she'd been to believe she might have had a future with him.

By midafternoon, the Boone's Lick Company had caught up to Caleb and Frank and set up camp. Since the rain had ceased and the clouds cleared, those who were anxious for supplies and a dose of civilization were making the short ride to the outpost before supper. Anna rode toward Rock Creek with Mutter, Caroline, Hattie, and Lorelei Beck. Großvater rode just ahead of them with Arvin Beck and the two Rengler brothers.

Rock Creek wasn't as big a settlement as Anna

had hoped. A small cemetery. A mill. A handful of cabins. It was about twenty buildings short of a town.

Resting her hand on the pommel, Mutter leaned toward Anna. "It's not as nice as Independence, but it's stationary and there's at least some civilization."

Anna drew in a deep breath. Mutter wouldn't consider staying here, would she?

"I know you want to go all the way to California, dear, but I would be happy to stay here."

"You wanted trees."

Mutter sighed. "What a person wants and what they'll settle for are not the same thing."

Anna shook her head and turned to her friends.

"Hmm." Hattie tapped her chin. "Where *shall* we go first?"

All the women laughed but Mutter. Anna smiled. They followed Hattie and tethered their horses to the hitching rail in front of a cabin with a shingle hanging out front identifying it as a general store. Minutes later, Anna and Mutter had sold their candles to the bald storekeeper. Each of the women purchased minimal supplies. Mutter added a nickel's worth of horehound.

"Ooh, he has a soda barrel." Hattie turned toward the assortment of stools placed in front of a rough-hewn counter. She nearly brushed Lorelei's forehead with the brim of her hat in her excitement. "Doesn't a soda and a leisurely visit sound delightful?"

"It does to me." Anna looked at Mutter. "It might wash out some of the dust."

The portly storekeeper shuffled behind the counter. "Warm sarsaparilla's all I got for you, ladies."

"Sarsaparilla is what we'll have, then. Thank you." A grin tipped Hattie's mouth as she seated herself on a stool across from the storekeeper. "The men will be awhile, availing themselves of all the finery the lumberyard has to offer."

Lorelei slid onto the stool beside her. "I'm in no hurry to return to camp."

Anna nodded and sat on a stool. She didn't blame Lorelei in the least for wanting to make the most of her time away from camp. Her husband seemed nice enough, but her father-in-law almost always looked and acted like he'd been sucking lemons. Even in Mutter's worst moods, she seemed a harmless ant compared to the cantankerous Emery Beck.

Mutter laid a hand on Anna's shoulder. "You go ahead, dear. I'll find Vater and ride back with him. That way I can start supper nice and leisurely like."

Anna stood. "I don't have to—"

"Stay?" Mutter slid her hand down to Anna's arm and squeezed. "Why wouldn't you?"

To police you. Anna swallowed her first answer

and then forced her concerns down. Of course, Mutter was tired. And, really, these were her friends, not Mutter's. "If you're sure."

Mutter looked from Hattie to Caroline to Lorelei, then back to Anna. "I'm sure. You stay and enjoy yourself. Enjoy your friends."

"All right." Anna drew in a fortifying breath. "I'll be along shortly to help with supper."

When Mutter closed the door behind her, Anna rejoined her friends at the stools.

Caroline patted Anna's hand and smiled. "I'm glad you stayed."

Hattie set her hat on the counter between them. "I'm glad too."

"This will do you good, Anna." Lorelei looked at her and smiled. "We're all glad you decided to stay."

Anna nodded, trying her best to be glad.

The proprietor carried tin cups to the barrel and looked up at the whiskey bottles on the shelf overhead. "Don't get much call for genteel drinks here."

Anna fought the lump forming in her throat. She was either going to trust Mutter—to trust God with Mutter—or she was not. Still, she couldn't help but be thankful Mutter wasn't here right now. She didn't need the temptation.

Her soda came in a tin mug. Taking her first sip, Anna allowed herself to relax. The settlement wasn't big enough for anyone to get lost or into much trouble. Besides, Großvater and Boney would both look out for Mutter.

Anna glanced at her friends. "It's not lemonade on Mrs. Brantenberg's porch, but it's good that at least a few of us can be together."

"I remember those chats." Caroline ran her fingertip around the top of her cup. "And I remember what Elsa used to say when I was waiting for news about Phillip."

Hattie raised her finger as the leader of the quilting circle had. "Worry is something the devil will use against us."

Anna nodded. "To distract us from the truth."

Caroline cleared her throat as Elsa Brantenberg would do. "God is in control, not us."

They all fell silent as they raised their drinks for a sip.

Hattie pressed a fingertip to the corner of one eye. "I miss her and Emilie and Jewell—all of them."

Caroline nodded. "I'm anxious for word from them."

"Have you written Jewell to tell her of the upcoming nuptials?"

"I wrote her about my horseback rides with the captain, but not about the result yet." Caroline quirked an eyebrow in a coy grin.

Hattie set her tin cup on the counter. "Once you and the captain wed, you may wish to, uh, change your living arrangements."

After Mutter had brought up the subject of where Caroline and the captain would live once they married, Anna had considered offering to take Caroline's place as the Kamdens' nanny. She'd immediately dismissed the thought, however, well aware she had her hands full caring for Mutter and Großvater.

"We've talked about it." A blush colored Caroline's face and reached her red hairline. "Me and Rhoda."

Lorelei swiveled on her stool. Leaning forward, she looked at Caroline. "How is Rhoda faring? I heard the pain was back again last night."

Caroline nodded. "Yes. Sadly, it seems more frequent. She hasn't eaten well the past couple of days."

"And she's not pregnant?"

"She and Dr. Le Beau both insist she is not." Caroline brushed stray curls into her bonnet. "Dr. Le Beau recommended Rhoda see a doctor at Fort Kearney. He said a surgeon might even be necessary."

"Oh dear." Lorelei shook her head. "I'm sorry to hear that."

"Garrett and I talked about postponing the wedding, but Rhoda wouldn't hear of it."

"She doesn't want to interfere with your happiness." Lorelei lifted her cup to her mouth and faced Hattie. "I'm sorry for the interruption. You were saying?"

Hattie smiled. “My mother and I talked, and I could take over as nanny for the Kamdens, if they’d like me to.”

A grin brightened Caroline’s face. “As it happens, your name came up in my conversation with Rhoda. I suggested you might be a good replacement, and she thought you would do well with the children and her mother-in-law.”

“Wonderful! Perhaps we could talk to Rhoda when we return to camp.” Hattie tilted her head and sighed. “If she’s feeling up to it.”

Anna glanced toward the open front door, looking out at the dusty road. Mutter had surely found Großvater by now, and they were on their way back to camp.

At least that was what she had to hope. She couldn’t be Mutter’s keeper, try as she might. Mutter’s well-being was between her and God. All Anna could hope to do was pray for her and love her.

Caleb sat astride a fallen tree with the wagon’s tack laid across his lap. He let out a deep breath. He should’ve gone into Rock Creek. It might have afforded him an opportunity to talk to Anna. If nothing else, he could’ve helped her keep watch on her mother. He wanted to go, if only to make sure the peddler wasn’t anywhere near the place. But Anna had made it clear she wanted nothing to do with him. Besides, Otto and

Boney had both accompanied the women. He would have only been in the way.

He dipped the rag into the neat's-foot oil and spread it onto the leather. The changes he'd seen in Wilma Goben since he pulled her from the river and sat with her in the draw were stark, almost day and night.

Come to think of it, the change in Anna had been just as drastic, and around the same time. More than two weeks had passed since she'd quit speaking to him. Outside of the obligatory niceties, anyway. Unless he counted her indignation that day he'd found her on the hillock and interrupted her *thinking* time, and then the following Saturday, during the evening music. Since that awful day at the river, he hadn't even caught her looking at him during the morning Bible reading the way she used to. And she didn't speak one word to him when she found him and Mrs. Kamden at the graveside.

More importantly, Anna had lost interest in listening to him.

On the hillock, she claimed she wasn't embarrassed by her need to be rescued. Wasn't embarrassed knowing he'd seen her toss a bottle into the fire or witnessed her mother's behavior. During their very few dance steps Saturday night, she said she wasn't angry with him, but at herself.

None of it made sense. He would've guessed Anna had learned the truth about the raid at

Centralia, but she couldn't know. He was the only person alive who knew what had truly happened there. He'd talked to her mother some, but hadn't told her any of that. No, it was most likely she felt guilty about her mother's behavior and was all the more determined to look after her.

Either way, it didn't seem he could do anything but wait. And hope the feelings Anna had for him the day they kissed were still there and would one day surface again.

He prayed it would be soon.

He'd just stretched the harness out on the log to dry in the sun, when he heard horses approaching and looked up. Wilma Goben sat atop a borrowed chestnut, looking every bit fine. Boney and Otto rode on either side of her. Where was Anna? It wasn't like her not to be at her mother's side.

"Caleb." Boney waved his hat toward the harness. "You get my work done for me, did ya?"

"You know me better than that." Caleb looked at Anna's family. "Otto. Ma'am. How did you find Rock Creek?"

"A very well-named town. About all there was to it." Otto chuckled. "A rock and a creek."

"You're forgetting about the lumber mill and the general store." Wilma turned toward Caleb and smiled. "That's where Anna is. She stayed behind to enjoy a sarsaparilla with her friends."

"Oh?" The word came out as a question. He could have been knocked over with a feather right then. Anna had actually done something for her own enjoyment.

"I was surprised too," Otto said. "They won't be far behind us. The captain, Arvin, and Tiny are in town to see to 'em."

Perhaps it was a good sign that Anna was feeling comfortable letting her mother go—to get out from under the dark cloud that had settled over her. A good sign that she might soon be ready to talk to him again. To listen to him.

Right now, he'd settle for a smile.

41

Anna looked up at the crescent moon set in the graying sky. She breathed in the cool evening air and rode Molasses past the grouping of wagons. Großvater waved to her from the back of Ian Kamden's Conestoga where he was helping to grease a wheel.

Mutter had been right—it had done her good to enjoy some refreshment with friends. There wasn't much to Rock Creek, so it wasn't the place that did her so much good, but the company. Even lukewarm, the sarsaparilla was a welcome treat after so many weeks on the road.

All the while, Mutter had been back here cooking the stew and baking fresh biscuits. Anna needed to help and catch Mutter up on the news from her friends. She guided her horse around a gaggle of children playing stickball.

At their camp, Anna stepped down from the stirrup and tethered Molasses to the tongue at the front of their wagon. She looked around. Three empty stools framed the worktable. Carrots and potatoes lay peeled but not cut. Water boiled in the dutch oven, which hung above a dying fire.

"Mutter?"

Had she gone to the stream for water? Or maybe into the wagon to lie down while she waited for Anna's help?

Anna climbed the wheel spokes. She had no sooner reached the wagon seat when the bitter stench of liquor assaulted her senses.

How? Mutter didn't have any left in the wagon. How had she gotten her hands on more? She'd left the general store without it. Mutter wouldn't have gone and found a saloon . . . not with so many from camp right there.

Why had Anna trusted her? She shouldn't have. She needed to get the liquor away from Mutter before the captain found out about it.

Anna scrambled over the seat and in through the canvas opening. A half-empty bottle of amber liquid lay on the floor. "Where did you get it, Mutter?"

Mutter lay in her hammock in one of her drunken stupors. She didn't answer.

"Mutter!" Anna rose onto her tiptoes and nudged Mutter's shoulder more abruptly than she should have. But she was tired of this. She'd believed Mutter had finally given up the drink. "Wake up!"

Mutter didn't even stir.

Anna's heart hammered in her chest as she laid her hand on Mutter's cheek. Her skin was still warm, but waxy and damp. Heat raced up Anna's neck into her face. "Mutter!"

She shook her.

"Wake up!" What was wrong? She'd seen Mutter in a drunken stupor countless times, but never this bad. Her gaze settled on Mutter's chest.

It wasn't moving.

Terror clutching her, Anna pressed her fingers to Mutter's wrist.

Nothing.

"What have you done?" Anna didn't realize she'd yelled until she heard a commotion headed their way.

"It came from the Goben camp."

"Something's wrong."

"Get Otto!"

The sarsaparilla soured in Anna's stomach. She couldn't let them find Mutter like this. Couldn't let them find the bottle. And what about the smell?

What would Mutter do?

Her hands shaking, Anna corked the bottle and

shoved it into her own trunk. Then she yanked an onion from the hanging sack, dropped it between two barrels, and stomped on it.

Tears burned her eyes.

God help her, Mutter was dead.

And Anna was still trying to protect her.

Caleb glanced out at the road in the direction of Rock Creek. He'd lost count of how many times he'd done the same thing in the past hour.

"I like dominoes good enough."

Caleb gripped his double-seven and looked up at Oliver Rengler, who sat across the table from him. It was a real good thing he wasn't doing anything that required a lot of concentration. Between his rolling thoughts of Anna and Oliver's love of gab, he wouldn't stand a chance.

"It's just that I miss playin' checkers with ol' Mister Heinrich. We talked about the river and Germany. And he always had somethin' new to show me. Like a stcroviewer."

Caleb nodded. "We left a lot of good people behind in Saint Charles." He opened his hand and played his sevens.

"Woo-weee." A grin widened Oliver's face. "I was hopin' you'd play a seven. That's all I needed to win you."

"Again." Caleb raised his hands in surrender. That was it for him. He'd seen Anna and the others ride into camp. Not that she'd be looking for him, but he might just decide to take a stroll that direction before supper.

"I'm real good at games. That's what Owen says."

"Well, your brother is right. And that's the last trouncing for me today." Caleb started stacking the tiles into their wooden box.

Oliver grabbed a handful of dominoes and made stacks on the table, then looked up at Caleb. "Did Madam-eezle Camille talk to you today?"

Caleb shook his head. "Was she supposed to?"

"I told her to tell you or the captain when she told me about her father's pill case."

"The doctor's? What about it?"

"Well, it's missing. She said they looked high and low for it."

"So, she thinks someone stole his pill case?"

Oliver nodded, his chin practically brushing his coveralls. His head suddenly still, he opened his hands and raised them. "And I didn't take it."

"She said you did?"

"The Madam-eezle?" Oliver shook his head. "No. But Sally thinks I took all those things."

As far as Caleb was concerned, Oliver's sister-in-law and Emery Beck belonged in a camp of their own. "But you didn't take any of it."

"No sir. I like to look at nice things, but stealing is a sin. Says so in the Ten Commandments."

"What have you done?"

Caleb's spine stiffened. The shout belonged to Anna. He could tell that even in the distance.

Oliver's bushy brows shot upward. "That was Miss Anna."

"Yes." Miss Anna very upset, which probably meant her mother had been drinking again. Caleb stood and grabbed his hat from the table.

"I'm coming too." Oliver shuffled behind him. "I like Miss Anna."

There was a good chance Wilma had snuck a bottle out of the general store. And this time, everyone in camp would know about it.

When he and Oliver arrived at the Gobens' camp, Boney looked out through the pucker of canvas at the front of the wagon, through the gathering crowd, and straight at Caleb.

"It's Wilma." His voice quavered. "Get the doctor!"

Caleb darted to the Le Beaus' cookfire and returned with the doctor and his daughter. When they stepped up into the Gobens' wagon, Caleb waited at the edge of their camp with most of the Company. The sound of Anna crying inside the wagon foretold misfortune and tightened his chest.

Caroline and Mary Alice Brenner braced each other. Hattie stood with Maren Wainwright. Lorelei with her mother-in-law, Irene. All of Anna's friends from the quilting circle. Sally and Owen Rengler stood off to the side, at a distance.

Murmurs mixed with prayers buzzed about him until he thought his head might burst.

When Garrett stepped out over the seat, the crowd quieted. “Folks, it is with deep regret that I must announce very sad news. Mr. Otto Goben and Miss Anna have lost their beloved daughter and mother, Wilma, this evening.”

“Is it the plague?” Sally Rengler’s voice carried over the rising murmurs.

“Folks, there are no signs of an illness that could be considered contagious.” Garrett looked across the crowd, his hands out, palms down. “Now, out of respect for the bereaved, I ask that you all, except for Otto’s and Miss Anna’s close friends, return to your camps and go about your business.”

Caleb’s insides twisted. His guess was Anna’s mother had bought some rotgut. Trade whiskey.

And it was his fault.

He knew the problem she had. He also knew the power of its grip better than anyone who went to town with her. He should have protected her.

Now there was nothing he could do for any of the Gobens. Willing his legs to move, Caleb turned toward his camp.

“Caleb!”

Reluctantly, he looked over his shoulder as his boss walked toward him. “Bring Otto’s oxen up. You’ll go into town with him.”

Caleb shook his head. Not when it was his fault the man’s daughter was dead.

"You're the right man," Garrett said quietly.

"But, Boney—"

"Trust me."

It didn't seem he had a choice. Caleb swallowed the rest of his argument and nodded.

42

Caroline knelt in front of Anna. "You need to at least drink something, Anna." She held out a steaming cup of black tea with a sprig of mint. Her poor friend sat on a mattress in Maren's wagon, wrapped in the circle's friendship quilt, her knees bent and her head bowed. Rutherford had taken Maren and Gabi to Mary Alice's camp for supper.

Anna looked up, her eyes puffy, circled in red.

"You won't feel like eating or doing much of anything for a while," Caroline said, "but please try to drink this."

Anna reached for the cup, her movements slow. "You shouldn't be here. You have a joyful wedding to plan. You shouldn't have to see me like this."

"Mrs. Brantenberg was fond of saying, 'Here in this quilting circle, none of us are alone. Not in our sorrows, nor in our triumphs.' " Caroline watched steam rise from the tea. "This is what friends . . . sister-friends do. What you did for me when I learned Phillip was dead."

"Only Mutter's death is my fault."

"You did everything you could for her. Some things are out of our control."

"I wanted to make her well." Anna sniffled. "I thought I could."

"I know." Caroline glanced pointedly at the tea.

Anna raised the cup to her mouth. "My grandfather should've let me go with them." Caleb had gone with Otto to drive Wilma's lifeless body into Rock Creek. After one sip of tea, Anna lowered the cup to her lap. "I should be with my family. What's left of it." She took a short, sharp breath. "What if she wakes up? What if—"

"Anna, you found her already gone." Caroline rested her hands on Anna's knee. "Garrett checked her. And Dr. Le Beau—"

"I know. But my heart can't believe it." Her lips quivering, Anna shook her head again. "I should have left the store with her."

Caroline knew about *should have* feelings too. Anytime someone you loved died, you second guessed your actions. And they always came up short.

"First, he buried his wife, then his grandson. And now his daughter. Poor Großvater. I should be with him."

"Caleb will take care of him."

Anna hung her head.

Caroline took the cup from Anna and set it on a barrel. After lowering herself to the mattress, she drew her friend into an embrace. Anna's head nestled against Caroline's shoulder as they let fresh tears fall. "Lord Jesus. You see us."

God had nudged Caroline forward, drawn her into a brighter future. Anna's situation was different, but God would do the same for Anna . . . in time. Caroline had to believe that for her friend.

Caleb walked alongside Otto on the road to Rock Creek, holding the oxen's lead rope. He chose his path carefully to avoid jostling the wagon. Otto stared straight ahead, but Caleb doubted he saw much. His chest scarcely lifted, his breaths shallow. Otto hadn't spoken a word since leaving camp.

The image of Anna in pain haunted Caleb. All he'd wanted to do was stay. Hold her. Comfort her. But on the one occasion she looked directly at him, all he could see was anger. The only words she'd spoken to him were in protest, saying she should be taking her mother's body into town, not him. But Otto had insisted she remain there with her friends.

Caleb took his hat off and put it right back on. In the silence, his past was on the attack. He could have done more. Whether Anna would listen to him or not, he could have said more to Wilma. If he'd told her everything, maybe he could have made her see the destruction that lay ahead of her. Maybe he could have saved her.

There had to be some way to make his own redemption from the bottle beneficial to someone. If he couldn't comfort the woman he cared for, he'd at least try to be of some help to her grandfather.

"Sir."

Otto drew in a halting breath.

"Are you all right?"

Otto shook his head. "I'm carrying my daughter's dead body to be buried among strangers. It will take time."

Caleb knew about the passing of time but wasn't as confident about time making that much of a difference.

"Alcohol killed her."

Caleb felt his throat tighten with a fresh onslaught of remorse, and nodded.

"Wilma was in the store with Anna. I didn't know—" Otto's voice broke.

"You did all you could for her."

Otto shook his head, kicking a clot of dirt in his path. "You know my Wilma got hold of rotgut? It's poison."

"I suspected as much. Saw a merchant's wagon and heard bottles rattling inside. Even suspected trade whiskey." Caleb blew out a long breath. "Thought he was far enough ahead of us . . . I should've done more. I'm sorry."

Otto groaned and wiped his face with the back of his arm. "We all tried to help her. Especially Anna. She tried so hard to stop Wilma from drinking, to protect her from the bottle."

Caleb nodded, fighting the lump in his throat. "My family tried to do the same thing for me."

"You drink?"

"I did. I was lost to it. But not anymore. Not since the war."

"How could you give it up, and my Wilma couldn't?"

"Something terrible happened. I might have been able to stop it, had I been sober."

"The trouble I saw in your eyes?"

"Yes sir."

"You told Wilma?"

"About the drinking. Told her I understood alcohol's appeal."

"That explains my granddaughter's sudden change of heart toward you."

Caleb stopped to face Otto. "It does?"

"Wilma would have told Anna." Otto dragged a weathered hand over his face and glanced back at the wagon. "God rest her soul, it wouldn't surprise me if my Wilma didn't say the drinking was in your past." He hung his head. "She may have even used that to keep Anna from holding her to account."

His heart stinging, Caleb wiped his mouth. Why hadn't that occurred to him? Could Anna have really thought him an ally, supporting her mother's drinking?

"My girl didn't know your whole story, then, and in her own struggles, Wilma couldn't believe anyone could walk away from the bottle for good."

A fact Caleb couldn't expect Anna to believe either, or even care about. Not after tonight.

43

Anna opened her eyes, looking up at the first hint of dawn. Diffused light edged a gray sky. Surely last evening had been a nightmare, and Mutter was really asleep in her hammock inside the wagon. Soon, when Isaac blew his horn, she would grouse about the noise.

Seeing the two wagons that supported the ropes for her hammock brought another wave of tears to Anna's eyes. Neither belonged to Großvater. She'd spent the evening with Caroline at Maren's wagon. If she looked out about twenty feet into the meadow, she would see where Rutherford and Garrett had kept watch over the Wainwrights' camp. Watch over her.

Mutter really was dead. And although Großvater's intentions were no doubt noble, he had indeed left her here.

"Miss Anna."

Anna turned toward the sound of Gabi's sweet voice. The little girl climbed down from the wagon, her woolly brown curls bobbing. Gabi took slow steps toward the hammock, carrying her quilted dolly, an inseparable appendage.

"Are you awake?"

Drawing in a deep breath, Anna sat up, letting her legs dangle over the side of the hammock. "I am awake, sweetheart."

Gabi peered up at her. "PaPa told me about your mutter. She died."

Anna nodded.

"My mother died too."

A new wave of tears welled in Anna's eyes. She remembered Gretchen Brantenberg Wainwright.

"When I was a baby." Gabi's blue eyes glistened. "I'm sorry about your mutter, Miss Anna."

"Thank you."

"I have a new mother now."

"Yes. Mother Maren." Maren had climbed out of the wagon behind Gabi and busied herself at the grub box.

Gabi studied Anna from her disheveled locks to her stockinged feet. "You're prob'ly too big for a new mother." Suddenly extending both arms, Gabi held the doll out to her. "But you can use my Baby Mary."

Anna opened her mouth to speak but couldn't.

"She helps me when I'm sad. When I miss my Oma in Saint Charles real much, I hold Baby Mary like this." Gabi hugged the quilted doll to her chest. "Mother Maren says Baby Mary catches my tears and gives them to God."

Blinking against the tears now brimming her eyes, Anna slid out of the hammock. Kneeling, she pulled the little angel into an embrace.

Großvater had been right to leave her here. This was the perfect place for her this morning. Here, receiving love from sweet Gabi, Anna felt God catching her tears.

Less than two hours later, Anna rode toward a small graveyard on the outskirts of Rock Creek. Boney and several of the others from camp rode with her.

Pulling up on the reins, she slowed Molasses's gait. None of this was real. It couldn't be. But when she and the others approached Großvater and Caleb, the truth was impossible to deny. They both sat on stools in the shade of the wagon, only a few yards from a hole in the ground.

Großvater stood, then Caleb. Black Nebraska soil from the grave still clung to the folds of their trousers. It didn't make sense. Caleb didn't seem like a man who would let drink get the best of im. He worked hard, and nearly every time she aw him, he was helping someone. The only time ie spent alone was when he went off to read his

Bible. But if it weren't true, why would he tell Mutter he liked to indulge in the drink too?

When Großvater stepped up to Anna's horse and offered his hand, she lifted herself in the stirrup and swung down into his tearful embrace. The others dismounted in silence and gathered around the grave. The slight whistle of the wind accompanied Anna and Großvater on the slow walk to their place beside the grave.

Why had she insisted they go west? Why couldn't she have just let Mutter remain in Saint Charles? Why had she insisted they leave Independence?

Anna looked down to see a form wrapped in a sheet at the bottom of the grave. Lifeless and anonymous in this vast wasteland of the prairie. Mutter finally lay in peace, free of her torment.

If only it were peace Anna felt. Instead, sorrow and regret pushed tears from her eyes and chased them down her face.

Boney read from the Twenty-third Psalm and talked about Mutter's kindness to him when he was a child. He talked of Mutter's German potato salad and shared a story about her helping him find a hiding place when Dedrick kept beating him at hide-and-seek. Good memories of a good time.

And now that was all Anna had left of Mutter—memories. The good and the bad ones.

When Boney had finished and the others walked

back to the road where they'd tethered their horses to the fence, Anna remained at the graveside. She knew it was only Mutter's lifeless body there in the ground, but she couldn't leave. She couldn't stop trying to make life easier for Mutter.

Großvater stood beside her and wrapped an arm around her shoulders. "It's time, Anna."

She shook her head, tears streaming her face.

Großvater turned her toward their wagon. The wagon where she'd found her mother dead.

Her breaths shallow, Anna looked at Caleb. He stood beside the front wheel, holding his hat in his hand.

"Anna, I can't begin to express how sorry I am," he said.

She nodded, biting her top lip at a flood of swirled emotions. Sorry for her loss? Sorry he hadn't seen the damage Mutter's drinking could do? Sorry he drank? Sorry he kept dark secrets?

Her whole body trembled. How was it possible that she could hate him and love him at the same time?

She hated the sorrow and sincerity she saw in his eyes.

She hated that he hadn't cared enough to tell her the truth about himself.

She hated that her heart ached for him, that her hand felt cold and she longed to set it in his.

Anna looked at Großvater. "I can't stay here."

Großvater took the lead rope from Caleb and shook his hand. "Thank you. If you'll ride Molasses back to camp for us, we'll see you there."

Caleb nodded, and without looking at her, walked back toward the grave, where Boney waited with a shovel.

She hated the fact that she and Caleb couldn't be together.

After one last glance at the fresh grave, Anna joined Großvater on the road that led to their camp. The road that would take her into a life without her mother.

Großvater cupped Anna's elbow and pulled her close. "Thank you, Anna."

She reared back, startling the oxen. "You have nothing to thank me for, Großvater. I failed Mutter. I failed you. "

He shook his head. "If you failed anyone, it is only yourself."

Anna opened her mouth to speak, but he pressed his finger to her lips.

"And that's because you expected of yourself what only God could do."

Anna's lips quivered. She could almost see Mutter nodding in agreement with him.

"Anna, you did what I couldn't do." His shoulders sagged. "You took care of your mutter, when she seemed bent on making the task impossible. It wasn't fair to expect more of yourself."

Her chest tightening, Anna wiped the tears from her cheeks. "I expected more of Caleb."

Großvater's brow creased. "What did you expect from him?"

"Honesty. Caleb knew about Mutter. He pulled her from the river and found her in the draw that night and brought her back."

Großvater nodded. "Yes, that is all true, but I don't see where he was dishonest."

"Because he drinks and never told me. Telling Mutter only made her think her drinking was all right."

"He drank," Großvater said. "Past tense."

"That's what he told you?"

"Yes. And I believe him. Anna, he's spent time with us. Lots of it. Helped us."

Anna moistened her lips, trying to push the memory of his kiss from her mind.

"Have you ever seen or heard or smelled any evidence of alcohol in him?"

"No."

"You don't think Boney would notice? Boney loves you like a sister. He knows your heartache. You don't think he'd tell you if he had any reason to believe Caleb was given to drinking? You don't think he would protect you?"

"He would." A fresh issue of tears stung her eyes.

"Caleb isn't your enemy. He never was. He tried to help your mutter."

"Instead, he dug her grave." She needed to stand behind her decision to dislike him. It was for her own good.

Großvater sighed, his shoulders sagging. "God is with us on this road, Anna girl. And He has been all along." The words seemed to flow as if Großvater hadn't just lost his only daughter. "I don't know. I don't understand." He sent a reverent gaze heavenward. "Only God knows."

But did God know how furious she was? How afraid she was to give her heart to someone she couldn't trust? How afraid she was that Caleb had already captured her heart?

44

Caleb shifted in the saddle. The memory of watching Anna mourn her mother tore at his heart. *Why, God, why?*

Boney pulled a slab of jerky from the pack on his mule. He ripped off a hunk and held it out to Caleb. "After all that work you did today, you should have a bite."

"Thanks." Caleb took the jerky. "You think Anna will be all right?"

"That depends."

Caleb looked at Boney with his eyebrows raised, waiting for the rest of the answer.

"On you."

"How do you figure that?"

"I reckon you'll either decide to tell Anna the whole truth, or you won't. And whatever you decide will affect her." Boney bit the end off of his stick of jerky. "You know you're that important to her, don't you?"

"I can't be."

"Just 'cause you used to drink?"

Caleb nodded. "How'd you know?"

" 'Cause of what you didn't say about Wilma. Idle gossip comes from folks who haven't done a particular thing but are afraid they might."

Caleb nudged his hat back and looked at Boney. "How'd you get so smart?"

"My mama said I come by it naturally."

Caleb chuckled.

"You told Anna you used to drink?"

"No. But I told Wilma that night in the draw. I planned to tell Anna—time and again." Caleb shook his head. "You see why I can't tell her now. Her mother just died because of it." He choked back a sudden catch in his throat. "And other people died because I drank."

"You know I'm mindful about all that, but sorrow is sorrow. And it seems to me, the way you and Anna feel about each other, you two could be lightening each other's load."

Boney was right. He needed to talk to Anna. The sooner the better.

He had just pulled his horse off the road and toward the line of wagons, when Boney grunted. "You seein' what I'm seein'?"

Caleb looked up. Anna was fairly marching up the line toward them, her skirt pinched up at the sides.

"Which one of us you figure she's aimin' to fire at?" Boney asked.

"Probably an easy guess. She had plenty of time to talk to her grandfather."

"You told him?"

"Uh-huh."

"You need a little moral support?"

Caleb shook his head and climbed down from his Pacer. "Thanks, anyway."

"Well, good luck to you, then." Grinning, Boney turned his mule toward the chuck wagon.

Her shoulders squared and her lips pursed, Anna looked straight at him. As she approached, he started to ask if she was all right and thought better of it. She obviously was not.

Anna stopped mere inches from him and looked him in the eye, her eyes narrowed. "You didn't think I had a right to know."

"I did."

"You said you were fond of me."

"I was . . . I am." He reached for her arm, but she pulled it away. "I am fond of you, Anna. Very fond."

She shook her head as if a fly had buzzed her.

"Yet, you told my mother about your past and you didn't tell me?"

He drew in a breath to calm himself. "I wanted to tell you. That day I said I needed to tell you something before you and your mother went into Independence. That day on the knoll. The night of the dance. You wouldn't listen. I wanted you to hear it all from me."

"Instead, you let me believe you were like her, that I couldn't trust you." Her fists balled, Anna leaned into him and pounded his chest. "You let me believe you would drink yourself to death and die on me too."

He cupped her wrists, allowing her to continue hitting him. When Anna broke down into sobs, the pounding subsided and she melted into his embrace, her face buried in his chest.

Her breaths shuddering, she pulled away from him and looked up, her eyes full of questions.

"Anna, I can't express how sorry I am it came to this. I cared about your mother. I tried to help her. Yes, I used to drink. I drank to hide. I drank to be brave. I don't anymore."

She shook her head. "I lost count of how many times Mutter said she had stopped."

Caleb rubbed his bristled cheek. "I need to tell you more."

"It won't bring my mother back."

"Anna, I am truly sorry for your loss, but your mother is not all there was and is to life."

Fresh tears glistened in her eyes. "That's all I've known for so long now." She wiped her face with her sleeve. "Trying to please her. Make her better. Keep her safe. That's all I've known."

Nodding, Caleb ached with her pain and the pain he had caused his own family.

"That day on the porch, you said you'd allowed past experience with women to cloud your judgment of me." She moistened her lips. "A bad past experience with a woman, is that why you drank?"

"Susan and I were sweet on each other in school. From the time I was twelve, I wanted to marry her. I expected to. She was sixteen when I left to fight in the war. While I was gone, I learned she had married someone else."

Anna sighed. "That explains your assumption that I had jilted Boney. Your defensive reaction."

"Yes, but it didn't excuse it. You aren't Susan." Caleb shifted his weight. "As it turned out, I was far from being ready to marry anyone. I was wallowing in self-pity when I met some other soldiers who hung around the public houses. They gave me some liquor, and it made me feel better. Soon I *needed* it to feel better." He shook his head, remembering Anna's recent loss. "I'm sorry. If this is too hard for you—"

"I want to know."

"My parents begged me to stop. So did my sister. Even in the times I wanted to, I felt powerless. I pretended not to drink anymore and became an expert at covering my tracks."

"You knew the signs. That's how you knew my mother favored the drink."

"Yes." He hung his head then looked up at her. "My squad was at Centralia. Enemy soldiers rode up on us, surprised us, and killed all eight of my friends."

Her breath caught. "You were the only one to survive? How?"

"I carried a bottle in my pack." He looked down at the graveyard mud on his boots, willing himself to continue. "While the rest of them were eating, I took my liquid lunch to my sentry post."

"Oh." Her response came out as a groan.

"From my position, if I hadn't been soused, I could've seen them coming . . . maybe done something to save Billy . . . any of them."

Anna's shoulders slumped and tears fell. No doubt tears for the other sisters who had lost their brothers. Tears for him. Tears for her mother. And tears for the daughter who had lost the mother she loved.

He pulled a dusty handkerchief from his pocket and handed it to her.

Dabbing her face, she looked at him. "I'm sorry. What a terrible thing to have to live with."

"That's why I've shared so many scripture verses about God's grace. That's also why I don't touch liquor of any sort."

"I'm so sorry you had to go through such a horrific experience." She tucked strands of golden-brown hair behind her ear. "I'm thankful you were my mother's friend. She liked you, you know."

"She didn't know the truth about me."

"She knew enough to know you are a good man. She knew you saw her, befriended her, and tried to watch out for her."

Caleb nodded. He had tried to watch out for her. Like Anna had. He enfolded Anna's hands in his and looked into her eyes, bluer than the deepest lake he'd ever seen. "Never mind that your mother couldn't do what you asked of her and quit drinking. She loved you, Anna. I love you. You captured my heart the day you stood on that porch in Saint Charles and asked if that was all there was to my apology."

Anna drew in a deep breath. "The night I walked away from our dance, I said I couldn't care for you."

"I remember."

"I lied. All I have been able to do is care for you. I love you too."

Caleb raised her hands to his chin. "Anna, your resilience and grace in hardship inspired me to want to know God deeper, to embrace His grace so I could have a heart that was whole and free to love you." He pressed her hands to his lips, kissing each one. "Forgive me. Love me."

Nodding, Anna rose onto her tiptoes and gave

him a light kiss on the lips. Her touch may have been tender, but the effects had him seeing forever in her eyes.

Friday evening, Anna sat alone in the wagon. Großvater had hung their hammocks outdoors. When he'd retired for the night, she'd come inside to brush out her hair and change into her nightclothes.

Instead, she leaned over a barrel, staring at Mutter's brightly stenciled trunk. Hungry for a taste of her mother, Anna considered opening the tin latches and looking inside.

Mutter was dead. Not coming back. The trunk now belonged to her and Großvater, and it was doubtful he would care to meddle in Mutter's private possessions.

Kneeling, Anna unlatched the lid and lifted it. The sweet scent of lavender sachets filled her nostrils, bringing the best of her childhood memories to mind. Snuggling with Mutter while she read. Making candles with Mutter. Watching her make potato salad.

The letter Mutter had addressed to Aunt Elva lay on top of a Soldier's Cot quilt Mutter had made in the quilting circle before Dedrick died. Sighing, Anna took the envelope from the trunk and sank to the floor. She leaned toward the light from the candle lantern and unfolded the sheet of stationery.

The words on the page were written in perfect High German.

My Dearest Elva, Sister of my heart,

I regret that I have not written you in nearly two years.

My dear son, Dedrick, succumbed to death during this country's dreadful war between its States.

A tear fell to the page.

Since that dreary day, time has marched to a beat that I cannot keep. Losing my son has left me lead-footed and weak in spirit and flesh. Out of step.

Another tear.

Your plans to join me in America, and my thoughts to return to Germany, have not come to pass. Now I fear I shall never again look upon your face or hear your voice.

Had Mutter simply given up on Elva coming to America, or did she know her time on earth was short? Was that why Mutter had been so concerned about Anna's future and pressed her to find a husband? How could she have known

Her death was an accident. Was it possible God had somehow given Mutter that sense?

Elva, dear, you were always smarter, more comely, and stronger than I. My sweet Anna is now eighteen, bequeathed with all the good things I knew in you.

Anna set her hand to her heart, remembering Mutter calling her a saint. It wasn't so much that Mutter believed Anna was a saint as much as she thought herself a sinner beyond saving. "Oh, Mutter. My poor mutter."

Sister, my admittance pains me, but my failings are as numerous as the stars here on the prairie. I fear I have worn Vater to a nub and driven my daughter's heart from mine.

Anna's vision blurred. She swiped at the tears and forced herself to read to the end.

Be well, my dear sister.
With my deepest regard, I am,
Your loving sister, Wilma

Anna leaned against the trunk, letting the letter drift to the floorboard. Fresh tears flowed. "Mutter. My dear mutter. Even when your bottle tried to convince me that I hated you, I still loved you. Oh, how I loved you."

God, please tell her, because I waited too long to do so.

When Anna had spent her tears, she returned the letter to the trunk and peeked under the quilt. A lacy sleeve stuck out from a paper bundle. Carefully, as if unwrapping a swaddled newborn, she peeled back the covering and stared at the silk chiffon dress. The peach color reminded her of dawn's first light. She brushed the lace collar with her finger. Beautiful. Something lay tucked just inside the collar. Her fingers trembling, Anna pulled the wedge of paper free and saw it was a note in Mutter's handwriting.

For you, my dear Anna.
This lovely dress belonged to my own mutter. In it, she said her vows to your großvater. They knew nothing but love for each other.

May you wear it in joy on your wedding day, whenever that comes.
With my undying love, Mutter

Mutter had saved the wedding dress for her? The letter and the dress were well-creased. Probably written and folded years ago and tucked away. This was an act of the mutter she knew from her childhood, always planning for a better future for her and Dedrick.

A sweet surprise, after all these years. Anna held the dress to her bosom, enjoying the comforting embrace of Mutter's love.

"Mutter, I know just the man I want to wear the dress for."

She smiled, knowing Mutter would approve and add her blessing.

She already had.

45

Thursday, the first day of June, Anna's steps quickened as the Company approached the rise just east of Fort Kearney. Although the wagons would arrive at the fort at midday, this wasn't just a noon break. In honor of Garrett's and Caroline's exchange of wedding vows later that afternoon, the train had rushed to arrive earlier in the day and planned to stay over until Monday.

The past two weeks had been bittersweet. Bitter without Mutter at her side, but sweet with Caleb there for her at every turn. Earlier in the day, Caleb and Isaac had ridden ahead to prepare a camp spot. The last mile had her giddy with anticipation, and she couldn't wait to see him again.

Großvater had no sooner pulled the wagon into line at the camp when Caleb sauntered toward them.

"I missed you," Anna said.

Caleb grinned. "I missed you too."

"So did I." Großvater's eyebrows arched with the monotone assertion, but his mouth tipped into a grin.

Caleb chuckled, then returned his attention to her. "Any chance you could be ready soon to go into town and find a preacher?"

Anna looked into Caleb's eyes, which sparkled like gold dust today. "For Garrett and Caroline?"

He dropped to one knee. "Actually, I've been thinking."

She nodded, unable to speak.

Taking her hands in his, he sent a warm shiver up her spine. "It seems a waste to go to town and busy a preacher for only one ceremony."

She tilted her head as if in deep thought, then smiled at Caleb. "I'd have to agree."

"Anna, will you do me the honor of becoming my wife? Today?"

"Yes! Gladly. Yes."

Caleb leapt to his feet and lifted Anna into the air, spinning her around.

On their second turn, Großvater cleared his throat, drawing their attention. "Nobody asked, but I'd be proud to be a witness."

Anna kissed Großvater on the cheek, then waved good-bye to both the men in her life and dashed to the wagon.

She had a special dress to change into.

• • •

Caroline accepted the tortoise-shell mirror from Anna and angled it to take better advantage of the diffused light shining through the white canvas of the tent cabin. Hattie stood behind her, tucking a last lock of red hair into a soft french twist.

"You really do have a way with hair, Hattie," Caroline said. "And out on the prairie too."

"I'm glad you like it." Hattie stretched the ringlets she'd left dangling at Caroline's neck.

Anna cleared her throat and turned in the caned chair. "I don't think Garrett would mind if your hair hung straight in pigtails."

Hattie gave a theatrical sigh. "The poor captain nearly ran headlong into a cottonwood tree earlier, so distracted was he by your beauty."

"Oh?" Anna giggled. "I'm sorry I missed that."

Smiling, Caroline studied Anna, from her softly plaited locks snuggled in a beaded snood to the lace hem on her chiffon dress. "One look at you and Caleb is liable to lose his footing entirely."

"Caroline is right." Hattie slid the hairbrush and pins into a sack. "You look beautiful, and your grandmother's dress is sure to leave Caleb speechless."

Anna giggled again. "*Speechless* would've been nice that first day on the road."

Hattie chuckled. "Caleb certainly had the hair the back of my neck standing on end with all that talk of Company policy. But, who knows, that protective passion might have been what made you fall for him."

"One of many reasons I love him." Anna's face pinked. "But I still can't believe I'm getting married today. And this time any jitters are due to excitement and anticipation, not to any uncertainty."

"Married in a double wedding, no less." Hattie looked at Caroline, her dreamy smile emphasizing her singsong tone. "It's all so romantic."

Caroline sighed, smoothing the lace at her neckline. It was romantic, making her a firm believer that God was a God of second chances and fresh starts. Quite the opposite of how she felt the day she first held the letter from the Department of War telling her of Phillip's death.

Anna stood and ran her hand over her dress. "Mutter would be pleased."

Caroline reached for Anna's hand and squeezed it. "She would, and so proud of you."

Her lips pressed together, Anna nodded.

"Pardon us." Garrett's voice came from outside the tent and froze them all in place. "Ladies?"

Anna and Hattie both looked at Caroline. She stood and drew in a breath. "Yes?"

"Me and Caleb pride ourselves on being patient men, but—"

"We're ready." Anna and Caroline spoke nearly in unison.

"That is indeed sweet music to my ears." Caleb gripped one flap of the tent entrance and Garrett the other.

Caroline followed Anna outside and turned to face Garrett. Her dashing groom wore a black frock coat, a white shirt, and a string tie, but it was his slack jaw and wide hazel eyes that made her smile.

Garrett pulled the hat from his head and held it over his heart. "You're just going to have to get used to me staring, ma'am, that's all there is to it. I didn't think it possible that you could become more beautiful, but today . . . stunning. I may not know—yet—who took Mrs. Zanzucchi's teapot, Otto's timepiece, or Dr. Le Beau's pill case, but you are surely the one who stole my heart."

Caroline raised her gloved hand and fanned herself, ready to rush headlong into her new life as Mrs. Garrett Cowlishaw.

Midafternoon, Anna and Caleb paraded into Fort Kearney with many of their friends. She sat sidesaddle in front of Caleb on his Tennessee Pacer. Caleb's arm was wrapped around her waist, and her shoulders rested against his chest. Boney and Großvater framed them while Oliver, Hattie, Lorelei, Mary Alice, Maren, and Rutherford followed.

Anna didn't know if Mutter had pictured her in the silk chiffon and lace dress atop a horse, but Anna felt no less the princess. Caroline rode Molasses and Garrett, his stallion, just ahead of them. Caroline's shining red hair and green velvet dress flowing over Molasses's croup made her look like royalty too. God had truly blessed them.

All of them.

As they approached the short boardwalk at the mercantile, Garrett waved at a couple of men sitting on a bench out front. "The parsonage?" he asked.

"That way, Mister. Only one church in town. You'll see the steeple once you round the curve."

Caleb nodded and smiled at Anna. "Much obliged." He doffed his derby, then rested his chin on Anna's shoulder. "You won't be Miss Anna Goben for long." His warm breath on her ear sent a shiver through her arms.

"Suits me just fine. Real fine."

The party reached the end of the main street and turned the corner. About two blocks down stood a small building with a steeple. The hitching rail wasn't long enough for tethering all of their horses and one mule, so Oliver and Boney took advantage of the fence.

Caleb and Großvater escorted Anna through the sanctuary doors. It was a modest room but well cared for. The pastor and his wife peeked out of the attached one-room parsonage.

Garrett stepped forward. "We're hoping"–he looked at Caroline, then at Caleb a

Anna—"there might be time on the preacher's schedule to perform a couple of weddings."

The door opened wider and the couple's eyes did the same. The petite woman looked from Oliver to Mary Alice and everyone in between. "Biggest wedding party I've ever seen."

Anna giggled. "Just guests, ma'am."

"Well, seein' as how you're all here and there ain't no other church, I guess I'll just have to clear my dance card for ya." A smile graced the preacher's round face before he disappeared into his quarters. His silver-haired wife shuffled out into the sanctuary.

After proper greetings and introductions, Mrs. Zimmerman dragged an intricately carved pulpit from a corner and set it in front of the window. She stepped back and tugged her skirt straight over her plump middle. "Now, then." She began directing the crowd with both hands. "We'll form two bride and groom groupings. Each bride will have a friend stand with her." The pastor's wife looked at Caleb and Garrett and sighed. "Our very handsome grooms will each need a supporter as well."

Anna swallowed the giggle tickling her throat. Their director was right—Garrett and Caleb were both looking quite fine, Garrett in his frock coat and Caleb wearing a blue shirt under a gray waistcoat. Boney and Großvater both stood beside Caleb while Rutherford stepped up to Garrett's side. Maren joined Caroline.

Hattie leaned toward Anna and squeezed her hand. "I love weddings."

Anna nodded, especially fond of this one and the man who stood at her side, beaming a brown-eyed smile that sent shivers up her spine.

They had just taken their positions when Pastor Zimmerman emerged from the back dressed in a starched shirt, his face clean-shaven and his white hair slicked back. He made his way through the tightly packed room and stood before them with his Bible open, while his wife played "Sussex Waltz" by Mozart. The lively tune was a perfect match for the joy welling inside Anna.

When Mrs. Zimmerman reached the end of the tune, the pastor straightened his string tie. "Mr. Garrett Cowlishaw, it looks like we'll begin with you and your bride."

"Yes sir." Garrett looked at Caroline. "I like the sound of that. My lovely bride."

In a swirl of emotion and soft sighs, Garrett and Caroline exchanged their vows and kissed. Beaming smiles that rivaled the sun, they stepped aside, allowing room for Caleb and Anna to take their place.

Anna set her hand on Caleb's taut forearm and took light steps toward the pastor. She had waited, and the right man had found her. Centered in front of the window, she couldn't help but look outside. One lone wispy cloud floated in the blue sky, reminding her that Mutter was with her spirit. Anna glanced at Großvater and returned his warm smile.

"Miss Goben?"

"Yes." Anna answered the pastor but looked up into Caleb's inviting brown eyes and said, "I do." Her heart overflowed with praise that God had directed her path to intersect with Caleb Reger's, and to give her a hope and a future with him.

Readers Guide

1. The Civil War brought devastating change to Anna Goben and the other women in the Saint Charles Quilting Circle. Anna joins the caravan of wagons going west, hoping the move will heal her family. Have you ever tried to "move" away from your problems? Did it work?

2. Caleb Reger set out on the journey west with a secret. He'd made mistakes that had possibly played a role in ending the lives of others and definitely scarred his own. He struggled with not feeling forgiven. Ephesians 2:8–9 says, "For it is by grace you have been saved, through faith—and this is not from yourselves, it is the gift of God—not by works, so that no one can boast" (NIV). In light of the Scriptures, what would you say our *feelings* have to do with the reality of God's grace?

3. Did you see other characters in *Prairie Song* who weren't living in the rhythm of grace? Who? What was their struggle? What would you say to them?

4. In one scene, Caleb finds Anna in the pastu[illegible] singing a hymn to an ox. Or is she? Do [illegible]

sing in your daily routine . . . while doing chores? Any favorite songs we might hear you singing, dishcloth or the vacuum in hand?

5. Caroline Milburn left her sister, her nieces, and nephew behind in Missouri. Do you think she was right to do so? Why? Why not?

6. Garrett Cowlishaw is the captain of the wagon caravan. What leadership traits did you see in Garrett? What qualities do you look for in a leader?

7. Before the women in the quilting circle parted ways, they each contributed to *Friendship* or *Album Quilts*—one quilt remained with the women who chose to rebuild their lives in Saint Charles while the other quilt went on the road with the women who chose to rebuild their lives elsewhere. What was the significance of the quilts? What did the women in the Boone's Lick Wagon Train Company do with their quilt?

8. Do you see meaning in the title *Prairie Song* for Anna, Caleb, Caroline, or Garrett? Has God given you a prairie song?

9. Caleb had studied for the pastorate and committed Scripture to memory, but he had not allowed his heart to accept God at His

Word nor allowed God's Word to change his heart. Is there a method of Bible study you use that moves you into applying Scripture to your daily faith walk?

10. Anna worked so hard to "fix" and protect her mother. Still, Wilma Goben's behavior proved to be troublesome and embarrassing at the very least, and even dangerous. What truth did you take away from Anna's efforts and her eventual loss?

11. Is there someone in your life you need to release to the Divine care and purposes of our Sovereign and Loving Lord?

Mona is available for conference calls where she joins your book club or reading group for a pre-scheduled conversation via Skype. When possible, Mona is happy to add an "in person" visit to a Book Club in a city she's visiting. For more information, please contact Mona through her website: www.monahodgson.com.

Author's Note

Thank you for joining me on the road west with Anna Goben and several of the other women from The Quilted Heart stories.

I enjoy featuring actual cities and places, but in keeping with my commitment as a storyteller of historical fiction, I am sometimes required to play with facts and actual locations to best meet the needs of my stories. In *Prairie Song*, I adjusted the name of an animal.

Buffalo was the nickname given to the American bison due to its resemblance to the Old World water buffalo, although the two are only distantly related. For ease of reading in my stories, I've chosen to use the more common name, *buffalo*.

What you might call a recipe, others might call a *receipt*. Both refer to a set of directions for cooking a particular dish.

Speaking of recipes, remember the Company potatoes Boney served in the dutch oven at the campfire? Well, it's a modified version of the Company Potatoes recipe by Jodie and her mother, Marjorie, who won my Wagon Train Recipe Contest. The recipe came from Jodie's grandmother. Good news! It's included at the back of this book. Congratulations, Jodie and Marjorie!

The unusual letter ß (esszet) you see in the word *Großvater*, translated as Grandfather, is the letter used for the double *s* sound in the German language.

Also, while I'm not writing my personal or family history in my fiction, bits and pieces of my experiences do make their way into my characters' journeys. That's the case with Davonna Kamden's memory loss and personality shifts. Her symptoms are that of what we now recognize as dementia, and in some cases, Alzheimer's disease, my mother's unruly dance partner.

Please join me for the next two novels in my Hearts Seeking Home series. In *Mountain Whispers*, the folks in the Boone's Lick Company set out from Fort Kearney with their wagons, intending to complete their trek west. At the end of their journey, will they enter the promised land or discover they've left it behind?

I look forward to our time together, discovering the width and depths of our true home—God's heart. Until then, love and hugs.

Your Friend,

Mona

THE WINNER OF THE WAGON TRAIN RECIPE CONTEST

COMPANY POTATOES

by Jodie & Marjorie

1 lb. frozen cubed hash brown potatoes*
(We cubed fresh Yukon Gold potatoes.)
1 pint Greek yogurt (Or sour cream, Grandma's original ingredient.)
1 can cream of chicken soup (Boney wouldn't have had a can of cream of chicken soup on the trail, so he most likely would've used chicken broth, cream, and flour as a substitute.)
1 cup chopped onion (Adjust to your preference.)
1 cup shredded cheese
Salt to taste (We didn't add salt to the recipe.)
Crushed potato chips (We used about a cup, crushed, to evenly cover the top.)

Preheat oven to 375 degrees. Spray a 9 x 13 pan with cooking spray. Combine everything, except the crushed chips, in a large mixing bowl. Spoon into baking pan and level. Spread a bit of extra shredded cheese on top! Cover the pan with foil then bake 45 minutes.

Remove the foil, add the chips to top, and bake another 15 minutes. Allow it to set for a few minutes, then cut and serve. Enjoy!

* If you're using frozen potatoes, allow them to thaw a few minutes before attempting to add them to the other ingredients.

Acknowledgments

I am so thankful for all who moved through the various stages of this story with me.

My hubby, Bob, who takes care of everything else.

My agent, Janet Kobobel Grant of Books & Such Literary Agency.

My editor, Shannon Hill Marchese.

The entire WaterBrook Multnomah–Random House team.

My prayer partners.

A big thank-you to all of those listed, and to all who aren't, who made it possible for me to accomplish my dream of writing novels for you.

About the Author

MONA HODGSON is the author of The Sinclair Sisters of Cripple Creek series; *Dandelions on the Wind*, *Bending Toward the Sun*, and *Ripples Along the Shore* in The Quilted Heart series; and nearly thirty children's books. Her writing credits also include hundreds of articles, poems, and short stories in more than fifty different periodicals, including *Highlights for Children*, *Focus on the Family*, *Decision*, *Clubhouse Jr.*, *The Upper Room*, *The Quiet Hour*, and the *Christian Communicator.* Mona speaks at women's retreats, schools, and conferences for librarians, educators, and writers, and is a regular columnist on the *Bustles and Spurs Blog.*

Mona and Bob, her husband of forty-one years, have two adult daughters, two sons-in-law, and a gaggle of grandchildren.

Learn more about Mona, find readers' guides for your book club, and view her photo album of current-day Saint Charles, Missouri, at Mona's website www.MonaHodgson.com.

You can also find Mona here:

Facebook at www.facebook.com/pages/Mona-Hodgson-Author-Page/114199561939095

Twitter at www.twitter.com/monahodgson

Pinterest at http://pinterest.com/monahodgson/pins/

And be sure to follow Mona's blog at MonaHodgson.com.

Center Point Large Print
600 Brooks Road / PO Box 1
Thorndike ME 04986-0001 USA

(207) 568-3717

US & Canada:
1 800 929-9108
www.centerpointlargeprint.com